THE HUM

The HUM series, Book One

Michael Christopher Carter

Golden Hill Publishing

Cover design by: MiblArt

To my wife Sherrie, and her kind and beautiful mother who we love and miss every day. Trish, may you rest in peace. I know you would have been so proud of my writing.

CHAPTER ONE

A strange noise again.

Nuthampstead, a small village in Cambridgeshire, England, November 1984.

The noise had been constant for days. It was at night when all other sounds were missing that it received the most attention. The husbands of the village, woken and sent to find out the cause, each discovered it wasn't the refrigerator, or the washing machine, or the music centre, or the boiler.

Upon deciding the source of the noise was outside, and venturing out to their respective patios or lawns in the dead of night, they were all still none the wiser.

It was a low humming, similar to a diesel engine a short distance away, or perhaps a helicopter nearing. Only it never changed. The engine couldn't be located, and the helicopter never moved closer nor further. The listener might stand outside forever and yet be unable to disern a direction. It came from everywhere and nowhere at once.

Noise travelling for miles in this fenland village was common, but the curiousness of the omnipresent oddity proved perplexing. Theories abounded as to its source. The consensus blamed the council for secret drilling, or mining, or construction.

Farmers bemoaned how their own planning permission was turned down left, right and centre while it was okay for the authorities to do whatever they wanted. Everyone felt uneasy with the inconclusive speculations, but uniting against a shared perceived enemy extended some comfort.

The sound even offered advantages to some: those chastised by the parish for their own noise pollution. One resourceful farmer who had turned part of his land into an Olympic quality clay shooting ground, despite rigorous efforts to block the echo of gunfire received rife complaints from locals at parish meetings.

And another, who ran a successful go-kart track, meeting only on the first Sunday of the month, found protests were common about that too. Even noise associated with general farming, such as harvesting, and incredibly, cows mooing, drew complaints nowadays. The humming took attention from them, at least.

It hadn't always been like that. Nuthampstead had once been a tolerant, neighbourly community where everyone knew everybody else and was willing to lend a helping hand. Most saw the recent influx of new-comers as the culprit. Steep house prices meant those born and bred in the village couldn't afford to buy a home there anymore. Families in residence for generations were being usurped.

Some of the so-called new-comers had lived here for more than a decade. But it took a lot more than a mere ten years to be seen as 'not new' in the Fens. A three-generation presence was a prerequisite.

The Ellis family were genuine new-comers. Having moved into the corner white house in the centre of the upper village eighteen months ago, they still felt new.

They didn't know it, but they always would.

Although Geraint Ellis wasn't actually responsible for the area, the villagers treated him as the local police officer despite his duties laying in the nearby city of Cambridge. Every missing sheep, and tool misplaced, he would be expected to investigate as though it were life or death. Particularly the lost sheep incidents, as their relocation from the Valleys of South Wales meant he was presumed to be something of an ovine expert.

Geraint endured these inconveniences, and the inevitable nick-name of 'Taffy,' in order to fit in; along with a real sense of duty. He was a very diligent police constable.

The large white house, now their home, had been carefully saved for whilst taking advantage of the security a police house gave them. A couple of years saving, and another year in a caravan, meant they now lived in an enviable home.

Geraint named it *Nutters* after the fond shortening of Nuthampstead he and his wife Diane had adopted. It was a name he bitterly regretted since doctors upgraded her diagnosis of postnatal depression to Bi-polar disorder when it had failed to clear up after over three years of distress. The rest of the community whispered of the appropriateness of *Nutters* behind the family's back.

It was in the home of this family of unwelcome, odd, new-comers that the hum was feared most. Six-year-old Carys Ellis had heard the talk in the village, and at school, about what the noise might be. She wasn't sure why, but she knew exactly what it was. She knew her mother was right to be afraid and wasn't a 'Nutter' at all.

No-one at school was privy to her secret because she had no-one to tell. The hostility she experienced as a funny sounding newcomer made it difficult to make friends

Today, after a tense journey home from school enduring her mother's erratic driving, she noticed a subtle but unwelcome change. The awful humming noise had grown louder. Neither of them mentioned it to the other; Diane's jitteriness was of no reassurance to Carys, whilst Carys's youth made her only a last resort comfort to her mother.

She slumped on the sofa in front of children's television for two hours before the evening news signalled the imminent return of her father. Diane fumbled noisily in the kitchen as though a home cooked masterpiece would greet them all soon. Instead, the clattering, cursing and swearing, was from her attempts to produce an entire meal in the new microwave.

The large, boxy appliances with the appearance of portable televisions were all the rage at the moment; and since buying theirs, Diane had barely cooked using anything else. Reading and re-reading the instructions for each element of the mass ready-meal, and the effort of keeping them all hot while the next component was 'cooked' caused immense agitation to the hapless chef in the kitchen.

The front door slammed, announcing the arrival of the man of the house. A fact they were both grateful for. The unmistakable smell of processed food chemicals filled the air and declared dinner to be almost ready. With a final screech of louder expletives, and urgent cries for the table to be laid, it was upon them.

Geraint always did well with the dubious offerings. He must have worked up a heck of an appetite at work, Carys envied him as she struggled to swallow hers without retching.

"I'm sorry," offered Diane. "The instructions aren't worth toffee on those packets. I've had to work out all new timings for the lasagnes and I haven't quite got it yet. They'll be better next time, I'm sure. Just eat what you can for now."

Carys was grateful for the get-out clause. Her mother at least recognised she was a useless cook. The effort she put into second-guessing microwave times must be greater than the effort it would take to prepare lasagne from fresh ingredients.

"It's this bloody noise making it impossible to concentrate," she said, a little tersely. "I swear it's louder!" she excused herself, keen to broach the so-far-undiscussed matter of the hum.

Geraint raised his eyes to heaven, careful it went unseen by his wife. Carys saw. He meant her to. 'Isn't Mummy silly worrying about the funny noise?', was the message. But Carys worried too. She was sure the noise was making her mummy ill.

"I can't understand how you can keep so calm," Diane was saying. "We all know what it means. Or have you forgotten what happened to me not so long ago?"

Geraint glared at her for risking upsetting their daughter. There was a time and a place, away from little ears, this sort of thing should be discussed, if at all.

He softened his gaze, careful not to upset her.

When Diane became agitated, placating her was the best practice. Taking the blame and agreeing with her every fancy was all he could do. Once calmer, she rarely remembered what the fuss had been about anyway.

With an urgent jerk of his head at their daughter, and back at Diane to imply later talks, he wasn't sure if she'd got the message, but she stopped speaking and made moves to retire to the living room. Her countenance changed abruptly. Beaming at Geraint, she requested a cup of tea and left to 'warm up the telly,' ready for Coronation Street, leaving Geraint to clear the table, and the alarming mess left by the 'cooking.'

He and Carys joined her in the lounge just as the opening theme to the show they watched religiously began. Carys realised with a sense of foreboding that she had only half an hour until her bedtime. Stock still, dreading going upstairs to bed, she hoped if she feigned interest in the next programme, and sat ever so quietly, she may go unnoticed for a while longer. Especially if it was something in which she might have a conceivable interest.

Her heart skipped for fear she was being sent straight away when she heard her mother say her name at the end of Coronation Street. She needn't have worried. Like most children in the 1980s, she was employed as the family television remote control. Skipping—not-at-all-tired—over to the small boxy set, she pressed the buttons to change through the four stations.

When David Attenborough's distinctive timbre wafted intelligently from the tinny speaker, she was virtually guaranteed a late bedtime. Sure enough, she sloped quietly back to her seat and settled down.

Despite her genuine interest in the planet's biology, she began drifting off to sleep, making bed certain. She wasn't sure, but shared glances between her parents showed a reluctance from them to make the move as well. Tearfulness at the suggestion she should go to bed still got her a telling off. Geraint didn't tolerate being manipulated by children's crying and only gave him determined resolve to complete whatever parental task was in hand.

Strong arms scooping her up, he carried his little daughter upstairs to her bedroom, commenting she would soon be too big for him to carry at all. Carys suspected an ulterior motive; that he was reminding her how grown up she was, now she was six—far too old to be bothered by silly noises.

But she couldn't help it.

So, with irresistible doe eyes, she asked her daddy for a bedtime story. He weighed things up. She gulped. Staying up late would usually be in lieu of a story, but she risked his displeasure because being left alone was unthinkable. When he agreed to, "Just a short one, then." Her heart fluttered in relief.

After choosing a not particularly short one at all, she settled under her covers, listening to the comforting tones of her daddy's sing-song, Welsh lilt; an accent she was unaware she shared. Whenever they went back to The Valleys to visit her grandmother and uncles, there were always comments of how English she and Geraint sounded. The Nuthampstead locals would be incredulous if they knew.

Up and down singing tones lulled her to sleep, and she drifted away. But, as soon as Geraint reached her bedroom door to leave, she sprung awake, anxious and tearful again. Returning to her bedside with a tut and a shake of his head, he sat on the edge of her duvet and prepared to have a talk.

Tears stung the backs of Carys's eyes as she listened to her daddy's instructions. 'Take no notice of Mummy,' he said. 'Did she remember how she hadn't been very well? That was why she should trust Daddy, and not worry her.'

It was too much for a six-year-old to understand, but she promised to try her hardest to be Daddy's brave little princess and go to sleep.

She really did try. She tried so hard, forcing her eyelids shut against the flutter-flutter of her pulsing veins. But sleep, inescapable listening to David Attenborough, snuggled up on the sofa, evaded her now, unsafe and alone.

The hours crawled by until, at last, she heard the heartening sounds of doors being locked and light switches flicking on and off as her parents prepared for bed. Maybe she'd sleep now she could hear them coming upstairs and they'd be close by.

As they passed her door, slightly ajar, shushed whispers floated in from the landing... Her parents' voices arguing about the humming noise as Geraint had alluded they would 'later'. The whispering paused, and they both peeped their heads round the door-jam into her room.

She was sure they could tell she wasn't asleep. Eyelids quivered rapidly as she strove to keep them shut. Air seeping slowly in and out of her lungs to disguise her alertness made her short of breath; an explosive gulp only a moment away.

As the loving gaze of her parents examined her for signs of awakeness, Carys fought the urge to call out 'Mummy, Daddy, I don't want to be on my own. I'm scared.' Swallowing down a wad of emotion, she fought to make good on her promise to be courageous.

Surprised when her unconvincing pretence at unconsciousness seemed to do the trick, she heard the door creak quietly back on its hinges and click shut. From beyond, the hushed conversation resumed; Diane's whispered tone still harsh, reminding Geraint of her terrifying experience and demanding his support now. Everyone else had decided it was one of her 'episodes', but the family knew, didn't they?

Carys knew. She remembered that time clearly.

Her mother had gone to stay in a hospital for weeks, and she'd been heartbroken. Whatever upset her then had something to do with the same humming tormenting them now. As they continued down the landing, their talking faded, but their talk of the hum reached Carys's delicate ears.

Their nearness provided scant comfort; the calm dissolving further when her daddy's violent snores filled the air. Mummy must be sound asleep too, or she'd hear her waking him with shouts of '*Turn on your side, Geraint. You're snoring!!*'

There was no other sound but her father's snores.

And the hum.

Growing louder.

How could her mummy and daddy sleep through it? The continuing snoring confirmed they could.

And that's when it happened…

CHAPTER TWO

Carys's Terror

Louder and louder, the noise shook Carys in her bed. Fighting the instinct to pull her covers over her head, her little body quivered as she prayed it was just her imagination. With the duvet covering half her face, her eyes skimmed around her bedroom.

She squirmed, digging her heels into the mattress, squinting at a sudden searing white light bursting through her curtains, piercing the darkness. Different to daylight. Brighter somehow, but didn't fill her room as sunlight would. Her hands gripped the duvet so hard, her fingers numbed. Aching to pull them over her again and make it all go away, she couldn't. She had to see what was there.

Her little mind, seeking a harmless explanation, forced a laugh as she decided it was just a police helicopter; colleagues of her daddy out searching for a bad man. The beam shining back and forth from the sky shone into her room, and her covers proved too tempting.

Abruptly, the noise stopped. The light, so bright it had burned to look at, was gone. All she heard was the thump, thump, thump of her heart as it beat furiously against her chest. All she saw was the weave of her duvet inches from her saucer eyes.

Torn between the illusion of safety from hiding, and a macabre curiosity, slowly, she pulled the covers from her head and peeped into the room.

At once, she wished she hadn't.

No longer did the brightness shine through her window, but Carys would prefer if it did. Because now it glowed through the crack at the bottom of her door.

It was inside the house.

Gulping down the bitter taste of bile, she peered, wide eyed, knowing that it couldn't be a helicopter. Whatever it was, had to be outside hers and her parents' bedrooms.

White knuckles gripping the covers up to her nose, the cotton tickled her nose and she pulled it a fraction down so she wouldn't sneeze. She stared at the door, her heart beating so hard and so fast, it might burst from her chest and run away. Her short life flashed before her eyes, streaming with salty emotion.

A clatter made her gasp. Timidly, her gaze darted in time to see the handle rattling up and down. A whimper turned to a cry as it shook more before turning just the amount needed to open, and it creaked ajar.

Long, grey fingers gripped the edge of the wood. 'Who are you?' she wanted to scream, but no sound came and she stared, eyelids sucked so far back in her sockets her eyeballs felt they might fall and tumble across the floor.

From deep within, terror expanded like foetid gas in a rotting rat. And when the inhuman hand pushed the door fully open, the screech which escaped her dry lips startled her. She wished she could've kept it in, so that whoever, or whatever, was creeping through the blaze of light from the doorway might be persuaded the room was empty. But she could be Daddy's brave little princess no longer.

Her mind struggled to hear her words as she screamed. Detached, she strained to comprehend her own hysterical squeals, barely recognising her trembling voice. Over and over she cried for her mummy and daddy. But they didn't come.

No longer creeping, a figure swiftly entered the room. Not her mum or dad; something else. And when Carys saw it, she relinquished control of her bladder and bowels. The smell made her gag but she couldn't give herself away. Lips pressed tight; cheeks billowing, she fought to swallow down the sourness.

Her mess felt hot at first, then cold as the wetness stung her skin. The concern was only fleeting. Physical discomfort barely breached the terror that kept her welded to her sheets as the stickiness dried and stuck her bodily, too, as sucking sniffles vibrated through her trembling lips. There was nowhere to go. Nothing she could do but watch it prowl closer.

Closer.

So close she might touch it if her arms weren't clasped tightly around her shivering body.

Despite the sickening stench, the refuge of her duvet beckoned, but she couldn't tear her gaze from the repugnant reality inches from her skin. Enormous, cold, black eyes bore into her from a featureless grey face. Its line mouth opened and it shouted at her in a language she didn't recognise, but somehow understood immediately.

Whilst the creature screeched its instructions over Carys's own screaming, her dad's tell-tale snoring broke through; telling the tale she was to face this monstrosity alone.

It loomed over her, taller than she would be standing, but smaller than any adults she knew. Its orb head perched precariously on a pencil neck, emerging from naked, almost translucent shoulders. Huge eyes bore through her, chilling like death. Its impassive pallor exhibited no emotion, but Carys burned from the heat of its unseen rage.

The sight was more than she could cope with and she could hold back the vomit no longer, adding to the disgusting mixture of sweat, urine, and faeces clinging to her claggy skin. An uncontrollable whimper escaped her resolve as she strained to understand the barked orders.

"Be quiet," the voice commanded. "No-one can hear you." Words sounded in her head, whilst at the same time, the creature's screeching filled the room like an injured animal. "You must do as I say. I will not hurt you if you do as I say."

It seemed cross with her. Petrified of making it angrier, Carys committed to do exactly what it asked. But she couldn't. She simply couldn't stop screaming.

"You *must* be quiet. You *must* do as I say," the creature demanded with the authority and surety its will could be enforced.

Her dry eyes staring at the beast, she futilely fought more squeals as they rose from her throat, echoing around her room but barely perceived, the alien instructions so dominating her head.

Looming nearer, it stretched spindle thin fingers toward her and she recoiled from a touch that nearly was. In a daze, Carys shook in violent shudders as her well of coping ran dry as more of the creatures pierced her peripheral vision. The fingers moved in slow motion to her face. Closer and ever closer until they could be no more without stroking her.

Touch. Her forehead jolted from the icy sensation.

The same bright light burned her eyes, but there was now an almost peaceful surrealness.

The creatures busied all around her, talking in the screeching animal shrieks Carys had witnessed before, but this time she couldn't understand a word.

A glance down soon shattered her calm and brought a gasp of disgust and terror to her lips as the spindle fingers tapped her tummy. Skin puckering in vile disgust, sucking in her stomach was the only movement she was able to make to repeal the advancing claw hand.

Paralysed; forced to oblige the gruesome examination, terror expressed from every pore, standing each tiny hair rigid as poles. A tear brimmed in her eye. As she lay flat, it domed, obscuring her vision, and she was grateful as it blurred the sight of several other of the creatures operating large machines over her, ready to perform God only knows.

Still flinching from their touch, she cried as again she couldn't move. Her limbs would not obey her desperate directive to kick and hit, and get the hell away from them.

And then, from nowhere, the calm serenity returned and engulfed her, consuming her.

She smiled.

It was all a dream.

Just a lovely, funny dream.

She awoke with a start. The sticky, odious wetness reminded her she was lying in a puddle of her own excrement and vomit. Jolting, she squirmed from the cold, wet, mess. Nightclothes sticking, she clawed at them, gripping and ripping at her sore skin before she finally threw them off only to grope on the floor to retrieve the driest of them to use them as best she could to wipe herself clean.

Relief tempered with uncertainty that the room was really empty. There was no light, and the humming noise was back as it had been when she'd first come upstairs. With a gulp of courage, she streaked naked across the landing and leaped under the covers with her mummy and daddy, who incredibly, after snoring through all the screeching beforehand, woke at the merest touch. "What are you doing, young lady?" he questioned hoarsely "Go back to your own bed, please."

Words wouldn't come. She shook her head slowly at first, then harder as terror streaked down her cheeks. Geraint propped himself onto his elbow and faced her with a concerned frown. "What is it, sweetheart? Bad dream?"

Carys's neck cricked as the vigorous shaking turned suddenly to nodding. "There was something in my room. Something from out there..." she waved to outside with a sweeping arc and hoped he understood. "I was so scared, Daddy, and I called and called you. I was really scared, and you didn't come."

He cuddled her, squeezing her tight. "It must just have been a nightmare, sweetheart," he stroked her head. "Of course I'll come if you need me. I will always protect you. Always." He smiled his warmest daddy smile (or the best his groggy numb face was capable of at this time of the night). "Now, shall I take you back to bed?"

Panic gripped her, and then she remembered her perfect excuse. "I can't." she said, sheepishly. Tears streaking her cheeks she said, "I had an accident... In my bed..."

Geraint became aware of the smell and screwed his face as he considered cleaning up momentarily before deciding it would better be a job for Diane tomorrow and so he snuggled back under the covers cuddled up to his little daughter.

Almost at once, he began snoring loudly again. Diane, instead of waking and berating him, slept through the racket with only a frown flecking her pretty face.

Carys's ears pricked, catapulting her back into extreme consciousness as the humming noise grew louder again. Violent shakes rippled her daddy but again he slept as, once more, the house flooded with intense, searing light.

Why must she be the only one awake again? Sandwiched in-between her parents, she managed to force down her fear and repress her screams as the glow filled the landing and bedroom with an intensity she feared would melt flesh if it were to touch.

She gasped, wide eyed, wrenching the covers so only her eyes and hair peeped from beneath.

Body arching closer into the warm protection of her daddy, she stared as the creatures shuffled past the doorway and down the stairs, disappearing from view.

But this time they paid no heed to the three occupants of the double bed, and as swiftly as they had arrived, with no noise of the front door opening or closing, they were gone.

The light was gone.

The hum was gone.

CHAPTER THREE

Mrs. Robbins

Carys opened her eyes, exhausted and alone in the large double bed of her parents; surprised she'd woken without prodding. Noisy bustling noises from the kitchen led her to surmise that's what woke her.

Making her way sleepily to the source of the sounds, she was astonished to see her mummy washed and dressed and cooking breakfast. Diane usually stayed asleep when she left in the mornings. Daddy would give her cereal and maybe some toast, and drive her to school on his way to work.

Gawping in disbelief, she didn't know who could possibly be expected to eat the enormous feast being prepared. Her typical bleary-eyed breakfast would get pushed around her bowl, forced down out of duty whilst stifling sleep, her head resting on the palm of her hand.

Eggs of two varieties (poached and scrambled), fried bread, fried tomatoes, sausages (a quick count revealed either they expected guests, or there were four each!) Bacon was being added to the immense pile while her mother put the final touches to lava bread cakes (edible seaweed from Swansea—her daddy's favourite) in the frying pan with cockles, winkles, black puddings and hash browns.

The microwave whirred in pride of place on the worktop, but not to make anything processed, just baked beans turning round and around in a Pyrex bowl. Carys, shocked, stood stock still in the doorway. Her mother actually cooking was a very rare sight indeed.

"Carys, darling!" Diane greeted enthusiastically. "Be an angel and get the sauces from the fridge, please."

Carys did as she was bid. Her father entered the room, beaming. He obviously approved of the great breakfast banquet.

"Is it school today?" Carys asked, confused with morning normally so rushed. How would they manage to eat all this in time?

"Of course," answered Geraint with a frown. "Your mother got up extra early to make us this super breakfast, that's all." Chuckling, he added, "We shouldn't need any lunch!"

Why her mother had got up so early was conspicuously not deliberated. Unnerved, the jovial good humour of both her parents became contagious, so Carys smiled and joined in, surprised to find she had a hearty appetite.

Lava bread and cockles were favourites of hers, too; particularly because people at school thought they sounded disgusting. She felt very grown up for liking what her mum and dad called 'brain food.'

They voraciously, making jokes in between mouthfuls. It would probably be safe to talk about last night's events, Carys decided. Diane was just getting up from her chair to replenish the sausage and bacon platter when Carys spoke. "Daddy?" she began.

"What is it, angel?"

"I saw the things again. When I laid in bed with you and Mummy they walked down the stairs. I wasn't as scared with you, but it wasn't a dream."

The noise of the clattering pan as it hit the table, knocking Diane's plate and the bowl of baked beans onto the floor, was deafening. Carys jumped back in her chair. Geraint stiffened.

With a steely, deliberate, glare at no-one, Diane strode to the door leaving the mess of tomato sauce covered beans glistening on the floor.

she Her footsteps stomping up the stairs rocked the walls until the bedroom door slammed and the noise was replaced by an eerie silence.

Geraint turned a woeful smile to his daughter and bent to clear up the spilled food. Straiting with a rehearsed carefreeness, he hummed a happy tune and proceeded to scrape the remains of the breakfast banquet from the table, wrapping leftovers in foil and loading the dishwasher. "Pop your clothes on, cariad, and brush your teeth," he said, mid-clean.

Before they reached the front door, he galloped up the stairs, two at a time, and called goodbye as if it was any other day. Silence was the unnerving reply. Geraint hurried back down the stairs, smile still plastered on his face but Carys could tell he wasn't feeling it. "Time to get in the car, bach," he said, bustling things he needed for work into a bag. "We're late, I'm afraid."

Carys nodded her acceptance. Numbness stifled anything else.

With Carys was strapped into her car seat correctly, Geraint clipped his own seat belt and pulled away. As the scenery flashed by and their home grew further, they both began to relax a little.

"What was wrong with Mummy?" Carys felt able to ask at last.

Geraint sighed and his fingers tapped either side of the steering wheel as his gaze fell to his daughter. "You know your mum's frightened of the aliens you talked about," he began, discerning her nod. "They're not real, bach. It must just have been a dream; a nightmare. I think Mummy being afraid has put strange ideas into your little head." He reached to ruffle her hair., then, conscious it sounded unsympathetic, and not wanting to be disloyal, he amended, "She doesn't mean to scare you, she isn't well, that's all." He planned to finish there but added, "It's probably best if you don't mention nightmares in front of Mummy in future. Just tell Daddy." Then he added with wide-eyed assertion "When we're alone, okay?" He spoke with a questioning intonation, but Carys knew it was an order. Never could she accept the alien creatures weren't real, but still she agreed. They travelled the rest of the way in silence.

Arriving at the school, Geraint stopped abruptly and kissed Carys's head by way of a goodbye.

"Can you take me into school?" she pleaded.

Geraint nodded and got out with a tut and a terse shake of his head. With an overly-firm grip on her small hand, he led her down the path to the school and explained to the woman at reception that they were late due to Carys's mother being unwell. Tears cupping in the backs of her eyes, Carys waved half-heartedly as she watched him turn back to the door and waited until the police car disappeared. Lips trembling, she shuffled down the corridor and forced her mouth to curve upwards when she turned the corner to her classroom. Mrs Robbins, looked up and a small smile acknowledged her without interrupting the flow. Carys shuffled into her usual place, next to a boy called Max.

The classwork swam over her. Mrs Robbins' words floating away from her ears unabsorbed. The lateness made her naturally behind, of course, but it was more than that. With every blink, the looming faces of her night time intruders filled her thoughts, and they seemed so real. Shaking her head to dispel the images, her eyes burned and frustration reddened her cheeks.

"Miss. Miss!" bellowed Max witnessing Carys's tears and stifled sobs. "Carys Ellis is crying, Miss."

Mrs Robbins looked up, and seeing the distressed face of her pupil, cooed, "Whatever is the matter, Carys?" she invited an undertone of annoyance unmistakeable. Carys could not speak. Not in front of everyone.

Conceding her need for privacy, Mrs Robbins held out her hand and led her to the reading area. Not quite private, but rather like a hospital cubicle curtain, it gave the illusion of discretion to a six-year-old.

Secluded from her class, Carys let her emotions abound. As she sobbed and sobbed, Mrs Robbins' concerns grew. "What is it, Carys, dear? Is it something at home?" she instinctively inquired.

At this, Carys wailed louder, filling Mrs Robbins with a determination to find out what was bothering this child. Her professionalism dictated it. Of secondary importance was providing comfort and solace for this poor wretch. And, thirdly, she had to understand what had disrupted her carefully planned lesson. She was a stickler for the national curriculum.

Grasping Carys by her young shoulders, a reminder of her authority and trustworthiness, she peered through large spectacles into the black holes that were Carys's eyes, wet with streaming tears.

"Carys, listen to me," she implored. "Whatever is upsetting you so, you must tell me about it. I have a duty to care for you, and I'm sure I'll be able to help." Said with professional detachment from a determination not to coat her words with superficial saccharine, it was no empty promise. "Now," she said, readying herself for what she might be about to hear. "Tell me."

Carys recounted every detail of the night before, and of course, Mrs Robbins' assumed it had just been a nightmare. Night terrors were something about which she knew little, but this sounded like a probable example. But when Carys described her mother's fear of the creatures, she revised her theory.

She'd heard the unfortunate rumours of Diane's poor mental health. Psychosomatic suggestion (again something she knew little about) joined simple night terrors as the likely truth. Despite her complete lack of actual expertise, Mrs Robbins accredited herself with acute common sense. Quickly, she made a plan.

With a brief hug to show her understanding, she proffered a few "Now, now's" and "There, there's," before taking action.

Concerned her mother's problems clearly had

such a detrimental and upsetting effect on her pupil, she conceived to propose a meeting, stat, with Carys's parents and the appropriate authorities' social department. She was sure there must be a counselling service available for Mrs Ellis to relieve her burden to someone trained to deal with her type of difficulties and not her young daughter.

The opportunity would arise sooner than she planned.

She still had the job of comforting her pupil, hoping her influence as her teacher would play trumps. "Carys," she opened, firmly. "The creatures you are scared of... Aliens," she said reluctantly. "They're not real. Your daddy is right," she assured. "It must have been a nightmare."

Carys looked up at her with wide eyes. Mrs Robbins continued. "Sometimes, we experience something called 'night terrors.' Do you know what they are?" Carys shook her head. "They are nightmares where people *think* they are awake," she explained. "Very upsetting, even for grown-ups. You must have been terrified. But please trust me that it was just a silly dream."

Carys felt better for having told this grown up. She didn't quite believe her, but wanted to so desperately, she allowed herself to be convinced.

"How is your mummy at the moment?" Mrs Robbins probed. She'd received the message from reception about Diane being unwell, and she thought she understood what that meant.

Carys told her how her daddy warned her that Mummy wasn't well, and to take no notice of anything frightening she might say. With Mrs Robbins's look of complete comprehension, Carys knew they were probably right.

"I think, perhaps, when Mummy isn't very well, you might hear things you shouldn't. Things that give you nightmares and these awful night terrors."

She placed a sympathetic hand on Carys's head and stroked her hair. "Are you feeling a little better now?" she asked, already sure of the answer. Carys nodded and followed her teacher's instruction to return to her seat.

Before long, the bell rang to signal play time. Concerned Carys might suffer jeering from the other children after her emotional and unbelievable outburst, Mrs Robbins gave her the chance to stay inside.

Well aware she was not a popular child—always polite in class, always diligent with any out of school work, along with her undoubted beauty, made the others envious, she supposed. They picked on her Welsh accent, and accused her of telling tales because they knew her dad was a policeman. So, playtime inside might be best for her today. "Would you like to wipe the blackboard for me, Carys?" she inquired, kindly.

Carys nodded enthusiastically. She'd been dreading the usual teasing and name calling in her fragile state. She wiped the board clean, then helped Miss to get sheets of colourful paper from a box and place them on each pupil's desk, ready for when they returned.

At the end of break Carys was allowed to do the job all the girls and boys thrilled to do - ring the hand bell to decry play time's end. Taking the large, heavy, brass bell in both hands, she walked outside the classroom through the back door used as entrance and exit at playtimes and waved it robustly. She found the deafening ding-dong, as the clapper struck the cup again and again, immensely satisfying. Her line smile curved at her grown up responsibility.

When the children playing heard the pealing tones, they sauntered back to class. As Max got closer and realised who was ringing the bell, he adopted a funny walk. Arms and legs unbending, he marched in a robotic fashion. Some other boys joined in, all squawking in a spiteful monotone, "I am an alien... I am an alien."

"That's enough!" yelled Mrs Robbins from the doorway. "Into class, now, and sit down!"

The children hushed at once and walked sheepishly past her into the classroom. Yet despite the displeasure of their teacher, a few unkind comments about aliens, and even that her mother's crazy a floated to Carys's ears. The teasing wasn't so different from every other day. And at least today Mrs Robbins was being nice to her.

After a lunchtime sitting alone, and further

lessons in the afternoon writing stories—which Carys loved to do—home time was upon them. The children all waited for their mums, and, occasionally, dads, to collect them. When Mrs Robbins recognised a parent, she would allow the appropriate child to venture off home.

One by one each child left. One by one, that is, except Carys. Once all the others had gone, Mrs Robbins asked Carys to wipe the blackboard for the second time that day. It wasn't unprecedented for Diane to be late. Living in Nuthampstead meant she was prone to delays where pupils' parents who lived in Royston were not.

When more time elapsed than might be explained by usual unpunctuality, Mrs Robbins asked reception for Carys's home phone number. She rang, but there was no reply. She dialled a further three times before deciding the lack of response probably meant that Mrs Ellis was already on her way.

A further twenty minutes passed. Mrs Robbins had run out of things for her to help with, and Carys was becoming upset. She decided there was nothing for it but to phone Carys's father who, fortunately, was nearby.

Soon, the jam sandwich, topped with an upturned blue bucket light, pulled up. Geraint ducked out of the squad car and marched with unnatural calm to the front door of the school, striding on to Carys's classroom.

Mrs Robbins struggled to hide her frustration

and decided Geraint probably deserved some of her ire for not anticipating such a problem. "Mr Ellis. Sorry to call you out of work, only, as you can appreciate, I didn't know what else to do with young Carys."

"No, no. You did the right thing."

Mrs Robbins arched her brows and hoped he got the message that she had never intimated that she might not have. "How is Mrs Ellis?" Fingering her hem until the tips of her fingers whitened, her eyes bore into Geraint's, searching for confirmation. "Carys has been telling me about dreadful night terrors she's been suffering. She's been terribly distraught, poor lamb, and well... Not to be too subtle, she mentioned your wife's, er... Fears. I wonder if they may have something to do with it?" Her hands paused in pressing and re-pressing her skirt's hem. "Should I be concerned for Carys, Mr Ellis? Is Mrs Ellis needing more support than she's getting at home, perhaps? There are people who can help," she stared to make sure he got the message. "I trust I can leave the matter in your capable hands?" she frowned, the threat of involvement from social services lingering in the air.

Geraint choked on his reply. "You can rest assured, I'll handle it. This won't happen again."

He and Carys left for home over an hour late. Neither spoke; both uneasy for what they might find. As Geraint glanced in the rear view mirror, it horrified him to catch sight of his grey pallor.

Any attempt to reassure his little girl would be unconvincing at best.

It was with mounting dread he steered the rover squad car round the narrow lanes leading back to Nuthampstead and 'Nutters.' Cringing again at the unfortunate choice of house name, he continued their short journey.

Even from the driveway it was clear all was not well at the Ellis family home. The untrained eye may be fooled, perhaps, although any on-looker might notice a few things not quite right; to Geraint, and doubtless little Carys too, the signs were all too obvious.

With every window flung open, spring clean-ing was clearly the order of the day—give the house a good blow through of fresh air. A not un-common sight in many homes in springtime, but given the wintry temperature, decidedly odd.

Diane's favourite, ABBA, blared from the open windows, and the two newly arrived Ellis's walked with trepidation up the shingle drive. The front door was locked and Geraint had to fish around for his keys. Absurdly loud music assaulted their eardrums as it swung open. En-tering the hall, they strained against the loud-ness toward the source of the sound. The 'music centre' crackled away beneath its Perspex lid, bellowing out the vinyl L.P. of ABBA's greatest hits. Diane was nowhere to be seen.

A clatter coming from the kitchen gave away her whereabouts. Another mammoth cooking escapade taking place? The lack of food smells should have alerted them, but didn't. As Geraint pushed the kitchen door open, they were shocked at the sight which greeted them.

The cupboards' contents were lined up all over the floor, which fortunately looked freshly cleaned. Diane wasn't immediately obvious, but then Geraint spotted her, kneeling in front of the oven, her head buried inside. He rushed, side-stepping saucepans and tins of everything from spaghetti hoops to figs, and packets of rice and pasta; desperately hoping he wouldn't be too late to purge the deadly fumes of domestic gas from her lungs.

Skidding on an unseen posse of penne pasta tubes, he halted bashing his hand on the cream-cleaner covered hob. A startled Diane shot her head out from the oven and beamed up at him.

Her reason for being in the cooker, obvious now: she was cleaning it. "Hiya, you two! What are you both doing home?" she asked, seeming genuinely surprised.

Geraint found it hard to repress a seething rage, but had long since learned that showing his displeasure only exacerbated the problem. Relief that she wasn't gassing herself (the lack of smell should have been a clue to a seasoned professional policeman anyway, he noted ruefully) helped keep him calm. He knew he shouldn't be cross, anyway. She wasn't herself in this state. She wasn't rational. He had to mention Carys, though. She had to know what she'd done. "We're home because I had to collect our daughter from school."

No reaction.

"I had to do that, because you forgot to pick her up."

Comprehension dawned with a dark cloud in her eyes. Explosive, irrational anger bubbled just beneath the surface; a volcano on the verge of creating utter devastation to its surroundings. A pinprick of light; of hope, pierced through the brewing storm as Diane fought through. "I've been very busy spring cleaning," she announced, as though that was a valid excuse; as if that were a perfectly normal reason to abandon a child at school.

Carys hid behind her father, sensing the tension in the air. Turning away, Diane sprayed more oven cleaner vigorously before declaring, "Right, I need to leave that for no more than half an hour." She paused before rising to her feet and announcing cheerfully, "I'm glad you're home. You can help me get the curtains down in the lounge. They're absolutely filthy." Geraint could see nothing wrong with them. They were actually fairly new. But he knew better than to argue.

Carys lingered, not knowing what to do with herself. She didn't want to be around her mother in this strange mood. And the lounge, and therefore the television, would be out of bounds whilst they dealt with the curtains.

She had most likely missed her favourite programs by now anyway, being so late arriving home. Outside, darkness already wove its cloak round the house. A step towards the stairs, and her bedroom, brought flooding back the images of dark eyes and grey skin. Trembling hands clutched her belly, the sounds of the whirring machinery beat in her ears at the fading memory. She couldn't move.

"Whatever is the matter, Carys?" her mother demanded. A simple enough question, but loaded with undisclosed magnitude.

"Nothing." Carys replied, her voice a quiver.

"Well, something is obviously wrong. Why don't you go and watch television? Like *normal*?" A command, not a question. Carys nodded that she would. The next comment, on the face of it throw away, chilled Carys with the implied threat. "I was beginning to think you didn't want to spend time with your mummy."

Carys turned and strained a smile. The moment passed but was too soon to breathe a sigh of relief. Diane followed her into the lounge barking orders to Geraint to fetch the step ladder.

"Now then, young lady," the tone less harsh as Diane smiled at her little girl, dispelling her fears at once.

Her mummy was lovely and kind, really. Carys understood when she acted oddly it was only because of her illness. She became a different person. That somebody didn't show itself often, and

Carys still saw the loving truth of her mummy smiling at her. "What did you do at school today?"

In the warm glow of motherly love, Carys had no reason to censor her reply. "I was upset in the morning and cried about horrible night-mares. Mrs Robbins told me about night terrors and let me stay in at playtime so the other children wouldn't tease me. I wiped the blackboard, and I got to ring the end of play time bell. I felt better then," Carys babbled. "She asked about you and said when you're unwell you sometimes say things that give me night..." Carys froze as she spotted the shift, "...mares," she whispered hoarsely.

Geraint breezed in with a chirpy whistle, carrying the stepladder under his arm. His apparent good mood, a transparent placatory act, disappeared the moment he saw her face. Dark eyes, whose gaze it was impossible to hold, stared hatefully out at the world. Catatonic, her breathing barely discernible.

He stood motionless, hesitant about what he should do. Saying the wrong thing now could be enough to push Diane over the edge. Over *her* edge. He decided to remind her of her excitement at washing the curtains; ignore her awful mood in the fruitless hope of pulling her through before she slipped too far. "Well then, cariad. Where do you want me?" he gushed, ever the enthusiastic helper.

Careful not to suggest any way of proceeding—she would likely object if she wasn't in charge—he was all too aware he might be making a huge mistake. Sometimes she *needed* gentle prompting for it to be palatable for her to cope with.

There must have been signs. An MO built up over the years, but Geraint struggled to make any sense of it. He was always sure he'd done the wrong thing and made things worse. But he couldn't put action off forever. "Shall I start on the right-hand side?" he queried in desperation, and then, realising he'd made a suggestion, began to panic.

Diane sat in stony silence for a full heart-wrenching minute before piercing the stillness with the cold steel of her tongue. "Aren't you going to ask me what's wrong?"

Geraint, who dealt with the dregs of abusive society; who'd seen more horrific things than most people could cope with and stay sane, was struggling. Wincing at his stupidity, he felt a failure. Not just for Diane, or even for himself, but for Carys. Doing things right and keeping his little family safe was his responsibility, and it was all going wrong.

Deep within, Diane, yearned to reach out to her husband; to place a reassuring hand on his and tell him everything would be okay. But the part of her that had breached the surface now was too strong and too clever to let her.

Voices. Always the same. They knew her - knew

when she was at her lowest, and exactly what to say to get her to react and lure her to do things she'd never think of otherwise. So compelling, so irresistible; her only salvation.

Threats of terrible consequences for telling anyone kept them a secret. They, and only *they* understood. That left everyone as the enemy. That part of her that wanted desperately to be free knew it was all lies; the voices were the enemy. But she could only fight them for so long. They never, ever gave up.

Today, the simple incident of her husband negating to ask her 'What's wrong?' became confirmation he didn't care about her. He didn't love her. On top of the indisputable fact that her daughter was obviously afraid of her, it grew too much. All in all, she was certain now. They'd be better off without her.

Before Geraint had delivered a suitable reply to her heavily laden question, she calmly stood and removed herself from the room leaving him faltering; paralysed; unable to do anything but stand and watch as she strode to the stairs and out of view.

The door to their bedroom slammed, followed by banging and clattering to signify what, Geraint and Carys could only guess.

And neither of them supposed it to be good.

Geraint always did his best to keep Carys from the worst; the self-harm, the threats of suicide. It was so unexplainable to his logical mind. There was no one to ask to unburden himself. He kept it all dangerously inside.

If Diane could talk about it, she'd explain that far from making anything worse, he was her rock. There was no right or wrong way, just an inevitability that couldn't be fought; a bath filling from a dripping tap—eventually it would overflow. One drip might be the final drop to cause the cascade, but if it wasn't one thing it would be another.

She would explain the abuse of cutting her arms as a reaction to the incessant beleaguering by disembodied voices; but partly, contradictorily, to exercise some control. Medication, prescribed by her psychiatrist to help her stay calm, detached her from her emotions. Pain made her experience something. It was cathartic. It made her feel alive.

If she recognised the compulsion creeping up on her, she could sometimes head it off with controlled, socially acceptable self-harm; jumping on tattoos, or piercings, as a solution, she had quite a collection of both.

It had been a while since she'd sliced her flesh with some random sharp object. Kitchen knives, and obvious instruments of injury were kept under close scrutiny by Geraint, but Diane would always find something: a belt buckle, a broken cup, even jewellery would be used to gash her wrists and arms alarmingly. Not life-threatening injuries, or even bad scars, but they caused pain, and most of the time, that was enough.

Always, upon discovery of Diane's wounds, Geraint would be mortified, punishing himself with the sight, certain he should have done more to protect her. He loved her desperately—he had to, or he couldn't have coped with their marriage. Conversely, loving her and caring so much made it more difficult to cope when she was ill.

The self-harm would often be too hard for him to bear, and he'd recommend a stay in hospital. Cared for by strangers who didn't love her would be the tonic that brought the real Diane rushing back to the surface. It was rare she would ever need to be hospitalised for more than a couple of weeks. Her stays were voluntary, so discharging wasn't a problem.

It always struck both Diane and Geraint, and would have Carys too if she'd been more aware, that it was a shame she couldn't check into hospital whenever she felt the need. But the system didn't support that. Instead, it was a prerequisite she be completely over the edge before it would even be considered.

Unfortunately, being over the edge was something she hid effortlessly from health visitors, and the so-called Crisis Team, who could actually help her. They would only ever call at the house when it was far too late. Still then, they showed hesitancy to do anything. Geraint's position in the police force was often the only thing that swayed their judgment.

But it could have been worse, they were both aware. Mrs Thatcher's 'care in the community' project, which had been talked of for years, was finally taking effect. Prior to now, Diane would simply have been sectioned under the mental health act and left to rot in the nut house as a paranoid schizophrenic.

On the whole, they were all grateful Diane was home for the vast majority of the time. For a lot of that time she was an extremely capable, intelligent, kind and loving member of society; and the invaluable linchpin of the Ellis family.

Filled with apprehension, Geraint raced up the stairs. Pausing outside his own bedroom, he felt the need to knock even though he knew it was pointless. There would either be abuse, or worse, no answer at all. At least if she was screaming at him, she was alive.

'*Knock, knock*'... No reply. Geraint tried the handle and pushed the door but it wouldn't move. There was no lock, so she must have pushed something in front of it.

What was she doing in there?

He imagined the worst.

"Open the door. Come on, cariad. Please, let me in. Don't be daft. Open up, now!" He rattled the handle again before giving in with a sigh.

A sigh instead of a scream.

CHAPTER FOUR

The ladder and
The wardrobe

Geraint tramped down the stairs and opened the red, plastic flip up telephone book at 'C' for Crisis Team. He dialled the long number and waited as it rang and rang. Eventually, a female voice answered in a manner suggesting perhaps the fridge had been ringing and had confused her. "Yes?

Not 'Crisis Team, how may we help?' or the name of the medical centre, or anything even vaguely professional. Geraint, used to the difficulties, continued with the necessary farce. "My wife is a patient of Doctor Richards. We're experiencing an emergency and need your help... Please." He thought to add the polite nicety despite a welling contempt for the service he'd learned to loathe.

A sighing sound, like they really had better things to be doing than dealing with his pathetic so-called crisis, escaped from the earpiece.

"What's happening, then?" she grunted.

Geraint described Diane's worsening mental state, culminating in her locking herself in the bedroom.

"Well, what's she doing in there?"

"Obviously, I don't know, but I don't suppose she's bloody knitting! You are aware of her history, aren't you?" Geraint hissed. "She has past cases of depression and self-harm. I'm seriously concerned she may be doing something we'll all regret."

There was no response, other than the irritated clicking of a computer keyboard. When no reply came afterwards, Geraint spoke again. "Can someone come out and bring medication or something?" he pleaded. "I really think she needs to go into hospital."

He barely finished his sentence before "We're full," was barked at him down the phone line.

"Well, there must be room somewhere she can get help. It might not come to that if the team get here in time. I don't know. You're supposed to be the experts."

More silence, then she suggested, "Can she come to the phone?"

Geraint struggled to repress profanities. "Have you been listening to me at all? She can't come to the phone. She's locked in the bedroom doing goodness knows what to herself. I need you to help us!"

"We are very busy," she began to answer

"Doing what? We need you, and we have no-one else to ask. What are you going to do?"

The receptionist, or CPN (Community Psychiatric Nurse), or whatever she was, didn't seem in the slightest bit phased by Geraint's angry outburst. She must be used to dealing with the perpetually unreasonable mentally ill, he supposed.

"I can put you on the list. The home-call team are out with patients at the moment. I'll pass on the message as soon as they get back and they'll give you a ring. In the meantime, you need to know what she's doing. Get a ladder and look in the bedroom window. If you're worried, call an ambulance and the police."

As annoying as her suggestion was, it made sense. If he saw Diane lopping an arm off with a piece of broken mirror or something, then he didn't have time to wait for the Crisis Team. If she was sleeping, then perhaps waiting would be okay.

He checked on Carys, now happily ensconced in front of the television, watching Crossroads. Geraint supposed it was a distraction of sorts. "I'm just popping into the garden, Cariad. If you want me, you'll need to call outside, okay?"

Carys nodded without looking away from the thrilling scene on the wobbly set of the long running evening soap opera. An altercation between a man in a wheelchair and a blonde lady was taking Carys's full attention.

Geraint made his way to one of the outbuildings that the house boasted. After removing the extension ladder he'd borrowed from his father-in-law when he had cleaned out the guttering, he walked carefully to the back of the house, managing to avoid tangling in apple trees and clothes lines.

Propping the ladder as gently as he could against the white rendered wall of 'Nutters', he took a deep breath and slowly exhaled. As soon as his foot met the first rung, he realised his careful attention to silence had been wasted. The ladder creaked and groaned in such a startling manner he was shocked he'd not noticed before.

There was little point in creeping up now. Diane would definitely have heard him. He was keen to get to the top fast and to reassure her that he was here, that he cared, and perhaps, that help was on its way.

The house proved surprisingly tall. He hadn't extended the ladder quite far enough to get a completely unobstructed view through the window, but he saw enough. The reason he'd been unable to gain access was plain to see. The large triple wardrobe, hewn from solid antique oak, which had needed four removal men to move it up the stairs (and even then, they'd taken part of it to pieces), was pushed in front of the door. How she had managed to shift it was dumbfounding.

On tiptoe, he glimpsed Diane sitting catatonic on the edge of the bed. She looked haggard. As if she hadn't slept for a week. How long she'd been trying to cope with the demons of her incessant, savage thoughts, Geraint could now begin to imagine—and to blame himself for not having noticed sooner.

Beside Diane on the bed lay a selection of items she'd selected for the purpose of harming herself. Geraint didn't recognise all of them and was sickened to realise she must have surreptitiously amassed them over time. Over how much time was unclear. She might always do it. Maybe she'd collected suitable objects over the last few days, or they may have been stashed away, hidden since her last episode.

As far as Geraint could see, the selection comprised broken crockery, a letter opener (that was surely too blunt to achieve anything, wasn't it?) and a packet of razor blades. Fortunately, they were the multi blade variety and unlikely to cause much harm.

Then something else he saw surprised him. Something that demonstrated more planning than he realised she was capable of. She had absconded with a handful of her mother's replacement needles for her diabetic testing kit. She'd used them to great effect too, as she still had one between the finger and thumb of her right hand while blood dripped to the floor and bedclothes from her left wrist.

Despite deep scratches on both arms, she had evidently been unfulfilled, or she deemed to try every tool in her collection and now chanced upon the very thing, because whilst she still clutched the sharp little object, she was no longer cutting.

The sight of her own blood had perhaps stopped her. Maybe that would be it now, Geraint unrealistically hoped. What should he do? Despite his certainty she must have heard him climbing up the ladder, she seemed wholly unaware. Like a turtle he'd once seen David Attenborough approach while she lay her eggs, who had been oblivious to his presence as he performed his piece to camera. Diane displayed that same distant look in her eyes, as though she wasn't really there.

Whilst Geraint wondered whether he should tap the glass, she suddenly stared at him. Like meeting a sleepwalker on the landing, she looked but didn't see. Geraint smiled, but no reaction came from his poor wife.

He had to get her out of the room. The ladder wasn't extended sufficiently for him to attempt climbing in through the window. The double glazing was supposed to be very secure, but Geraint knew a trick or two. He could remove the glazing bars from the outside with a chisel, and then he would lever the double-glazed unit from its sealing tape to remove it. The resulting gap would be easily adequate for him to get to his wife.

Unable to reach without adjusting the ladder,

he hurtled back down. After fiddling with it a bit, he soon realised the reason he hadn't adjusted it in the first place was the ill-remembered fact of the ladder's extreme stiffness in operation.

With a grimace, he remembered his plan to oil it when he'd finished cleaning the front gutters, which were, because of the slope of the garden, much lower than the back ones. He knew there was oil in the small barn he'd fetched the ladder from, as well as the tools required for removing the glass from the window.

Leaving the ladder, he scurried back to the shed. It struck him as strange the thoughts you have in a crisis. As he ran, he mused on the different names the shed got called; anything but shed, practically. Barn, outbuilding, garage, or, bizarrely: 'Tim's Room,' due to the words scrawled in messy paint on a door within the barn which led to another room containing old model railway pieces. They must have belonged to a previous owner, and for now, they had left them as they'd found them. Tidying them was one of many jobs they planned, and had been for all the time they'd lived there. But it wasn't a priority.

What was priority, urgent priority for Geraint now, was finding oil and tools. Struggling in the only light escaping from the small kitchen window nearby, Geraint cursed himself. When they did finally get round to clearing out Tim's Room, they were planning to use it as a pottery—a useful hobby for Diane. As he stumbled in the dimness, Geraint wished they'd pressed on with their refurbishment plans sooner. That way he'd surely have electric lighting, and not be attempting the near impossible task of finding what he needed in the dark disarray he floundered in now.

Lurching forward, his shin struck something hard. The gloop, gloop noise denoted kicked over engine oil which he'd topped up the squad car with earlier in the week and apparently neglected to replace the lid properly.

He bent down to right the can and gasped. Not what he was looking for, but oil was oil, wasn't it, and would suffice in this emergency. Now he only needed to find a chisel, and he was fairly sure he knew where one was. How good a state it was in, he'd soon discover.

Creasing his brow, he could picture it near Carys's Wendy house. Not long ago, he had adjusted the door which had been sticking. He was sure he could remember leaving it in the nook of the old apple tree.

Keen legs stumbling down the garden through slimy fallen leaves and steadily forming ice, he slipped and slid to his destination a few feet from the edge by the Wendy house. He thrust his hand where he remembered leaving the chisel, and sighed relief at the sensation of cold metal.

Prize gripped, Geraint scuttled back, pausing at the barn to collect the Castrol GTX, then returned gratefully, without falling, back beneath his bedroom window.

Making quick work of removing the ladder to the ground, he poured more than sufficient oil into the rectangular openings where the tubular aluminium slid (when oiled properly.) But even with oil dribbling bountifully over the struts, it refused to budge. Geraint was too dismayed even to utter profanities. Instead, he offered a silent prayer.

Maybe the pause calmed him enough to modify his technique. Perhaps it gave the oil time to seep where it was really needed. Or, his silent prayer had been answered as suddenly the ladder rocketed to its extended length and Geraint jumped into action.

Replacing it at the window, he noticed almost joyfully that it now reached plenty far enough for him to complete his mission. He scuttled up, narrowly avoiding injury as he slipped on the engine oil covering much of the middle treads. No longer concerned with keeping silent, only with reaching his distressed wife.

The pinnacle of his journey reached, his heart stopped. Now the view into the room was unobstructed, he was horrified.

Diane was no longer there.

Somehow, the wardrobe had been hauled back into place, away from covering the door, which gaped wide open.

His heart caught up with his racing thoughts

as he leaped down the full height of the ladder, breaking his fall with only a couple of rungs. He raced round the house to the front, not wasting time bothering to check the back door which was always locked. Beads of sweat peppered his brow, despite the bitter cold. The door slammed back on its hinges as Geraint barged through, wracked for his wife and their daughter.

With time to think, he would concede he wasn't worried Diane could hurt Carys, although it would be foolish not to consider it a possibility, in his rush he was more concerned that Carys seeing her mum in such a state would be distraught.

Stood in the doorway of the lounge, little hands wringing one another, she cleared her throat and announced, "Mummy's gone." Her tone matter of fact, but the dewy glint of her eyes betrayed her distress.

"Did she say where she was going?" Geraint asked with a nonchalant nod.

Carys shook her head. "She said to tell you to leave her alone. And she had a bag."

His eyes closed slowly as the seriousness clawed at his heart. "Wait there a minute, sweetheart," Geraint directed, forced to act fast over his reluctance to leave his daughter alone for longer. Surely Diane with a bag couldn't have gone very far.

He raced back through the front door and out of the house. Reaching a way down the lane leading out of the village, there was no sign of her. Breath held, he listened. Sound travelled far in this flat village, but none of a bag being hauled. No sound of heavy strenuous breath. No scuffing shoes, or stones being kicked, or twigs snapping; nothing.

He retraced his steps and continued past the house toward the woods. It seemed hopeless. There was still no sight or sound of her. And hiding here would be far easier for her, with tree coverage, and Red, and little Muntjac deer to disguise the noise of her flight.

Reluctantly giving in, he realised the futility of continuing his doomed pursuit, and returned to the house and his daughter. Calmer now, his responsibility was to his little girl. Convinced of what he had to do for his wife, he didn't bother calling 'Crisis Team'. It was too late for that. Much to his embarrassment, he knew exactly who he needed: his colleagues at Cambridge constabulary.

CHAPTER FIVE

Geraint's Vision

Geraint elected upon the swiftest way to contact his colleagues and dialled 999. It was an emergency now. She was a danger to herself, and to others; and to antique oak triple wardrobes.

It was with relief and surprise he greeted the prompt attendance by two of his contemporaries from Royston station within quarter of an hour. A tall police constable with short cropped hair, accompanied by a studious and efficient looking woman police constable. He hadn't met them before, but they seemed to know who he was.

He was relieved their manner in no way suggested he should be embarrassed for needing their help. Relief and pride gave a gratefully accepted reprieve from the enormous anxiety which had dominated his mood for hours. "Hells bells, you've got here fast!"

"We find the sooner the better in these situations," said the tall constable.

Geraint and the WPC nodded along in grave accord. "Do you have a recent photograph of your wife?" she asked with a raise of her eyebrows. The Ellis family weren't big on photographs. Compared to most families, they had pitifully few on display; a fact Geraint regretted and sometimes sought to remedy. Brief, spasmodic periods of avid photography, typically at the beginning of holidays or special days out, led to discarding many feeble attempts upon their collection from the chemists.

There was, however, one very recent photo of the family. It was after being accosted exiting the local Fine Fare supermarket for a photo opportunity with a smiling Father Christmas. Carys had been a little unsure, but the picture had been taken and duly paid for; the Polaroid instant now displayed proudly on the door of the fridge. It depicted Geraint to the left, Father Christmas in the middle with Carys on his knee, while Diane stood beaming on the right of the photograph.

Geraint fetched the snapshot and handed it to his colleague who stared at it, taking it all in.

"She looks so happy here," he commented. "How could someone go from this," he pointed at the photo, "to being so 'unwell' and depressed?"

"She's the one on the right, you know," Geraint teased the grinning Santa in the middle might be causing confusion. After a shared look of shock at the inappropriate humour, what began as a polite chuckle turned into a full belly laugh. Geraint surprised himself with his flippancy, but more that the show of good humour had briefly helped relieve tension.

"We'll take this, if we may?" the WPC said, pocketing the photo. "We can bring it back, but if we have a search now, we may find her before the dogs get here."

"Dogs?" Geraint shrilled, surprised but heartened Diane's disappearance was being taken so seriously.

"Yes. We do consider that she's at risk and a danger to others. We want to find her urgently." They exchanged scathing, yet always professional, comments about the unhelpfulness of the Crisis Team.

◾"They wouldn't have had time to do anything, to be fair. It's all happened so quickly," Geraint excused. The two officers looked at one another.

"I'm sure there must've been clues to Diane's mental state if the right people had been involved sooner. Anyway," he said, changing direction, "Let's just get her found. Has she taken anything from the house she could use to harm anyone? Any type of weapon?"

Usually, Geraint would be asking these sorts of questions. Being so close to the situation meant it hadn't even occurred to him. A quick perusal of the kitchen revealed a very conspicuous gap in the knife rack where a large carving knife should have been. Geraint's colour drained. This was worse than he thought. His fear was of her harming herself more than harming anyone else.

He'd witnessed that. Believing she'd stab some-one was harder.

"If while we're out looking, you could keep the doors locked. We wouldn't want her to return while you're unprepared. It would be so easy for her to knock you over the head with something. You'd be unconscious and we'd worry for your daughter."

"Diane would never…"

"I'm sure you're right, sir," the constable inter-rupted, "But let's be on the safe side, eh?"

As the pair of police officers left to begin their search, they waited to make sure the door was se-cured behind them. They really did believe Diane was a danger.

Carys walked calmly up to her father as he en-tered the lounge in a daze.

"It will be okay Daddy," she reassured. "Mummy will be okay. She's just scared, that's all."

Carys's calmness comforted. The pair of them sat watching nothing in particular on the tele-vision, cwtched up on the sofa, lulled into fitful sleep out of sheer nervous exhaustion. It can't have been long before they were roused fully conscious again by the rapping of knuckles on the door, and police officers' voices. "Mr Ellis? It's the police again."

Geraint let them in and waited expectantly. Carys sat on the couch stifling a yawn.

"We've looked everywhere we can in the vicin-ity, sir. There's no sign of her, I'm afraid. Clearly, she doesn't want to be found."

Seeing the distraught look on Geraint's face the officer looked to reassure. "I'm sure the dogs will find her. The unit is already on its way."

Once the dog and handler arrived and they'd been introduced, the original officers bid farewell and left the situation to their newly-arrived colleague.

"I'll need something with your wife's smell. A pillow would be ideal, or an item of her clothing. Do you have anything, sir?"

"She was in the bedroom before she left. I suppose her smell would be strongest there. I'll fetch something."

"You're Welsh, aren't you?" the gruff voice of the dog handler asked. Upon Geraint nodding, he said, "I go to Wales sometimes, for holidays. Barry Island?" he said, arching his eyebrows.

"Not too far from where I'm from," Geraint exaggerated. He wasn't in the mood for chit-chat about his homeland, particularly the jibes that often went with it.

"Is your wife Welsh as well?" asked the dog handler.

"No. She's very English. Very prim and proper," he added in answer to the querying gaze from the other policeman.

Geraint disappeared to the bedroom and returned with bedding and a jumper for the German Shepherd Dog to get the scent. Then he and his handler went on their way.

"Don't worry. Sabre here will find her. She can't have gone far in this weather."

Geraint watched as the pair disappeared down the driveway and began their search. Surely it wouldn't be long before Diane was found. And then what? She couldn't just come straight back home, surely. The crisis team was still needed. She had to recover properly in a hospital. If she came home against her wishes she'd just do more harm to herself.

It was with dismay Geraint answered a gentle tapping at the door a while later to witness the dog and his master standing forlorn in the porch. "I don't know if it's the cold or what. Sabre kept picking up the scent for a few hundred yards in different directions, and then losing it again. Sorry. I really expected to find her."

Geraint hadn't realised until this crushing disappointment that his thoughts and concerns had been of what to do with her afterwards. It hadn't occurred to him she could escape the dog. "What now?" he managed to utter.

"Well, it'll be up to the helicopter crew. I don't know if they'll find her, though."

"Helicopter?!" Geraint could scarcely believe his ears.

"Uh-huh. Our best hope is that she's holed up somewhere warm. I'm sure she'll be fine," he added unconvincingly. "You get some rest."

"I need to. I've got to be at Cambridge station

tomorrow."

"Oh yes. I forgot you're one of us," he grinned. "If we hear anything through the night, we'll let you know, but I'm sure she's safe until the morning. We'll carry on looking anyway though. Good luck," he offered by way of goodbye.

As he locked the front door for the night, he knew sleep would be impossible. Perhaps he'd try reading, or maybe watch some more television.

Slumped in his usual chair, he'd long-since given up on his book (he was a slow reader at the best of times) and instead had watched until the end of service on all four channels. He'd seen the news four times on ITV and BBC, all of it bad, as always, which did nothing to alleviate his suffering, and now he was back to contemplative silence.

The shrill ringing of the telephone exploded from the stillness. With a jolt, Geraint checked his watch: 11:02pm. "Hello," he asked tentatively.

"May I speak to Diane Ellis, please?" a female voice inquired.

Geraint's thoughts caught up as he realised who it was. "This is her husband, Geraint, speaking. Is that the Crisis Team?"

"Yes, that's right. How are things?"

"Nice of you to ask. Unfortunately, I'm afraid you're far too late and she's gone. I've called my colleagues in the police force and they're looking for her with a helicopter as we speak."

"Ah, okay." the voice responded, sounding not in the slightest bit surprised and not acknowledging any responsibility for the situation. "You won't be needing a visit then?"

"No. Thank you. I don't think so. But if she does turn up tonight, which seems unlikely—the police expect she's hiding somewhere warm until morning—then we may do," Geraint controlled a sneer.

"Well, call any time," she said cheerfully. "I hope we won't be so hectic," she added an inappropriate, chuckle.

This sort of thing was par for the course for her, Geraint assumed. "Okay, I may call later."

Wide awake again now, he sat in the hallway next to the phone, gazing through the large window onto the driveway of Nutters. He smiled thankfully at Carys sleeping soundly on the couch, covered in the tartan blanket he'd placed over her. He'd leave her there for now, in plain view. A guilty lump grew inside at the thought of letting her down. He should have seen the signs. How would she cope without her mum if the worst happened?

Choking down his dread, he took comfort in watching his peaceful daughter before his gaze drifted back to the window, staring out forever. Mind meandering over the events of the last few days, blame weighed heavily. He should have called someone for help way before tonight. It was obvious things weren't right. That bloody humming noise had driven her to distraction. Even when she'd appeared to be coping there must have been signs. Why had he ignored them?

If anything happened to her; he corrected himself, things were already happening to her; if it was anything irreparable, he'd never forgive himself. How had it got to this? His beautiful wife; unstable; roaming around with a dangerous knife on her, and being searched for by a helicopter? No. He'd never, ever forgive himself.

Distant bright lights pulled him from his self-deprecation. Frowning, he strained to decipher what he saw. As they came closer, Geraint wondered if his colleagues had spotted her. Avidly he stared to see where the spotlight would fall, keen to catch a glimpse of where she might be.

Something about the image puzzled him. He couldn't work out where the helicopter's tail was. Strange colours he didn't associate with aviation creased his eyes. What was causing them? A trick of the light? The sound was wrong, too. It didn't move with the light, just echoed; a strange, directionless hum.

As the lights grew closer, Geraint's heart beat wildly in his chest. The shape made no sense. His brain couldn't work out where the helicopter was in relation to him. All sense of perspective was lost to him.

The bright light which had drawn his attention wasn't directional like a spotlight as he'd first thought, but filled the sky with its luminescence. Shaking his head, he fought to comprehend the spectacle. But as the strange lights began to take shape, he was stunned to disbelief. He couldn't believe his senses.

He was forced to defer to them as what could only be described as a saucer shaped craft came clearly into view. The bright light he'd presumed to be the helicopter's search light effervesced from every surface of the ship, giving an ethereal incandescence like those depicted in science fiction films. But this was real. He hadn't realised how a two-dimensional film struggled to portray such brilliance; or that those films were anything other than fiction.

Despite displays of credence in his wife's tales of alien abductions and UFO sightings, he hadn't believed them for a second. He knew she was ill. She believed them and he wanted to support her, but now?

The lights moved closer, becoming brighter until they were blinding; the brightest lights Geraint had ever seen. Dazzling. So intense, they were painful to look at.

And then, as suddenly as they'd arrived, they disappeared, returning the sky to darkness. The craft was gone. In its place hovered the police helicopter, its searchlight weaving back and fore. 'I must be cracking up,' Geraint muttered under his breath.

CHAPTER SIX

Psych View

Geraint was surprised when Carys woke him, tugging at his sleeve. "Daddy? Daddy? Is Mummy home now? Is it time for school?" she asked.

He realised he had no idea. "Er... No. She's not home yet, sweetheart. As for school, what's the time?" Carys shrugged. She didn't know, but had been awake for ages.

Having observed her daddy resting on his arms against the glass of the hallway window for long enough, hunger had led her to investigate the kitchen. She'd left empty handed as it was still a shambles from her mummy's house cleaning yesterday. With no choice, and despite wanting to leave him rest, she'd roused Geraint from his sleep.

Poor Daddy. He felt guilty, she knew; but there was no right way to treat Mummy when she wasn't well. Sometimes, because she understood that, she was the only one who could bring Diane back to normal.

Geraint managed to focus his eyes enough to decipher his wristwatch, and to realise his daughter had woken him just in time for them both to make it to school and work on time. A feat all the easier for them already being downstairs and dressed having slept in their clothes.

"Come on, Cariad. Let's get in the car. We'll get breakfast on the way."

There was no news yet of Diane, which Geraint found strangely comforting. Assuming she'd kept herself safe and warm somewhere, it was natural she wouldn't be found until she came out of hiding voluntarily.

They opened the front door to leave but the shrill ringing of the telephone stopped them. Geraint rushed to the hallway and grabbed at the receiver. In his eagerness, he dropped it to the ground where it landed with a crack. Nervously, he picked it up and put it to his ear. "Hello?" he inquired, half expecting the phone not to work.

"We've got her. Safe and sound!" Geraint's sergeant announced, recognising his voice.

"How is she?" Geraint asked, meaning more than just her immediate physical appearance.

There was a lengthy pause before the sergeant answered. "Not good. We've requested the psych' to come and have a look at her."

"What's she doing?"

Another pause. "She's quite feisty, isn't she?" he breathed, his huge sigh belaying the understatement. "We can't get anywhere near her in her cell. "She came in quietly enough. A fireman found her on his way to work. She was trying to get into the medical centre, but it was way too early. Good she knows she needs help though."

"Mmm, I suppose. I'll be there as soon as I can. Thank you."

With watery eyes, Geraint replaced the receiver. "They've found Mummy, Carys bach," and then in response to her raised eyebrows, "She's fine. Fine," he assured in a less than convincing croak.

His immediate worries eased, he fretted what would happen next. She wouldn't be safe at home. Not yet. The same terrible, compelling thoughts would still reside firmly within her. A night in their crazy control might have served to make them all the more powerful.

His cheeks reddened at the memory of the vision he'd seen whilst drifting off after his phone call from the Crisis Team. Could he ask his colleagues if any of them had seen anything strange, too? Shaking his head to bring him back to his senses, he knew it was madness. He must have hallucinated with the stress of it all and woken still dreaming. The alternative was too outrageous to comprehend.

Desperately pushing the thought aside, a nagging doubt pulled at his resolve like a snagging thread. If it had been real, the helicopter pilots would have seen it. He shook his head, not knowing if he'd have the gall to ask them. Crazy talk like that might cost him his career.

The thread of thought was left to hang, unre-solved, dangerously ready to unravel, leaving Ge-raint with a sickening knot in his stomach. Past-ing a pale line of a smile onto his grey pallor, he ushered his daughter towards the car.

He walked Carys into school, pausing at recep-tion, his thick throat allowing no words to pass.

"Is something the matter?" the receptionist peered at him from over her spectacles, leaning over a large book in which she was writing.

Geraint cleared his voice with a cough. "Er, Yes. Carys might be a little fragile today. She didn't get much sleep... Her mother, you see? She's not too well at the moment..." He struggled to explain more.

"Yes, yes, of course. We'll keep an eye on her." Standing up, she walked from behind her desk and stood beside Carys offering her outstretched hand. "Come on. I'll take you to your classroom." She smiled at Geraint. "Don't worry, she'll be fine."

With a teary wave goodbye, Carys disappeared around the corner. Staggering a little, Geraint made it back to the car. The disquiet now filled his chest, ready to explode out in a mighty force of pent-up agony.

Driving a short distance up the road, just far enough to be sure no-one would see, he pulled over, buried his head in his hands and sobbed. Briny snot oozed from his nose as silent, salty sobs shook his broad shoulders; the silence finally breaking to hideous screeching howls of despair.

Of course, things were already better now. Diane was safe. She would get better. It would be okay, just as Carys had promised. But the grief of guilt and fear had to be purged. With his wife the responsibility of his capable colleagues, at least for now, he was at last free to release the dam and let some of it out before he burst.

It was a twenty minute drive to the station, and thanks to giving into his emotions, he was already late. A stab of anxiety returned, so soon after its relief, at the thought of how Diane might be behaving; and how much that behaviour might be denting the respect of his colleagues.

He arrived, grateful for the available parking space. The large grey building loomed over him in dreary reflection of his mood. Entering the building, he was expected. "Geraint, the psych's not arrived, yet. Perhaps you could go and have a word with her."

The edgy tone struck Geraint. When he walked to the cells and saw Diane, he understood all too well. Before he'd even entered hers, she noticed him through the peephole.

She couldn't hurt him through the door. Geraint hoped it was her knowledge of this that explained why she threw herself at it with such force.

"You did this to me!" she shrieked. "You called

these bastards. I told you to leave me alone! Don't come near me. I never want to see you again!!"

Geraint slid the peephole closed. "I'll leave her to the experts." With a cough to disguise his rasping voice, he rushed to his cubicle, slumped in his chair, and planted his face in his palms. Sitting bolt upright, he slapped both cheeks a few times and sighed.

It wasn't the first time she'd said such things to him, and he was sure it wouldn't be the last. One day, he might cope better. Today, he felt it raw. An excruciating pain for which he knew no relief.

He didn't know what would make Diane better, nor if feeling better would be enough for her to act differently; or even if one day she might not get better at all and remain hospitalised forever.

The institutions she'd inhabited over the years were full of people who weren't expected to get better. People who had given up trying to be normal, whatever that meant. They'd probably been just like Diane once. What would it take for one of her episodes to become permanent?

After she'd recovered enough to come home, when might the next incident be? Months? Weeks? He could count on it being sometime, definitely. There was no suggestion, and never had been, that she'd ever be cured. All he could hope was that next time he'd have regained enough strength to survive.

And how about Carys? She always coped better than him, but now she was frightened of aliens, too. Was she destined for the same affliction as her mother?

He shuddered, recalling his own sightings last night. Surely it was a hallucination; fuelled by psycho-suggestion from all that had gone on. And sheer exhaustion. A hallucination might even be an over-statement. A dream. That's all it had been. Just a dream.

With that certainty catalogued in his mind, he threw himself diligently into his morning's work. He'd just begun looking at files from the day before when the phone on his desk burst into shrill cries.

He looked at it for a moment before answering, anticipating, he wasn't sure what. Sitting up straight in his chair, he answered on the fourth ring. "PC Geraint Ellis speaking."

"Mr Ellis?" the caller still wanted to qualify.

It was a vague, airy-fairy voice Geraint was sure belonged to a male, but wouldn't fall over with shock if the caller turned out to be a woman. "Yes. That's correct. Who's calling?"

"Mr Ellis," the caller repeated, happy now, that it was fact. At least everyone was clear on that point. "Good morning. I'm Doctor Richards, Consultant Psychiatrist from Addenbrookes Hospital. I've just been in to see your wife," he/she stated, pointlessly adding her name, "Diane Ellis," before getting to the point. "She seems to have calmed down now. I just wanted to check you're happy to have her home before I sign her release papers."

Geraint spluttered into the receiver, "You can't be serious?! Calmed down! It was less than an hour since she was screaming she never wanted to see me again, and throwing herself at her cell door!" A wave of nausea piqued by anger and fear creased his face into a grotesque scowl. "You can't have done any proper assessment. She always pulls the wool over your eyes, you lot. It's me and my little daughter who have to pick up the pieces."

A stab of regret at suggesting Carys might be compromised stuck him in the chest. He had no desire for the infamous interference of Social Services. Carys's teacher had already threatened that. His error appeared to go unnoticed. "What will happen to my wife if I'm not happy to have her at home yet?"

A brief pause followed before Dr Richards answered. "I could phone to see if we have a bed on the ward, but, to be honest, it was quite full last night. We may have to consider a unit further away. It might mean travelling to visit your wife."

"That's fine. Whatever it takes I'm worried about her, doctor. I wouldn't be comfortable caring for her when she's so unwell. She needs to be safe in hospital."

It felt like betrayal. Even though he knew it was

right, the real Diane hated being in hospital. But she wasn't being the real her at the moment, and hospital was the best place to achieve that.

There always seemed an unwillingness to admit Diane whenever she volunteered herself to their care. "Hospital is such a horrible place to be," they always said. He was never sure if a bed shortage wasn't their biggest concern. "No-one in their right mind would want to go there." They'd actually said that, Geraint shook his head recalling. There were concerns other inmates might be a bad influence; or worse, harm her. Hospitalisation, therefore, had to be a last resort.

The ambiguity of her imminent departure fell to the side of relief rather than guilt. Clouds of despair parted and Geraint's eyebrows un-knit and his shoulders relaxed. She was safe, and she'd be his beautiful, wonderful wife again soon.

He had to stop himself bursting into uncontrollable laughter and sufficed with a heartfelt grin. With tension melting, he set about catching up on paperwork with a new found aplomb. He allowed himself a small chuckle and soldiered on.

CHAPTER SEVEN

Stella

When he'd finished most of his paperwork and was about to leave the station to follow up some enquiries, his desk phone shrilled into life again. It had been a couple of hours since his last contact with Dr Richards but he knew it would be him.

"Mr Ellis?" Once confirmed, the purpose of his call was revealed, and he was pleased to confirm Diane a place on Addenbrookes A5 ward. It was a section of the hospital separate from the main building to facilitate mental health care.

Visiting times were whenever he wanted, so long as he appreciated he might arrive to find he wouldn't be allowed entry after all. Things could change rapidly on the psychiatric ward. Geraint said he understood, which he clearly did. Diane was becoming a frequent user of their facility.

He had to leave work early again to collect Carys from school. Childcare would need to be arranged urgently. There were no family members to call on for help. Geraint's were back home in Wales, and Diane's had kept their distance since her diagnosis. Disgusted, Geraint had long since accepted their shortcomings

They'd used a child-minder before who Carys was fond of, called Stella. A robust, wholesome, slightly scruffy former teacher in her late fifties. She could be relied upon to collect Carys from school, and entertain her with paints, or cooking, or even (under strict supervision) using Stella's potter's wheel. It was Carys's favourite thing to do, and almost made Mummy being unwell worthwhile.

Stella had fired a few of Carys's creations which now adorned shelves in her workshop. Some had even made it into the house.

Diane was always a little embarrassed in Stella's company. The circumstances at such times were usually unfortunate. But she too was a fan of the potter's wheel. It was after dabbling they'd decided to make 'Tim's Room' into their own pottery. Stella kindly offered that if a wheel was purchased, she would fire the first few attempts in her kiln.

Thinking of Stella, and why she was in their life, brought a pang for home. In his melancholy, the ruler-drawn horizon riled him. Things would be so different in the bosom of his family.

Diane found the wonderful 'Nutters' after exhaustive telephone calls and mailings to estate agents when the opportunity for his career had been too tempting to dismiss, prising him from the lofty peaks and sandy shores of his homeland.

There were days when he conceded some preferences for his new surroundings. Every house lining the leafy lanes of Nuthampstead was full of character; a far cry from the grey breeze blocks deemed suitable as a finished surface so commonplace in Wales.

He held little fondness for the row upon row of long terraced housing in the valleys, despite a recent upsurge in their popularity. Geraint preferred the charm of thatched cottages and brick facades. Recently, he'd learned that Nutter's displayed its own thatched roof once. A senior villager had enlightened him.

Slate (probably from Wales), had long since replaced the reeds after severe weather damage over its hundred and fifty years of history had prompted the modification. The cost of restoring it to its former glory was too pricey for Geraint's police wages.

Daydreaming his way despondently through the bland countryside, a thin smile played on his lips at another source of joy: the wildlife the area boasted. The first time he'd seen deer in the woods and fields behind the house he'd gasped with surprise; and been ecstatic upon discovery of hoof prints in their garden! Deer roamed in

Wales, too, but in the Swansea valley's it was all mountain ponies and sheep.

A slowing of traffic forced his view left and made him judder. The reason for his disdain, the road sign noting his location: Caxton Gibbet; a pretty village named after a hideous execution. The gibbet itself sat gruesomely on the outskirts of the village. In Geraint's mind, a dangling cadaver still hung grotesquely silhouetted against the sky.

When the traffic finally moved, the relentless flat fenland was unyielding, provoking within Geraint a feeling of almost agoraphobia. Atop a Welsh mountain so open and free, the peaks and troughs of the undulating landscape gave scale and perspective. For a Welshman, this flatness was hard to endure.

It was with mild relief that he reached Royston, boasting as it did the highest point for miles on the pinnacle of Therfield Heath. Famous for rare species of orchid, there was nothing higher than the grassy upland on a direct line across the channel. On a clear day, it was said you could (just) make out the Eiffel Tower, but never on any of Geraint's trips to the summit. He almost felt more home sick knowing this was as high as he could get, and it still not providing the scenery he yearned for.

He wondered if this kind of home-sickness might be uniquely Welsh. Wherever he was, he knew he'd never be truly happy unless he stood on Welsh soil; his feet bedded into the Cambrian bedrock that was even a term geologists used to describe rocks of immense age.

He'd been warned of it by family, and fellow Welshmen and women, before their move across the water. The Welsh had a word for it, 'Hiriaeth', that they say has no direct English translation.

Geraint always choked on it, driving over the four mile long Second Severn crossing; always singing the same song. And when he got to the line, '*We'll kiss away each hour of Hiriaeth, when... You come home again to Wales*', he'd struggle to get the words out.

Arriving at school along with the other parents, mostly mums, Geraint and the squad car received plenty of attention. Not being one of the local town Bobbies, it was with suspicious murmurs that the crowd parted. After a few broad smiles and 'good afternoon's' in his friendly Welsh accent, he was soon winning them over.

Carys ran out from her class. "Daddy!" she cried, dashing towards him. He grabbed and lifted her to the sky in one brisk motion, nuzzling into her woolly jumper, her giggles filled the air.

The atmosphere in the car was strained. Fear from the day before had given way to a sadness. Worrying how Diane was coping, they missed her; the loving, nurturing wife and mother the enduring memory.

The pleasant drive back home washed over them comfortingly, but Diane's absence hit harder closer to home. Passing 'Lower Green', the first of the two halves into which the village was split, 'Nutters' stood proud and white at the end of a long shingle driveway just around the corner at the start of 'Upper Green'. Its roof pitched slightly oddly, a little too steeply. It must have looked grand thatched. The 'Nutters' sign Geraint had carved before they'd even moved in, hung from its purpose made post taunting them.

No signs of seasonal cheer adorned the Ellis home, and it was later than they'd usually start. The neighbours hadn't succumbed to the festive pressure. With a silent prayer, Geraint acknowledged there was still time to have a normal Christmas.

Geraint couldn't face visiting tonight. It hadn't been long since the violent outburst from her cell, and it wouldn't be fair on Carys to drag her out again. She looked exhausted. Maybe tomorrow, if Diane was any better.

He phoned Stella, who, apart from her concern for the family, was delighted to have Carys after school for a few days or so. Then, after poached eggs on toast for tea (three eggs each, because he was a bit greedy, and Carys only ate the yolk), he led Carys to bed.

Halfway up the stairs he remembered the mess Carys had confessed her bed to be. Pushing her door open, flinching at the anticipated gagging, he smiled when he was greeted by an agreeable, flowery smell. Before Diane had tackled the kitchen in her cleaning frenzy of the day before, evidently, she had changed Carys's bedding.

Carys was a bit tearful as he tucked her in. It took three stories of quite considerable length for Geraint to make it back downstairs. When he did manage to settle her down, he sat with a cup of tea in front of the television. Some new comedy series was starting on BBC One. It amused him in his fretful state. He chuckled a couple of times during it and made a note to perhaps watch 'Birds of a Feather' again next week. It was followed by the news. He was usually an avid fan but tonight he fell into a deep sleep.

He awoke to a fuzzy screen and an excruciating high pitched humming noise. He'd heard the noise plenty of times before. Often he'd fall asleep during the news before the weather forecast (his favourite part.) Tonight, though, it jolted him awake. He hadn't realised how on edge he was. It wouldn't have surprised him to see little green men surrounding him

"Bloody Hell's bells!" he cried. "We'll all end up in the nuthouse at this rate!"

He stumbled over to the television and depressed the button under the wood effect speaker. The telly fuzz reduced to a small white dot before disappearing. The screen was black and the humming noise, intended to alert viewers to the schedule ending for the night, sounded no more.

Static haze from the screen prickled Geraint's shirt as he brushed past. Jumping back, he snorted before realising what it was and steadied himself against the wall. Climbing the stairs to bed, further sleep evaded him as he lay awake wondering what his wife was doing.

Was she having the worst time? Maybe she was sleeping peacefully with a good dose of medication. His mind tracked back to before she'd started her episode, or rather, when he'd recognised she was struggling. The trigger was obvious. The bloody hum; and Carys's nightmare. With a chill, he found himself giving it credibility. What was happening to him? He shook his head on his pillow and tried to laugh it off.

When the room flooded with bright sunlight through the curtains, he was convinced he'd not slept at all, but soon realised otherwise. He had a little visitor. Carys lay across his chest, duvet wrapped round her like a sausage roll, and Geraint cold and uncovered.

"Wyt ti'n iawn, Cariad? You okay?" he asked with a frown.

"Yes Daddy," she mumbled. "I'm fine. I thought you might be lonely on your own without Mummy."

Geraint squeezed her tight, glancing at the time.

Last night's apprehension flooded his mind in a nauseating wave. 'Get a grip, you fool' he chided himself. How could he be a comfort to her, or care for Diane when she came home if he believed in aliens too?

"Come on Carys," he said with a smile. "Let's get you ready for school."

CHAPTER EIGHT

No Remorse

Parking could be a nightmare at Addenbrookes, but easier in a police car. Finding a spot with double-yellow lines, he parked near the entrance and walked inside. The receptionist at the main desk looked up reverently. "Can we help you, officer?" she inquired.

Geraint flinched at what he saw as his disloyal embarrassment at his wife's condition, but found himself reluctant to explain his presence. Maybe he was protecting her. "No, thank you. You're okay. I know where I'm headed," he assured, barely pausing on his well-trodden route to A5 ward.

It was quite a walk through the large busy hospital. When he arrived, one of the psychiatric nurses acknowledged him and went to a small window. Seeing him in his uniform would be no surprise. Patients were often brought in by police, particularly if they'd been sectioned against their will.

"I'm here to see Diane Ellis," he stated, and the same nurse left the room to let him in. A moustached man in pyjamas approached her. Geraint saw her mouth form the words, 'In a minute', and what looked like she said 'Steve'

When she turned, he made a grab for her behind. Un-phased, she pushed his hand away and walked toward Geraint. She typed in a code that Geraint's police brain couldn't help but memorise.

"Come in, come in," she bustled. The pyjama man advanced again, pleading (Geraint could scarcely make out his mumbling) for his cigarettes. His barely discernible muttering, easily comprehended by the nurse, was indecipherable whale music to Geraint.

"Wait a moment, Steve," she instructed firmly (he'd been correct). "I'm just showing this nice policeman to one of the side rooms." He reached down and managed to tweak her bottom before she silently moved his hand back to beside his body. Steve mumbled something in reply and shuffled away.

The nurse unlocked a door to the left with two keys and asked Geraint to wait while she fetched Diane. He wiped sweaty palms on his uniform trousers and struggled to pose in a natural way to receive his wife.

Time dragged as he raised his head for constant glances along the corridor for the first glimpse of her. Should he leave the room and make his way back to reception to see if they'd forgotten he was waiting?

Pacing to the window, he gazed through cell-like bars and fought back a surge of claustrophobia. He read every poster on the wall a dozen times, then tried to decipher what the lesson might have been, on the large flip chart.

A sudden racket echoed down the corridor. He thought he recognised Steve the mumbler's voice, shouting now, like thunder; echoing from every surface in eardrum-shattering uproar.

Then, he saw her; stony faced, flanked by the nurse, oblivious to the cacophony of Steve's whale song and walking towards him. Reaching the door, she stood, starring through the narrow pane of wired security glass, and straight through him. The catatonia was mildly preferable to the violent screaming.

Ushered in by gentle shoves from the nurse, she was guided to a chair where she slumped heavily. Turning to Geraint, the nurse plastered on a professional smile. "Do you need anything? Tea? Coffee?"

When he declined, the smile remained, but the nurse left, locking the door behind her, leaving Geraint feeling like he was in one of his own cells.

Detesting the excruciating silence, he ventured to break it with the warmest of greetings. "Hello, cariad," he soothed, leaning in to kiss her on the cheek. Her head shot away, leaving him pucker-lipped, mid-air.

Standing straight again, he fought down his irritation at the rebuff. He knew it wasn't really her. "How are you?" he asked to stony silence. His mouth dried in the face of her loathing of him. No words came to his lips, his mind pre-edited stringently every notion, deciding each topic of conversation was perilous.

Carys visiting was certainly out of the question for now. He shouldn't expect miracles so soon.

"What are you doing here?" she hissed through gritted teeth, her gaze, if he'd met it, surely would've turned him to stone. "Have you come to admire your handy work?"

"What do you mean?"

"You put me here, to rot. You can't love me. You've never loved me. Conniving, lying, scum, that's all you are! Get out! Go on. You've got rid of me like you wanted. You may as well go home."

The spat out words hung venomously in the air. Geraint smiled. He understood that deep within, the real Diane was being desperately hurt by this alternative personality. Pained at the thought of upsetting him, the part of her exhibited now wanted to cause her pain. It wanted to prove to her that she was unloved and on her own.

Geraint knew his role well. It was vital he didn't bite on his agitation, that he understood what she really needed, which was unconditional love. Whilst it cut him to the quick when she said such horrible, hurtful things to him, he made a good show of absorbing it harmlessly and giving back only love.

He made a few more chit-chat attempts, but Diane only stared at the floor. Her icy exterior did little to hide the furnace of fury inside. Rage combusting with every word, threatened to explode. Geraint stopped dead. His wavering lips terrified of giving reason to react.

The silence calmed her. Geraint offered his strong hand across the chasm between them; a show of affection without words that were so easy to misconstrue.

"Don't TOUCH me!!" she screamed.

He should have expected it, but he jumped, attempting to withdraw his hand calmly. There was no more he could do today.

After half an hour of excruciating silence, Geraint was glad when the nurse returned. She must've seen through the glass that the visit was over. She unlocked the door and came smiling into the room. "Everything okay?" Geraint looked at his wife. The nurse caught his eye. That was answer enough.

Standing to leave, he rasped "Bye, bye, Cariad," choking back a great gulp of emotion. Silence was the stern response until he made it to the door when a deep sob escaped from deep within her.

Shooting his head to look at her, she hadn't moved. But just visible in the corner of her eye, getting larger and larger, a steadily growing tear threatened to breach its salty skin. Mesmerised,

Geraint watched as it stretched to bursting point, cascading down her nose. The droplet grew on the tip, until it too fell. Geraint wasn't sure if he imagined the small thud as it hit the carpet. "Diane?"

She carried on staring at the floor. The nurse looked up at him and squeezed her eyes almost closed in a fashion Geraint took to mean 'It'll be fine. I'll take it from here.'

He nodded, darting his moist eyes away before she could see his pain. Striding down the corridor, he used the code he'd memorised and left.

Thankful Carys hadn't witnessed her mother's mood, when he arrived to collect her from Stella, he found her having a wonderful time. They'd baked cookies and ginger bread men, and Carys had been given a free hand with the decoration.

"Wow, they're fantastic, Carys, bach," he said as she threw her arms around him.

As Carys carefully arranged her creations into a Tupperware tub to take home, Stella took the opportunity to ask after Diane. Geraint shrugged, the emotion he'd been free from distracted at work threatened to embarrass him again. Stella understood implicitly and went back to help Carys with the lid.

Grabbing a takeaway on the way home, the proprietor of the local Chinese (a bizarrely named Norman Smith) had given a few extras, free of charge. Geraint's uniform often had that effect.

Having put Carys to bed, Geraint watched television until he fell into restless unconsciousness. He wasn't sure what time it was when the telephone woke him, but it felt late. Rushing to the hallway, he snatched at the receiver, almost dropping it in his eagerness "Hello?"

"I'm so sorry," Diane rasped before breaking down into sobs. "I want to come home now, please".

Heart racing, he reined himself before agreeing, 'Yes, come home.' Was it too soon? What would have been achieved in such little time? "Of course, I want you back home, cariad," he replied before adding, "But what do the doctors say?"

A long pause followed before she admitted they wanted her to stay.

"I think you should, then. If they want you to. You were very ill."

Diane's deep sob reverberated the handset. "I know," she choked. "You're right. I'll try to stay, I promise. But I haven't started Christmas shopping yet. And there's the decorations, and..."

"Huussshh..." Geraint soothed. "I'd rather postpone Christmas and have you properly well." He wasn't sure if he meant it, but it was important she understood the priorities. He still trusted she'd be out in time.

They made tentative plans to bring Carys in the next night, and Diane calmed. She seemed like her normal self. The Diane, looking back, Geraint realised hadn't been around for weeks.

They chatted like love struck teenagers for an hour before a nurse interrupted suggesting Diane leave the phone call to have her night time medication.

"Okay," Diane's voice sounded muffled as she turned away from the mouthpiece. "Night, night, cariad..." she returned with. "I Love you."

"Dw i'n di gari ti, (I love you), angel," he replied. "Nos Da." (Good Night)

"Nos Da," she said before the phone went 'click'.

Everything was going to be okay. On his way past her room, he popped his head in to check on his daughter, as he did every night. Turning away, certain she was sleeping, a little voice from the darkness croaked, "Is mummy coming home soon, Daddy?"

"Soon, cariad, soon," he assured her. "We can put the Christmas decorations up then, eh?" She beamed at him.

"Yes. Ooh, I can't wait". She snuggled under her duvet and Geraint made for the door. "Night, Daddy."

"Nos da, Carys," he smiled, eyes twinkling. Walking across the landing to his room, he allowed himself some optimism. "She's coming home for Christmas," he sighed.

CHAPTER NINE

Never Speak of This Again

He strapped Carys into her seat in the back of the squad car and grinned at her. Perhaps he was being a bit too upbeat. "You know mummy probably isn't coming home today, don't you, sweetheart?" She nodded. "It'll be nice to see her though, won't it?" A statement more than a question.

Driving from Cambridge to Royston in the rush hour, then almost immediately straight back again was the best plan Geraint had come up with for tonight's visit. Tempted to use the blues and two's, his conscience stepped in and removed his finger from the switch.

Stood in the foyer, Geraint pressed the door buzzer. As they waited, they could see into the corridor. Through one of the doors Carys spotted a pool table. "Can we play pool, Daddy?"

"Maybe. But we'll have to see how Mummy is first. Okay?"

Geraint told a different nurse to yesterday

who they were there to see, and she answered through the little window before leaving the room to key in the code allowing them entry. He had been concerned bringing Carys might be frowned upon, but they welcomed her warmly.

"Would you like a drink of squash, or a milkshake? How about a biscuit?" Carys was thrilled. "Hold on. I'll just empty the family room for you."

She walked through double doors to the room they had seen from outside where two men played pool. A tall man, slightly built with lank, greasy hair, and his very large opponent, bristled with bubbling rage. A glance from his ferocious face could kill at fifty paces, but the nurse ordered him from the room like a naughty toddler. "Can you finish up, you two, please? I've got a young family needing to use this room."

They showed no signs of resistance, and the large man in particular was thrilled to witness Geraint in his uniform. Muttering to one another, as if in the presence of a prized celebrity, they ushered from the room saying, "Good evening officer," almost in unison.

A soft look in the larger man's eyes as he smiled at Carys surprised Geraint. She appeared unafraid and returned the gesture. Geraint, impressed with his daughter's compassion, thought he may have judged too soon.

"You can come in now," the nurse directed. "I'll go and get Mummy, shall I?" Carys smiled and nodded enthusiastically.

She walked off down the corridor, locking the door to the family room as she left. Carys looked longingly at the pool table. "Looks like we'll have a game then, bach," Geraint conceded.

It wasn't long before a changed Diane came beaming into the room. Carys beat Geraint's reflexes in her rush to hug her. Diane swept her up, and Geraint joined them for a group hug.

"I'm so sorry, you two. You must've been so worried about me. I'm sure I was just dreadful to you both." She broke free from the hug just enough to make eye contact.

"You mustn't take anything I said to heart." She squeezed them both in her arms. "Don't take any notice of Mummy when she's unwell, darling, will you?" Said to Carys, it was meant more to Geraint. Her eyes couldn't meet his. She knew how much she hurt him when she was ill.

Too choked to speak, he sufficed with placing a reassuring hand on her shoulder and giving a gentle squeeze. Their eyes met at last. "It's okay," he managed, swallowing in quick gulps. A large tear made its way to his cheek and he turned away. "Shall I rack 'em up?" he gushed with false cheer, batting more tears from his streaked face before his girls could notice.

The nurse came back to inquire after tea or coffee requirements, and then returned with them presently, along with Carys's milkshake and an assortment of biscuits.

Carys rushed across, grabbed a couple, and eating them greedily, was forced to answer questions about her age and what school she went to with biscuit crumbs falling from her mouth.

"You're welcome to use the room for an hour or so. Watch the telly and use the pool table, by all means. There's some board games in the cupboard too," she said, indicating a wood-effect melamine unit with graffiti of every patient's name (in-between cigarette burns) achieved with various techniques—Typex, biro, scratched on, and some in what looked like blood. "I can't guarantee all the pieces will be there," she said. "You might have to improvise." She beamed at them as she left and locked them in again.

Over the hour, they played pool, watched telly and tried playing a couple of board games by using pieces from several boxes. Drafts with tiddly-winks was a challenge, but not as much as Cluedo. When Colonel Mustard murdered Professor Plum with a Ludo counter, they gave up.

"When are you coming home, Mummy?" Carys squeezed into her, gazing up with innocent doe-eyes.

Shuffling in her seat, she looked at her husband.

"Will you be home for our Christmas?" Carys blinked.

Diane took a moment to compose herself. She was obviously back to her lovely self but didn't want to rush things. "I'm sure I'll be home for Christmas," she seemed glad to commit to. "It might not be until next week though."

"Take all the time you need," Geraint piped up. He was proud of her for taking her treatment seriously. "I worried you might've been tempted to rush things."

"I was. Things aren't quite right yet though..." She drifted off, troubled by whatever that meant, but wouldn't say in front of Carys. "The doctors are pleased," she assured. "They're sure I'll be home soon if I keep up the good work. But I don't want to come straight back in again, do I?" a phrase she immediately regretted noticing the micro-expression of horror on Carys's angelic little face.

The nurse came back and stood smiling expectantly.

"I'd better get this little one to bed," Geraint fought the sorrow to announce, causing a group hug to launch again. "I'll pop in tomorrow, after work," he promised as they prepared to leave. Diane nodded, hiding a tear with a timely glance away.

Waving their own tearful goodbyes, they paused for the door to be unlocked and walked back out into the cold night air. Before starting the car he sat in silent thought for a few minutes. Turning in his seat to face his daughter, he smiled and paused again before speaking, unsure how to begin.

"It's going to be lovely having Mummy back, isn't it." Carys nodded. "Carys?" Geraint began his question. He wanted to reiterate his request from days before. It seemed even more vital now the ordeal was almost over. Speaking in a firm, calm tone, he saw her peering expectantly, her eyebrows raised. "If you have those horrible dreams again... tell Daddy, okay? Don't mention them in front of Mummy again, will you?"

Carys didn't bother saying, "They're not dreams." Somewhere in her young head she understood that her daddy already knew. He was putting his head in the sand and pretending nothing had happened.

Her mummy was no fool. Carys knew she was afraid for good reason despite sometimes becoming ill and acting like a different person. But was it her talking about her nightmares, and the awful humming noise, that tipped her over the edge? Or was it the lack of support from Daddy? Why didn't he believe her?

Carys was certain he'd seen those strange lights when he'd stared through the hall window. The lights which seared their eyes just like before. The flashing, multi-coloured beams glowing from the huge spaceship. She knew he'd seen it too, but there was no point saying.

As for his request, Carys didn't need telling. She'd resolved already never to mention, ever again, anything about it to her poor delicate mother. No matter what happened.

Twelve years later...

July, 1996

CHAPTER TEN

The Invitation

"Bye Stella. Wish me luck," Carys called, leaving the house. Ambling down the path, she opened the wooden gate to the busy main road roaring past Stella's house. Unfazed by the waft of a passing juggernaut, she strolled past the well maintained park, its tennis courts full of carefree kids beginning their summer holidays; Wimbledon fever was having its usual effect on the Royston youth.

She continued her journey, passing the old cinema which had closed down last year and was scheduled for demolition. Carys wasn't keen on change. She'd learned to live with it lately though.

Her mum and dad had left England to return to Geraint's homeland. Her father had witnessed too much horror, and it had broken him. He could do no more for the community he'd chosen thirteen years ago.

The Ellis's might still have been seen as the new

family, but Geraint would definitely take the love of the locals back to Wales. He had gained the respect of the Nuthampstead residents when he'd showed himself to be the hero he was. At what cost though, Carys mused as she recalled…

On a dark night in the autumn of '94, warmer than some which had gone before, but wet. After countless days of rain, frantic knocking echoed through Nutters.

Her dad had opened the door to a hysterical looking neighbour. "Geraint! PC Ellis!" Farmer Walker stood wringing his hands, cold rain running down his grey countenance. Shakily, he croaked out the words, "It's my boy…"

Geraint had grabbed his coat and rushed off with the farmer without asking the details. She supposed he'd questioned him on the way to wherever they were going.

She'd been too young at the time, but she understood now. Her dad had never been the same after that night. He never told her or Diane what happened, but she'd read about it in the Royston Crow newspaper.

'Heroic policeman, just too late to save boy in the dyke'

Diving into unthinkably deep water forming part of the fen drainage system, he'd taken a while to even find the boy. It was a miracle he found him at all, the report alluded.

The current had been so strong after the still falling torrential rain, but Geraint had refused to give in. He just wouldn't leave without finding him.

With no thought to his personal safety he'd dived under the icy water again and again. When he'd discovered him, he'd transported him under the chin in the style concordant with lifesaving procedure, and swum to the dyke bank.

Old Farmer Walker was no use lifting his son from the water. Gripping onto the lifeless body, it had taken all his might to stop his son drifting under again while Geraint hauled his own exhausted frame from the inky blackness.

At once, he'd turned to relieve the dad of his burden, and with superhuman strength, he'd raised the lad out of the water, dragged him onto flat ground and begun CPR.

There had been no hope, of course. And after more than half an hour of supreme effort, Geraint had looked at the farmer, and the farmer back at him. The glance had confirmed it. Both men had known it was time to stop. They'd both known the boy was dead.

Not mentioned in the newspaper report was the reason the farmer's son had ended up in the water. The reporter must have presumed he'd simply fallen in, as had everybody else.

It wasn't reported at the time; neither had Carys heard it herself until much later when village rumour abounded, but it was the humming noise which had spooked the Walker boy.

He had, according to the friend he was with, gone a deathly shade while they were out setting bird-scarers in the woods. His friend had heard the noise as well, and had assured him it was just a distant tractor or something. Walker had said he knew every type of tractor there was, and this definitely wasn't one. With that, he'd bolted for home and the friend had been unable to keep up.

From a distance, he'd seen him leap into the dyke, unsure if he was trying to cross it as the fastest route home, or was escaping the noise. He had seen where he'd entered the water and then not seen him again. Ever.

He'd scurried to sound the alarm, but by then, of course, it had been too late, Carys remembered, eyes dewy, the prick of emotion threatening to burst forth.

Andrew Walker had been one of very few people who Carys believed liked her. He never joined in the teasing from the other children. Carys blushed. There had been a time when she'd had a little crush on Andrew. Why did he have to go so young? Swallowing a surge of bitter bile, with a jolt and a shake of her head, she forced her mind from the disturbing reverie.

There had been periods over the years when Carys too thought she'd heard the noise. Usually late at night, craning to decipher it before falling into unnaturally deep sleep. It coincided, she was sure, with her mother's jittery moods.

Her condition had been much better controlled in recent years with a range of uppers
and downers. Sometimes, she'd be too sleepy to
worry about anything much. Other times she
was hyperactive and neurotic. But there were
lengthy periods where she functioned at close to
her full capacity. But her mood always worsened
noticeably whenever the humming noise echoed
through the village.

Carys kept her promise and never mentioned
it to her again. Beyond diligence, she'd become
less and less convinced about what had happened on that fateful night when she was a
young girl and had no desire to mention it to anyone. Maybe it had just been a dream as everyone
had told her.

More change hit her as she walked: an Indian
restaurant on the site of what had been the old
'Green Gunge' public swimming pool, as everyone at school had called it. Its official name: The
Green Plunge wasn't much better.

Turning into Garden Walk, past her old middle
school, where she'd stayed, as all the children did,
until she was thirteen, and next door the reason
she'd not yet joined her parents in Wales.

When she'd started at 'Meridian', the upper
school, she'd felt so small and vulnerable and
she realised now the feeling of being new had
never left her. Fourteen years with many of the
same people pointed to the feeling being a prob-

lem with Carys rather than her environment, she conceded. As a young adult, away from her parents, she was only just beginning to consider her own peculiarity. And given her family history, it was an affliction she was reluctant to give much deliberation.

She was treated differently. Was it her shyness that pushed people away? Or them making her shy? Her mum had always told her 'They're just jealous,' and Carys had always wondered what they could be jealous of. 'You're the most beautiful girl in the world,' she would say, but the compliment would stick in her heart and she'd quickly temper it with, 'If you weren't such a tomboy.'

She didn't consider she was boyish. Her hair was long and she had curves which needed underwear not stocked in most stores. Okay, she wasn't girly and favoured jeans and T-shirt for every occasion and her fingernails were usually filthy from woodland walks and helping with all the work at 'Nutters' but she didn't think that made her boyish. In fact, the very notion that particular activities were seen as male or female angered her and had become a pet topic. But maybe that was enough to put off boys.

No one in Nuthampstead was her age so her style mirrored the middle-aged villagers she spent her time out of school uniform with, so she never felt pretty. Occasional compliments reached her ears at school, but she didn't believe they were anything more than a set up for more teasing.

She cringed when everyone turned whenever she walked the corridors of the large school building. P.E. and swimming lessons never went by without at least one wolf-whistle.

Certain she was being made fun of, she never responded to advances. Disbelieving she was genuinely revered, loneliness in her perceived unpopularity was a bitter burden. If she really was admired, she must appear stuck up, but she wasn't about to let her guard down.

Reaching the school hall, it was a hubbub of excited and nervous fellow students. Carys needed to find where to get her results. There was a girl crying in the corner with her parents and Carys felt glad hers were hundreds of miles away.

Her intelligence was not in question. There had been an IQ test in her class before she even joined the sixth form and her score, an impressive 137, was by far the highest in her class. Most break times she could be found, if anyone had been looking, in the library (she'd volunteered so as to avoid the need to socialise with people she was sure disliked her at worst, and ignored her at best.) So, if other students were asked, they'd surely predict good results for Carys Ellis. She wasn't so sure.

Keeping on task was a struggle noted on many a report card. Scenery through the window would take her away from school and she'd finish each day feeling she'd learned nothing. Revising the same 'nothing' for exams was impossible. Pages whizzed by at a blur and refused to stick in her head. As soon as she had sat in the exam hall, she'd been certain she would do badly.

Bristol, Cardiff, and Swansea universities had received her application, simply because of their proximity to where her home would soon be. Staying behind when her parents made the move back to Wales had been hard. She knew they were loath to leave her, but her dad couldn't stand the city crime anymore.

When a position as sergeant became available in a small town in West Wales boasting the lowest crime rate in Britain, he'd decided to take it easy there until he could benefit from the generous police pension.

He'd more than paid his dues, but there were just too many horrific things he'd had to deal with every day: too many drug related murders, too many rape victims. Sometimes, things that weren't crimes were the worst.

Visiting a family to deliver the devastating news they were to be without their father because he'd been killed on yet another fatal accident on the Great Cambridge Road. Being called upon to yet another cot death to make sure it wasn't suspicious. It had all taken its toll. He needed to be in a small community.

There were only three thousand people on the voting register of Narberth in South West Wales compared to thirty thousand in Royston, and close to two hundred thousand in Cambridge. It had to be better for him. Less people equated to less crime.

The last straw came for Geraint when he'd been called to a suicide. Another train jumper. He felt awful for people so down they could jump in front of a train, but also a terrible guilt at his irritation.

The horrific mess left behind was gruesome, but he'd forced himself to build a resistance to it. He thought them selfish and hated himself for it.

One day, the ordeal had been worse than he could ever have dreaded...

He discovered the mutilated body of a female jumper. Terrible any day, but when he saw her dress, it looked familiar. His heart leapt to his mouth. Diane had the exact same dress.

With a violent shake of his head, he forced himself to disassociate from the possibility it could be his wife. Her mood hadn't gone downhill, had it? In fact, she'd been good, really good, for months.

Squinting at the body, vomit reached his mouth and he swooned as blood rushed from his head, because that's all it was; a body. A conspicuous space existed where her head should have been. But the body wasn't Diane's. No. It didn't look like Diane, did it? Or was he fooling himself?

The effort to turn his head to find the decapitated head was too much, but he spotted it twenty feet away, straight ahead. Long brunette hair, just like Diane's, laying at the side of the track.

Thankfully (or was it delaying the inevitable?), the head faced away from him. As he staggered slowly towards the sickening sphere, his legs filled with adrenaline, shaking violently. Shudders rippled through him, rattling his keys and handcuffs on his belt. The last oxygen-carrying blood drained from Geraint's addled mind and reality merged with a surreal soup of disbelief. Falling to his knees, he collapsed in a heap still several feet from his worst nightmare.

His colleague, a WPC who had no idea what was wrong with him, rushed to his aid. She checked on him before she saw the head. Instinctively she moved to collect it, to place it respectfully with its body.

Geraint lay still now. Staring, unable to tear his gaze away as the head was picked up. Wincing as it turned slightly toward him in his colleague's grasp, he squinted, straining to make out the features. Would this nightmare never end?

As it paraded past him, the face was visible for the first time; a motionless wax work; a necessary disassociation. When reality hit, he wept as relief relaxed the bear-trap on his heart. The waxwork head looked nothing like his wife...

After that, he had suffered a complete mental breakdown. The stress of his career, on top of mortal concerns for her beloved mother was more than he could take.

She forgave him his fall from calm capable father, and supported his move back home. He'd needed persuasion that she'd be okay finishing her A-levels with them both away. She was a big girl now, she encouraged. It had been vital for him to secure his new Sergeant position in Narberth.

She went to the line of tables set up in the hallway as a long desk. She saw her Head of Year, Mrs Clark. As she approached, Mrs Clark smiled. Despite a warmth in her greeting, there was something Carys detected that told her she wouldn't be surprising herself with better than expected results.

When handed the sheet of paper with her grades in different modules of her exams printed on, she had to take a deep breath to bring herself to glance down at it. A half-smile played on her lips. She'd scraped what could narrowly be described as a pass, but not at a level that would impress any of the universities to which she had applied. Mrs Clark bobbed keenly, ready to support her pupil. "How are you Carys? Did you get the results you hoped for? What you expected?"

Carys felt apathetic. She hadn't hoped for anything. She'd expected to do badly, and those expectations had been met. Nodding, she turned and walked away without saying a word. It would be nice to feel proud of herself. But mediocrity fitted in better with her low self-image.

She wasn't sure if she should hang around for a while. Walking to the school hall, confirming her low expectations, then walking straight back home seemed a little pointless. With a sly twinkle in her eye, she had an idea.

No-one need know her poor results. Her move to Wales was imminent. And whilst her own expectations had been low, she knew her contemporaries anticipated great things from her. She didn't have to correct their misjudgement, did she? In the middle of her thoughts a voice broke through.

"How'd you get on?"

Carys looked round to see one of the few people she could recognise and name. Not because the two of them were friends, but because everyone knew him. Stephen Holmes was popular with boys and girls alike, He had it all.

His swarthy, Mediterranean looks were incongruent with his Scottish accent, but that only added to his charm. Sports of astonishing variety were under his mastery, representing the school, and the county, at running, and swimming, and gymnastics, and Judo.

His name was proudly displayed on a number of brass plaques in the school foyer with his blisteringly white smile beaming down at visitors to the school.

He was no jock though, to coin an American-ism (even if he was a Jock, coming from bon-nie Scotland). Boasting academic skills as well as athletic, his GCSE results had been exceptional, and much acclaim had been given to his lead role in the school's latest production.

It was no secret his education was pointing him toward becoming an airline pilot. The future was rosy indeed for Stephen Holmes. And he was talking to her! She couldn't speak, but managed to nod to suggest that she had done well.

"I did better than I expected," he volunteered. "Oxford, here I come!" Carys still didn't manage to find her voice and could think of no appro-priate gestures either. Staring at him, her cheeks reddened.

Stephen was so immensely confident, he took the apparent lack of interest for the shyness it was. Rejection of his attention was unthinkable. "We're going out to celebrate tonight. Wanna come?"

Carys's cheeks flushed redder. She would have beamed at him, but was momentarily unable to meet his gaze. She accepted at once. That is, she nodded vigorously to the invitation, and to the following instruction to meet at *The Green Man* pub at seven.

It wasn't that she fancied Stephen (although she had to admit he was handsome), but his at-tention made her feel accepted. Not the social leper she always felt.

Unwilling to spoil the high, Carys hurried back home clutching her almost forgotten results in her fist. Stella was busy in her pottery. Not expected back so soon, she rushed upstairs to plan getting ready for her night out.

She knew that whilst everyone would be excited, mainly due to finally having their long awaited results and being able to map their futures a little more, she'd be the only one nervous about the social shenanigans this evening promised.

Maybe she wasn't as unpopular as she had imagined. Stephen could've asked anyone and been sure of a positive response. Aware he'd only said 'We're going out' and hadn't specified she would be with him, she was still sure the invitation was personal.

A brief perusal of her wardrobe produced no notion what to wear. She could list every item without opening the door anyway. Standing with the door ajar only confirmed her hopeless task.

She checked her purse. It was full enough; her mum and dad left her with sufficient pocket money to appease their guilt at bolting to Wales at such a crucial time for her education. She could easily walk into town and buy a new outfit. But there was a reason her wardrobe was so unappealing. She had always bought clothes with her parents. Every item chosen for its practical purpose. Geraint, in particular, had seemed more than happy for her to dress that way.

Occasional visits to the Woodman Inn, in Nuthampstead, and mingling unwelcomely with the young farmers, had not provided clues to what was fashionable. They all shared her parent's tastes.

Determined to make the most of tonight's social opportunity, Carys set off to the town centre to take advice from the shop assistants.

Not bothering to say goodbye to Stella (she wanted to put off answering questions about her results), and sure she hadn't noticed her return anyway, she strode off with a spring in her step.

Crossing over the busy London road and past the park, she walked through a small alleyway leading her to the square where various eateries could be found. Norman Smith's Lotus House Chinese takeaway still thrived, next to the inevitably named 'Taj Mahal' Indian restaurant, kebab shop, burger bar, a Thai restaurant and a very popular cafe opposite the obligatory fish and chip shop. Carys resisted the temptation and continued on.

Glancing in the window of Ladds newsagents/ cards/ and stationary supplier, brought a pang of childhood memories and she missed her mum and dad. She'd bought every Christmas or birthday card she could remember from there.

Snapping back to task, she strode away towards a boutique she'd not visited before (why would she have?) just next to a small arcade of covered shops.

Temptation to abandon her hunt for clothes in favour of visiting the bookshop she loved drew her attention for a moment. If there was time, she decided, she could buy more books to add to the ever-growing collection.

She entered the boutique with the discouraging name of 'Suzi's', as one of very few choices in the former market town. Two assistants bustled, sliding clothes along rails, clicks and scrapes grated as hangers were nimbly moved for no apparent reason. One scarcely looked up as Carys walked in. The other failed to look at all.

Carys thumbed through the items on display, adding to the racket. Unwilling to ask for advice from the unfriendly staff, instead she noted what they wore and selected similar from the shelves.

With a frown, she decided she wasn't so keen on the way either of them looked so instead assumed everything in the shop must be fashionable and just choose for herself. With an armful of various garments, all considerably more girly than anything she had at home, she made her way to the changing rooms.

Upon glimpsing her reflection in the little cubicle's mirror, her favourite of the new clothes adorning her curves, she stunned herself; scarcely able to believe the beauty smiling coyly was her.

Venturing back onto the shop floor to search

out accessories, she laughed as the two assistants nearly tripped on their open jaws rushing to help. Wow, I must look good, she contented herself as she allowed them to suggest embellishments.

It was a stylish and confident Carys who left the shop having purchased enough clothes to not have to leave in her unfashionable old ones. Resisting again the temptation to go book shopping in favour of new shoes, she was surprised she was enjoying herself. The rude assistants had made her feel even more special in their turnaround performance than if they'd been pleasant from the start.

In the shoe shop she was treated at once with respect. The male assistant had trouble serving her without stuttering. For the first time in her life, she felt as though she was fancied. Mildly disconcerted, she considered, on balance, she probably liked it.

CHAPTER ELEVEN

Carys Regrets

When Carys explained to Stella about her plans to meet up with friends (and especially Stephen Holmes), she was thrilled. It diverted her attention easily and deliberately from her exam results which Carys had diffused with "All in good time. There's something else I'm excited about..."

Stella hadn't been around Carys in Nuthampstead and witnessed how lonely she was, and had assumed (as most people would) that this charming, beautiful young girl was inundated with offers of friendship and more.

She wouldn't know Carys's fashion statements were anything but. And she was unaware how isolated Carys felt; how detached. Not understanding the significance of tonight's social meeting, Carys's coyness at the mention of a boy met with a knowing look from Stella.

Carys's eyes twinkled at the misunderstanding. Although sure she had no interest in Stephen romantically, it was heartening to receive some positive attention.

Excitement coursed through her veins as she laid out the new clothes on her bed and then a flush of panic again as she realised she didn't have any make up.

Stella might have something she could borrow. She wouldn't need much. Her long, dark eyelashes were already as thick and lustrous as anyone could want. She might use eye shadow and lipstick. Just so her face looked different to her normal unglamorous self.

By six thirty, and almost time to make her way to the Green Man, she was a nervous wreck. Happy with her clothes, she still worried that despite her best efforts, and the admiration of the respective sales assistants of the day's shopping, she still wouldn't meet the expectations of the girls from school with their cruel tongues. "Don't be such a neg-head," she muttered. "You look good!" Lips pressed together, her mum's comments about jealousy were almost believable as she looked in the mirror. And even she wouldn't make any 'boyish' comment, surely.

Her mum always suggested the bitchiness was down to jealousy. She could almost believe that now. Grabbing her coat from the bed, she made a move before the feeling ebbed.

Stella seemed surprised when Carys called

'Bye'. Despite mentioning the time of gathering, she must not have heard as she was warming up the telly for the Friday edition of Coronation Street the family and Stella still followed devotedly.

Stella, once she realised Carys's departure would clash with the planned viewing, offered to video it for her.

"Er, okay. But I probably won't get around to watching it," she smiled. In her parent's absence, Cary's interest had blasphemously diminished. Bidding farewell received wishes of good luck in return, and Carys pulled the front door closed behind her.

At first, she couldn't hear it. The busy road effectively masked the noise. A disquieting shiver ran down her spine before she was even aware of the low humming filling the air. Stopping abruptly, it was with a nauseous shudder that she identified it. She'd subconsciously attributed it to air-conditioning units on the rear of shops, pubs, and restaurants she passed on her route; or perhaps the bus which was stopped at the pelican crossing nearby.

As she stood in the market square, which doubled as a car park at different times of day, she was certain the humming noise had remained constant. She knew now it wasn't coming from any of those other things. Uncontrollably shaking, she squinted in anticipation. Why was it here? Over twelve years in Nuthampstead she'd all but convinced herself the sound emitted from farms in the village. But that can't be true because she wouldn't hear it in the town, would she? Yet, the noise was undeniable.

Was it following her? A wail of despair startled her as it escaped her lips. Those dreadful creatures. Were they coming for her again?

Fighting the urge to run straight back to Stella's and hide under her duvet, she hissed, "No," under her breath. "Stop it!"

A long time had passed since she'd heard that noise which had so many dreadful connotations for her. It could be a different farm. Or whatever it was could be present in town and village. She didn't know, but that didn't make it sinister.

She had a choice: worry, or enjoy herself. Worrying would achieve nothing. A psychologist might suggest she simply associated the humming with unpleasant occurrences in her childhood. Like Pavlov's dogs, trained to expect food at the sound of a bell and who salivated accordingly, Carys had conditioned herself to be fearful when she heard this noise.

Encouraged by her logic, Carys resumed walking the remaining short distance to the pub. As she tentatively pushed open the door to the lounge bar, she gained a view of the room beyond. Butterflies sent nausea wafting through her as she entered alone.

She was relieved it was empty. And a huge advantage to being inside was the inclusion of music, easily loud enough to block out any noise from outside. A flat screen television on the wall next to the bar displayed in silence some sport that didn't interest Carys at all. Her tom-boyishness was restricted to loving being outdoors, not to a love of boyish things.

Walking up to the deserted bar, considering calling for service, a young barman appeared from a door behind the bar. He looked approvingly at Carys.

"Be with you in a minute," he announced as he disappeared briefly, evidently to wash his hands, as he returned still wiping them with a green Greene King IPA towel. He placed the towel down near the till in an untidy heap. "What'll you have?"

Carys didn't drink often, but enough to have built up an idea of what she liked. Consumption of quite large quantities of alcohol left her unaffected, and she wanted a more immediate effect to quell her growing apprehension. "Do you do any cocktails?"

The barman shook his head. "Not officially." Briefly turning, he plonked a cocktail shaker on the bar. "But I know a few of my own." He rattled off his repertoire, and Carys chose whichever sounded the most pungent. But despite her best efforts, she was still startlingly sober by the time Stephen walked in.

He wasn't alone. A number of girls Carys recognised from sixth form gathered around like a

VIP entourage. Spotting Carys instantly, he broke free and bounded over.

Leaning in to hug her made it perfectly clear he was there to meet her. An awkward moment followed as the pair went to the wrong side of one another to kiss cheeks. Stephen laughed it off effortlessly and offered her another drink, which she accepted happily.

The gaggle of girls made their way to join them and were included in the round. Carys gave them a big friendly grin. She wasn't sure if they were being as rude as they appeared when they completely ignored her gesture.

As was Carys's norm, she assumed the worst from her counterparts. They did seem to be persisting in their want for causing her distress, she thought. She didn't fancy Stephen, but it was painfully obvious the other girls did.

She believed, for the first time, her mother's assertion they were jealous, and understood why these girls were being horrible to her. She didn't care so much anymore. A wry smile creased her pretty face in amusement as she downed her drink.

She would damn well drink everything Stephen bought for her. If only she could feel drunk, she could genuinely not care and thoroughly enjoy herself.

Stephen drank only soft drinks, Carys noticed. He explained how he'd driven here so wouldn't be drinking.

"Aw, that's a shame. You can't celebrate your brilliant results properly," Carys sympathised with an exaggerated frown.

"Don't worry," Stephen replied with a knowing smile on his face, the meaning of which, Carys, either through mild inebriation or more likely, complete lack of experience with boys, was completely oblivious to. "I'm sure I'll have a great time." The smile was welded to his face as he waited for confirmation of his intentions. "Another drink?" he generously offered.

Carys nodded her consent. She couldn't remember quite how many she'd consumed, but it was not inconsiderable, she was sure. She realised that apart from the drink she bought on arrival, her hand had remained strictly out of her pocket.

"Let me pay for these," she offered, not wanting to appear greedy. Stephen ignored her and continued paying.

"It's too late now," he insisted. "You can buy the next round."

Carys was enjoying herself. She wasn't drunk. Definitely not drunk. But she had to admit to feeling a little... uninhibited. Things she'd normally avoid mentioning at all costs, she had a sudden burning desire to broach. "Did you hear that strange noise when you came in? Before you came in," she corrected. Stephen and the two girls frowned blankly back at her. "A humming noise. A bit like a diesel engine, or a helicopter."

The blank faces continued and were joined by expressions of disinterest. "It doesn't come from anywhere, or go anywhere. It's just... there."

The two girls sniggered and began their own whispered conversation. Stephen made attempts to humour her, having already exchanged derisive glances with the girls. "I didn't hear anything," he shrugged. Turning away, he rolled his eyes.

Carys was cross. And for once, a little inebriated. Having been denied talking about this for years, she didn't care that she might appear foolish. She wouldn't see these people again after her move to Wales anyway. With a dogged determination, she carried on.

"There is a noise, whether you heard it or not. And you two..." She directed her comment directly at the two girls, "Are *very* rude!" They snapped to attention, surprising Carys who'd expected them to continue ignoring her.

"I've heard it before. I know what it is."

'Why are you telling them this?' the voice in her head demanded. 'You can't be certain of anything. It was just a dream.' But she couldn't stop now. The floodgates which she'd kept firmly shut since childhood had breached, and now, she was determined to be listened to.

"When I was five, or six, Alien creatures came into my room and did things to me, horrible things. In their spaceship, well, I presume it was a spaceship," she pursed her lips in thought.

"They were all around me, saying things I couldn't understand, and touching me." A shudder prevented her from describing them, but she didn't want to stop. Letting it out after so long felt good.

Eyes wide, like a celebrity performing absently down a camera lens on Jackanory, she was oblivious to her audiences scorn. "I could see all their machines, and the bright lights and everything. It was so real. It definitely happened," she announced.

The girls snorted in unison. Carys babbled on further, filling in details. When they could contain their amusement no longer and exploded into drink spraying guffaws, Carys couldn't help herself. "Fuck *off!*" she shrieked.

Carys's outburst caused more mirth as the pair huddled in cliquey cahoots. Turning sharply away, she strode purposefully toward the door. She'd reached it and had it open a crack when she heard one of the girls squawk, evidently to Stephen.

"Just leave her. She's crazy!"

Carys couldn't bear to hear more. She stomped from the pub ready to walk home. Stella might be surprised to see her back so soon, but the hot glow of embarrassment was from disappointment in her own lack of social graces.

Why did she have to blurt out her stupid alien abduction stories? And ignoring those bitches would have been better than her humiliating outburst. She'd definitely burnt her bridges. But she could learn. "When I get to Wales, I'll keep my mouth shut!"

Tapping her pursed lips with an elegant index finger, she decided wandering round the town before going home could kill some time. Anticipation of Stella's probing was too much (and she hadn't told her about her exam results yet.) Maybe she'd get something to eat.

Looking up at the clock above the indoor market, she was surprised to see it was after ten and immediately felt less disappointed and happier with her plan. When her thoughts calmed from her social faux pas, the hideous humming noise filled her head again; so loud, how had she been able to ignore it, even for a second?

As she stood and pondered, a car pulled up beside her. An electric window whirred down and Stephen popped his head out. Struggling to focus, she realised for the first time that she was feeling rather unwell.

Staggering forward, she steadied herself by leaning against the car. Through a foggy giddiness she shook her head in an attempt to rid herself of the shame of mishandling her drink.

"Sorry about those two," Stephen offered, excluding himself from the insults. He noticed Carys's wobbling. "You alright?"

Carys didn't quite know how to respond. She'd never felt like this before. Of course, she'd been drunk in the past (after a lot of alcohol), but it hadn't been like this. Woozy. Groggy. Distant, almost. And drowsy. Not herself at all. Struggling, she peered up at the sky in a slow laboured manoeuvre, before exaggeratedly looking back at Stephen. "Do you hear that?" she slurred. "That's the bloody humming noise I was talking about."

"I'm sure it's just machinery. There are a lot of farms around here."

"I give up!" Carys scowled (it was more of a smoulder in her befuddled state), hoping desperately that Stephen was right, she knew he wasn't.

"Hop in the car," he offered with a sideways nod. "I'll give you a lift."

Warning bells sounded in Carys's brain but went unheeded. Between the humming noise and its associated anxiety, and the fug in her head, she was in no position to make clear decisions.

A lift home probably was a good idea, she considered. Despite a certainty the house was close by, she couldn't quite remember in which direction. Peering one way, and then the other, gave her no clue where to head to begin her journey.

She struggled with Stephens's car door and flopped into the passenger seat. "Thank...you," she rasped from dry lips.

After setting off, it took Carys a while to notice they were travelling out of town; leaving Royston and heading into the countryside; and then a while longer to work out why this might be. Of course, Stephen didn't know where she lived.

He probably thinks I still live at 'Nutters.' That he'd have no reason to know where she lived, and that he'd certainly never been to 'Nutters,' didn't rear any warning. "I don't live in Nuthampstead anymore," she instructed. "My parents have moved back to Wales and I'm living with a family friend for a while."

Stephen smiled in understanding. "Don't worry. All will be revealed." He tapped the side of his nose with his extended index finger. Carys smiled and shook her head, clueless. The car rolled onward. The journey making no sense to the passenger gazing at the darkness flashing by outside her window.

"You are a very beautiful girl, Carys Ellis." Stephen informed her.

"Thank you," she blushed, genuinely pleased.

After bumping over the country lanes and swerving round bend after bend, Stephen turned in abruptly and pulled the nose of the car into the gateway of a field. He nudged the car forward until it brushed the rusting bars of the gate, causing it to fly open.

He tapped the accelerator with deft care, jolting the wheels over the muddy entrance in perfect time to accommodate the swing back of the gate as it creaked on its hinges.

Carys's muzzy mind marvelled at the precision she witnessed in her door mirror as it rocked back at just enough speed to end up where it had started moments before. That is, moments before she found herself in a field, in a car, alone with a boy who was looking at her peculiarly.

He edged close to her and reached a clumsy hand towards her right breast. She reeled at the touch, the horror of it waking her from her lethargy. "What are you doing?!"

"Don't act all innocent," Stephen scathed, moving to grope her again. She lashed out instinctively. Stephen seized her wrists. "You little bitch!" he gripped harder. "You happily drank my money for hours, and now you won't put out? Is that your game, is it?!" He manoeuvred her wrists into the vice grip of his left hand and raised his right ready to hit her.

Carys trembled. She was strong, at least a boy's equal, but he was so much stronger. If he struck her it would hurt. But she couldn't *not* struggle. Her instincts forced her, even though in her mind she'd resolved that compliance was safer. He was sure to have his way, why get hurt as well? She couldn't stop herself.

Fight as she did, she was no match, and Stephen had her utterly immobilised. His knee prevented her legs from moving whilst her wrists remained in his iron clench.

"Get off me!" she screamed at him. And then she thought to add, softer, "Please".

"Oh no you don't!" he spat. "Keep still you fucking bitch! You fucking owe me!"

His free hand didn't hit her. He had her well within his control. Instead, he used it for something else. Carys's eyes widened in disbelief at the realisation.

Straining a little at first with the buttons of his fly, one handed, soon though, he was free and pumping vigorously up and down his shaft. Carys let out a huge sob; the sound of it lost in the guttural grunts and moans of the grotesque act being perpetrated upon her.

Suddenly, from nowhere, an incredible bright light lit the sky, scorching the field in its white glow.

"Shit!" Stephen howled. "What the… ?"

Carys was surprised at his apparent fear. He must think he's been caught trespassing by a farmer. But Carys knew. She had seen the light before.

In response to his imminent capture, Stephen tugged more hastily at his throbbing member. Carys had never seen one before, but lessons in school meant she knew what to expect. But she never saw it. Her drowsiness hadn't been from plain alcohol, had it? Now, too late, she understood. Stephen had drugged her.

Evidently the effects were overwhelming as she could maintain her consciousness no more. Her last thoughts, before giving into oblivion, were of how she was powerless to Stephen's desires now. That, and the strange figures she saw surrounding the car in the burning blue and white light.

CHAPTER TWELVE

The Suspect

Carys awoke in her bed with no recollection of getting there. Hazy memories of being in Stephen's car refused to sharpen their focus. But then, with a rush that made her retch, came the awful image of Stephen, (Ugh! She could barely utter the name) manhandling himself, forcing her wrists. It was almost not a memory; more a production in her mind. Whatever drugs he'd given her were doing a good job of blurring the lines.

Squinting up into the middle distance, cajoling her brain's neurotransmitters into action, she wasn't sure why. Wouldn't it be better if she couldn't remember? The rage at the impertinence, the abuse; that's what was fuelling her curiosity now.

A sudden flash. There had been an interruption,

and yes, the humming noise. With a sigh of resignation, she eased herself from the safety of her duvet and padded to the window. Yanking back the curtains, she was surprised to see it still dark.

With the sash pushed open, it was clear; the humming had stopped. Carys exhaled slowly, freeing tension with the releasing breath. Shaking her head, she tutted at seeing she still wore her new outfit. She grabbed a nightie from the floor and fumbled her clothes off.

Fatigue set in fiercely again. With her appropriate attire making bed more inviting, she lay down again. Images of Stephen loomed at her closed eyelids. As she threw her head from side to side in her struggle to be free of them, Stella's well-plumped eider-down pillow slowed her movements until she succumbed to slumber.

Stella knocked on the door. Receiving no answer, she entered anyway, carrying a steaming cup of tea. Her eyes fell to the sleeping Carys with a fond twinkle. The night out must have been a success. She hadn't heard her come in. It must have been late because she'd gone to bed herself after midnight and read for a while.

Pleasure in Carys's enjoyment was short lived. As she placed the cup onto the bedside table, her fingers hadn't left the handle when Carys jumped awake causing Stella to spill a little of the tea. "Oh hello, dear. Did you have a lovely time last night, sweetie?"

Carys threw her arms around her waist and burst into tears. Through the sobs, Stella just made out her words. "It was awful. The girls were mean, and when Steph... (she couldn't bear to say it) gave me a lift home..." she frowned. "I don't know why I even needed a lift. It was only The Green Man! Oh yes, I was feeling really groggy, I remember. I think he drugged me... and anyway, we ended up in this field and..." the sobs became too loud to discern more but Stella had already guessed how it concluded.

She stroked Carys's hair as the tears and wails abounded. When they abated a little, she pulled away to look her in the eye. "We don't have to let him get away with this." Carys blinked. She had said 'we'. Her support brought more sniffs.

"No, no," she croaked. "I don't think he even did anything in the end. Not really. We were... he was," she amended, "interrupted."

"Just because he didn't get his way, doesn't mean he should get away with it. He would have raped you. And he obviously scared you. What would your father say?"

Carys knew. He'd want to throw the full weight of the law at Stephen; if he could refrain from killing him.

"Okay," she agreed. To protect other girls from this predatory bastard, she could be brave. A couple more weeks should see her move to South Wales. She could definitely be brave until then.

Stella telephoned Geraint and told him of

Carys's troubles. It took a lot of Stella's calm persuasion to prevent him jumping straight in the car to show this boy what would happen to him, touching his daughter. But he agreed to leave it until his day off tomorrow. Today, he'd make a phone call to ex-colleagues in Royston and prepare them for taking his daughters statement.

The stairs creaking at Carys's step caught Stella's attention as she was about to hang up. She held the receiver out to Carys who shook her head. Stella smiled with half-moon eyes and returned her attention to Geraint. "Me and your mum will be with you as soon as we can, tomorrow. We'll leave early. Don't worry, cariad, we'll look after you."

Carys spent the day occupying her troubled brain, slumped on the sofa. Scowling at a black and white film, its un-taxing images and tuneful music gradually un-knitted her brow and she began to unwind.

A pang of hunger grumbled in her belly and she reluctantly left her nest to search out snacks. Fortunately, Stella's larder had a choice of Carbohydrate laden munchies bought especially for Carys.

Slumping back on the sofa with a thwump, relief at her parents' arrival tomorrow was tempered with anxiety at her decision to speak out against her perpetrator. But that's what he was. And what he'd done; what he'd attempted to do, sickened her.

She could only guess at how it might affect her future relationships. She decided not to think about it further. Tomorrow her parents would pick her up and dust her off. They would take responsibility and ensure what needed to be done, would be done and she would feel safe. Until then she had only to occupy her thoughts. Nothing bad could happen to her in the comfort of Stella's comfy lounge.

She didn't see the end of the film. When she was awoken by Stella wanting to discuss dinner options, she realised she'd slept away most of the afternoon. Stella thought a takeaway might prove a nice comforting treat for her young charge.

They decided upon Chinese. After a brief discussion, Stella phoned their order through to Norman and settled back down. When Carys got up to go and collect it, she realised what last night's ordeal had done to her fragile mind. The front door became a barrier she couldn't cross.

Standing with the latch in her hand for a long minute before retreating tearfully to the sofa again, she slumped down, a lump of raw emotion preventing her from speaking.

Stella understood. After a hug and comforting words, she went to collect the food herself, praying Geraint and Diane could rebuild her.

Saturday night television did its best to entertain, but every time Stella looked Carys's way she wasn't even looking at the screen and it was obvious where her mind was.

"Why don't you go up to bed? Rest will do you good." Stella reached to pat her leg, her hand left in mid-air as Carys flinched. Slowly, she drew her hand away and smiled. That was a silly thing to have done, but offering comfort was an ingrained instinct. "I'm going up now, unless you want company for a little longer?"

Carys shook her head in rapid jerks. "I'm fine. Thank you." The numbness of unconsciousness would probably be the relief from racing thoughts like Stella suggested, but having been asleep for so much of the day, she wasn't tired so she settled for a night of cable television instead.

Sleep must have claimed her thoughts at some point because as she jolted awake, she knew she wouldn't have chosen to watch the paid commercial presentation about car polish featuring a particularly irksome man who insisted on setting car bonnets on fire every chance he got, and then showing the damage-free shine underneath. Stella walked in offering a cup of tea and a bacon sandwich.

She hadn't finished eating when the troubled figures of her parents entered her view. Swallowing the last mouthful of dry crust and bacon rind was out of the question as she choked with emotion. Forcing down her food with the help of a glug of cold tea, she leapt to her feet and threw her arms around Diane.

Cuddles from Stella had been a comfort, but

the raw emotion which sprang forth in the arms of her mum was purging. Elemental sobs sent shudders through the pair as they clung onto one another. Pulling away, she rubbed her eyes and smiled. "Hi," the first word she'd said in five minutes.

Perching on the end of the couch, she waited. What would happen now they were here? Geraint placed a gentle hand on her head and sat beside her.

"I've arranged for your statement to be taken, this morning," he said. "So if you want to get showered and dressed, we'll get down there."

As soon as she was out of earshot upstairs, Stella filled them in on what she knew of Carys's night of abuse.

A knot tightened in Carys's stomach at the thought of leaving the house when it was time to head to the police station. With a sigh, she clutched onto her mum's arm. Her mum and dad were with her, she'd be fine.

Huddled in the back of the car, she felt the trembling before she saw it, but holding a quavering hand in front of her face reminded her how nervous she was. The police station was minutes away. They'd be there too soon. How could she calm herself enough to talk?

As they entered the station, Geraint's official presence reassured. She had to persuade no-one. Her dad had already done that. She took a gulp of air and let it out slowly.

The desk sergeant knew Geraint and why they were there. Winks and head movements signified he'd see to them in a minute

"They're on your side," Geraint assured. "Just tell them exactly what happened. What you remember of it. They don't want arseholes like him getting away with it any more than we do."

A door opened a short distance away and a pleasant looking uniformed officer popped his head round to invite them in. The three Ellis's entered the small interview room and sat down. The police officer introduced himself to Carys, but Geraint and Diane were already familiar.

"I'm Sergeant Collin Freeman. A friend of your dad's." he sounded confident and authoritative. Carys settled down and prepared to go through the events of Friday night. "Just tell me in your own words," Collin invited. "Take your time."

Carys described the night in The Green Man, omitting the humming noise and the brief disagreement with the girls. She didn't see the relevance. "I was feeling really drowsy. And I'm sure it was down to more than drink. Looking back, I reckon he drugged the drinks he bought me."

Collin looked up sympathetically, then back down to write Carys's statement.

"He drove me out of town, I think towards Nuthampstead. Well, I kind of presumed, because then I still thought he was just giving me a lift home. I don't even live in Nuthampstead anymore... Anyway..." she babbled.

Staring at her shoes, unable to maintain eye contact, she mumbled, "We ended up in a field... That's when he..."

Collin looked up at the silence. He smiled and nodded. "This isn't going to be pleasant, especially in front of your parents, but it is important to tell me everything."

Carys coughed. "Can I get a glass of water, please?" she whispered. After Sergeant Freeman returned with a cup of tepid chlorine water, Carys surprised herself when she started talking, it was difficult to stop. She described how Stephen had no trouble holding her down; how he'd exposed himself to her shouting at her that she owed him because of all the drinks he'd bought her. "He would have raped me if we hadn't been interrupted."

"And did you say 'No' at any time?" the policeman asked.

Carys tried to think back. She meant no. She definitely meant no. But had she actually said it?

"I... I don't really remember," she stammered. "As I said. I think I was drugged."

The Sergeant smiled with a comforting nod before he spoke. "You did admit you'd had plenty to drink, didn't you?"

She nodded but added defensively "I had drunk a fair bit, but not more than I've had before." She shot an embarrassed look at her parents before continuing.

"Alcohol doesn't normally affect me. This was definitely different, without a doubt."

"What are you playing at, Collin?!" Geraint intervened. "She's not lying!"

Collin put two placatory hands in the air.

"I'm not suggesting she is, Geraint. But you know how it is. He'll just deny it, say it was consensual..." He paused before looking directly at Carys

"Thinking back," he said "Is there any way Stephen could have believed you wanted him to...? I mean you don't remember saying no, do you?"

"No!!" Carys slammed her palm on the table. "If he thought I wanted him, why did I try to hit him? Why did he hold me down?"

Sergeant Freeman carried on, a brief squeezing of his eyes his only concession. "How did you get home?"

"I don't know." she muttered blankly. "I remember bright lights. Farmers shooting rabbits with big spotlights on their roof, I think. I saw figures approaching the car, but by then the drugs had taken effect and I was unconscious."

"When I woke up in bed with no memory of getting there, I assumed the farmers brought me home. I must've roused enough to tell them where I lived and get myself upstairs to bed. Or maybe he," (she didn't want to say his name) "told them. It's all that makes sense."

Collin turned the written statement around for Carys to peruse and sign. "Make sure that's all correct and we'll bring him in for questioning."

Carys signed and the three of them stood to leave.

"I know Stephen. He's good at sport, runs with my Nathan," he said. And then, aware that sounded like he was supporting him, added, "Arrogant little shit!" Shaking everyone's hand, he added with a reassuring smile, "I'll keep you informed how we get on."

"We'll cwtch down at Stella's for tonight," Geraint said. "We can head off in the morning then. Get you moved to sunny Pembrokeshire, is it!"

Carys had forgotten her eagerness for the move home to Wales. It had never felt like home here, even though it was a lovely place, and Royston a very attractive period town with an interesting history. Every time they crossed the bridge to visit family in Barry Island, she had been at her happiest. Carys had always adored the ocean. And Barry Island's funfair and amusements had been a reliable source of joy as a child. She loved that her dad had grown up there too. It gave a shared connection to both their roots. The locals sounded like her and Geraint as well.

When they arrived back at Stella's, it was with an animated rhubarb of move related chatter. The main reason for Diane and Geraint being there, briefly forgotten. They wouldn't be able to forget for long.

Stella left to answer a hefty knocking and ringing at the front door. Following her into the lounge on her return was Sergeant Freeman. He smiled at the group, but without the warmth they might have expected.

"I have some news," he announced. "Two of my constables visited the home of Stephen Holmes this afternoon." He paused and straightened his shoulders, shifting his weight from one foot to another. "Unfortunately, they were not able to arrest him as planned: because he wasn't there. He hasn't been seen since Friday night."

The Ellis's and Stella didn't appreciate the significance of the information. Collin continued with his explanation.

"His mother is frantic and has now registered him as a missing person."

The Ellis's and Stella gasped. Peering at their frowning ashen faces, Sergeant Freeman was happy to give full disclosure. "We have begun a search. Under the circumstances we thought it pertinent." He directed the next statement to the room but mainly at Carys.

"We have recovered the car," he announced. "It was in the field as you described. But there were no tyre tracks, other than those of the entry to the field by Stephen's vehicle. The bright lights you saw must not have been from a land rover as you suggested."

Carys thought briefly before concluding, "It must have been parked in the road then."

"We considered that. Whilst the floodlights on

top of farmer's vehicles are dazzling, the car was a good distance from the gateway and had turned a corner. We have concluded it to be an unlikely occurrence."

Carys shrugged, not understanding what he was getting at.

"We are wondering whether you think it might have been torches. Whilst there's no tyre tracks, there are footprints around the car."

"I wouldn't have thought so, but given what you're saying, I suppose torches makes more sense. Maybe one of those million candle ones. They must be pretty intense, right?" she answered.

"Indeed," Collin agreed. "The footprints don't come from anywhere." He frowned at the perplexing notion before carrying on. "We are imagining a pursuit around the vehicle. Do you think you may have regained consciousness and been involved in a chase?"

"I don't think so. But I suppose as I don't remember, I can't be absolutely certain."

"Exactly," he agreed. "It's very important that you try to remember. You see... We've found blood at the scene. As you don't have any cuts on you, we're expecting it might be Stephen's blood. We're waiting for confirmation, but it's obviously probable."

The room sat in stunned silence. Colin examined the whorl of Stella's lounge carpet with unhealthy interest before glancing at them all in turn. He cleared his throat and delivered the next statement staring at Carys.

"The situation is this: We have a boy missing. We have an abandoned vehicle. We have blood. *You* were the last person to see him before he disappeared."

A sudden realisation at where this was heading drained any remaining colour from Carys's taut face.

"The last people to see him were whoever was holding the torches!"

"You're right. And we've questioned the farmer whose field it is. He and his family have confirmed they weren't out shooting rabbits." Carys's mouth opened and closed but no words formed from her delicate lips.

Collin let a thin line of a smile enhance his dour continence briefly. "Of course, that doesn't rule out other people with torches. They may have harmed Stephen. Then again, it might not even be Stephen's blood. But at the moment you are the last confirmed sighting of Stephen, and by your own admission you don't remember what happened. You don't know how you got home and you don't know where Stephen is."

"What are you saying, Collin?" Geraint demanded.

Collin softened into a smile.

"I'm not saying Carys has done anything wrong," he began to defend, "But we have a protocol to follow. You know that, Geraint."

"And what's that?" a nervous Carys asked.

Sergeant Collin Freeman took a deep breath. "Until we get more information, or until you re-member what happened," he paused, staring at Geraint, Diane and Carys slowly in turn... "We have to ask you not to leave town."

CHAPTER THIRTEEN

Appealing to
a guilty conscience

"That isn't going to work," Geraint protested. "We have to set off tomorrow. Carys is moving down to Wales with us."

"You're going to have to delay your plans, I'm afraid."

"Why? Come on Collin. You know Carys hasn't done anything."

Collin didn't want to offend his friend and colleague but he knew nothing of the sort. "You understand I have no choice but to follow protocol. There'd be complaints. Complaints I'd have to agree with, might I say. "Imagine, we allow the last known contact of a missing local sports hero, whose last known blood stained whereabouts were - by her own admission - with Carys, because she's the daughter of a police officer! The press would have a field day!" He realised he'd become a little too animated.

Geraint and Diane bristled with animosity. Carys stared ahead.

"I'm not suggesting," Collin added, looking at the three of them, "that Carys is guilty of anything at all. Just that we cannot afford to be seen assuming her innocence based on her parentage. You do appreciate that, I'm sure?"

He made his leave. In his opinion they should be extremely grateful he hadn't arrested Carys then and there. He didn't suspect her of any wilful wrong doing. Not that he was willing to admit. But the truth was, she couldn't remember what happened after Stephen had exposed himself.

Well aware of Diane's 'episodes,' he knew she could be aggressive and violent when she was unwell. The sweetest, kindest lady you could hope to meet when she was well. Not dis-similar to her daughter, he nodded to himself.

And didn't Diane always struggle to remember what she'd done in her unwell state of mind? Geraint had been really shaken by some of the things he'd come into work and told him.

Tapping his pursed lips, he frowned. Carys's story fit perfectly with a crime perpetrated by someone mentally ill. The stress of the situation could easily have triggered a dark side of her, making her lash out in self-defence. She looked a strong, robust girl. He'd seen what fear could do to someone. The adrenaline could have made her superhuman.

It was too early to be drawing conclusions, but one thing he was certain of: there was a lot more investigation needed before he'd allow Carys Ellis to go anywhere. They were very lucky indeed that he hadn't arrested her. It was a fact that he expected to change.

The Ellis's were speechless, sitting motionless in Stella's lounge. Geraint accepted with a rueful shake of his head that Collin had been right. It wasn't just protocol, Carys could be in serious trouble. Until now, Stephen Holmes's whereabouts hadn't been a consideration.

"So, what do you think 'av 'appened to 'im, Cariad?" Geraint's Welsh accent, stronger in his time of distress especially having mixed with his countrymen for several months.

Carys shrugged. She'd hated Stephen, but now desperately wanted him to be okay. Partly, mostly, because she wouldn't wish that sort of harm on her worst enemy. But also, she had to admit, because if he had met a bloody demise, she couldn't be sure Sergeant Freeman's not-so-subtle accusations weren't absolutely spot on.

Trembling turned to shaking as she looked to Diane for comfort, "I'm scared, Mam," she quivered.

"Don't worry, chicken. He'll turn up safe and sound. You know what teenage boys are like. He probably went on a bender after you spurned his advances. Lick his wounds."

Carys thought about it. That couldn't be right. Why would her memory block out Stephen walking away with nothing worse than hurt pride, but keep intact his disgusting conduct moments before? It didn't make sense.

What made a lot more sense was that whatever had happened after he abused her had been terrible. She had zero recollection of anything after the bright light shone through the window.

"Unless there's something you're not telling us, bach?" Geraint intimated and regretted instantly with the glares he received from his daughter and wife.

"I've said what must've happened," Diane reproached. "I'm right, just you wait and see."

"And if you're not?" Geraint persisted.

"I am!"

Diane had spoken, and that was that. But there was another possibility Carys hadn't wanted to admit, even to herself. Friday wasn't the first time she'd seen bright lights accompanied by that horrible humming noise, was it? Where was he? Where was Stephen? She couldn't bear to continue the thought. Doing so would unravel all the convincing herself, over the past dozen years, that it had just been a nightmare.

Geraint, ashamed of his accusation but unable to keep from thinking with his policeman's head, cuddled his precious daughter. She pressed herself into him and a huge sob released from deep within her chest. She pulled back and looked up at him. "We need to be practical," she said, bravely. "We can't have you losing your job over this.

"I won't leave with this up in the air," Geraint interrupted

"No," Carys insisted. "This might not be settled for a while. I haven't done anything, so everything will be okay."

"I'll stay," encouraged Diane. "If we need you, you can come back up, can't you? It doesn't take that long."

Geraint nodded slowly and agreed to head back in the morning so as not to miss any work. "I'll try to keep abreast with inside developments. Put your mind at rest as soon as possible, eh?" None of them were greatly comforted. They would need to be strong and hope Diane's theory proved correct.

Takeaway food gave comfort again. Having spent years in a tiny village, the temptations of this small town were surprisingly alluring

So with an Indian feast and Sunday night cable TV to entertain them, they put out of mind the troubles which on a metaphorical flip of a coin would prove to be a storm in a tea cup, or a complete disaster. Nothing they could do would influence the outcome. Stephen was either okay, or he wasn't.

Stella, perhaps being less attached compared to Carys and her parents, had an idea.

"What if he's deliberately staying away? He might be afraid."

Geraint leapt to his feet. "You're a genius! Why didn't we think of that? We should put out an appeal, or his mum could. Promising he won't be in any trouble if he just makes contact. Carys will be home and dry. It would mean him getting away with it though," Geraint winced at the thought

"I disagree," argued Diane. "If he's staying away deliberately then maybe he's learned a valuable lesson. I'm sure he'll have a lot more respect for girls in his company. Carys has protected any further girls from going through the same thing. That's the most important thing, now."

Carys agreed. She just wanted to put it all behind her and move to Wales. Recounting the whole ordeal with Sergeant Freeman had been difficult enough. It would be so much harder in court.

Geraint had no choice but to go along with it. He telephoned and left a message at Royston Police Station for Collin to call him first thing. Putting his plan into action straight away, with radio broadcasts and television appeals assuring his pardon, they could only hope Stephen might make contact soon.

They awoke early to see Geraint off, back to Wales. Diane and Carys wiped tears from their eyes as they hugged him goodbye. As the car disappeared round the corner of London Road, Diane turned to her daughter.

"What are we gonna do today then, sweetheart?" she asked

Carys shrugged. "I was expecting to move house." She grimaced dramatically. "How about helping me pack my stuff. I haven't done anything, what with everything going on."

Whilst making piles of washing, packing and throw-away, Diane gave several pensive glances toward her daughter. "Are you keeping something from us, Carys bach?"

Carys clutched onto the stack of CDs in her hand and stared in disbelief. "No, why?"

"The lack of details for the lights you say you saw. You seemed so certain about Stephen and his..." she hesitated, searching for a palatable word. Giving up, she continued her point. "But you don't seem bothered by what might have happened after..."

Carys looked down. Why did she feel guilty? Her cheeks burned and she couldn't look back at her mum.

"You just let it go. It's not like you." Diane paused and placed a hand on Carys's knee, gazing into her eyes. "I think I know the reason."

Carys's heart stopped. Her mind whirred at what her mum might be about to suggest.

"When Collin told you about the footprints and your story's discrepancy, you remembered what happened but you didn't want to say."

"That's not true at all," Carys protested. "I don't remember. I saw people in the spotlight but I'd been drugged," she said with a frown. "And sexually assaulted if you recall!"

It was harsh. Diane was trying to help, but what was she getting at? Amid wondering what to make of it and questioning her own memories she caught sight of her mother and her blood drained. She sat motionless with 'that look' on her face. Carys's mind raced back through the brief conversation to what might have upset her.

It took only a second for her to wonder if Diane had considered her worst nightmare too: the footprints came from nowhere because they weren't farmers, or anyone else's. They were... *those* creatures'. She shuddered. Pushing thoughts of them aside, her mind raced to make things better.

"Beth syn bod, Mam? What's wrong?" she used Welsh to placate her. To remind her of Geraint and her new home. Diane, as was her custom in these black moods, failed to respond in any way. Carys's dry mouth withered with her ideas, as she attempted a facade of normality. "I didn't mean aliens, Mam," she said with a cough. "It must've been people with floodlights. Maybe not the farmers, but someone else, defo!" The cogs of her jaw ground to a halt and allowed no more sound. Her train of thought bumped up behind, buffering against the colliding words.

It was in slow-motion, the film of regret played

on the screen in her mind. Grey-skinned, naked aliens running around a field in a comical Benny Hill montage. What if Diane hadn't thought of aliens? What if Carys had completely misread her mood and had just put the idea in her head? "Where are you going, Mam?" Carys probed as Diane stood and walked from the bedroom staring blankly ahead. She gave no answer and none had been expected. When the sickening sound of stomped stairs and the front door slamming reached Carys's ears, she knew things were serious.

Clenching her fists, she pounded them into the mattress. How could she be expected to cope with this? Why couldn't she have a normal mum? She should have fucked off to Wales with her dad if she was going to be like this. She was no support.

Guilt at her angry outburst washed over her like a barrel of freezing water. Smoothing back the covers, rubbing away her rancour, she frowned and raised her eyes to the scheming sky. She was supposed to be enjoying a scenic drive to her new home today. How could things get any worse?

At that moment, Stella made her fortuitous arrival from the pottery. Wiping clay stained palms on her striped pinny she, spoke without looking up. "Just going in the shower before dinner. I thought I heard you go out?" Glancing at Carys for the first time, she gasped, hurrying into the bedroom and scooping Carys's hands into hers. "Whatever's the matter?"

Carys choked out the words, "It's Mum... She's... upset" Stella needed no more information. She'd gathered enough about Diane's episodes over the years to appreciate the magnitude. "I'll go and find her."

"No, No!" Carys pleaded. "She won't let you!"

Stella gazed at the terrified look on her lovely face and wondered what damage a childhood with a mentally ill mother had done.

"It's my house! She'll do it my way," Stella pronounced. "Don't worry," she soothed. Carys, both reassured and surprisingly hopeful, watched as she disappeared from view. With relief, she slumped onto the bed and fell asleep.

When she awoke she was surprised at the sight greeting her. Her mother. Back from the abyss and smiling down at her, arms outstretched.

"Sorry, cariad. Mummy's back now."

CHAPTER FOURTEEN

*Are all boys
like that?*

Stella stood in the doorway, eyebrows raised in answer to Carys's unvoiced question: 'How did you do that?' Shrugging and shaking her head slowly, it was clear she didn't know. It was one of the rare occasions where the gravity of the situation had thankfully brought Diane round. Carys smiled.

"What's gonna happen to me, Mam? If he has been... You know?"

"I don't think they can charge you with anything. It's all a bit circumstantial, isn't it?"

"Maybe. But too incriminating for comfort."

She understood with today's forensic techniques they didn't even need a body to get a murder conviction. Murder! Is that ultimately what they were alluding? She shuddered. The weight of it threatened to overwhelm her.

'Please, God; make him be just lying low,' she mouthed, hands together in customary fashion. 'What about Stephen's blood?' the voice in her head refused to be silenced with a feeble prayer. Everything pointed to her, she was sure. She was the last known person to be seen with Stephen, a fact she had signed a statement to attest. She had motive to kill him, another fact she'd confirmed with her signature. If he didn't show up soon, things would be bleak indeed.

Forensics would verify his last appearance in his car in the field. Carys's best hope was if whoever had hurt Stephen had left evidence too. Unless that person *was* her. She winced

Another fact gnawed away at her. There was no blood away from the car. It was too easy to imagine some extra-terrestrial device whisking him into the sky. Heart racing, her eyes squinted, as though a rational explanation might be perceived if only she could focus on it.

But then it came. Stephen could have injured himself before going into hiding, couldn't he? Of course! He could've fashioned a tourniquet, hence no blood away from the car. Yes! That made sense. More sense than Carys having killed him, then somehow moving his heavy body without spilling any more blood. And, thankfully, more sense than her other outlandish notion. For the first time since yesterday's accusation, she felt genuine hope.

Smiling, she suggested the rest of the packing could wait, and the three went downstairs. Stella left to cook, leaving mother and daughter to talk.

"Me and your dad have been going to church in Pembrokeshire," she began. A revelation that raised Carys's eyebrows. The family had dabbled with religion before. When they lived in Wales before Carys was four, they'd gone to chapel every Sunday. And when they first arrived in Nuthampstead, they went to church to ingratiate themselves with the locals.

Although well attended, people came from further afield than the village. Without the benefit of getting to know their neighbours, and considering Diane's poor mental health, their attendance dwindled until they'd stopped going completely. The family always made the effort for Christmas and Easter to be about more than trees and eggs though.

"We're involved with a lovely contemporary church who congregate in the town hall. It's a bit 'happy-clappy,' if you know what I mean," Diane explained. "I was planning to tell you after the move. No pressure of course. You don't have to come if you don't want, but I thought you might enjoy it." There was an edge to her tone, Carys picked up on. "I'm just saying now because... I wondered if you might want to pray. What do you think?"

"Okay," Carys accepted, pleased to see her

mum's enthusiasm after her earlier wobble from sanity. "If you reckon it'll help," she encouraged. "Stella? Do you want to come and pray with us?"

Stella pushed aside her natural reluctance and joined them. The three sat on the edge of their seats, eyes closed and hands clasped together. It was a while before Diane spoke and Carys wondered if she was supposed to be silently praying.

"Almighty God," she began at last. "Please help Carys in her time of need. Shine your light of truth onto her, and everyone involved, so that Your Peace and Truth can reign supreme. Help Stephen to be found safe and well, and for Justice to be done for Carys. We give you our love, oh Lord and trust that you will make it so... Amen."

"Amen," Carys and Stella joined in appropriately.

"I haven't done that before" Diane apologised, embarrassment raging in her flushed cheeks and neck.

"Well I thought you sounded very ministerly," Stella offered. Diane blushed more.

"Thanks."

"I'd better get back to dinner," Stella said, already at the door.

"Tell me more about this church then, Mam," Carys suggested. Keeping her mum happy her main motivation, but she was strangely intrigued.

"I've told you, really," she said, "But well, the Pastor is so nice. He's from Italian descent. A lot of people in South Wales are. He's just come back from doing missionary work in Malawi and taking over from the old Pastor who is retiring."

"What's his name?" Carys asked.

"Dan. Dan Paulo."

"Are you sure he's Italian? That sounds more Brazilian or something."

Diane shrugged. "They have a band and everybody sings. They do healings and communion. It feels like a real community. Dan's son saw pictures of you and I think he likes you!" Noticing Carys's look of horror, she added, "Sorry. That was insensitive. I thought because he's the pastor's son..."

Carys nodded and the subject was promptly dropped.

"I haven't left the house since Saturday," she remembered, a sudden resentment of the fact surfacing. "I could go to the shops. Is there anything we need?"

"Check with Stella. I'm sure she'd appreciate it."

Stella had a well-stocked and organised larder, but impressed with Carys's progress, she made a list anyway.

Carys put her shoes on, gauged the weather and debated changing. Outside looked warm. Wanting to just get going before the anxiety set in again, she went as she was in jeans and T-shirt. It was nice to be out. People were again playing Tennis in the park's courts like they had been when her only worries had been how bad her A-level results might be.

She walked through the park and past the library to get to the shops, despite the crowds. As she made her way, she passed a mob of teenage boys; a gang with the addition of a few token girls. She thought she might recognise them, probably from the year below her at school.

As she walked past, they nudged each other laughing and jeering. Carys stumbled, glowing with self-conscious heat.

"Heyyy. You is ffiiit!!, innit." Whoever was speaking began to jog after her, thrilling the rest of the gang. "Hey, don't be walkin' away from me, innit. Not without a kiss!"

He jumped in front of her waggling a lewd tongue in a grotesque fashion. "Come on baby!! You know you wanna." He grabbed his crutch in vulgar gyration.

Several of the pack joined in, cheering and imitating the first. Carys tried to keep on walking, but the boys blocked her path.

The first boy barred her way, grabbed her shoulders and moved in to kiss her. Tearing her head away, she couldn't believe this thug expected her to yield to such boorish advances. But he was fast and his lips brushed hers. It was a mistake he would regret

Fuelled by the bubbling rage from Stephen's abuse of her, she kneed him violently in the place he'd been so keen on promoting to her moments before. He fell in agony to the floor.

"Oi! There's no need for that!" one of the others yelled, grasping for her and missing as she sidestepped. The punch she threw caught him full in the face whilst she screamed a blood curdling yell. Whether it was the swiftness she dealt with them, or the attention her shout had attracted, the gang moved away, mumbling vile language under their breath.

Carys glared back, resuming her walk. The boys scuttled off like kicked puppies, and the girls glowered their judgement that she'd seriously over-reacted. Carys was breathing heavily, fists clenched tight, ready to fell anyone who got in her way. Were all boys just complete jerks?! She had preferred it when no-one noticed her.

She strode on through the market square and car-park, past the restaurants and takeaways. Trudging up the gentle hill to the high street, she intended fulfilling Stella's list.

As she reached the top and prepared to turn left, she stopped dead. On a newspaper headline display stand outside the newsagents, she saw two familiar faces prominently exhibited on the front page: Stephen Holmes, and her own.

The newspaper, a national tabloid, seemed set on the possibility that Stephen had come to a sticky end, and that Carys was responsible.

She paused to read more. Her story of self-defence against a sexual attack was held in scant regard by whoever the journalist had interviewed. But the 'source's' opinion that she was a frigid recluse who overreacted to Stephen's perfectly normal, respectful advances, received full editorial support.

It detailed Stephen's celebrated local sports heroism and confirmed he'd always behaved like a true gentlemen in the company of the 'source.' To make sure the reader got the full picture, Diane's struggle with mental health was paraded for a few paragraphs along with Carys being described as weird. It even mentioned her alien abduction! Whoever helped the journalist with their testimony knew her.

The story was peppered with enough '*allegedly's*' and '*according to our source's*' to protect the writer from any libel claims.

Carys stood in shock. She hoped the story hadn't been on the television news as well. If it had, her mum, dad and Stella must have kept it from her.

"There's that stupid bitch!" Carys heard the shriek from across the street. Whirling to face them, she recognised one of the girls who'd been with Stephen in the 'Green Man' on Friday night. The girl was marching aggressively towards her, flanked by a skinny emo and another much larger androgyne.

The familiar one walked straight up to her and shoved her. Catching her off balance, Carys tumbled to the floor.

"What have you done with Stephen, you weird Welsh cow?!"

Pushing herself up from the floor, Carys screamed back with a furious frown, "What are you on about? Your precious Stephen tried to rape me!" She brushed grit imbedded palms on her T-shirt and stood her ground.

"In your dreams, you frigid freak!" the girl screeched at her. "He didn't even fancy you. He told me. He was only trying to be nice to you because he's a nice guy, and he knows no-one likes you."

"And this is how you repay him!" the much larger girl growled. "Telling your little lies." She took her turn shoving Carys too, catapulting her straight to the floor again. Staring up at the leering girls, their eyes glared at her, full of hatred.

"You gonna tell us where he is? Or does Sharron have beat it out of you?"

There had been times when Carys would have taken a pounding. Her low self-esteem made her believe she deserved it. Today though, with the injustice of her accusations and the leery lads in the park, this proved the final straw. She refused to take an unfair hammering lying down.

Still sat on the floor, propped on her arms behind her, she half-listened to the continuing jeers from the girls but her expression had changed. Her eyes no longer saw. They had the glassy look anyone encountering Diane in one of her episodes would have recognised instantly.

She took the jeering and prods from the three girl's feet in considered endurance until the pot of fury within her boiled to such a pressure, explosive force became inevitable. With one terrifying leap from the floor, combined with a scream of unimaginable ferocity "Diawwl!!" she floored the girl she recognised and her skinny sidekick with an arm to each of their respective throats.

As they lay spluttering for breath on the pavement, the larger girl, Carys now knew to be Sharron, reluctantly made a grab for her. The confidence she'd felt due to her superior size faded in the strength of Carys's effervescent fury.

Her feeble flailing matched poorly against Carys's swiftness. Snatching her hair, she yanked her face with incredible speed and force towards her knee which she drove with equal vigour to meet it. The resultant collision left Sharron's previously fairly unpleasant features, a bloody, toothless mess.

"Fucking leave me alone. All of you!" Carys screamed.

Neglecting Stella's list, she ambled back in a daze, entered the house undetected, and went straight to bed. Heaving the covers over her head, she sobbed into her pillow, falling into a teary, snotty, self-preserving sleep.

CHAPTER FIFTEEN

*The consequences
of violent action*

Carys slept for hours. She didn't hear the knocking at the front door, or the ringing of the doorbell. Diane and Stella were worried. They'd last seen a fragile looking Carys shuffling into town on errands, and hadn't realised she was even back.

She was eighteen and capable, so they both felt a pang of guilt at their concern. But the very nature of why Diane returned from Wales to be here, justified it. Loud knocking and ringing of the doorbell, and the presence of a uniformed officer looming in Stella's doorway inquiring after the object of their anguish, deepened their concern.

"Good evening madam," the policeman began. "Oh, my god. What's happened?" The officer raised two placatory palms.

"I'm PC Webb. This is my colleague, WPC Gardener," he nodded towards a small birdlike woman who Diane had failed to notice. "May we come in, please? We'd like to speak to a 'Carys Ellis?' of this address," he said with an Australian questioning intonation.

Diane stuttered slightly, but invited them in with a mumbled "Of course," before remembering Carys wasn't home. "She isn't here, I'm afraid", she said, her mind bolting to the worst conclusion. Stella, acting on instinct had already made her way upstairs to check Carys's room. Upon finding her sleeping, she woke her and informed her of the visitors.

Carys, by this stage, had little recollection of her violent outburst in the town and came downstairs smiling happily. It came back to her when PC Webb spoke.

"Carys Ellis?" He inquired, and she nodded. "I am arresting you for the assault of Sharron Wilding, Jennifer Mitchell and Denise Brown. You do not have to say anything, but it may harm your defence if you do not mention, when questioned, something that you later rely on in court. Anything you do say may be given in evidence. Do you understand?"

Of course she understood. She had no option but to accompany the two constables to the police station; the last place she wanted to be. The police declined Diane and Stella a lift alongside their daughter and friend, and encouraged them to stay behind.

"You're welcome to visit after Carys's interview, but I warn you, it might take a while."

Carys was duly booked into the custody suit of Royston Police Station. Cringing with embarrassment at the thought of her father learning about her incarceration at the hands of his former colleagues, a tear streaked her cheek and she stared at nothing.

Cooperating fully with requests to remove jewellery and valuables (she considered it the least she could do) she was led quietly to her cell. "You will be questioned presently. Do you have a lawyer, or would you like us to provide one for you? Free of charge."

"My dad must know some good ones. Can I call him?" Carys asked with a sheepish smile.

"We'll arrange for that shortly," the officer assured and proceeded to close the cell door, locking her in.

The finality of the slamming steel echoed through Carys's troubled head, and she let out a silent sob. Concealing what she saw as her pathetic weakness, she hid her face behind sweating palms. "Who are you hiding from? You're the only one here," she spat the comment to herself.

Why? Why had she done it? She was her mother's daughter, wasn't she? The realisation held as much fear for Carys as anything the police could contrive. She'd attacked them from no-where. And why didn't she remember? If so little of what had happened just a few hours ago was lost to her, what more was she capable of?

A flash of sudden clarity saw her forcing her forearm into the girls' jugulars. She realised with a shudder, she could have killed them! She had no choice but to admit it was possible she might have dealt Stephen an outraged fatal blow to his jugular, too.

Her failing memory frustrated her. The large girl this afternoon she'd thrown around as though she were a doll. Enraged Carys was stronger than she dared to contemplate.

The magnitude of her thoughts were becoming just too much. When a WPC opened the door to escort her to make her telephone call, she gasped. Carys sat on the floor, rocking back and fore, arms wrapped round her knees in a fashion which would fit in nicely with her mother's co-patients at the various mental health facilities she'd inhabited over the years.

The police officer coughed, peering at Carys from a safe distance across the cell. "You can make your phone call now, Carys."

She looked up at the voice and shook her-self into action. Hauling her exhausted body to standing, using the bench-cum-bed, she fol-lowed the policewoman through to a secure area outside the cells, away from the front desk.

There, stood a telephone with a cowl around it

for the illusion of privacy. Chained to the wall was a telephone directory and a yellow pages. Both of which were much thinner than they had been in years gone by, but would probably yield a firm of solicitors for those requiring their services.

Carys panicked realising she didn't remember her parents new phone number to speak to her dad. She wasn't to be allowed a second phone call, so she phoned Stella's and blurted instructions as soon as she heard her mum's voice. "I'm gonna need a solicitor, Mum. They haven't questioned me yet, but I've asked if I can have legal representation. They can't question me until I have a lawyer present,"

"I've been trying to reach your dad since your arrest. No joy yet. I'll have to keep phoning."

Platitudes of 'Keep your chin up,' were countered with reassurances from Carys she'd be fine, until the allotted phone time was up.

The police lady led her back to the cell to await her interview. She waited, shuffling in her seat; standing facing the door, then the window; counting the painted bricks on the wall, until another officer popped in to say that due to the lateness of the hour, and still having not secured legal representation, she would be questioned tomorrow instead.

A kind night-shift policeman offered her buttered toast and hot tea. She hadn't been aware of her hunger, but gobbled greedily the savoury treat. After the sweet milky cup of tea she was left to rest. Sleep eluded her the entire night. But once the sun peeped its first light through the high barred window, she at last dropped off.

Three hours sleep felt like mere minutes to Carys when she jolted awake. "What ridiculous time is this?" she squeezed from her mouth, pasty and slothful. It was, in fact, a rather reasonable eight-thirty.

"Get yourself up. We're ready to question you now," a policeman Carys hadn't seen before instructed her through the peephole in the door.

She got up as hastily as her groggy morning stiffness permitted. As she followed the officer to the interview room, she shook her head vigorously in her effort to lose her bleariness. Being alert was crucial.

They arrived at a door which the officer knocked before entering. Inside the room sat a serious looking grey-suited man of around thirty-five. He was tall and thin with ash blonde hair. Glancing at Carys as they walked in, he attempted to get up, but by the time he had moved his briefcase and papers, and pushed his chair back, Carys was already across the room.

As the policeman introduced him as her duty solicitor, Mr Bright, he'd managed to stand only half way. Hunched, he greeted Carys over spectacles perched on his long, slightly red nose and sat down whilst wafting his arm in invitation for her to take the chair opposite.

"Miss Ellis?" She confirmed with a nod as he reached his hand across the desk and shook hers. "Damien Bright. I'm the duty solicitor appointed by the station. I work completely independently and I'm very experienced, so you're in safe hands," he gushed, trying to convince himself more than Carys.

"I thought my dad was going to find someone for me. Someone he trusted."

"I understand he's been somewhat difficult to track down," Mr Bright informed Carys. "I'm sure everything's fine, but the police are wanting to press on with their inquiries."

Carys didn't attempt to hide her disappointment.

"I have worked with PC Ellis a number of times. A very diligent police officer." Reassured, Carys consented they should get on.

"Quite," Mr Bright concurred. "Now then. You know why you've been arrested, yes?" Carys nodded.

"And what is your position?" To answer Carys's confused expression, he further explained, "Did you do it?"

Carys thought this was a stupid question and wondered at just what level of knowledge this man was operating. "It would be pointless to deny it. I'm sure they can back each other up, and I must've left pathological evidence."

"Quite," he agreed again. It was beginning to grate. "Are there any..." he looked meaningfully into her eyes, "extenuating, or mitigating circumstances?"

"What sort of mitigating circumstances?"

Mr Bright sat up straight and inhaled a deep breath.

"Well," he started to explain, "I don't think self-defence will wash. Not with the injuries the three of them sustained and the complete lack of injury to yourself..." he coughed before continuing. "I er... understand there might be a history of mental health issues in your family?"

He didn't bother asking if he was correct. His information was from an impeccable source. Carys reluctantly granted that if the police wanted to charge her for assault, her family history should be taken into consideration. She was sure they'd want to give her a break, what with her father's respected career, but she had to help them to help her.

The door opened after a while and a police Detective Inspector walked in along with her female sergeant. They introduced themselves, made a show of recording the interview and began their grilling.

"I am Detective Inspector Jackson", a presentable but haggard looking woman in her mid-forties, Carys estimated, began. She had a redness to her face and hands that belied her vice of cigarettes. That and the smell of stagnant tar on her pungent breath.

"Also present is Detective Sergeant Cooper," she

said before indicating to Carys and her legal representation to speak their respective names,

"Mr Bright, attorney."

"Carys Ellis."

They questioned her whereabouts, and she gave a statement detailing what little she could remember of the incident. Details eluded her, but she grudgingly accepted the police version of events. It made sense.

Whilst signing, she paused, keen to make sure they knew it wasn't her usual character, and to perpetuate the possibility of a mental health plea.

She would soon regret it.

"With your difficulty in remembering your violent behaviour of just a day ago; would it not be fair to say your recollection of Friday night's events might be equally elusive to your poor memory?"

Carys gasped sharply. She'd taken only surreptitious breaths throughout the interview until now, filtering the air through the corner of tight lips. The idea of inhaling fully the bitterness slowly filling the room, circulating putridly from her accuser's mouth, made her want to vomit.

Mr Bright leaned in and suggested quietly that she didn't have to answer that. Carys wasn't sure if she replied, or if she somehow indicated with gesticulations that she concurred. Everything was becoming such a blur.

Detective Inspector Jackson's next words were

enough to render Carys stricken.

"I am further arresting you on suspicion of the murder of one Stephen Holmes. You do not have to say anything…"

CHAPTER
SIXTEEN

*A turn up
for the books*

After Carys's shock, she was again left to take counsel with Mr Bright.

"So you're not sure if DC Jackson is correct in her accusation?" he asked.

"I told you. I don't remember doing anything to Stephen. I don't remember *not* doing anything either. I don't remember!" Carys was losing patience.

She had yet to be charged. The evidence stacked against her was circumstantial. The police took the step of arresting her in connection with Stephen because they were genuinely concerned for what else she might do. Two possible serious crimes within a few days meant they'd had to take action.

Investigation into Stephen's disappearance persisted relentlessly. The severity of his injuries, as established from the blood stains in the field were inconclusive. He could have lost that amount and still be alive, but he could also easily have died.

With no sign of him obtaining medical treatment from any hospitals, it pointed to the latter. But the police were acutely aware that a rapist on the run may have sought alternative care.

There were plenty of dodgy doctors willing to supply their skills to criminals unwilling to put their head above the ground to receive the help they needed; for a price. But Stephen was a clean-cut boy. He'd never been in trouble before and it seemed unlikely he'd have those sort of contacts.

The scientific evidence: Carys's fingerprints, threads from clothing and various other signs were present. If nothing in Carys's favour turned up before they were forced to either release her or charge her, they made it clear to Mr Bright: they planned on charging. For her own security, and the public's safety!

They believed her excuse that she was suffering from poor mental health, but they couldn't risk her getting into even more trouble. If they did end up charging her, she would have to be remanded in custody without bail.

Having been escorted back to her cell, to remain until a decision was taken (at least the next thirty six hours), Carys tucked her knees to her chest, lay on the bed and stared unblinkingly at the wall. This was bad.

Days passed and Carys was charged, as promised, with the assault of the girls, and for the murder of Stephen Holmes. The cell she was already sick of, her home for the foreseeable future.

Suggestions of moving her to cells in Cambridge left her cold. Carys didn't care. She was losing the struggle to maintain her sanity. During the long, sleepless nights, she'd become convinced she must have killed him and was just waiting for the bad news to be confirmed.

If ever she did fall asleep, she woke screaming, shouting not about Stephen, but of alien monsters coming to take her away.

Diane, too, was struggling to hold on to her equilibrium. She sat, as she had for days, motionless on Stella's couch, news from one channel, then the next, blaring from the old boxy television. With Stella's cable, it was a twenty-four-hour a day assault.

The frequency her daughter's name caused her heart to beat wildly increased by the hour. Debates about murder trials without a body on 'This Morning,' were followed by experts' critique of mental health services and care in the community. The question featured on every bulletin was, "Mental illness; is it a get out of jail free card?"

It all washed over Diane. She wasn't really listening. Just staring, ready to pounce if reports of Stephen Holmes's safe return reached the airways.

And then they did. Stephen Holmes turned up. A farmer spotted him dazed and confused, wandering in the middle of his field. The farmer put himself in the frame for Stephen's assault briefly, but there appeared to be no case to answer.

Stephen's expected horrific injuries were nonexistent. He had no recollection of the farmer having harmed him or keeping him against his will. He had no recollection of anything since his night with Carys.

Mention of her name flushed the colour from him like a dial on a television, leaving no doubt to the truth of Carys's testimonial.

Mainly though, he was confused. Extremely confused. Baffled where two weeks had gone. He only remembered being with Carys in his car and then blinding lights shining through the windows; glimpses of people surrounding them. The next moment, he was still in the field but it was daytime and his car had disappeared!

With any other possibility too disturbing to consider, he drank up the explanation offered by the police. They told him he must have sustained an injury and suffered amnesia as a result. The reported blood loss must have been somewhat overestimated.

Carys no longer had the stomach to pursue the assault and attempted rape charge after the worst two weeks of her life. Stephen was free to go. He apologised through others to Carys for any 'misunderstanding.'

The girls, pleased to have Stephen back and warned by him how difficult Carys could make things, dropped their charges too. Four assault charges, an attempted rape and a possible unlawful killing were wiped out by the sheer exhaustion of the two main parties. Carys, at last, was also free to go.

Carys, Diane and Geraint wanted to put the last two weeks behind them and get the family move complete. Carys couldn't wait. She'd been saved from the brink of disaster in the nick of time. Diane's prayer had, it seemed, been answered.

CHAPTER SEVENTEEN

On the move

A rather shamefaced Geraint arrived to move his daughter and wife to their new home in Pembrokeshire. His whereabouts when they both needed him only glossed over.

He couldn't cope. The stress he'd endured during his time policing in Cambridge came flooding back, overwhelming him like a sandcastle to the tide. He'd forced on his suit of saviour armour in his initial rage at his daughter's abuse, but returning to the quiet suburbia of his new Welsh beat, he allowed the cracks to break him.

His job was safe; compassionate leave had been granted for as long as he needed; the reasons for his move well known. But he hadn't rushed back to Stella's to be their rock. He'd hidden in the new house, beavering away from dusk 'til dawn with unnecessary D.I.Y chores (predominantly involving knocking down walls and painting things blue.)

But he was here now, and taking on a role of authority over the gaggle of press who had congregated at Stella's gate. Diane felt unable to be disappointed in her husband, understanding all too well how not feeling oneself could affect behaviour. And Carys couldn't bear to admit his limitations. She'd long learned to live with her mother's shortcomings, but her dad too? Where would that leave her?

Seeing the throng of press from her bedroom window, she was grateful she had little to organise to join her parents in Wales. She and Diane had thrown out any clutter two weeks ago. She had no furniture or anything of any size to pack, and she wasn't into clothes. A couple of pairs of shoes and her laptop loaded into the car and they were ready to leave.

They all said a grateful goodbye to Stella, awkward under the scrutiny of the men standing feet away, telephoto lenses collecting magnified images of them.

"You take care of yourself, young lady," she choked, squeezing Carys in a tight hug. When she pulled away, she turned to all three of them. "Don't be strangers, you three, will you?"

They smiled and said of course not. Realistically, though, they all knew the Ellis family would have no reason to come back to Royston any time soon.

"Stella could come and stay with us in Pembrokeshire, couldn't she?" Carys suggested.

"Yes! Come down for a holiday. It's a lovely place. We're close to some really special beaches."

"Thanks. I'll take you up on that!"

Desperately trying to avoid giving the press the satisfaction of their growing rage at the invasion of privacy, they got into the car and waved fond, albeit hurried, farewells through open windows as the Saab pulled onto the Great London Road. Four or five hours later, their new life could begin.

Hurrying south towards the capital and away from the ordeal the charming yet regrettable area had subjugated them with, Geraint breathed a sigh of relief. For the first time in weeks, the irrepressible father and husband returned to something of his usual vigour, cracking punny jokes and boring the others with little known facts about the areas or wildlife they passed.

"They'd barely finished this road when we moved here, do you remember?" Of course, Carys didn't remember, and Diane looked as though she had no idea what he was talking about as the London Road joined the M25 London Orbital.

"Which way do you want to go round? We could go via Dartford. We go over two bridges then. And that one wasn't built when we moved here. We may never see it again. Although the other way is a lot quicker, and there is a small toll…"

His wittering mind seemingly wanted to catch up on weeks of despondency. The girls shrugged. They just wanted to get there as soon as possible, but wouldn't deny him his sight-seeing bridge.

"Do whatever makes you happy, darling," Diane said in a faultless but clipped tone.

"Mmmm hmmm. No. We'll go anti-clockwise. A true Welshman would never want to pay twice!" Diane forced a smile and settled down for a nap.

As they sped and occasionally crawled around the capital's by-pass, the scenery remained flat and boring. Occasional outposts of light industry, indistinguishable from one another, were all that broke the monotony until they turned abruptly onto another concrete carbuncle.

"Wake me up when we get to the big bridge," Carys asked, shifting into a comfy position for a nap as well, leaving Geraint to endure the scenery of the M4 alone.

She slept soundly. As the miles passed, the troubles of the past fortnight shrank in the distance. By the time she was awoken by Geraint's obligatory rendition of *'We'll Keep a Welcome in the Hillside,'* she was more relaxed than she'd felt for a long time.

"I love how you have to pay to get into Wales, but getting into England is free!" Geraint chuckled as they approached the Second Severn crossing. Traversing the huge expanse of water high above, they clocked up four miles before they reached the one-way tolls.

While waiting for the barrier to rise, Geraint's impatient fingers tapped the steering wheel as his right foot prepared for pole position in the race for the normal road lanes. Carys flinched at his disquiet. His enthusiasm had a ring of falsity to it that worried her.

"Who's gonna be first into Wales?" he asked, unfairly reaching his arm forward to claim the win.

'Croeso i Gymru', 'Welcome to Wales,' the sign declared.

"It's good to be home," Geraint sighed.

The mighty Severn estuary marked an ocean like boundary between the two nations. United against warring with one another for five hundred years, since the act of Union, they still shared an uneasy resentment of one another.

The Welsh resented the seat of power in Westminster, and the English resented them resenting it.

With his audience awake again, Geraint treated them to articles from Geraintipidia once more. "Cardiff was the busiest port in the world in its day, you know." Carys was impressed, but she'd heard it all before. It was an obligatory monologue they endured every time they crossed the border.

"Of course, none of the money was seen by the Welsh. All kept by bloody English and Scottish lords, wasn' it. Marquis of Bute, it was, built most of it. Then the iron barons from Yorkshire. The industrial revolution might have started in Wales, and we may have roofed half the world with slate from our hills, but damn few pennies stayed with the Welsh, I can tell you."

And tell them he frequently did. The fact his countrymen of yore had been too busy tending livestock to make the most of the opportunities their environment offered, was a notion lost on Geraint.

Carys shared her father's distaste for what the development had meant for the scenery, but did wonder if Wales would have been by-passed by civilised society were it not for the land's exploitation. People living in simple dwellings off the fat of the land, like newly discovered tribes in far-flung places in deepest Amazonia. With a smile to herself, she couldn't be sure if that might not be better.

"Look at that!" he roared at the Port Talbot steelworks. Carys thought it possessed a certain beauty. There were only so many mountains that needed to remain 'unspoilt,' surely?

"We're just a dumping ground for things too unpleasant to have in England!" he ranted. "If a power station's needed, stick it in Wales. Unsightly industry? Wales is the place to put it. Droughts in England? Why not flood a Welsh village and make it a reservoir?"

"Alright, Dad. Calm down," Carys squeezed his shoulder affectionately."

"No. I bloody won't. Do you know, the great city of Liverpool has given a public apology to the flooded Welsh village of Capel Celyn, now Llyn Celyn! That's Celyn Chapel to Celyn bloody Lake," he translated unnecessarily to his English wife.

Diane shared a glance of concern with her daughter. He really was going off on one, this time.

"It wasn't just Wales, Dad. It was a time of Empire, wasn't it. It was happening all over the world. I think it's more about the rich exploiting the poor, and that's still happening. I think you're being a bit racist."

"Racist? Me? I'll tell you who's racist. Do you know where the name 'Wales' comes from? Do you? We called ourselves 'Cymru'—'People.' The bloody English, in Saxon times, called us 'Weles'—'Different!' Now we're named after that. *Different!* That's bloody racism for you."

The irony of bestowing for hours his opinion that his countrymen and women *were* different didn't seem a point worth making to the ranting zealot driving them home.

"I suppose the industry is part of our heritage, cariad," he mellowed. "Beyond the mountain beside us," he indicated with a nod right, "is the 'green desert of Wales.' That's mile upon mile upon mile of undulating mountain pasture. You could climb to the top and not see a man-made structure as far as the eye can see."

Carys was interested, but Geraint's monologue burgeoned on obsession as he blathered on.

"That's the Cambrian mountain range. The oldest rock known to geologists is named after them. They give way to 'Black Mountain' and the

'Brecon Beacons' ranges to the east and to the massive Snowdonia ranges of 'Cader Idris' to the north."

Carys nodded, struggling to maintain interest, debating suggesting she wouldn't remember any of this, but decided against it in case it set her dad off with greater fervour.

Several other mountains were named and heights given but Carys was unable to keep up. It had been a big mistake to keep this Welshman from his homeland for so long.

"Look down to your left and you'll see the great sweep of Swansea Bay." Frustrated as Carys was becoming, she was pleased to see the sea.

The gorgeous crescent of golden sand meeting calm blue ocean was exquisite. The city of Swansea hugged the bay and surrounding hills, with Mumbles islets and pier in the far distance leading to Gower, Britain's first Official Site of Natural Beauty.

"How long now, Dad?" Carys moaned.

"About an hour," he said, beaming at her in the rear-view mirror. Diane had dropped off again.

"You okay, Dad?" she asked, meaning more than just how he was now. She knew he loved his homeland, but his enthusiasm struck her as odd; a touch manic. With a sigh at him not answering, she gave in, vowing to keep and eye on him "You've been driving for hours." The less serious question prompted an immediate response which added to her suspicions.

"Fine thanks, cariad. Just excited to get you home."

Carys hadn't even seen home. Journeys down to view it had all been done when she was in school and revising. A bubble of anxiety welled within at the realisation she hadn't followed up any of her applications to Uni. She'd be lucky to be accepted so late now. She sighed, determined not to let it spoil her day.

Pictures from estate agents had shown a pretty impressive house. Prices in Pembrokeshire hadn't caught up with Cambridgeshire and the difference was obvious.

Just on the outskirts of the town of Narberth in the centre of the county was Ty Hedd (House of peace.) They'd seen it as a sign because the Welsh word for police is heddlu, roughly translating to 'peace army.'

Their journey took them around the picturesque little town and out towards the coastal resorts of Tenby and Saundersfoot. A short drive up a steep hill and Carys gained her first glimpse of the new Ellis family home.

In appearance, it was comfortingly similar to *Nutters*. A large, white, double fronted house with a slate roof that unsurprisingly (as *Nutters* roof was also Welsh slate) had a reassuring familiarity. Whilst equally steeply pitched, there was some subtle difference which meant it suited the house much better.

As with their old home, there were a number

of outbuildings. Carys wondered if her mum's pottery might finally get completed. The garden boasted several acres, and accordingly, there were plans for horses, goats and perhaps even a business as a garden centre.

Enjoying an elevated position, the house offered wonderful views of the Preseli Mountain range, ten miles to the north. It was a dramatic difference to the infinite flat fenland Carys had grown up with and she liked it. The town nestled in a valley below the mountain reminding Carys of a model village. She couldn't wait to enjoy the amazing coast which brochures promised was unspoiled.

She had no idea what she wanted from her life. She had no friends. But a new optimism drove through her veins and she giggled.

If she'd been in touch with any sort of prophetic knowledge, if such a thing existed, then her optimism would be very short lived.

Maybe the hope she felt now was crucial to give her the strength to cope with the turn her life was about to take.

CHAPTER EIGHTEEN

Carys's Unearthing

Carys had applied to several close by universities but had yet to receive any offers. Without tempting fate by contacting them she attempted to relax in her ignorance. Geraint and Diane recognized the pitfalls of this approach but also, how much their daughter had endured. They didn't want to push her.

Both delighted in seeing Carys relishing the area and encouraged her daily trips to the beach. Swimming in the clear sea and soaking up the sun gave her a fresh outlook, and indeed a fresh look. 'Surf girl' suited her. Maybe she should arrange surfing lessons, she thought.

Ty Hedd had been home for a couple of weeks now and everything was great on the surface. Geraint seemed fine, but photos dotted around of them working on the place in her absence showed a crazed looking man she barely recognised. Sporting a bushy beard and a permanent manic grin, she supposed he must have smartened himself up to come back to Royston; not wanting his colleagues to see him like that. And maybe the forced return to his usual look had made him feel better, because he did seem okay.

Carys's worries had mainly settled, apart from one other concern. Putting it down to her different routine and super active lifestyle, she couldn't ignore it forever: she hadn't yet had her period. It was too early to panic, but it had become a nagging worry.

Their first family attendance of the church Geraint and Diane discovered months ago was planned and Carys was looking forward to it. It might be just what she needed: to finally make some friends. She wouldn't admit it, but surprised herself that she was quite keen to meet the Pastor's son who'd taken a shine to her photo. The idea of it weeks before had been horrific. With all that behind her, she was relieved to have those sorts of feelings again.

Everyone was up and showered in plenty of time to arrive at church (held in the town hall) before the sermon started—testament to Carys's keenness. An expectant buzz charged the air as people busied about setting out chairs and testing the sound system. It was like a concert. Not what Carys associated with church.

An elderly entourage ambled over to greet them, recognising Geraint and Diane. "So lovely to see you again!" an enthusiastic septuagenarian in a smart suit hailed, vigorously shaking each of their hands.

"This is our beautiful daughter, Carys," Diane introduced. The elderly man, so full of life, was delighted to meet her and wished her a wonderful time.

Next they met the Pastor, Dan Paulo. An air of majesty exuded from him as he welcomed his flock to the large hall. He wore typical ministerial smock but with a tie rather than a dog collar of priesthood. Not a handsome man, but he commanded the room with a magnetism.

His son, nicer looking, and commanding some of the holiness his father emanated, came over. "You're Diane and Geraint's daughter," he said with a wink. "I recognise you from your photos. Even more beautiful in real life." Carys blushed suitably.

"Marco," he said by way of introduction. He turned away and spoke to someone involved with the sound system. Before leaving he turned back to Carys

"We'll have to grab a coffee later?" Carys smiled a timid approval. He seemed nice. Half jogging away, he jumped onto the stage, strapped an electric guitar to his chest and preceded to tune it. Carys swooned. She could get used to this.

The family took their seats in the middle of

the congregation. It wasn't long before the music started. Praise songs played with the backing of the full band, sung by a mousy girl with the voice of an angel.

Marco took lead vocals for some of the songs. His tone was nothing special, maybe a little whiny, but the fact they were about love (albeit the love of Jesus), and that he sang them directly to Carys made them lip-bitingly alluring.

Marco's father did a great job of raising hallelujahs from the congregation who sang and clapped through a frenzy of worship. Carys could have found the whole thing appallingly self-indulgent, but she was smitten.

From the moment the old gent at the door had looked so genuinely delighted to meet her, she'd felt like she was with an extended family. Beaming faces alighted every time she caught the eye of another member of the flock. It was all most heartening.

She enjoyed coffee with Marco along with others in the group. Biscuits, other refreshments, and impressive cakes were offered to a crowd insatiable after the energetic morning. The Ellis's left happy, full of treats, and the love of their Lord and his herd.

A few social engagements were arranged under the guise of Bible study groups, and Carys had particular interest whenever Marco Paulo was expected.

Realising, when she'd sounded his name for the first time how unfortunate it was, she would (as she expected would everybody else) be forever put in mind of Marco Polo. She'd refrain from mentioning it for fear of repeating countless others before her.

At one of the study sessions, Geraint and Diane decided they'd take the next important step in their Christianity and become baptised. With their names on the list, they were told to invite family and friends—partly to celebrate, and partly to spread the word. Of course, they invited Stella.

Two weeks passed. The baptism was booked and due to take place on Sunday with Stella arriving this afternoon.

Carys's concern for her absent period had turned to acute anxiety. She'd have to buy a pregnancy testing kit. She'd have to try to block it from her mind until then.

Stella was met off the train by Diane and Carys at the little unmanned Narberth Station. She had a small green suitcase that fit easily into the boot of the little Fiesta Diane had recently bought. A car had proved rather more of a necessity here in Pembrokeshire than in Royston.

Diane was pleased to see her comrade from the terrible fortnight in Royston of a month ago. Carys greeted her former guardian with a sense of relief. There were delicate issues she wanted to air. Spoiling her parent's baptism wasn't an option, but she had to find out.

Having persuaded Diane that taking Stella for lunch in one of the excellent café's the small town boasted was a good idea, under the guise of getting money from the cash point, Carys popped to the pharmacy to buy the box that would end her misery, or begin a whole new one.

She met up with the two ladies further up the street where they were deliberating the pros and cons of various eating establishments. They went for a Spanish themed deli-cum-café with the confusing moniker of Ultra-Comida.

Walking through the rustic shop-front, delicious smells titillating their senses guided them to a flag-stoned area beyond, bathed in brilliant sunshine from the high glass ceiling. Their table was overlooked by a busy kitchen visible over the counter.

After choosing various tapas displayed on blackboards dotted about, Carys excused herself. She hoped taking her handbag to the toilet hadn't aroused suspicion. Opening the door, she glanced back at the table, relieved Stella and her mother weren't looking in her direction.

Once inside, fumbling fingers struggled to find the testing kit in her bag. Exhaling through puckered lips, she unearthed it with a victorious flourish and discarded the wrappers, grateful they wouldn't be discovered in a bin at home. Yanking her jeans and knickers down, she squatted over the toilet.

As her right hand held the little stick receptacle, she peed on it and pulled it out. Shaking off the excess, she placed it carefully on the basin to develop its answer while she finished.

She sat welded to the toilet seat, unable to bring herself to look at the life changing little line. With a resolved stomp, she re-dressed and washed her hands, the calm, pleasant, fragrance of the flowery soap seemed incongruent with her darkening mood. Ready to leave, all she had to do was get her result. Picking it up without looking at it, she needed to be sure. She couldn't risk glimpsing an uncertain conclusion.

"Oh, my god. I'm shaking!" she murmured under her breath. When she could put it off no longer, she clutched the stick the perfect distance from her face to see it clearly but kept her eyes closed. Forcing them open in a burst of blinking lids, she stared at the window of fortune.

She'd done the right thing, buying the expensive, no-room-for-ambiguity, tell-it-to-you-straight, type of testing kit, because even in plain English she couldn't quite believe it.

'Pregnant, 4-6 weeks,' the little piece of plastic informed her. Colour drained from her pretty face. Steadying herself on the wash-hand basin, slumping back onto the toilet, she sat with her head in her hands.

The only carnal experience she'd ever known

had been the disgusting night with Stephen Holmes. She didn't even remember anything baby producing. It must have happened though. The evidence was clear. She'd have to reconsider pushing charges of rape.

The University offers mattered little now. She would keep her baby. Shocked, definitely, but part of her was even pleased. In fact, as an enormous grin bisected her face, busily regaining some of its normal colour, she had to admit she was thrilled.

Her life had lacked a point. Her parents had always assumed she'd go to university, but for what purpose? She had no particular career in mind. Her life just stretched out aimlessly before her. But all that had changed in a second. She may have had no idea what she would do with her life, but now she did. She was going to be a mum.

With a quick exhalation, she remembered her dining companions. Reopening the door back into the café, she could see food on the table, and the concerned faces of the two ladies peering up at her.

"Everything alright, bach?" Diane asked as she got close enough.

How did she know? Carys shook her head, she didn't, of course. Her reflection in a mirror above the seating shocked her. Pale and drawn, no wonder her mum had asked. "Yes, fine now, thanks. Just a bit of a dodgy tummy that's all."

Diane frowned, but with nothing practical to suggest, sympathetic glances sufficed until they began to eat.

Carys didn't know how she'd tell her mum and dad. Would they be angry? They'd be angry with Stephen for sure. Would it set her dad off on his weird busy-bodying again? At least it might give him a focus. He'd clearly not recovered from that dreadful day on the railway.

Glancing from her plate to Stella's kindly face, she was desperate for her advice, but she had to wait. Furtive glances controlled, she stared resolutely at the end of her fork. Her parent's special day in church had to come first. There was no hurry. The baby wasn't going anywhere.

The obligatory tour of the house and land followed immediately their arrival at Ty Hedd. Diane enthused about plans for a garden centre or whatever they decided. Stella made all the right noises, but she'd heard this sort of thing before.

"Hello, stranger," Geraint's ever-deepening Welsh accent hailed from the driveway as they stepped past the gateway from the field. "What do you think of our new place, then?" he grinned. From a distance he looked the picture of happiness, the pain in his eyes only detectable closer up.

The months away from Cambridge were healing him. Carys hoped his new faith would tip the balance firmly in favour of contentment.

Her own anxiety caused her to need to keep distracted so she made a suggestion.

"Shall we take Stella down to Tenby?" Seeing the glances at wrist-watches, and Stella stifling a yawn, she tried hard to overcome any objections before they gained a majority. "I know you must be tired after your long journey, Stella, but it really is beautiful, and you might not get the chance again before you leave on Monday."

Carys could almost see the thoughts taking place, and as the faces softened it was no surprise when "Oh, alright then," fell from each of their lips.

The views didn't fail to impress. As soon as Stella saw the palm-lined crenulated castle walls of the mediaeval old town she gasped with delight. And her grin when the car swept round the Esplanade as she glimpsed her first sight of the mile and a half of golden sand, fringed by turquoise ocean, made it clear she was pleased they'd come.

Fish, chips and an ice-cream were devoured before they headed back inland and the nagging anxiety tugged once more at Cary's good mood.

She filled Saturday with an itinerary of castles, undiscovered coves and a long scenic drive through the wilds of the Preseli Hills. Guilt that her tour guide act was mainly a manic excuse to avoid the inevitable discovery of her secret piqued when Stella announced she could see her-self moving down.

"That's known as the 'Pembrokeshire Pull,'" Geraint beamed proudly. "There's so much nat-ural beauty here," he gushed as though he was the leading authority, wafting his arms left and right, demonstrating it was the view outside he was talking about, in case there was any doubt.

"Drive ten miles in any direction and it's hard to believe you're in the same country, let alone the same county." His hands wandered danger-ously from their job of steering the car with his gesticulations. "Everything's so varied. You can be on a mountain top in the morning, walking through waterfalls at lunchtime and be on a se-cluded secret cove or bustling golden beach for tea!"

"Sounds tiring," Diane scorned, wondering where all this enthusiasm had come from before biting her lip. Even Stella was lost for words and forced a nod and smile. Maybe it was excitement about tomorrow.

Carys awoke to noises of people getting ready. Stumbling sleepily to the bathroom, a glance into her mum and dad's room revealed Diane applying full make-up. Why, thought Carys? She'd be dunked in a pool in an hour.

Drying off after her shower, boy-style - with a vigorous rub with a towel, Carys put on clothes she considered her best, but they were just newer versions of the jeans and top she wore all the time. The outfit she'd bought to celebrate their exams results had been hastily discarded after the consequences they'd achieved

"Fifteen minutes," Geraint called up the stairs. Carys did her best to put her own make-up on and came downstairs a more glamorous vision of her usual perfection.

Nerves spoiled her desire to see Marco. Any hopes she'd had of something happening between them had surely been quashed by Friday's discovery? Oh well. You can't miss what you've never had.

They arrived at the swimming pool which served the town and two of the local schools. Today it served Narberth Christian Fellowship for the baptism of Geraint and Diane Ellis.

Around the poolside stood the congregation who usually filled The Town Hall, precarious in their Sunday finery.

Pastor Dan Paulo was in fine form, commanding his audience with some relevant scripture. By the time he invited Geraint and Diane to join him in the shallow end of the pool everyone could feel the love.

Everyone except Carys. Her heart dropped and beads of cold sweat highlighted her brow as soon as her mind assessed the sound. Gripping the hymn sheet she'd been handed on arrival until it almost ripped in her fingers, Carys took some much needed deep breaths.

The humming she'd left behind nearly three-hundred miles away was here. Faint, but undeniable. Glancing from one person to another, Carys shook. Serene smiles on faces swaying from side to side in god-loving bliss assailed Carys's solace. Couldn't they hear it?

Putting a hand over her mouth to stop from calling out as well as prevent her being sick, trembling turned to violent shaking. One or two of the congregation began giving her concerned looks.

"Are you alright, dear?" was the last thing she heard before everything went black.

Everyone was clapping and cheering. Her mum and dad were out of the pool and dripping wet as she sat on a chair she had no recollection sitting on.

"You fainted, bach," a kindly lady, squeezing her shoulder told her. "It can be overwhelming, can't it?"

Not waiting for a response, she turned to join the congratulations flowing to Diane and Geraint. In the hubbub, Carys sat, allowing it to wash over her. That's what it had been. Not the hum again. She'd fainted. She was pregnant after all.

The expectant faces of her parents peered across at her 'What did you think?' their raised eyebrows implored. A peace shone from their effervescent faces and Carys knew at once she wanted what they had. She needed it.

The congregation made their way to the Town Hall for the customary coffee and bible chat.

"So, tell me, Carys," Pastor Dan prompted. "How did you feel about your parent's baptism?"

"I loved it," she blurted, surprising herself. "In fact, I'd like to do it. Be baptised, that is."

"Excellent, my dear. Most splendid news." But before she'd even finished asking, she bit her lip, and fell silent. "What is it? What's worrying you?" he asked with a frown.

"You mustn't tell anybody. Promise me! Especially not my parents!" she whispered. "I'll have tell them soon, but you see… I think I may be pregnant."

Dan stepped back, jutting out his jaw and Carys was certain he was furious with her. Wishing she could melt into the floor, she stared at her feet and awaited her rebuking. Then with a shake of her shoulder, a familiar rage bubbled within. She'd done nothing to be ashamed of. "I was raped," she glowered. "A few weeks ago, back in England," she said, eyes widening as she realised the accusation was with absolute certainty for the first time.

Dan Paulo's expression softened as he regained his holy sympathy. "I'm sure we can still offer you a Baptism. It's what it's all about: putting the past behind you and moving on in Jesus Christ."

"I will tell Mum and Dad," Carys assured. "I only

found out myself a couple of days ago and I didn't want to spoil today for them."

Dan nodded. "Very noble. We'll set a date. It'll be fantastic, don't you worry!"

The Ellis's and their house guest arrived back at 'Ty Hedd' and prepared for a traditional Sunday roast. Whilst the cooking was going on, Carys knew it was her best opportunity to gain Stella's help. Knocking gently on the guest room door, she was surprised at no answer so pushed the door open.

Stella gasped. Sat on the edge of her bed in just a bra, Carys could see her mind stalling. "Come in, dear. I'm just putting something comfier on. Don't mind me."

With a step inside, Carys averted her gaze as Stella pulled a sweatshirt over her head. "I'm so sorry. I don't know why I did that."

"That's okay. It's your house. I don't expect you're used to guests taking up your space." She could see the dewiness to Carys's eyes and held out her hand. "Come here," she smiled.

As Carys clutched her hand, she stared at the floor between her feet.

"Whatever is the matter, my lovely? You can tell me, you know that."

Different ways to broach it whirled around her mind until she plumped for the most concise and blunt version. "I'm pregnant."

She must have know when it occurred, but she

didn't ask, recognising how difficult it must have been to tell her. "When you tell your mum and dad, I'll back you up if you think it'll help," Stella offered. "We should tell them over dinner." Noticing Carys's, slender shoulders slumping, she placed a reassuring hand on her knee provoking a moist sheen to her floor-ward gaze. "Don't feel bad. It's not a normal situation, is it? And it's not as though you're fifteen or anything."

Carys sighed and wiped her eyes. It would be fine. She felt better about telling her parents that they were soon to become grandparents with the calming presence of sensible Stella on her side. Even so, as the smell of cooking became more pronounced, so did her nerves. By the time she sat at the table, them noticing something wrong was inevitable.

"You don't look right, Carys bach. Did you not enjoy church?" Geraint probed.

Stella stepped in before things got awkward. "Carys has something delicate she needs to tell you both." Diane glanced at Geraint then they both stared at Carys. Her tongue felt dry and welded to the floor of her mouth. She didn't know why she was so jittery.

Stella, not wanting any of them to suffer the long silence whilst Carys struggled to make a sound, stepped in again. "She's pregnant," she announced abruptly.

It was Diane and Geraint's turn lose their voices. They looked at their daughter in shock, as though it might be possible Stella had made it up. Carys confirmed with a nod that she hadn't. No-one needed to ask who the father was.

"That little shit!" Geraint couldn't help himself. "He'll have to give you maintenance. And we'll open up the case again." He glared at them with seething fury. "He can't get away with this."

A cough from Diane stopped him in his stride. "If you still want to go off to Uni, I can look after your baby for you," she offered with a nervous smile. Carys's grin widened. She was so proud of her parents. Her dad might be strict, and a bit stressed and manic lately. And her mother might lose touch with reality once in a while, but they were truly wonderful and supportive and she loved them dearly.

"You haven't asked Carys what *she* wants to do," Stella interjected. Diane was taken aback.

"Of course. Sorry, darling. I didn't think..."

"We struggled so much to have you, anything else... Well, it wouldn't occur to us. But, no pressure, cariad," Geraint grappled with the words.

"I'd never dream of not keeping my baby! Being a mum will be wonderful."

The adults, with tears of joy in their eyes, all hugged Carys until she was suffocating and had to fend them off.

CHAPTER NINETEEN.

Carys's Disbelief

Clutching the phone number her dad had provided, Carys sat in front of the phone. Picking the receiver up, putting it to her ear, she slammed it down for the third time, heart pounding in her ears. What was she afraid of? Hearing the voice of her rapist? But she was in the position of strength now. She hadn't decided exactly how he'd pay, but he should be afraid; not her.

Picking up the receiver for a fourth and final time, she dialled the number, determined to have it dealt with before her mum and Stella returned from their walk.

It rang four, five, six times. Carys expected it to be picked up by answerphone by then so was surprised when an actual human, sounding the right age and tone to be Stephen's mother, answered.

"Hello?" the woman inquired.

"Hello," Carys replied. "Is it possible to speak to Stephen, please?"

"Hold on. I'll see if he's in. Who's calling?" She must be used to girls calling her son, she thought. Debating saying a different name so as not to alarm the mother, she decided alarm would be a good thing to cause and said confidently, "Carys Ellis."

There was a long, silent pause from the other end, as though she were weighing her options. "Hold the line," she said and left to fetch (or rouse, Carys suspected), her son.

There was a lengthy pause while the phone was left off the hook. Carys was sure she'd be told he wasn't in. Or perhaps they were arguing over what she could possibly want. Getting their stories straight.

After an inordinate length of time, Stephen finally answered. "Hello?" his voice, quieter, more timid than she remembered.

"Stephen. This is Carys Ellis." She knew he already knew but was keeping business-like and matter-of-fact. "I won't bother with 'How are you,' because I don't particularly care. I'm phoning out of common courtesy to inform you that you are going to be a father. I'm six weeks pregnant."

The announcement was greeted by complete silence. Carys had to prompt him for a response. "Did you hear me?"

"I can't be," he stated calmly. "Nothing happened. Don't you remember?" It was Carys's turn to be stunned into silence. "Look. I am truly sorry for my behaviour. I thought you liked me. Every other girl does. I was frustrated. I thought you were ..." he was going to say something more accusatory but settled on, "Playing hard to get."

Carys didn't say anything, but something in the manner of her silence assured Stephen she was still listening. He continued. "You don't know, do you? It's taken a while for things to come back to me, and I don't remember everything. But some things are crystal clear. Believe me."

Carys was in a whirl. Stephen's calm tone had the resonance of truth about it, but how could that be? If she believed him, where did that leave her?

"Like I've said," he persisted, "I deeply apologise for how I behaved, but nothing happened that could cause you to be pregnant. I promise. Nothing." His tone changed to incredulity.

"You must remember the bright light? And those... those things?" Carys could hear the judder in his voice. "I couldn't have done anything with you then, even if you'd begged me!"

Carys didn't remember. She couldn't. But what Stephen had said chilled her to her core. If Stephen wasn't her baby's father, who was?

A nausea like she'd never known hit her like a punch from a heavyweight. She couldn't speak. Her mouth opened and closed, but no words came. It didn't matter; she had nothing to say.

Replacing the handset with a slow deliberation, the silence was filled by the pound, pound, pound of her racing heart. A wail fell from her lips as she jerked round in her seat, eyes darting, searching for a hiding place; anywhere to get away from where her thoughts were taking her.

She knew. She had known all along. The baby wasn't Stephen's. It was *theirs*.

Clutching her tummy, desperate to protect the burgeoning life within her, she scrabbled up the stairs, steadying herself with her upper arm against the wall when her peculiar posture almost caused her to fall.

Bolting the bathroom door behind her, she slumped on the floor, the cold tiles sending a shiver through her.

"What are you running from, Carys?" she taunted herself. "You know you can't run from them. They'll take the baby. It's not *your* baby any more than it's Stephen's; and they'll take it away. You won't be allowed to keep it. It's Rosemary's baby: like the film."

"But I want it!" she shrieked. "So, so much. I love him already. He's been with me for weeks, and I know I only just confirmed it, but, deep down, I knew. I'm sure I knew..." She broke into silent sobs, snot caking her nose and mouth, deformed by the red swelling of her grief.

"Please don't take my baby... Please don't take my baby...," she begged. And then, as though on cue, the noise she dreaded; the noise which always proceeded terrible things happening in her life echoed through her head.

Her face shot up, eyes piercing every corner of the room, daring them to appear with a wounding intensity.

"Go AWAY!" she screamed, tears streaking her horror bloated face. "Go away. Please, please, go away…," she begged. But the hum continued, resonating from everywhere and nowhere as it always did; reverberating in the chamber of terror in Carys's head, destroying any other thought.

Clutching her knees to her chest, Carys checked out, rocking back and fore… back and fore… back and fore.

The humming endured.

CHAPTER TWENTY

Sinking in

A sudden nausea forced her back onto her feet. Throwing the loo seat up and catching it before it bounced back closed again, she could hold back the surge of bile no longer.

In-between retching torrents, gushing to form spectacular kaleidoscopes of stomach debris adorning the sides of the bowl, missing the small pool of water which might have eliminated some of the odour, she detected a gentle rapping at the bathroom door.

The sound from the real world immediately banished the hum to the annals of her mind. Carys shook her head. She was cracking up.

"You okay in there?" to which Carys's only answer was another bout of violent vomiting.

"I used to be sick every morning when I was carrying you," her mother's slightly concerned, amused voice came muffled through the wood.

"It might mean you're having a girl as well!"

A girl *what* though?

The unforgettable scene from the eighties' series 'V' assaulted Carys's thoughts: where a baby is conceived with questionable terrestrial parentage. Born, and plonked—still umbilically attached—onto its mother's chest; she sighs with relief at its apparent normality. But then a forked tongue slithers from its mouth, its face contorting into a demonic demeanour, denoting its part-alien lineage!

She remembered when she'd first watched the cheesy film, she'd found it amusing, in strict contrast to her current situation which was not amusing at all. It was absurd. Could she seriously be considering the baby inside her might not be human?

There had to be an alternative. The figures surrounding Stephen's car; why was she assuming they were Extra-Terrestrial? Wasn't it far more likely they were normal, everyday people? Just because the farmers who owned the field denied being there, didn't make it true. Especially if they had something to hide: like one of them had beaten Stephen and raped her!

But she knew, even as the thought grew solid in her mind, that she didn't believe it. Stephen wouldn't have called them *'those figures'* if they'd simply been some other boys. He'd been clearly terrified.

Another viable alternative that failed to gain a

foothold on her psyche was that Stephen may be lying. She was certain her parents would think so... well, maybe her mum might believe it. Carys gulped, memories from her childhood swirling in her mind, ripping at her resolve for calm as surely as a tornado.

She knew. He was telling the truth.

Dying down in the face of acceptance, the horrific hurricane of the realisation eased. What should she do now? Could she leave the alien embryo to develop into god knows what? Would it not be the best thing to arrange a termination?

More bile found its way to the back of her throat and she struggled to swallow it down. She couldn't. She wouldn't kill her baby.

And, she couldn't be the first. Other hybrid children surely roamed the world. There must be a purpose to their interference. It made no sense to Carys that she would be the only one; chosen out of all the millions and billions of women on the planet, now and throughout history. No. there had to be others. And if that were so, her child would look normal enough to not arouse suspicion, or...

Just when she thought she had a handle on it, she came out of the eye of the storm, straight back into the tumult of terror once again.

What if she couldn't keep it? What if she was just a surrogate? An incubator for *them*; until they could harvest her baby as mercilessly as a farmer culling a cow? Could that be the cause of many miscarriages? Maybe her own mother's miscarriages had been caused by exactly the same reason.

Carys slumped, flinching against the chill of hard porcelain, convinced she was the latest in a long line of mothers destined to provide safe gestation for an alien race until her fruit had ripened for picking. No wonder the hum so terrified her mother.

A cold lump of sick sat in her mouth, blocking the scream of anguished frustration which threatened to explode from the depths of her despair. Gazing down at her unchanged stomach, fear of what was there, and of what was to come, jittered in her chest making her giddy. She wanted her baby. She wanted to be a mother. Would that even happen, or could she be forced to relinquish an unrecognisable foetus? Would she even realise when it happened?

Talking to the one person who might know: her mother, was impossible. She'd never broken her promise to her father to keep her secret. Diane was more stable and happier since their move to Narberth than during any time in Carys's life so far. She couldn't risk ruining that; and for what?

Her mum could offer no useful advice, could she? It wasn't as though she had come through her own experiences unscathed. She was the very last person she should talk to. Her dad wasn't well enough to bother either. She was on her own, like always.

There was another knock. "Are you feeling any better?" The high pitch of her mum's concern wafted in. No, she definitely was not. Sighing deeply, she made a reluctant grasp for the bolt and opened the door.

Diane took her quiet demeanour and pale complexion as evidence of her morning sickness. She rubbed her arm reassuringly and accompanied her downstairs where Stella stood waiting, bag packed at her feet.

"I thought I wouldn't see you again before catching my train!" Stella said, laughing. "I hope you won't be sick for the entire pregnancy," she declared earnestly, regretting the humour when she saw the look on Carys's face. She wasted her breath with her reassurances that every pregnancy is different.

Morning sickness could be the least of Carys's concerns. But it was the perfect excuse to lie low. Feeling terrible was just the smoke screen she needed.

Having used her sickness as a defence for returning to bed, Carys saw no-one until dinner time. Geraint was home from work, and Diane had provided a hearty meal of traditional Welsh Cawl.

The non-availability of ready meals in the sleepy town's convenience stores combined with a subconscious acceptance of encouragement from a bombardment of 'Pembrokeshire Produce' posters adorning every shop window to prompt her to learn to cook.

After purchasing the latest books promising satisfaction for even novice chefs, she could now create a handful of signature dishes that weren't half bad. Disaster remained only ever round the corner if any vital ingredient was missing, or something didn't cook exactly to the recipe.

Tonight, though, the only dampener was Carys's miserable face. Geraint and Diane shared a few knowing looks before Geraint decided to venture into the troubled waters of their daughter's distressed disposition. "I heard from Dan Paulo today," he began. Carys's ears pricked. "He was wondering if you were ready to book your baptism."

Carys balanced cheese on crusty bread. Scooping up some of the lamby broth, she stuffed it into her mouth as the cheese melted into the bread so she couldn't possibly answer. Geraint continued without feedback. Years spent deciphering Diane helped him cope.

"I suggested you might be feeling a bit delicate," he continued. "I wasn't sure it was possible to be baptised in your... er, condition," he said, his cheeks reddening. "But he seemed to understand; catching on a little too quickly if you get my drift." Geraint's steadily increasing Welsh lilt floated on the air. "Does he know?"

Carys finally left enough of a pause between mouthfuls to speak. "Yes. Sorry. I told him first. It just came out. He said it would be fine for me to be baptised whilst with child. I'm not sure if I'll feel much like it any time soon though. I've been really sick today." She glanced across at her mum for confirmation. Diane, pleased to be included, smiled her support.

The next question made Carys splutter gravy onto the tablecloth. Geraint wanted more. He thought he knew it hadn't gone well but had to ask about the call with Stephen Holmes. Recovering with another cough, she froze. She should have expected it. She should have prepared some sort of believable response.

Just lying that Stephen had accepted the responsibility of impending fatherhood was impossible. They'd pressure him to be involved; to pay maintenance. Goodness knows what he might say in his defence. Lying could buy her time, but also more uncertainty. For her peace of mind, she had to face her dilemma head-on. "He denied any possibility it could be his," Carys announced with a feeble fake tone of annoyance, tutting like he'd been caught littering or some other banal misdemeanour; not denying the serious charge of rape.

Geraint stiffened with barely concealed rage. He wasn't fond of people getting away with things. "He can't just deny it!" he spluttered. "When the baby is born, we'll get DNA tests done and prove he's the father."

Carys remained silent. It's what she would

have expected from him, but she didn't know how to move on.

Geraint was riled now. "Don't you want him to pay his way?! He has to take responsibility! He raped you for Heaven's sake! If he says he's not the father, then who does he suggest is?!" He realised he was making assumptions about his daughter's virtue. But surely, they were safe assumptions. After all, she never went anywhere. And she had been so certain herself of Stephen's culpability. There'd never been any question of it up until today.

It was too much for Carys. Shoving back her chair, she fled from the room. She heard her name being called as she rushed upstairs, but didn't answer. Bounding up the steps, batting tears from her eyes, she leapt to the sanctuary of her bedroom, struggling to refrain from slamming her door. She didn't want to antagonise her father. She just needed to be alone.

Desperate days passed with Carys spending most of her time in her bedroom. Whilst she hoped her isolation was being blamed on her feeling lousy, she hadn't felt in the slightest bit nauseous. She just hadn't wanted to talk about how she was feeling, in case she couldn't help but betray her true worries about her unborn baby.

She was afraid of appearing foolish and neurotic, but more of what would happen if she was believed. It wasn't just *them* she had to fear. It wasn't just *them* who would take her baby away; he'd be wrenched from her and subjected to merciless examination if anyone in authority suspected what she herself believed.

She had only known about her baby for a short while; so, perhaps it wouldn't be so distressing if she couldn't keep it? And would she really want it if it was alien in some way? The knot in her stomach made her certain she would.

Love for someone you'd never met was an odd notion, but that's what she felt, wasn't it? Her parents had always loved her. With her peers, she never felt loved, or even liked, and now her parents' love struck her as a compulsory fate. They didn't have a choice, just as she didn't have a choice now.

Choice or not, her baby would love her. She would feel complete as never before, so, she definitely wanted, no, *needed* her baby, no matter what.

Remaining in her room, sleeping erratically day and night, she failed to notice how much sleep she was indulging in. With eighteen years' experience of her mother's descent to mental unwellness, perhaps the signs should have been clear. She should have known what was happening, but her own clinical depression was creeping up on her unnoticed.

Unnoticed, that is, by herself. Not by her doting parents. They were both acutely aware of the signs. Conscious of Carys's dark view of the

world and how people treat her, they'd long concluded she must have something of a persecu-
tion complex. How could anyone not adore their
delightful, charming child?

Carys put their kindness down to parental
bias. They had hoped their concerns were un-
founded and that Carys's introverted nature was
nothing more than that. But Diane saw too much
of herself at the same age to not worry.

Since she'd announced her pregnancy, their
monitoring of their daughters mood had amplified. Diane had suffered terribly in her pregnan-
cies. It seemed anybody could, and that Carys
was certainly pre-disposed to it. They had taken
action and Carys was about to learn what that action was.

Lying on her bed, staring into space, she became vaguely aware of some unusual exuberance
downstairs. Remaining detached, she considered
there must be a visitor. As anxiety bubbled to the
surface, it burst harmlessly into a smile of satisfaction that she was safe from unwanted social
graces in her room.

Her ears pricked alarmingly to the thud of footsteps ascending the staircase. Surely it was just
her mum or dad, but there was something in
the sound that was unfamiliar. She became more
and more certain the footsteps assailing her ears,
step after step after step were unknown. It must
be the visitor!

Why would her parents do that to her? They

knew she wasn't feeling well. They must be aware of her fragile state of mind. Why would they upset her this way?

Detecting the last creak of the stairs, it was most likely whoever owned the feet pounding Carys's heart in her chest, would turn left. That would mean they'd come upstairs to use the bathroom. Perhaps the downstairs toilet was occupied, or had a plumbing problem, or something.

Carys wouldn't know. She'd been ensconced in her room for days. Downstairs had been a nighttime domain she would visit to snack when she was certain Geraint and Diane were sleeping.

Her ears almost hurt with the strain of listening. Her hand shot to her mouth and she bit hard on her fist to control a cry desperate to escape the prison of her emotion. The footsteps did not turn left as she expected, but instead, turned right - towards her own room!

Surely the visitor wouldn't call on her? Diane and Geraint couldn't possibly have sent someone up to see her! They wouldn't even know if she was dressed. They certainly wouldn't know if it wasn't absolutely the worst thing they could do to her. She knew she couldn't cope with a visitor, and they must know too. Unless...

The visitor wasn't invited! The raucous behaviour she had heard might not have been as jovial as she'd assumed. And then she imagined the worst possible visitor. The one she feared most of all.

She worked herself into a frenzy, so that when there was a gentle rapping on the door, she was certain an alien was about to enter the room and perform some extra-terrestrial anti-natal procedure.

When, after the normal time for someone to answer a knock at the door, she hadn't responded, the knock came again. She couldn't answer. She couldn't say 'Come in'. It might be like a vampire in the films: unable to enter without an invitation.

There was no more knocking, but worse than that, the handle began to move downwards, ready for the door to open. Carys flew across the room, determined not to meet her alien foe lying down.

It had the effect that as Marco opened it a crack, and peeped cautiously around the jam, she met him inches from his face.

Relief, like a dip in a plunge pool after a sauna, giddied her and she was shocked to hear her own peals of laughter. Marco grinned back, certain she had expected him; that she'd heard his voice downstairs and known the footsteps on the stairs were his. Her greeting him face to face and laughing, to him, seemed like a good-natured joke.

A few short moments of exchanged amused glances and they were falling about hilariously, propping one another up in their hysteria. It was natural for Marco from that easy standpoint to offer to pray with Carys, and she accepted gratefully.

And then she felt well enough afterwards to accept his kind offer of a trip to the pub. Geraint and Diane smiled jubilantly as they watched the pair go. Their plan, which they both knew could easily have backfired, had paid off. Their daughter was back. For how long, they'd have to wait and see, but they were for now, grateful for small mercies.

They walked into The Angel Inn, a large (probably the largest of Narberth's half dozen or so public houses) white, Georgian looking building on the main Narberth high street, and tried to find a table.

"Wow. It's really busy in here," Carys commented. She might not have agreed to come if she'd realised the crowd she'd be walking into.

"Well, it is Friday night. It's usually pretty busy," Marco explained patiently. "What would you like to drink?"

"Just a lemonade, thanks." It wasn't only her pregnancy which prevented her ordering something stronger. She was surprised at her desire to make a good Christian impression to the son of a Pastor.

She felt a little foolish for this second point when Marco returned to the table with her lemonade and his pint of Double Dragon ale.

"You've not been feeling too great, your Mam

told me. Morning sickness, right?" Carys felt heat rise to her face, surprised Marco knew. She nodded confirmation whilst holding the straw of her lemonade between her slender fingers and rose petal lips. Marco couldn't help but find her endearing with those big brown doe eyes and thick long lashes looking up at him from behind the drinking glass.

Conversation flowed easily. Carys was relieved her confinement hadn't lasted long enough to miss the coming Sunday, Narberth Christian Fellowship, morning worship. And when Marco officially invited her to come and see him play, it felt like a date (but with the rest of the church being present, a safe date.) She'd make sure she wore something attractive for this week's Sunday outing though. Her excitement was undeniable.

Marco put her at her ease completely. He oozed confidence and charisma, yet suffered none of the cockiness so off-putting about the boys she used to know. Whilst his charm was undeniable, he made it clear, very clear, that his intentions toward her were honourable.

Not that she wasn't the prettiest girl he'd ever seen, she was to understand, but his holy values meant he was planning to wait until he was married to be intimate with a girl. She felt relaxed and safe.

She didn't know what the future held, and didn't much want to think about it. But she thought she could enjoy being with Marco until her baby fears surfaced and ruined everything. 'Stop it, Carys' she berated. Things might turn out okay... somehow.

CHAPTER TWENTY-ONE

What if...?

Carys had a letter. Receiving it provoked within her, a nervous response; a fear that she'd been able to distance herself from for the past ten weeks.

Things with Marco had developed. Not dramatically, but weekly or bi-weekly dates to the pub, out to eat, or to the cinema had proved very pleasant.

When he'd announced a solution to her university dilemma, she'd opened her heart even further. Unable to be away from home with a new baby, she'd resigned herself to not furthering her education. But Marco had suggested she do something closer to home. She could be there for her baby, and have the support of her family on hand.

As a result, she'd enrolled on an A-level Psychology (it seemed pertinent with her family history) course at Pembrokeshire College. It would give her an A-level, hopefully with decent grades, and a pathway into a degree course (also run from the college by Swansea University.)

She had a lot to thank Marco for. He'd given her the strength to change her life. She wasn't in love with him. She didn't think so, anyway. Him being sworn to chastity meant their friendship could skirt harmlessly into the territory of mild flirtation without fear or expectation.

The easy, relaxed feeling she'd become tentatively accustomed to was spoiled by the letter she held in her hand. At the top were the initials NHS, and the Welsh equivalent which looked bizarre even though she spoke quite a lot of Welsh. The address of Withybush Hospital and contact numbers, fax numbers and email were displayed as she would have expected. The reality of it shook her.

The Hywel Dda National Health Trust were inviting her to have an Ultrasound scan to check everything was fine with the foetus growing inside her. She shuddered. Would everything be okay? Or would it all suddenly be the furthest from okay it could be?

Carys had witnessed the process of an Ultrasound numerous times on television. They told you the sex of the baby and took all sorts of measurements to see if it was developing normally. Convinced her baby may be developing anything but normally, she gripped the letter harder, willing it to be okay.

With a deep sigh, she resigned to a more positive outlook. Maybe the scan would reassure her everything was fine after all. Then, only her judgement, and memory, not to mention her sanity, would be in question!

A further chill travelled down her spine as she imagined her parents, or even Marco inviting themselves along for moral support. She had to keep it secret. If she was going to learn her foetus has exceedingly large eyes in a huge skull, she wanted to hear it alone.

Reluctantly, she lied to Diane and Geraint that the appointment was on a later date than it was. That way, they wouldn't be tempted to chase it up, it being such a landmark in her gestation.

Once she'd been, she could explain her reason for keeping it from them was the genuine anxiety she had about the scan. She was sure they'd understand. Her mother had got away with all sorts of odd behaviour over the years down to her bipolar condition. Carys was sure that the stress of her pregnancy, conceived from appalling abuse, would be excuse enough for her.

She hid the letter in her bedroom and adjusted the appointment date in her mind in advance of any questions. Tuesday, October the twenty third would be changed to Thursday the twenty fifth. With a cough to compose herself, she collected up her college books and scurried downstairs.

Sitting at the kitchen table with a fresh coffee and various text books at her side, she hadn't been working for long when she was joined by Diane, trying to sit quietly and enjoy a late breakfast. Her attempts at silence were excruciating. The noise of the chair being slowly scraped across the tiles instead of the usual pick up, clonk down manoeuvre was far more disturbing.

Carys looked up from her reading to glare at the perpetrator. The sight of Diane's pursed-lipped, raised-eyebrows expression, straining to be quiet, struck her as hilarious. They caught one another's eye and cracked up. When she had recovered a little, Diane apologised for the disturbance, sat down in a normal fashion and proceeded to eat her cereal.

"That's okay. If I really needed privacy I'd work in my room. I wanted company. I'm a bit nervous."

"Why?"

"I've had a letter. It's my twelve week scan next week. I'm worried there'll be something wrong with the baby."

"Twelve weeks already eh?!" Diane looked thrilled. "Things might have changed, but I don't think the first scan tests for abnormalities. It's usually just a dating scan, I think. They'll tell you when you're due. Exciting!"

Relief poured its calming oil on Carys. A dating scan; that was okay. She could carry on fooling herself for weeks before any 'abnormalities' might become apparent.

Maybe she didn't need to lie about the date of the appointment after all. It seemed a shame to deny the anxious grandmother-to-be. "Would you come with me?" Diane's face lit up as she happily accepted.

"I wouldn't miss it for the world!" she beamed. She marked the real date of the scan appointment in her diary. After her breakfast and a little more chatting, she drifted off leaving Carys to her work.

Carys was diligent with her A-level studies. Her Tutor, Professor Simpson, seemed pleased with her. She liked him too. He looked like how a professor should: tall, with a bald head, apart from above his ears, and spectacles perched on the end of his nose which he would peer over at the class from his desk. An incongruous part of his attire was a cowboy shirt and string tie, alluding to a different life outside of college.

His enthusiasm for his subject was contagious and Carys developed a real understanding the more complicated conditions of mental health (surprise, surprise). She found the information from the course concerning her mother's condition enlightening.

She was finding it particularly fascinating learning about 'What is normal?' According to the textbooks, 'Normal' is a shifting parameter dependent on geographical location and place in history. For example, she was shocked to learn, someone of her mother's condition would have been locked away in an asylum only fifty years ago, joining thousands of others classified as schizophrenic, which was a word she thought she understood, but was surprised to find she was completely wrong.

She'd supposed that twin, or multiple personality disorders depicted in films was accurate, often wondering why her mother's diagnosis hadn't featured the word as it seemed wholly appropriate. But, it seemed, the term schizophrenic in her books simply meant 'mad'.

It was a term out of favour for some time as the definition of 'mad' changed as well. Fifty years or more ago, very everyday things could have led to a mad, schizophrenic tag, and Carys was alarmed to find out she was guilty of one of them herself; or soon would be.

Being an unmarried mother could have seen gained her a 'mad' classification. Along with homosexuality. Mad was simply classified as 'behaviour which deviated from the normal behaviour of society' (behaviour categorised by the same society!)

Back then, you'd have to be crazy to be an unmarried mother, or a homosexual, or think you were Napoléon, or believe in UFO's. Nowadays, she considered gratefully, many of the definitions had been revoked.

Whilst some people in New Age circles could freely suggest they were the twentieth incarnation of Moses, and that Jesus Christ was their spirit guide; and others could talk quite happily about their fervent belief in all things extra-terrestrial, still others were persecuted.

The class had discussed how most people had a very scathing view of a certain ex-footballer who now was more famous for his talks on the presence of the illuminati. How the class had laughed.

"Laughter aside," Professor Simpson calmed, "One definition you all agreed on was whether the person in question was coping in their society. But, I would argue that because the society decides what is normal and therefore what 'coping' may represent, is it not that society found them inconvenient?" He peered at them over his half-moon frames. "Food for thought." He stepped from his desk and scribbled on the whiteboard. "David Icke's views, for example, whilst seen as 'not normal' by many, are not inconvenient. In fact some conspiracy theorists might argue he's a smoke screen, but that's for a different class a different day. Think, though, could the David Ickes' of this world, instead of being popular celebrities, have been turned into dribbling imbecile's rotting in an asylum? One man's madman might be another's eccentric visionary, yes?"

He wrote indecipherably in purple marker. "Add to that, the mix of tranquillisers, anti-depressants, and anti-psychotic medications, and the previous generation's Freudian psychotherapy and electric shock therapy, along with brutal frontal lobotomies and such like, and it was no wonder the psychiatric wards were full of patients who became lifelong residents.

"Suffice to say Any answer to the question of what defines mad is subjective, even today. Psychology is not a science and never has been, and why?"

Carys raised her hand, "Because all its conclusions are opinion. Granted, opinion often backed up by great research; but opinion all the same."

"Exactly, Carys. Well done!"

Carys had liked that when she'd read it. It made her feel free, and so much better about her mother's, and her own, mental health that it was worth attending simply for that. She doubted Marco had known quite how genius his suggestion of college had been.

Her upcoming scan was unsurprisingly the subject of the family's evening meal discussion. Carys had offered to cook. It was something she did as often as she could without appearing ungrateful to her mother's limited repertoire. She excused it as wanting to take on some of the burden, and it was something she'd been looking forward to doing at Uni.

Diane tended to pick at the offerings and it was hard not to take offence, but the irony helped. Tonight, it was 'Roman Lamb': a recipe she'd found in one of her mum's new cookbooks comprising lamb (in this case from the local Preseli Mountains), and a sauce made with anchovies.

Diane struggled with its richness, whilst Geraint wolfed it down declaring it the tastiest food he'd ever eaten, then coughing and sharing a smile with his wife to say 'I'm just encouraging our delicate daughter.'

Leaving washing-up to her mum and dad, Carys took herself up to bed early for her college lectures tomorrow. Once under her duvet, she suddenly didn't feel tired anymore. Grabbing the huge tome of her psychology course book she began reading.

Re-reading line after line as her tired mind struggled to assimilate the long names and dates and theories, she knew she was wasting her time. It became most apparent when she woke herself by dropping the heavy book to the floor. Jolting awake, she expected her parents would come running in to see what the noise was.

Sighing with relief at the silence, she put the books neatly on her bedside table and turned off the light. Moonlight filtered through the curtains leaving the room in a soft glow. As her eyes became accustomed, they darted to things moving in ghostly ways: her cardigan thrown casually on her bedpost took on the shape of a child with long hair; her dressing gown hanging from the back of her door morphed into the grim reaper.

It was only her imagination, but it unsettled her. Perhaps reopening her textbooks would be a good idea? Before reaching across and heaving them from the bedside table again, her mind drifted to topics she might read about. Suddenly, in her peripheral vision, she caught sight of movement. Her gaze shot to the cornice of the wardrobe and she stared in disbelief as the unmistakable repugnant legs of a huge house spider wriggled into view.

She gawped in horror as the one spider turned into five.

And then ten.

And then hundreds, and thousands, of frantic legged monstrosities, cascading down the wardrobe like a hellish avalanche of wriggling revulsion.

Reaching the floorboards, the rat-a-tat-a-tat of a million scurrying legs grew Carys's terrified anticipation like a drum roll; the mass, tumbling over itself as the spiders hurtled towards her on the bed. Clutching her sheets to her face with only her nose and eyes peeping out, she could barely breathe.

Thousands and thousands of spiders still spilled over the top of the wardrobe. An unbearable unease gripped her, knowing she could no longer see the ones which had already reached the floor, obscured as they were by the foot of the bed. With nowhere to run, she paused in petrified anticipation for them to reach the top of the footboard and find their way onto her bed. Her pounding heart surged blood through her veins, sending tingles to every extremity. A scream poised in her mouth, waited for an order from her brain which would never come. Shaking her head, she knew they weren't real. They couldn't be

Then they were there, surging over the bottom of her bed, thousands and thousands of horrible black bodies, their legs moving as only spiders' legs can, onto the bedspread. As they tore towards her, she could contain her fear no longer and the scream bounced from every surface.

As soon as the first spider reached her, it vanished. And then, in a pulse of dream erasing consciousness, a dispelling tremor flowed back, eradicating all of them until, rapidly, the room was back to normal.

What was happening to her? She must be stressed with her pregnancy more than she realised; or perhaps it was the effect of her hormones. Whatever caused the hallucination had exhausted her, and she was finally ready to sleep. She gave one more nervous look around the room, and particularly at the top of the wardrobe, before cautiously laying her head on the pillow.

After a few minutes lying in tense silence her chest slowed to normal breathing. Sleep followed, but for only the briefest time. When she awoke next, she had another terrible shock.

She stirred to someone stroking her leg. Half-thoughts of Marco in her dreamy state made her smile.

The rubbing became rougher and more urgent - like a child tap, tapping their mother, demanding attention. She became more and more alert until her eyes sprung open. Immediately, she wished they hadn't.

There, sitting at the foot of her bed, its skeletal fingers upon her leg, was an archetypical alien being.

Hunched, expressionless, skin translucently pale and white, stroking her bare leg with its clammy, rough hand; it stared at her forever before indicating her stomach with a long bone-thin finger. Making noises like a cheap space toy, it shifted towards her.

Shocked the scream ringing in her ears was hers, Carys clamped her hand to her mouth.

The shriek turned to sobs as salty tears streamed down her face. Just as every time before, no-one came to her aid. From the creature's gesticulations, she understood: it wanted her baby. Flinching back, she scuttled up the bed as it shouted at her in a polyphonic growl.

She knew she had no choice but to do as it wished. There was menace in each movement. Frantic to wriggle free from its willowy fingers as they advanced toward her belly, her eyes bulged in terror as movement was impossible. Paralysed, the creature was unhampered to perform its hideous examination of her bump.

In a supreme attempt to scream, she shifted her parched tongue an inch, pressing what little moisture remained in her mouth dribbling down her chin. Even blinking appeared impossible, forcing her to endure an unwavering stare at her foe.

She so wanted to scream; wanted to punch it in its bug-eyed face; make it stop and leave her and her baby alone, lying immobilised, abused by the alien beast. A voice she'd never heard before cackled in the hush.

"That there's an eebomeenashon," the voice slurred in what Carys recognised as being bizarrely, Pennsylvania English.

Unable to see who spoke, from the corner of her eye a man came into view. Beneath a wide-rimmed black hat, he wore a white shirt and black waistcoat supplemented by an unattractive beard combined with wide sideburns, peculiar without an accompanying moustache. He was pointing at her tummy, unconcerned with the alien.

"That there insida youu is a eebomeenashon. You should get ridda eet," he drawled. As she looked away from the Amish stranger, the alien released her from her paralysis, stood straight, and walked out of her bedroom door. Free from her restriction, she finally screamed. The Amish man's hand shot over her mouth and he looked into her eyes.

"Hush now! You don't wanna be worrying your folks any," he grimaced. Carys nodded her compliance, and he released his hand from her face. Following the alien's path, he paused as he opened her bedroom door, and turned once more to speak. "You get ridda that thing, you hear?"

Mercifully, he didn't wait for her answer. And Carys was pretty sure he couldn't have been real. She rolled over into the foetal position and rocked back and forth until eventually, not long before dawn, she dropped into a fitful sleep.

The next day didn't get off to a good start as she'd forgotten to set her alarm (or slept through it through sheer exhaustion.)

She hated being late for college lectures. It was hard to catch up, and that made Professor Simpson less than pleased with her.

Disappointed to have missed the praise she'd learned to rely on, Carys was surprised when at the end of the lecture he asked her to stay behind. He was full of smiles so she knew she wasn't in trouble. Saying his goodbyes to the rest of the class as they departed, when he was sure the last of them had left: hearing the flapping closed of the double doors and fading chatter of the class along the corridor, he peered at Carys over his spectacles. His eyes twinkled from his lofty height, lessened by his posture leaning against his desk.

He slumped his shoulders in a pseudo-defeated

manner before speaking. "What's the matter, Carys?" he asked. "You don't seem yourself at all today." Carys shifting from foot to foot betrayed her internal struggle. "Trouble at home?"

Problems in the home were the usual cause of teenage angst, and speaking out often compromised their loyalties. His next presumption would have been boy trouble, but he had no need to guess. Carys was perfectly forthcoming.

"I think I've been seeing things: people. Well I definitely have seen them, but I don't think they're real."

Professor Simpson gasped. It wasn't what he'd expected. Broadening his smile for a moment, his lips pursed and he rubbed his chin in thought "When have you seen these people?" he inquired eventually.

"Well one of them isn't people, really. It's an alien. And the other one's an Amish bearded man in a hat. Oh, and there were thousands of spiders, everywhere; all over the floor and dropping from the wardrobe." The thoughtful look persisted on Professor Simpson's kind face.

"So, you're happy to admit these people, and the spiders were not actually there, but you saw them as though they were?" he nodded slowly, confirming his point. "You had a bad night by the sounds of it. No wonder you look so tired."

Carys nodded distractedly as she considered how she did feel. "I think they weren't real. Well, I know the spiders weren't real because they disappeared when they reached me." She paused, feeling embarrassed before continuing. "I don't know about the alien... it seemed true, and I could feel it touching me."

Professor Simpson smiled in amusement. "What about the Amish gentleman?" Carys shrugged. He chuckled. "So you're happy that the spiders, and Amish man aren't real, but you're not so sure regarding the alien?" he asked rhetorically.

"Given that we *know* Amish actually exist, it could be argued that it's far more likely the man was real, and *not* the alien? And as an Amish gentleman from Pennsylvania in your room, in Wales, in the middle of the night is extremely unlikely, it's probably fair to presume that neither were true."

"Not very scientific!" Carys argued. "What if the alien was real and tricked my mind with the other hallucinations to throw me off the scent?!"

"I love how your mind works, Carys. You are, of course, absolutely correct. I'm a Psychologist, not an expert in Extra-Terrestrial biology! We cannot discount any theories without proof, can we?" He smiled understandingly at her.

"I think, given our lack of knowledge in such areas; the world as a whole's lack of knowledge, we should treat them as hallucinations." He nodded in earnest agreement with his own evaluation. "In your condition, it's not all that surprising. But it would probably be a good idea to seek medical advice. You don't want them to get any worse. You might find you're prone to post natal depression. Go and see your GP," he advised.

Carys agreed. Perhaps more concerned than he was showing, Professor Simpson offered Carys use of the phone in the classroom. He looked up the phone number for the Narberth Surgery, and detecting Carys's reluctance, he even phoned for her.

Whether it was his status as a professor, or whether they were just having a quiet day, the surgery surprised Carys by offering an appointment for that afternoon. It fitted in with when the bus arrived back in Narberth, so she agreed to go.

She didn't expect to feel nervous, but found on the bus journey she was becoming more and more so. The bus stopped opposite Meddygfa Rhiannon, the Narberth Health Centre. The heaving waiting room convinced Carys of Professor Simpson's clout.

"O dan ei sang," she sighed, emulating her dad in any crowd. It was a Welsh idiom that translated as 'underneath it' but was said to mean really busy. Leaning against a wall in the absence of an available seat, she locked her legs for a long wait.

The receptionist who checked her in told her she'd be seen by Doctor Ferrero. The wall plaque declared her to be very well qualified; in fact, judging by the number of letters after her name, the most qualified in the building. She didn't know what the letters meant, but was pleased she had so many of them.

Of course, there was a lot more to being a good doctor than qualifications. Carys's sensitivity required an impeccable bedside manner; and when the stern face of Dr Ferrero appeared from behind her door and she bustled to reception, Carys wasn't convinced she had it. The receptionist jumped to attention as though in the company of a severe sergeant-major.

Carys's mind whirred. Should she ask to see someone else? Maybe she should leave and go home? She shifted from the wall and stepped towards the door. She'd rather take her chances with weird Amish men and aliens than the terrifying Dr Ferrero. But before she made it past the doctor's door, it flew open.

"Carys Ellis?" the doctor inquired, and when Carys looked into her eyes, she was relieved to detect an undeniable kindness. Carys smiled back. As they stepped into the room together, Carys towered over her diminutive frame. Recalling the receptionist's nerves brought a smile to her lips. "What can I do for you today?" she asked when they were both seated. Carys fumbled with the hem of her top. "Take your time", she reassured.

After a bout of nervous coughing, she decided to tell all. "I'm eleven weeks pregnant with a history of mental illness. My mother is bipolar, and last night I was awoken with what I suppose must have been hallucinations, but which seemed completely real at the time."

The doctor sat in attentive silence as she listened to Carys's tale of spiders, Amish, and aliens. Pausing for a moment, she tapped her pursed lips with an extended index finger. "It sounds as though you've had two types of hallucination. It's quite common for people to have them as they drop off to sleep. Spiders, in actual fact are not uncommon. It's called 'hypnagogic' hallucination." The technical words were both reassuring and interesting to a student of psychology.

"The second type, known as 'hypnopompic', happen when you are just waking. They're not unusual, either." The doctor sat up in her chair, obviously enjoying airing her knowledge. "Your body is going through a lot. You're more fatigued than you realise. People who are particularly tired or stressed are prone to this type of thing. You probably shouldn't be all that concerned."

Carys looked up at the 'all that'. Doctor Ferrero explained. "There's a slight risk it could be an indicator to a more serious mental health condition such as your mother's bipolar. I'll make a referral to the psychiatric department for further assessment."

Dr Ferrero's reassurance had calmed her, but Carys knew she hadn't told the doctor everything. If she were to find peace, it was vital she disclosed her darkest fear. "I am not convinced the baby I'm carrying is human."

Doctor Ferrero flinched and struggled to maintain her composure. Carys imagined her scribbling on her doctor pad when she left: "CRAZY!"

Smiling sympathetically, she reiterated her diagnosis. "It doesn't seem that odd to me. It is a stressful time for you. Stress can do some very strange things. I'll make the referral; I can make it urgent, if you like, and in the meantime, if you become more worried you can access emergency mental health services at the A and E department in Withybush. If you're really concerned, call 999. Is that okay for now? I could prescribe something, but in your condition it's a bit of a minefield, and I'd rather an expert cast their eye over you first."

"Thank you, doctor. I don't want to risk my baby at all, so I'll wait."

"And, do get in touch if you become more worried." The doctor stood and Carys wasn't sure if she was even shorter than when she sat at her desk. "Bye, Carys. Look after yourself."

The sound of computer keyboard keys tapping away emanated from behind the door as she pulled it closed behind her. The doctor was obviously getting straight onto her referral. So, until someone told her differently, she had to accept she was perfectly normal.

Memories of the hideous creature touching her sent a shudder down her spine. Dr Ferrero might be convinced everything she'd described was a hypno-whatever-it-was hallucination, but Carys wasn't. The alien was real, and no amount of telling her how normal she was could convince her otherwise. She almost hoped she *was* crazy. It might be her only hope.

As she walked slowly home, the doctor's scepticism offered a perverse comfort. If she could be told clearly that she believed her baby to be extra-terrestrial, and not consider it for a second, she realised with a smile that no medical professional would. Even if they did, they'd never risk their reputation by saying, would they?

Whatever measurements and scans the obstetrics department took, her baby was safe. No-one would suspect the truth.

CHAPTER TWENTY-TWO

Moving things forward

The twelve week scan went by without a hitch, and Diane had loved every minute. A due date of the twenty second of April 2002 was estimated, and her twenty-week scan booked. Carys received the news blankly. It would be a worry, but she aimed to put it out of her mind until then.

No more strange visits in the middle of the night had bothered her in the intervening weeks. She didn't like to tempt fate by thinking about it, but allowing herself a smile, she was blooming.

A-level studies saw her on top form again, and things were plodding along nicely with Marco. His company was easy. He never judged her. Gazing at him during church one Sunday as he played his guitar and sang, she realised she was actually quite smitten.

Holding the latest letter in her hand, she felt a dilemma. It was from the Psychiatric department, offering her an appointment to attend a clinic at the health centre next week. She was fine now. Was it worth even bothering with? In anticipation of what she might have to endure after birth, she grudgingly decided to go.

When the day of her appointment arrived, she arranged a taxi and arrived prompt. A scruffy looking gentleman and a very short, slightly obese lady were already in the windowless upstairs waiting room. As they sat rocking back and forth, the lady occasionally hitting herself in the face with the palm of her hand and shouting "Go Away!" Carys began to wonder what she was letting herself in for.

Sitting as far from the others as possible, her mood brightened when Doctor Rimmer entered the waiting room. Partly because she looked pleasant, and partly due to her taking with her the lady, whose face hitting had turned to punching, in-between opening up a gruesome scab on her wrist.

Left with the silent, rocking man for a good half an hour had the effect of making Carys feel unquestionably sane.

She was sane, wasn't she?

The lady came out, red-faced, and the man replaced her in the doctor's care. She was next.

After only a few minutes, the man emerged clutching a piece of paper.

"Carys Ellis?" The gentle Doctor Rimmer inquired. As Carys nodded, she invited her to follow her through double doors into a corridor. It was uncomfortable following the stranger. She didn't know if she should start a conversation.

Before she'd opened her mouth to speak, they'd arrived at a small room containing a few chairs and a desk shoved against the wall. As they sat down in the cramped office, Doctor Rimmer introduced herself as the registrar to the consultant Psychiatrist, and they began.

Having listened to Carys's problems, her diagnosis concurred with Doctor Ferrero's. And like her, she baulked at the idea of Carys's baby being 'not of this earth' dealing with it in the same way: by ignoring it

"Everything you've described is completely normal. When something traumatic happens our minds can create a more palatable version that then becomes a memory," she said, discounting the alien baby theory with one dismissive psychobabble-statement. Was it a test to see if Carys persisted with it? Or was it really normal to come up with outlandish theories to cope with traumatic events? "We don't like to give out medication unnecessarily. If you have further concerns, please phone my secretary at Bro Cerwyn and ask for another appointment."

Carys didn't disagree. She didn't want to take medication and hadn't been bothered for weeks anyway. Happy to be declared sane by a professional who should know, Carys left and made her way back home.

Sunday morning came round again and time for Narberth Christian Fellowship's primary worship. Marco had asked her virtually every day that week if she was definitely coming to church on Sunday. She had become suspicious and he had stopped asking. She'd been every week since moving to Wales. Why he was so anxious about this week in particular, she could only wonder.

The cold November morning provoked a premature festive feeling in Carys, who was already looking forward to her first Christmas in Wales. She'd easily forget her worries with the distraction. Especially as she now was in the bosom of friends from Narberth Christian Fellowship.

She was still daydreaming about Christmas trees and nativity scenes when Geraint pulled the car into the town car-park. They walked as a family to the Town Hall, and took their places near the front in their usual seats.

It was rare for them to make it to their seats without interception by well-wishers, but today they'd been left alone. Not that anyone was unfriendly. No, there were big beaming smiles and stifled words from every face they saw. Something, Carys was sure, was definitely afoot.

The band began tuning up. Marco jumped onto the stage to join them. He was wearing smarter clothes than his normal casual attire. Maybe there was a special guest expected today? The band played. Marco seemed oblivious to Carys's presence; strange since he'd gone on and on about her coming.

Fluffing a couple of notes on the guitar really threw him where normally he'd laugh it off. After his struggle to lead the congregation in Hymn, he sat down for his dad to take the sermon: a lovely message of love and family. Carys felt unusually lifted and sang along with unprecedented verve.

When the preaching paused, and the band came back on stage to accompany a few more Hymns, Carys waited for them to restart playing, but instead, Marco shuffled to the front of the stage with his microphone.

He looked at her for the first time that day; nervously, but with a glint in his eye she liked.

"Carys. Would you please join me on stage?" She was very shy. The unwavering attention sickened her and she stood motionless. A tug at her sleeve, and an encouraging 'Go on,' from her mum was enough to surge her on. Marco took her hand and helped her onto the stage.

No sooner had he done so than he was down on one knee in front of her. "Carys Ellis," he said into the microphone he already held. "I knew I wanted to be with you from the first time I saw your photograph. Since I've met you and had the pleasure of getting to know you, I have fallen deeply in love with you."

Carys couldn't quite believe what, now she

looked back, the whole day, the whole week even, had been pointing to. She flushed red with embarrassment and delight.

"I want to look after you. I want to be a father to the little gift from God growing inside you. Carys… Will you make me the happiest man on earth and marry me?"

She knew straight away, she wanted to say yes. It wasn't love, but safety he offered. He'd be a good provider. She certainly enjoyed his company. And the clincher was his joy at being a father. Surely, she could learn to love a man like that?

Aware she had taken a long time to answer, she flexed the biggest smile onto her face and gazed into his eyes. "Yes. Yes I will marry you."

He beamed back at her. "Sorry. Would you please say that again," he asked, head tilted coyly, microphone extended to her lips. "Yes!" she cried, amplified now by the sound system. The "I will marry you," she also repeated, lost in the cheers of jubilation and joy from the congregation. Carys suspected they'd been in on it from the start.

The rest of the day went by in a whirl of congratulations and well wishing. Carys couldn't remember ever having been happier. Something, intuition? Just her usual negativity? She didn't know, but something burnt away at her contentment as surely as a flame on a rope.

Willing a smile back to her mouth, her granite

gaze held at bay doubts which already threatened her traction on the treacherous ascent of her sanity. The cold steel of recognition of an old foe threatened to cleave her heart from her chest. Maybe it would be for the best. The further she climbed, the further she'd fall when the tenure snapped.

Who would want to be a father to an alien baby? She loved the life inside her no matter what. But could she really expect someone else to? Was it even fair to build up his hope? What if it wasn't born at all; snatched away by its alien creators? She'd be shackled to a man (albeit a nice, decent man) she didn't love.

"Drink that, dear. I think the excitement's been a bit much for you." The kind wrinkled hand of an elderly lady held a cup of tea close to her mouth. Sipping the hot nectar, its calming effects welcome, she took the cup in quivering fingers. "I'll just put it down here for you, shall I?" she said, taking it from Carys as a spill seemed unavoidable. Carys nodded and turned away to disguise the moistness in her eyes.

Clenching a fist, she forced away the shaking. For the sake of my baby, I'll learn to love Marco. And if I can't; and if my baby's never born, I'll deal with it then. Marco will get over it if things don't work out. But for me and my child, it could be our only chance. And she vowed to seize the opportunity.

CHAPTER
TWENTY-THREE

Facing the future

December was almost upon them, and the small town of Narberth prepared for its Christmas celebrations. From the colourful lights (yet to be switched on) draped like bunting from one side of the street to the other, to banners announcing the upcoming Winter Carnival and 'Civic Week', it was clear that Christmas was a big deal in Narberth.

It was a pleasing distraction for Carys with the twenty week scan date looming ever closer. This one, she was keeping close to her chest. She'd declined the invitation to perform on the carnival float of Narberth Christian Fellowship because of just feeling too heavy and hormonal to be a reliable help. But she supported from the side-lines with bacon sandwiches for her fiancé and the rest of the crew.

Being appreciated in the bosom of her new

church family made her feel popular for the first time in her life. And since Marco's romantic proposal, she felt like a princess.

Despite the date of her scan being etched into her brain, every morning she checked her diary and calculated the days to her appointment. She'd fumble at the pages and squint at the little squares on the calendar as though the simple addition was the most complicated of mathematical conundrum.

Denial at her odd, manic ritual served to protect her from an admission that she was spiralling downwards. If Diane was aware, especially if she understood the reason for her daughter's anxiety, she would have joined her, the pair tumbling to an abhorrent, emotionless abyss, like a tandem jump with no parachute.

Her obsessive anxiety meant bus routes had been planned well in advance, and she was acutely aware of the anxious waiting she'd have to endure when the bus reached her destination an hour early. Falling on a college day had provided an unsuspicious reason to leave the house with the excuse she needed to go in early for some advice.

The float her friends were working on was a clever replica of the Town Hall church on wheels. Dan Paulo was going to be at the front leading the congregation in clapping and singing, whilst Marco and the band would play accompaniment and provide lead vocals as they did every Sunday.

When Carnival night came, the float was praised for the religious theme, celebrating the true meaning of Christmas; conspicuous amongst the three Father Christmas's (a Welsh Sion Corn version made it four.) Nativity scenes from local nursery schools kept with the religious sentiment, whilst bigger schools represented films currently at the cinema such as Harry Potter and Star Wars.

Three of the pubs in the town chose Pirates as their theme. Two wore Pirates of the Caribbean garb, with Elizabeth and Cap'n Jack Sparrow in unconvincing costume, whilst the third depicted the richest pirate who ever lived, Pembrokeshire's own 'Barti Ddu', 'Black Bart'.

After the parade, the crowd lining the streets to capacity good- naturedly made their way to the pubs and social clubs to continue the day's heavy drinking. Others stood and watched the fireworks filling the air with their showers of fiery colour.

For Carys, the fizzing pyrotechnics symbolised the final distraction before the event she'd been dreading claimed her full attention.

The morning of the appointment arrived, and Carys showered and dressed in plenty of time for the bus, which was perfectly on schedule, despite the icy conditions of the cold December morning. Carys gazed out from the bus window grateful the Preseli mountains took her thoughts away from her fears.

Stepping from the bus, the imposing building that was Withybush General Hospital, glared at her from its myriad of oblong eyes, daring her to turn and run. But, no. She was going nowhere. Today was the day she'd dreaded for weeks, but she had to know - was her baby's development normal?

After checking in at the reception desk of the Antenatal Clinic, she sat with other expectant mums waiting for their scans in the stuffy waiting area. Her nervous gaze rested on each of them in turn, scrutinising their bumps, wondering who dwelled inside each one, busily budding for birth.

A prick of guilt at denying her mum this moment stung her eyes, settling on her abdomen above her own bump bringing with it a wave of nausea. Looking away to appease her guilt, she was the only one there without a mum or a partner with her.

She couldn't have had company though, could she? Unsure what she was about to encounter forced her isolation. But she missed the comforting hand of Diane, or Marco, or even her dad.

A noise grabbed her attention as a sonographer or midwife or someone else in a nurse's uniform opened a door off of the waiting room and called a name. In response, one of the girls, accompanied by her mother and husband got up excitedly from their seats and followed the nurse into the room she had come from.

They disappeared for fifteen minutes before re-emerging with grins on their faces and clutching a folded card Carys assumed was the scan photograph.

"We're having a little boy!" the girl announced jubilantly to anyone who was interested. The father looked quietly chuffed; his name set to live on for another generation.

The rest of the waiting room mustered fake smiles as their own babies took all of their real attention. Carys hadn't given thought to what sex her baby might be. She dreaded being unable to contain her distress at being asked "Do you want to know what the baby is?" What gender, or what *species?*

The same procedure played out a few more times before the moment she was dreading finally happened. The same nurse came out of the room and looked questioningly around.

"Carys Ellis?"

She got up, obviously by far the least excited of any of the girls waiting. She shuffled despondently into the room and followed the instructions to sit on the examining couch.

"No-one with you?" the nurse asked unnecessarily. Carys shook her head as the nurse adjusted her clothes and applied gel to her bulbous belly.

The lights dimmed as the nurse swung a monitor into both of their views. As the ultrasound paddle moved around her stomach, it made a sound similar to a vinyl record skipping until the whop whop whop sound of the foetal heart was detected.

"A good strong heartbeat. That's what we like," the nurse seemed delighted to impart. "Hopefully, baby will turn and give us a nice photograph. They cost three pounds if you want to keep it." Carys nodded that she would as she tried to recall the coins in her purse and her bus journey home. She was sure she had enough.

The nurse announced that she had a good shot, but didn't explain where everything was. Carys hadn't deciphered the image before it changed and the nurse began a different job looking at very specific parts of the foetus. Carys's heart felt as though it would burst through her chest as her anxiety reached new levels.

'Calm down,' she instructed herself. The taking of measurements began and Carys felt as though she might faint.

"Everything okay?" she rasped as she couldn't help herself but ask. The sonographer remained silent but seemed undeterred.

She moved the computer curser to a point on the unfathomable picture on the screen with a touchpad and a clicking noise followed. It was quickly followed by another brisk movement of the cursor on the screen and another click. The distance between the two points, Carys supposed, was a measurement that would indicate normal development… or not.

Carys began to decipher the image. Little legs, and the head was obvious, and then a hand moved briefly over the face. Carys stared as the fingers on the little hand appeared inordinately long. She looked at the sonographer for a reassuring sign, but she continued gazing with an alarming intensity.

When the freaky hand moved, the face it had partially covered displayed the most enormous eyes. And the head that housed them was large and disproportionate to the body.

Carys had seen pictures of scan pictures before in magazines and despite these startling features the foetus looked largely normal, but the sonographers prolonged silence, so different to the twelve week scan she had received, that was worrying Carys the most.

"Is something wrong?" Carys asked again. The hush was becoming unbearable.

"I'm sure everything's fine," the nurse began, "but I'm just going to go and get a colleague, okay?"

Carys nodded but tears stung the backs of her eyes. She'd feared it for months, but the reality was still a shock. Praying fervently the colleague would make it all better, she lay alone, the blank screen of the monitor offering no comfort.

The door flung open, making her jump, and two nurses, the sonographer from before and another woman, much larger in both build and stature, came striding into the room.

The bigger woman took the seat where the smaller woman had previously performed the scan. The niceties of introductions were remembered suddenly and distractedly and the larger woman turned briefly to Carys and smiled unconvincingly. "Okay, dear?" she turned away again before receiving any answer. After performing the same procedure as the original sonographer, she turned off the machine, wiped the gel from Carys's stomach and helped her sit round.

As she sat, legs dangling off the couch, the larger lady, with supportive nods and 'Hmmm hmmm's' from the other, explained the ultrasound findings.

"You aren't here with anybody, are you, dear?"

Carys shook her head. Why? Why did she need to be here with someone?

"I don't want to worry you," she persisted, "but I'm going to refer you to the consultant Obstetrician, Mr Overton. He's ever so nice."

"Wha... what's wrong?"

"None of the anomalies we look for were detected... but we are a little concerned with the size of your baby's head. It is unusually large. It may be that it will even out later on in the gestation, but you may have to bring your due date forward, and you might need to have a Caesarean section. Like I say, the consultant will tell you all about it."

The featureless ovoid heads of the alien creatures loomed in Carys's mind. They'd take her baby away. As soon as they saw it she was certain: they'd take her baby away from her.

The nurse placed a reassuring hand on her arm.

"Is there any reason to think that Mr Ov..." she'd forgotten his name already.

"Overton," the nurse reminded. Carys nodded.

"...will recommend termination?" she choked.

The sonographer frowned, shaking her head. "I can't predict what Mr Overton will say, but I very much doubt *that* will be his recommendation. It's probably nothing to worry about."

The photograph was handed to her in exchange for her three pounds. Either kindness or disinterest (Carys suspected the former) elicited silence in response to the freakish appearance of the photo. It looked so unmistakably alien to Carys that it could have been a science fiction poster.

Carys rode the bus home in stunned silence staring surreptitiously at her little picture, keeping it hidden from public view to avoid questions. She knew why the baby had a big head, of course she did. She'd known all along that the scan would turn out like this. And all the security she'd enjoyed since accepting Marco's proposal felt jeopardised.

She couldn't show him, or anybody else; or tell him how worried she was. Tears that had threatened to breach the dewy surface of her eyes while she lay on the examination couch, flooded unremittingly from her eyes now.

Face hidden, sobs subdued, she still attracted the attention of other travellers. Something in her manner, whilst attaining sympathetic looks, prevented anyone approaching her. Travelling from the hospital in her condition the answer was probably all too obvious, and what could they say?

What if he doesn't want to marry me once he sees the baby? She didn't even love him, but she knew she wouldn't find a better provider. The only attention she'd got before was from a rapist. It wouldn't get any easier with a child, would it? If Marco rejected her, she'd be alone, she was certain.

The wedding needed to be soon: before the baby was born and it was too late, and before she became too huge. She could say it had suddenly become the most important thing to her for the baby to not be born out of wedlock, even though biologically it made no sense.

Anxious now to get back to Narberth and start things moving, the bus journey seemed terrifically slow. She didn't have to wait long to speak to Marco though, because he was driving towards the bus stop as she climbed down from the bus. Spotting her immediately, he pulled up, rushing out gallantly to open the car door for her.

"Hello, beautiful!" he greeted loudly. "Need a ride?"

"Can we go somewhere?" she asked. "For a

coffee or something? I really want to talk to you."

A worried frown creased his forehead. "Er… okay. Everything all right?" He looked understandably concerned as to what the urgent topic of conversation might be. Was she getting cold feet? But as they sat enjoying Latte's in Lillie's Coffee Shop, his anxiety turned to elation.

Marco couldn't quite believe his luck that the incredibly beautiful girl he'd seen in a photo just a few months before was going to be his wife soon. And for a Christian boy who'd saved himself for his wedding night, it couldn't come soon enough!

CHAPTER
TWENTY-FOUR

The influence of Discovery

Christmas day, 2001

The guests at the wedding of Marco Donatello Paulo to Carys Diane Ellis were the usual congregation, with the addition of course of Stella; delighted to be invited to spend Christmas with her favourite family; and seeing Carys so happy was the best present ever.

The service followed a usual Christmas day service with the wedding tacked on. Getting married on what was Carys's favourite day of the year anyway had been Marcos special surprise to his bride. Unsure to start with, expecting guests to be few, and her own quiet family day compromised. In the end she'd succumbed to the romance, and thrown herself wholeheartedly into it.

Carys glowed like a royal bride in a dress from an intriguing boutique, *White Bride,* in Narberth's exclusive little town centre. Marco looked incredibly handsome, as only a tall dark Italian can. Geraint proudly wore his police uniform, complete with domed helmet on his daughter's insistence. And Diane wore a blue two-piece with a large hat, a proud smile, and a tear in her eye.

It was the perfect wedding day with the perfect guests. Afterwards, many of the congregation transformed the hall into the perfect reception venue, with live music and food prepared by the best cooks in the town. It was all… perfect.

They milled around the hall throughout the day, danced into the night and finally received their gift from the two parents, who had paid for two weeks to the island of Mauritius. The perfect honeymoon for the perfect married couple to begin their life together. The perfection wouldn't last for long.

The honeymoon was lovely, as it should have been. Fabulous weather, but not too hot for a pregnant bride. For Carys it was the last chance to relax before the countdown to an uncertain future raced to its conclusion.

When they returned from paradise, they were to move into their marital home together, not share either of their parents' houses. Marco had been encouraged from young adulthood to buy property and had already mortgaged a town house which he'd rented to a family whilst they found somewhere to buy. Their move out matched with Marco and Carys moving in.

Marco was so excited planning the nursery (or he was making a good show of it to impress his new bride at any rate.) Carys struggled to match his fervour but came up with an appropriate neutral colour scheme. What colours did extra-terrestrials like anyway?

Normality soon took over as Carys grew and grew. Marco worked every day and she continued waddling to college. On her free days, she spent time with her mum, who had given up trying to ignite excitement in her daughter for her up-coming big day (she'd been in hormonal hell her-self in pregnancy, so didn't push it.)

Sighing, Carys supposed it was all very normal; apart from how she was feeling. Already, she was convinced Marco had changed. And she was definitely irritated by him. Maybe her bedroom performance had disappointed after his months and years of waiting for intimacy with his bride (she was pregnant!) Maybe it was male cocki-ness after finally sowing his oats. Or maybe the honeymoon was over.

The previous occupants had installed satellite television. The receiver dish was still attached to the front of the house so it was an obvious choice to get the benefits for themselves. Marco, like most men it seemed to Carys, was looking for-ward to sports and maybe films. Whilst she liked a good film, Carys was excited mainly by the prospect of the documentary channels.

She imagined, with twenty-four-hour program choices, that there would be a lot of documentaries of huge interest to her. Among other things, she could expect programs, at least occasionally, about psychology and other topics of interest to students of psychology. Disappointingly, they were almost conspicuous by their absence. But there were other topics also sadly lacking.

What she did find, but had little interest in, was bountiful programs on topics as dull as Americans living in the Florida Everglades, Americans who drive on incredibly dangerous roads, people with lots of cats or dogs, or so much crap in their houses they could barely make it through the front door.

But there was another documentary subject that consumed the schedule more than any other. She watched at first with detached, slightly amused interest, but obsession was only around the corner. Carys was doomed now her attention had been grabbed by the most prolific of Discovery channel's output. Only sharks could offer comparable airtime.

It started off with the compelling account from a credible sounding policeman who swore blind he'd been abducted by aliens. Carys flinched at the artist impression of his description, peeking back at the screen though her fingers. She'd seen them. An uncomfortable knot tightened in her belly.

The policeman had experienced time missing he couldn't account for, just like Stephen! The creatures spoke in his head, looming over him in some scientific looking room, just as they'd done to her.

The narrator of the program sounded suitably sceptical and Carys felt indignant. The policeman being interviewed was good enough to have authority over civilians, and give evidence in a court of law, but suddenly he's a fool because he says he saw a UFO.

Other documentaries she watched followed a similar pattern. Airline pilots, high-ranking military, more police officers; all people she'd always respected, she was now expected to dismiss as fools because of their eye witness testimony.

Whilst she felt vindicated about her own experiences, she also felt more afraid. There were programs running one after the other, after another throughout the day and night, and Carys couldn't get enough. It was a dangerous obsession, but she couldn't stop.

Marco arrived home from work, parked, walked through the gate and into the kitchen from the back door, and frowned. Scowling, he presumed the loud blaring of a television was emanating from one of the nearby neighbours.

Expecting that Carys would have returned from college and made a start on cooking dinner by now, he was dismayed at the lack of confirmatory smells. Had something happened? Had the college bus broken down?

Pulling his phone from his pocket, his thumb scrolled to 'Carys Mobile' and pressed send. He ended the call as the voicemail began its message. Out of battery, he assumed.

With apprehension mounting, he walked from the kitchen into the hallway to the toilet. Drying his hands, he shook his head and squinted. The loud television noise was coming from upstairs. How was that possible? Bounding up, two at a time, he flung open the door.

Carys barely looked up before staring back at the documentary which had been showing throughout the day.

"What on earth are you doing?!" Marco demanded.

Stony silence was the cold reply.

"I thought dinner would be started! How long have you been back from college anyway?" Struck by a notion, he raised his voice. "Why are you watching television in the bedroom and not the lounge? Have you even been to college today?"

Carys still didn't look up or speak.

"You haven't, have you? Have you been in bed gawking at this... this... crap all day?"

The look Carys gave him in reply made him hanker for silence again.

"Leave me alone," she growled with quiet rancour.

"*I'll* make dinner then, shall I?" he hissed, half-placatory half-antagonistically.

"Do what you fucking want," she spat, her face glowing with hateful rage.

Marco retreated like a wounded puppy, went back downstairs and looked around the kitchen for inspiration. He became quite enthused as he prepared a Bolognese with fresh ingredients from the larder. He hoped the delicious smell might tempt his bride from her pit.

As it was quick to prepare, it didn't give very long for Carys to calm down; and he didn't want to risk more abuse by calling up that dinner was ready. He couldn't just eat without telling her, so he decided to let it simmer. "Let the flavour develop," he said out loud to himself.

He nearly died of shock when Carys put a placatory hand on his shoulder while he stirred the sauce. He hadn't noticed her coming downstairs.

"Sorry," she said.

Turning round, he gave her a huge grin. "Dinner's ready." He dished out and placed the two full plates onto the table. Carys didn't need coaxing to sit down, but despite assuring Marco the food was tasty, she pushed it around her plate eating little of anything.

"I'm sorry," she whispered. "I'm not feeling very well today."

Throwing his arms around her, guilt left a nasty nausea in his chest. Why hadn't he considered her feeling unwell? Why had he jumped to the worst conclusion? "No, I'm sorry. I was horrible to you, and you're not well."

Carys responded agreeably to the sympathy. Snuggling up on the couch together, Marco was happy again. He'd been really foolish. Everyone had warned him about the female hormones during pregnancy and he'd forgotten at the first hurdle. He vowed to be more thoughtful in future.

"What do you think about UFO's?" Carys blurted. Marco was relieved to have a pattern answer to hand that had been discussed at one of the Bible study groups he'd led.

"The church doesn't deny the possibility that other life may exist on one or more of the infinite number of stars and planets out there," he explained. "I'm not sure how I feel about it, but it's nice to think that God, and the concept of life on other planets aren't mutually exclusive." Carys was pleased too. She believed in God. Maybe Marco might accept their little bundle after all.

From shock, to contentment, to a restful night, Marco woke refreshed. Leaning over, he kissed his wife goodbye and wished her well enough for college today. Shrugging in reply, she hadn't decided.

She knew she should; that the mental stress would be helped by mixing with her classmates and learning new things from Professor Simpson. But she wasn't sure she could cope. She just didn't feel able to handle any of it: the class, catching the bus, finding clothes and getting dressed; even with getting out of bed.

In less than a minute's thinking, she'd reduced her options to one thing. Resolved to staying in bed, she flicked the on button on the TV remote and up came the pre-selected Discovery channel, which was already halfway through a UFO program. It was one she'd seen before, but it didn't matter. They were all the same, anyway.

Realising she needed the toilet, a reverberating dong echoed through her mind from the alarm that she was reluctant to move. These were signs of serious mental illness, not just pregnancy hormones. She wasn't ready to admit it to herself yet though.

She found that after the third or fourth documentary she'd already seen, they were losing their appeal. Flicking through the channels proved a revelation. She discovered a channel specialising in conspiracy theories. The eminent Mr David Icke, whom she had discussed with her classmates in college, was giving a talk to a rapt audience on the subject of the Illuminati.

It was all news to Carys. She'd never entertained such theories before, believing, on the whole, that government bodies were hard-working, and trying at least to get it right. Seeing her diligent policeman father may have swayed her judgement, she considered, in the onslaught of trailers for conspiracies programs advertised in the first commercial break.

David Icke, the butt of her classmates' digs, was talking so much sense. Amongst other theories, the proposal that government bodies, particularly the United States and British governments, were fully aware of aliens. So much so, they'd done deals with them, allowing a certain number of citizens to be abducted and experimented on, in exchange for certain technological advances.

He argued that not only were governments aware of the extra-terrestrials living among us, but that aliens were actually serving in office in some of the most powerful positions in the world. And the reason we weren't able to recognise these aliens? Because their true appearance was hidden, existing on a different frequency to our own perception.

Like a radio, he said: just because you listen to a station and then retune to another radio station, the first station still exists. It's still there, broadcasting the same information it would if you were listening to it. Only you're listening to a different frequency. It's no different. "I know how simple it sounds," he argued, "but the simplest explanations are often the correct ones."

The idea sounded preposterous yet plausible to Carys. She wasn't sure how to take the suggestion that heads of state (Her Majesty The Queen was even suggested!) were in fact aliens whose true identity were lizard like aliens known as

'The Reptilians'.

The 'Different Frequency' theory struggled to convince Carys with people she had been aware of since childhood. It was easier to believe some old presidents of America were not as they appeared; the past looked like a different world anyway, but the Queen?

Yet, he was so convincing. She tried to grip onto the doubts; to use them as a foothold back to the real world, but she was teetering.

The type of alien with which she was more familiar, Mr Icke referred to as 'The Greys.' There were others too: giant humanoids with blonde hair, tall ones, diminutive ones, all with different names and places in the universal hierarchy.

Staring, eyes wide and dry, it all got too much for Carys, and she drifted off to sleep during one of the subsequent broadcasts. By the time Marco returned from work, she was sat up, gently snoring. He bounded upstairs, expecting her to be in bed this time having established her being unwell. He stroked her forehead dotingly, asked if there was anything she would like for dinner, and offered to bring her a cup of tea.

In response, she turned up her lips in the pretence of a smile. He was being lovely. Why did she find him so utterly irritating? It hit her hard. When she'd told him yesterday she was feeling unwell, she hadn't meant physically. And she was certain he knew what she did mean. So why was choosing to ignore it? Pretending she had a fucking cold or something? Did her husband not know her at all?

And if he wasn't just brushing it under the carpet; if he really didn't know what she'd meant? Well, that showed such a lack of understanding of her, she felt disgusted. Grinding her fist into the bed sheets, she struggled to control the urge to spit the bitter contempt from her mouth.

The dankness hit Marco in the face like a wet fish as he lovingly brought the cup of tea he had promised. Attempts at conversation were met with indifference, just like yesterday. Her agitation was unmistakeable, so Marco retired from the room making remarks about his plans for dinner.

With every step Carys heard as Marco walked down the stairs, her irritation grew, until by the time he'd reached the bottom stair she was ready to scream. Instead, she knocked her cup of tea flying across the room. As it flew, scalding liquid burnt her skin in the few places it touched. It was all Marco's fault. Leaving hot tea next to someone clearly mentally unwell was stupid. Could he not see the dangers?

Marco hadn't even stepped off the bottom step when he heard the crashing noise and turned straight round again. He recognised it for what it was, but half-worried she'd fallen in her ill state, attempting to go to the toilet. Given the force he'd heard, the sight of Carys sitting calmly on the bed surprised him.

Glancing at the large tea stain on the wall, and then down at the broken cup on the floor, he was angry that his good deed had been rubbished, but he was scared as well. He didn't understand what Carys was going through, and understood even less what on earth he should do to make it better.

Instinctively recognising that demonstrating his displeasure at her behaviour would worsen the situation, he smothered his resentment and walked back down the stairs to prepare dinner.

Carys sat seething. She was livid. How could she be married to such an idiot with so little understanding of her condition? The moderate pain of the hot spilling tea galvanised a feeling within her to seek more. With a sick compulsion, she knew it was the only way past the anger; the only way to regain control. This seething monster wasn't *her*. She had to find herself again, and she thought she knew just how to do it.

The cup glistened, wet with cold tea, its broken pieces laying jaggedly on the floor. Her moth whet at the expectation; a sharp sense of herself a brave moment away. She knew what she would do and she would have that control again; feel that thrill again; feel alive.

And Marco would learn just how carefully she needed to be treated.

CHAPTER TWENTY-FIVE

The Amish Return

Marco found inspiration for dinner hard to come by in the tense atmosphere. After a brief look through kitchen supplies, he decided on sausage and mash. Not one of Carys's favourites, but what the hell.

When it was cooked, he debated eating alone but decided against it for fear of antagonising his wife further. He popped his head around the kitchen door and called up the stairs.

"Carys!" he waited, not expecting a reply, and none was forthcoming. "Carys!!" He called a little louder. "Dinner is on the table." Attempting to inject into his tone a sense of being considerate but firm. He was determined not to take any nonsense.

Sat staring at the food on his plate, he was dismayed at his lack of appetite. When it became clear Carys wouldn't be joining him, he pushed his meal away towards hers and sat a while in contemplation. He would have to go and check she was okay. It all was getting a bit ridiculous.

With a sigh, he slumped up the stairs, not bothering to disguise the sound of his footsteps, nor his displeasure. Pausing half way, the silence, disconcerted him. What was she doing up there? Sleeping? Maybe she'd wake in a better mood.

Hesitating outside the bedroom door, it was now closed when it had been ajar. Peeved that he should be made to feel unwelcome outside his own bedroom, he raised a reluctant hand to knock. There was no response to his gentle rapping. Twisting the handle, he pushed the door gently.

Carys sat in the middle of the bed rocking forwards and backwards. The blood on her wrists had clotted and was starting to scab. The wounds looked raw and painful. There was a red stain on the bed. "What have you done you silly, silly girl!? How is that going to help, hey?" he couldn't believe his beautiful wife of only a few weeks could be in such a state. He couldn't imagine why she would spoil herself in this way.

"God made those wrists that you're abusing!" he said self-righteously.

Carys flung what was left of the cup, missing him by inches. Either her aim wasn't brilliant, or she hadn't actually meant to hit him. It had the desired effect of shaking him up.

"Hey! There's no need for that," he cried.

Carys screamed. A primordial, hair-raising scream that shook the ceiling and hurt his ears. "You don't understand!" she yelled at him. "You don't care about me!" Marco gasped.

"Of course, I care!" he yelled back. She leaped up, and in one bound made it round the bed to him where she unleashed her clenched fists on his broad chest.

He wasn't hurt, but he was angry. This was a step too far for Marco. "Behave yourself. You're acting like a spoiled little brat!"

"You don't care. You haven't even asked what's wrong!"

She had a point, but he was loath to give her any leeway after her appalling behaviour. Looking again at her bloody wrists, he understood this wasn't a rational human being he was dealing with. He tried to keep calm.

"I'm sorry," he forced through gritted teeth. "You're right. I haven't." her shoulders dropped in response to his mollifying tone. "What's wrong, my darling?" he finally asked.

Relief that she was being taken seriously wasn't enough to calm her "I can't tell you," she said shyly. "You wouldn't believe me."

Marco soothed and reassured her that of course he would, but given her weird behaviour, he was wary of whatever it might be. Bracing himself, when he heard her say it, he grimaced.

"I have an alien baby growing inside me, and I don't know if I can cope." As soon as the words left her lips, her hand shot to her mouth to silence them. Wincing at the betrayal of her deepest secret, as well as from the wounds on her wrist. What had she done?

Maybe her baby would look completely normal, and there'd never be any need to tell him... ever. In one ill-thought blabbering moment, she had ruined everything.

Fiddling with her hem, she wouldn't endure the silence much longer. Why wasn't he saying anything? Glancing at him, then looking away, she couldn't hold his gaze. Please put me out of my misery. Tell me what you think.

Marco, of course, didn't know how to respond. He looked at Carys and noticed her twitching her hands from the corner of his eye. A sharp piece of the broken cup was gripped in her right hand, she didn't seem aware of it as she fidgeted with her nightie. He knew he would have to say something.

"Why do you think that, my love?" he asked softly

"I don't think it. I *know* it!"

Marco nodded slowly in compassionate understanding. "How?" was all he could think to ask.

Carys glared at him, as though she couldn't understand how he could be so thick.

"Because I only had one encounter before you. I don't remember it because that's what they do. They wipe your memory. At first I thought this boy, Stephen Holmes was the father, but after I asked him, I'm sure he's not. He sounded really adamant and really believable that nothing had happened between us. Then he told me about the figures walking towards the car."

"I know who Stephen Holmes is," Marco said. "Your mum and dad were frantic about him raping you. Why would you believe him? He abused you and got you pregnant. Of course he's going to deny it!" His voice was becoming louder. "I can't understand, for a second, why you'd buy anything he says!" He was shouting now. "And what have you come up with to excuse his lies? An alien pregnancy!"

Taking a deep breath, he carried on, his voice hoarse. "I know you have hormones raging through your body. And since meeting me the idea of that scum touching you probably makes your skin crawl even more, but come on. Get real!" He tried to cough away the frog in his throat. "He raped you. He's covering for himself by taking advantage of your fragile state. That's all. That's all it is." Too late, he added, "But I'm here now, and everything's going to be okay." He caught a glimpse of how he may have got things catastrophically wrong in Carys's catatonic stare.

"Let us pray," he suggested in desperation. Carys didn't want to pray. She didn't want anything from this man who understood her needs so little. She couldn't even raise enough energy to tell him to fuck off.

Marco prayed 'in the name of Jesus,' and 'cast

out the demons that dwell within her,' and a few other Christian platitudes. Carys wasn't really listening. When he'd finished, he hung around for a while before muttering something about food and disappeared downstairs again.

Carys sat on the bed for a while before lying back down and staring at the ceiling. She heard Marco's footsteps coming up the stairs. To avoid him talking to her again, she closed her eyes. Aware of him standing self-consciously at the bedroom door, his heavy breathing, the creaking floorboards as his weight moved from one foot to the other. She imagined him peering at her, trying to decide if she was actually asleep. Seemingly satisfied, he quietly crept back downstairs.

Pinging open her eyes, enraged by his mistake, she still didn't move. Like a coiling spring in a clockwork mechanism, wound ever tighter, ready for whatever its function was to be. Carys didn't know what her mechanism might produce when it was released, but she didn't think it would be good.

Part of her wanted to try deep breathing or even praying on her own, but another part of her wanted the clockwork to keep winding tighter and tighter. That part of her wanted to see the explosion of kinetic motion, like a jack shooting from its box. The thrill of the surprise, and the accompanying adrenaline, surging through her veins, was irresistible.

As she lay wrestling with the angel and the

devil on her shoulders, she heard the same creeping up the stairs. She closed her eyes again. Marco seemed to be pondering his options at the door. He waited for less time before turning and creeping back downstairs. He must have decided, as she hadn't moved at all and still had her eyes closed, that she was definitely be asleep.

Carys imagined his relief. Perhaps as he sat downstairs quietly watching the television, he pictured her waking her normal loving self again. She wanted that for him. Maybe she did love him. And maybe it would work. Maybe if she could go to sleep, she might feel better. Controlling her breathing, eyes closed tightly, she would try.

A breath from across the room.

Opening her eyes, she stared at the doorway.

No-one was there.

She'd clearly heard Marco go downstairs, so who did she just hear breathing? She forced her eyes shut again. The breathing stayed silent and she wondered if she imagined it.

Swoosh! The noise of breath rushed past her right ear. A jolt of alertness left her cold, made her jump out of her skin. This time she daren't open her eyes.

She lay motionless, eyes moving rapidly under their lids whilst she shivered in fright.

"That there is a eebomeenashon."

She heard the familiar voice of the Amish man clearly in the room. What could she do? She wouldn't open her eyes. He wasn't real, was he? So if she ignored him, surely he'd disappear back to where he came from.

"You look at me when I'm talkin to you," he drawled menacingly.

He's not real, Carys told herself over again. There's nothing he can do. She soon decided otherwise and opened her eyes abruptly when something brushed against her leg.

"That's better!" he said. "You can't keep that ee-bomeenashon," he almost spat as he prodded her tummy. She felt pain as he jabbed her hard.

Fight or flight response rapidly injected her body with a surge of adrenaline as she reached out to grab his arm. At the first touch of his slight, wiry limb, he vanished and she was alone in the room again.

Scrambling from the bed, she tripped over the entangling duvet. She had to get out of here. Reaching the stairs, foot poised to go down, Marco rushed to the lounge door and poked his head out.

"Want some food?" he offered bounding, puppy-like, to the kitchen to prepare or re-heat something.

No, thought Carys I don't want any of your sodding food. She followed him into the kitchen and watched his bemused face as she side-stepped him in his effort to get to the microwave with the plate containing her dinner from earlier.

She opened the cereal cupboard and took out

the large unopened box of cornflakes.

Marco didn't know quite what to do with the dinner. It was obvious she wasn't planning to eat it, but he didn't want to antagonise her by discarding it. Standing with the plate in his hand, he gawked as Carys slid her finger under the cardboard flap on the box and peeled open the plastic bag.

She didn't continue to prepare the cornflakes as Marco had expected. Instead, she poured the entire contents of the box onto the kitchen floor, sprinkling liberally, ensuring the whole surface was covered.

Enjoying Marco's stupefied expression, she walked to the fridge. The cornflakes crunched underfoot as she stepped. Removing six pints of full cream milk from the door, and opening it, Marco knew what was coming, but felt powerless to stop it. His mouth fell open in astonished silence as she predictably splashed the bottle of milk over the cornflakes on the floor.

When she'd finished, she turned to Marco. Before he realised what she was doing, she grabbed the plate of sausage and chips from his hand and threw it to the floor as well, showering food debris to mix with the cornflakes and milk and smashing the plate. Marco roused quickly from his daze and shouted out in objection.

Carys was already out of the kitchen and heading for the front door. Marco rushed after her. "Where are you going?" he called out. Panicking

At her rapid pace, he watched, powerless as the front door closed with Carys on the other side of it. Bounding to the door, he grabbed the handle, desperately aware of the final turn of the key the other side of the lock as he tried to turn the lever, pointlessly.

Dashing to the kitchen to get to the back door, he skidded on the milk and cornflakes, just making it across the room without falling. Fumbling the door open he stumbled into the garden and struggled with the temperamental catch of the back gate, bursting, breathless, onto the street.

There was no sign of Carys. Searching both ways to decide which direction to go. One way led to 'The Drang' (Pembrokeshire slang for an alleyway) and out to the town centre. The other way lead through the communal garden of a warden-controlled complex of flats for elderly residents. The only other way was straight ahead and clearly in view. She couldn't have gone that way.

The gates to the residents' flats creaking was usually a source of irritation. Marco was sure he hadn't heard it. That left The Drang, apart from a gap through the fence to the fire station, but at five months pregnant, that was unlikely.

Hurtling down The Drang, and into the main street, he could see a long way up and down the road. She wasn't there. He raced back up through the alleyway and up the road past the old people's complex onto the street the other side of the town. There were a lot more hiding places there and he couldn't see far up the street.

Breathless, he examined the area as far as he could see before deciding he'd be more help going back to the house and calling 999. He went to the front door automatically before remembering it was locked. Carys had left the key sticking out of the barrel, so he let himself back inside.

After the police, he tried to phone his father-in-law, but given the lateness, he was either asleep or working a night shift somewhere. He phoned his own dad too, hoping to mobilise a posse of Fellowship members to search for her. Embarrassing her was the last thing he wanted to do, but he had to try everything he could to protect her, and their baby.

There was no answer from his parents either. A glance at the kitchen clock revealed it was late.

Still wondering what else he could be doing; who else he could call, a squad car with flashing lights appeared at the front of the house. Marco answered the door before it was knocked and invited the police officers, a PC and WPC, into the lounge.

They took a statement of Carys's mental health and were particularly concerned that she was heavily pregnant. "Try not to worry. Easier said than done, I know, but we'll get colleagues out looking as soon as we have a description. I'm sure we'll find her soon." They took a recent photograph and left him to man the house. That way he could let them know if Carys returned, whilst they joined in the search.

If he had been able to speak to Geraint, Marco would have known how similar Carys's behaviour was to her mother's mental episodes. It wouldn't have helped. Geraint felt as ill-prepared now as ever he had, despite Diane's latest cocktail of medication proving the most effective yet.

Marco had no choice but to wait at home, wringing his hands. He'd be exhausted for work tomorrow, but he could call in sick. He just wanted his wife back. And he wanted the baby. Having his own children with her one day was the goal, but looking after the victim of the awful rape Carys had suffered was a calling he truly felt compelled to answer.

As he sat on the sofa with no television on or any distraction, he started to drift away into a fitful half sleep. The front door was knocked lightly and he leapt to his feet within half a second. Would it be news of Carys? It was. They hadn't found her. The police officer at the door announced himself as the dog handler.

"Could you bring something of your wife's for Rufus to smell while I get him ready?"

Marco nodded and raced upstairs, and deciding her pillow case was the most recent thing Carys had touched, he brought that down.

"Go on Rufus. Get that scent in your nostrils."

Rufus, an enormous German Shepherd Dog, was clearly excited to do his job. He soon picked up the scent of Carys from the pillowcase and dashed off with his handler past the old peoples' complex and up to the main road.

Marco raised his eyes to heaven as he realised how she had fooled him with her route. She could have walked fairly far in the short time before the police had responded to his call, but without her purse (It was still in her coat pocket) she should surely be easily caught by several police officers in cars and a police dog.

He went back inside to wait for news.

Hour passed after hour, after hour, until, as the light of dawn broke the blackness, he finally drifted off.

CHAPTER
TWENTY-SIX

A peculiar dawn

Carys ran from the house. Locking the front door had given her a minute's head start. She hadn't expected it to be enough, but it had proved to be. From her hiding place in-between some large communal bins in a covered archway next to the launderette, she could see Marco. She was quite surprised he couldn't see her as he ran back and forth.

When she noticed the police arrive she decided to move on. She walked along the road and turned right at the end onto the street that joined The Drang. When she reached the long alleyway that lead back to the house, she headed up it and debated going back home, but she couldn't. Not with the police there.

She reached the top and rocked on her heels in-decisively. Someone stepped out of the darkness and pointed into the large garden of one of the neighbours.

"They won't find you in there," the Amish man of earlier was stood in the street light. "The smell of Guinea pigs and chickens will put the dog off its scent." Carys didn't know about any dog, but believed the man's logic. Why he'd help her after his aggressive treatment of her previously was another matter. But then, he wasn't real. He couldn't be expected to behave consistently, could he?

As she stepped cautiously into the garden, she became aware of a second figure, a woman. She wasn't sure if she was Amish as well; in fact, she thought she may have been wearing traditional Welsh costume, but authentic, period clothes.

She didn't speak, but pointed to an opening in the tarpaulin covering the cages. It could barely be seen in the dull night light, but she fumbled her way through and discovered a dry area of discarded hay to sleep on.

She could hear the police striding up and down the alleyway, the excitement of the chase, electric in the air. Then she heard the dog. Just as her Amish ally had suggested, it didn't pick up her scent into the garden. Instead, it seemed confused by her earlier trail.

Making no allowance for the silence required for effective hiding, the Amish man yelled at her. One of the advantages of not being at all real, Carys supposed.

"When the powleese go, you gotta get rid o that

alien insider ya," he said in a 'confident he would be obeyed' voice. Carys's mind flooded with images of her extra-terrestrial child on her lap, suckling at her breast, looking up at her with vast black almond shaped eyes, clutching her with white twig fingers.

The Amish man was right. She couldn't have this baby, could she? But how could she get rid of it now? A termination was only a possibility if there were exceptional circumstances. What would the consultant say? If the measurements the sonographers took did point to a hideously deformed foetus, might they offer a termination?

Carys couldn't be sure. She also couldn't be sure if an abortion was suggested, that she might not fight tooth and nail against it. The bond she had with the little life inside her was strong. If it was from out of this world, then surely the aliens must have a plan. And if its true identity was kept hidden, did it really matter? Was an alien very much worse than carrying the child of her rapist?

The nausea swimming in her head indicated that it was. But the baby was a consolation, whoever the father was.

"If you don't get ridda that there baybee..." the drawling voice of her Amish tormenter filled her ears and her brain again, "then I reckon we'll just have ta do it for ya," he said indicating himself and the olden day Welsh lady.

"No!" she shouted. "You leave me and my baby alone."

The Welsh costumed woman moved towards her with her dirty pale fingers clenched in a strong looking fist. Carys jumped out of the way as the fist flew at speed towards Carys's stomach, only narrowly missing.

Carys threw back the tarpaulin and ran out into the garden. She was surprised that it was daylight. She didn't know she had slept, but nothing else accounted for the passing time. She kept on running down The Drang, and out the other end to the town centre.

For a woman five months pregnant, she had a tremendous turn of speed. The slight downhill gradient aided her rapidity. Her pursuers' footsteps echoed through the long alleyway as she hurtled down the road. She knew she was at the limits of her stability and her stamina. She'd have no choice but to rest soon.

If she was near people, they wouldn't be able to hurt her. They'd only ever showed up when she was alone in the dark. Her brain couldn't decide if that was because they wanted to avoid witnesses of their violence, or because they couldn't exist in front of other people. The boundaries were becoming perilously blurred.

She rushed down the hill and past the war memorial overlooking the dramatic ruins of Narberth Castle.

A collection of benches was arranged in a small

public garden next to the cell of Rebecca, the famous holding place for leaders of the Rebecca riots of 1839-43. Sat on the bench with the Dragon public house, and tourist information centre and the other shops and cafes close by, she'd be safe, she was sure.

Cramp clawed her calves and thighs. The cold start to fast running was taking its toll on her stiff muscles. Stumbling, exhausted, across the road and into the small garden with its benches and promise of safety-affording observers, Carys allowed herself to stop and gulp life-affirming oxygen into her lungs.

Breathing heavily on the bench facing the way she'd come so she could see if her attackers made it down the hill, she pondered if she wasn't better off hiding, but where? They had found her easily last night. Should she stick it out where she was?

"You can't run from us, Carys," the drawling voice sneered next to her. She hadn't seen where they'd come from but they were both there.

Being close to Rebecca's cell, she knew who the Welsh woman reminded her of. She looked like the picture of Rebecca on the cell door. Not a woman at all, but a man dressed in women's clothes, as was the disguise used by Rebecca and her children a hundred and sixty years ago.

Carys let out an involuntary scream. "Get away from me!" she cried. She had no idea what time it was. If she'd had her wits about her, the half-light and empty streets would have told her it was very early.

"Get away!" she yelled louder. The two aggressors moved slowly towards her. There was no hurry. It didn't matter where she went. When they were almost upon her, Carys made the choice that she was too exhausted to run anymore. She rolled onto the ground, instinctively protecting her bump from whatever cruelty she was about to suffer.

As she lay curled into as tight a ball as her gestational proportions would allow, she felt a hand on her shoulder, pulling at her. She could hear a voice, but her panic-stricken mind couldn't decipher the words.

Determined to defend herself, she rolled over just enough to free an arm. Pushing herself up with her other, she struck out hard in the direction of the voice. Who was that? She didn't recognise them. It wasn't the Amish man, nor the Rebecca. Who had joined the gang of tormentors now?

As her clenched fist made crushing contact with the jaw of the unknown face, the words she had just spoken reached Carys's ears too late. "Are you okay?" the words lost in the morning air. The owner of the face succumbed to the pounding blow, and fell unconscious beside Carys.

Carys's arms were suddenly forced behind her back; hand cuffs pinched into her wrists. Aware of another voice reading her rights, she didn't listen. She'd heard them all before.

CHAPTER TWENTY-SEVEN

Extra Biological Entity

Geraint was still unaware of his daughter's predicament, but his colleagues were, as she was currently languishing in cell three.

"Go and check on the girl we brought in this morning please, Steve?" the desk sergeant asked of one of the constables working with her on the detention block. "She's being unnervingly quiet after the noise she's been making all morning."

Steve walked nonchalantly to the cell. He slid back the cover from the observation-hole, and peeped inside. He could see Carys standing on the bed, and he was terrified she might be about to hurt herself. Her mental health problems had been quickly ascertained when they'd arrested her, so his immediate worry was that she'd found something to hang herself with, so he quickly unlocked the door whilst calling for assistance.

It took a while for Carys to realise it wasn't her

attackers lifting her up and plonking her in the back of a car.

"Keep them away from me. Keep them away from my baby," she shouted when she finally grasped the situation.

"Keep who away from you?" the arresting officer frowned, "There's no-one here!"

"They want to hurt my baby," she squealed, gesturing to the town hall and Rebecca's cell. Realising she was making no sense, the officer humoured her and assured her of a safe passage to the police station.

The journey, indeed, went without further incident. Since arriving at Haverfordwest Police Station and being booked in however, things had changed.

It took only moments alone in the cell before they both appeared. The Rebecca, now her identity as a man was known, was not bothering with her bonnet and looked the more menacing for it.

Amish man looked much the same but rather smug, knowing that after all Carys's effort she was now more at his mercy than ever. "Now, let's finish that atrositteey off, once and for all."

He punched Carys hard in her stomach, bringing her to her knees. Even though the Rebecca grasped her throat from behind, she was still able to shout for help.

The first few times the sergeant looked in at the

noise, she saw Carys in various contorted positions as though she was play acting. She put Sergeant Amy Evans in mind of her own six year old son fighting imaginary foe whenever he entered a room. He always added punching sound effects with his voice. Whilst he usually emerged victorious, he sometimes let the baddies have their day.

Watching a grown woman go through the same act was disturbing. The mentally ill had always been a bother to Amy. She just didn't get it. She certainly had no plan to open the door to check on her charge without reinforcements. A choke hold had almost been her demise, perpetrated by one very quiet drunk who was determined he was the reincarnation of Moses. She had definitely learned her lesson to be cautious.

As the door opened to Carys's cell, PC Steve Lewis winced at the sight of blood pooling on the floor. He sidestepped it in time to save a hazardous slip, but that distracted him just enough for Carys to perform what was rapidly becoming her signature move of a forearm to the jugular.

Steve went down in the bloody mess just as the assistance he'd called out for arrived to see it. Angered by the attack on one of their own, the two other officers waded into the room to give Carys what for.

"Careful, she's pregnant," Sergeant Amy warned them, causing them to restrain her in a far gentler manner than they'd intended.

"Keep them away from me! Help me! They want to kill my baby. They want to kill my baby," Carys repeated, breaking into hideous sobs.

In view of the blood, and Carys's condition, they called an ambulance. One of the officers accompanied her to hospital as she was still technically under arrest. Carys looked imploringly at him.

"Don't leave me. Please don't leave me. They can't hurt me when there's someone with me."

The maternity staff ascertained that immediate danger of miscarriage was small. They advised her to stay in hospital overnight to be sure. Whilst there, she received a visitor from Bro Cerwyn centre across the road from the main Withybush hospital, a separate unit that dealt with psychiatric patients.

A thorough examination took place in the side room Carys occupied, at the end of which the on-call psychiatrist prescribed medication for immediate use that could be reviewed once she'd given birth. She was reassured when he confirmed hallucinating people under stressful conditions wasn't that unusual. And help was available to eliminate them, or to at least help her cope with the delusions.

It was decided she should be de-arrested as charging her seemed pointless. The accompanying policeman wished her well, and she finally settled into a much needed sleep. The Amish man and the Rebecca stood in the corner of the room, but with the hustle and bustle of the ward, she knew was safe. Maybe they'd fade with the new medication. Sighing, she allowed a calmness to settle on her shoulders.

"Hello you!" Diane gushed as she walked in to visit her daughter. It was just about the best person she could have hoped to see. If anyone would understand what she was going through, it was her mental mum!

"Hi," Carys managed through her shame. "Have you heard what I've been doing? I rather lost the plot I'm sorry to say."

"It's your hormones!" Diane offered as an explanation that let her daughter off the hook. They both knew the truth: that she had inherited her mother's problems.

They chatted for a while about different medications that Diane had tried over the years. What she'd found effective, what had not worked. After their chat, Carys felt almost back to her normal self.

Diane left them to it when Marco arrived sheepishly through the door, uncertain of the reception he'd get.

When he met Carys's misty eyes, he knew she was back. Silently he walked over and hugged her. Carys squeezed a tear down her cheek. Trickling onto the upturned corner of her mouth, she sighed in contentment. He'd seen her at her worst now, and he was still here. Maybe she'd drop her guard; relax into things and trust Marco, and actually admit that maybe she loved him too.

With the scare for her baby's health, along with her mental breakdown, Carys received visitors daily. The community midwife, a little Welsh woman with Dana hair and a strange Greek sir name, visited twice a week. And the newly appointed CPN (Community Psychiatric Nurse), Eleri, visited on the other days.

Carys was invited to voice any worries she had about anything, especially regarding her safety. She would never reveal all her worries though. Despite mild tranquilisers and some anti-depressants proving undoubtedly helpful, there was nothing that could relieve her of the nagging burden that the baby inside her was of unearthly origin. She was happy to keep it to herself now though, and nod and smile like a good girl.

Her mood stabilised for a while. Carys resigned herself to her baby's fate when it was born, and even managed to rouse herself enough to get a little excited, about baby clothes. Her appointment with Mr Overton, the obstetrician was no longer necessary as she had seen him on his rounds during her stay on the maternity ward where he had confirmed her foetus did have a big head; unusually large. Indicators for spina-bifeda weren't present, but it was likely to be hydrocephalus - fluid on the brain. Carys wasn't surprised to learn this was a dire scenario which might cause a number of problems with her baby's speech or walking.

She'd smiled in acceptance, but her own explanation offered a new advantage. Her version didn't mean her baby would be disabled.

Marco was due to take paternity leave from his job in the council building. Carys was hoping to catch up with the college work she'd missed whilst she was ill, and planning to continue with college until the last possible moment (and hopefully even coincide with Easter break if baby was good and came when he should.)

Thirty-three weeks pregnant now, another seven to go, but with the extra-large head she had pushing its way around her huge belly, the due date could be any time after thirty-six. She was banking on it being three weeks, not seven because her hugeness was getting out of control.

The CPN had suggested she should get out on days she didn't have college. Today was one of those days so she'd elected to do the weekly shop. Gazing from the window of the bus to Haverfordwest, a dusting of snow on the mountain showed spring was late this year.

She thought it would be amazing to be on the summit looking out over most of Wales and Devon and Cornwall, and maybe even the Wicklow hills of Ireland on a very clear day like today.

Holding her bump, she mouthed 'Not gonna happen today, is it.'

The bus stopped at the supermarket and Carys stepped down onto the tarmac. She fumbled for a coin to release one of the trollies and set off on her journey around the aisles. She had a list in her handbag which she fished out and clutched like a map she had to follow.

Staring at the paper, the words jumbled together. Squinting down at them, she gripped the handle of the trolley, fearing she would fall if she didn't hold on. What was wrong? Her mind took a second to catch up with what had assailed it: an enormous pain in her stomach.

She'd felt nothing like it since the attack from her hallucinated Amish attacker. A flood of liquid from between her legs puddled on the floor, soaking her legs and her shoes. Panic exploded neurotransmitters in her brain, tensing her fist, but calming instantly at the sight not of blood, but of amniotic fluid from her womb.

"I'll call an ambulance," a savvy lady customer announced as she got the situation at once. A chair was brought for her to sit on while she waited for it to arrive. This is it, she thought, 'B' day!

The paramedics arrived promptly, the hospital being only a mile and a half away. She was booked into maternity and a midwife in-between her legs before she knew it.

"We're trying to contact your husband for you,

but is there anyone else you'd like here?"

Carys wasn't sure she wanted anyone to see her baby come out. If there was something wrong; one of the things Mr Overton had warned her about, or her own concerns, she would prefer to be alone.

Half an hour later gave a different story. "I need my mam!" she screamed, now the labour pains had fully begun. But she'd left it too late. Despite attempts to contact her, allowing for her journey would make her arrival the best part of an hour away.

"Six centimetres dilated," one midwife reported to another. "It won't be long before you can push."

"Can I have something else for the pain? This gas and air isn't f***ing working!" The midwives were used to bad language at this stage of labour, especially from young, first-time mums. They didn't want to upset her, but things were moving far too fast to consider an epidural now.

"You're doing brilliantly. Have another good suck on that and then we'll have a go at pushing, shall we?"

Carys could have been grateful that as it turned out, there had been plenty of time for her mum, dad and husband to get to the hospital. But the pain she was in gave her a different perspective.

Pushing hadn't gone to plan. After two hours with her mam and Marco taking turns holding her hand, and Geraint pacing the corridor, the obstetrician was called.

It was decided the baby's large head, even at only thirty-three weeks, was causing enough problems to necessitate a Caesarean Section. She wheeled away to theatre, past the faces of her family, fixed with tight smiles but with moist eyes betraying their true emotions.

"I'll be fine," she reassured from her lofty nitrous oxide perspective. Images of the fork-tongued baby from 'V' came back into her mind, and she laughed and was still chuckling as the anaesthetist gave her the epidural she'd wanted hours before.

The operation went as well as hoped, and the moment of seeing the life that grew inside her for eight months was upon her. Fears for its biological origins, and being tortured by mental illness and hallucinations all raw in her memory, but finally her child was here.

No sooner was the baby plucked from her womb, it was plonked unceremoniously on her chest and she saw it for the first time.

Its head had the appearance of a water balloon, swollen, and disproportionately large. Its eyes, too, were huge, and dark as the ocean. If you were so inclined, it would be perfectly believable that this baby wasn't human. But who, apart from Carys, would believe such a notion?

"Congratulations, it's a little boy!" the nurse announced as she placed him on Carys.

"Hello!" Carys cooed at the odd little face. After

the initial introduction, the midwife scooped him up again.

"Nothing to worry about, it's just he's so early," she said, and later, "He'll need to be incubated for a few days, and come out for feeding, so you'll stay in hospital until baby's ready to go home. Okay? Have you thought of a name for the little baba?" she said, glancing at Carys as she pottered near the incubator.

"Yes. Ebe. It's Dutch, and means God in abundance," Carys explained. If he'd been a girl, it would have the same name, but the explanation would have been that it's Egyptian, meaning 'wonderful'. Neither was the genuine reason.

She had decided on the name Ebe as an acronym: Extra Biological Entity. She thought it was most appropriate.

CHAPTER
TWENTY-EIGHT

Marco has a plan

Incubation wasn't all Ebe had required. Before they could come home, they had to wait for three weeks as Ebe's large head put him in danger of suffocation whenever he turned it to the side. Carys was beginning to succumb to the baby blues.

But when they did come home, still the relief she'd yearned for didn't materialise. Ebe was so demanding and never able to settle to sleep anywhere but on Carys's chest, either suckling, which was already becoming saw, or with his face pressed into hers. Claustrophobia didn't help lift her spirits any.

The midwife, a different one to the lovely Greek/Welsh woman who had visited throughout the pregnancy, now visited daily. Carys did not like her.

"The baby blues is perfectly normal," she told

her in a lazy Welsh lilt that irritated Carys every time she heard it (It was in fact very similar to her own which she had always liked.)

"It's a little bit early with you, but Ebe is quite demanding isn't he? It's him being prem, see. He don't wanna be out yere yet, do you, bach?" Carys bristled with every word.

She knew this stupid midwife had been told about her previous mental health problems; she'd even collected a prescription for tranquilisers and anti-depressants one time.

Carys wasn't a fool. She knew exactly what she should expect to feel, given that she wasn't allowed a single second to herself any time of the night or day without this weird little creature clinging onto her.

She knew deep, deep down she loved her baby, but she was growing to hate the clingy little shit too. It might be normal to you, she thought, but shouldn't we be a teensy bit concerned where this might be heading.

"It's a bit early to diagnose postnatal depression. Let's see how it goes, shall we?" Carys's protests were wholly ignored, but she flinched when Carys gave her a glimpse of what she was capable of.

"Let's wait until I've sliced my arm off and killed myself, shall we?" Carys mocked the midwife's tone.

"You have thoughts of suicide, do you?"

"Sometimes, yes."

The midwife looked silently down at her notes. "When does your CPN come round next?"

"Tomorrow," Carys mumbled, suspecting rightly that the buck was being passed.

"Okay. I'll leave something in your notes letting her know how you're feeling, okay?" she said with squinty, pseudo-care in her eyes. It was clear she couldn't wait to go. She put her hand on Carys's knee and increased the squinty look before standing up to leave.

"See you on…" she looked down at her diary again "… Wednesday, okay?" she didn't wait for an answer before walking briskly to the front door. "Don't worry. I'll see myself out," she called, closing the front door behind her.

I wasn't worried, Carys thought. But the idea of the midwife calling again in a couple of days raised an anger in Carys that frightened her. Ebe wasn't safe with her. She didn't know what she was capable of in the state she knew she could get. She'd already hurt strangers. What if she hurt Ebe?

She was driven to distraction by the little bleeder, but she couldn't bear the thought of harming him. And what about Marco, or herself? She knew she was more than capable of doing that.

The CPN came on Tuesday and made some notes, murmuring about getting Carys an urgent appointment with the psychiatrist to review her meds. 'Was she breast-feeding?' she had asked, 'It might affect what he can give you,' she had been told, as if she didn't know.

"If you feel worse in the meantime, call the Crisis Team, or 999. A and E will get you a psychiatrist quickly." Carys felt moderately reassured by this information. Maybe she would be okay.

Marco was worried. Having witnessed her fall from sanity once, he was wary. What concerned him most at the moment was her reluctance to go with him to church. Narberth Christian Fellowship had prayed every week for her good health. Her disinclination was excused by not wanting to bring Ebe with his certain propensity to wail when not pinned to her chest.

Although a genuine reason, she was using it to disguise her indifference, rapidly becoming dislike, for going.

"Come on, sweetheart," Marco encouraged. His upbeat insistence really starting to piss her off.

"You go," she said. "But I'm not getting up early to try to make this..." she gestured up and down her body, as though the disfigurement of pregnancy had left her a grotesque mess, "look anything presentable, and then sit and jostle Ebe on my knee in an attempt to quieten him, whilst you sing to your adoring public on stage, like normal!"

"You look lovely, my sweet," he asserted, but the sourness of his wife's countenance detracted from her usual splendour as she glared contemptuously at him.

"I've seen a mirror," she spat. "You go and have a *brilliant* time."

"I'll stay home with you then? If you want me to?"

Glaring at him, she left him floundering. Part of him wanted to be stern; to say, 'Don't talk to me like that.' But the last time he'd done similar, she'd ended up having a meltdown. And he knew it wasn't really her. She had always been sorry whenever she regained her equilibrium. He decided to stay.

After a couple of weeks giving her his full support and missing church himself, which was quite an inconvenience to the church band, he decided to fulfil his obligation to them, leave his wife and child at home, and go.

Carys showed no sign of caring either way if he was there or not, and he found his mood degenerated when he didn't go. He needed Jesus, God, and the love and support of his church in his life. Maybe they could think of something to help his wife.

He felt guilty the while, but relaxed enough to enjoy himself. His angst, obvious to all, received freely forthcoming advice. Between them, they hatched a plan they were convinced would be the answer. Marco felt excited to implement it as soon as possible.

When he got back home after church, he was

buoyant with anticipation of their plan. He called up the stairs to find Carys and suggested they go out for a well-earned meal whilst his parents' baby sat for them. They could go tonight if she wanted.

When there was no response to his call, he raced eagerly upstairs, expecting to find her asleep. Bursting through the bedroom door, citing the invitation again, he stopped mid-sentence when he saw what had been happening in his absence.

The look of rancour on Carys's face was replaced with one of fear and regret as she sat on the bed, blood seeping from jagged gashes on her arms.

Marco glanced around for what weapon she'd used this time, and soon saw the broken photo frame which had held a picture of the two of them on their wedding day, the broken glass from the front had carved gruesome wounds.

"It's okay. I'm here now," he soothed, rushing to cuddle her. "Everything will be okay." Where was Ebe? Why couldn't he hear him crying?

"It's okay," Carys whispered, sensing the tension in his embrace. "He actually settled to sleep."

She didn't object when Marco checked anyway, but sure enough, little Ebe was sleeping peacefully, chest rising easily up and down.

"I don't feel like going out for a meal, but I would like to get out of the house," suggested Carys in response to the invitation Marco had assumed went unheard.

"That's fine, babe," Marco said. "We'll drop our little man off with Mum and Dad, and we can decide from there." Marco was pleased with how it had gone. The meal was only the bait to initiate his plan.

Ebe carried on sleeping for a while. Marco promised to look after him, even if he cried, allowing Carys to have a much craved shower. She enjoyed getting ready. Not making a massive effort, assuming they'd end up having a simple bar meal, or some chips on the beach. Just getting out of the house, and Marco being so thoughtful, was something to be pleased about.

Repentance at cutting herself ebbed in the flow of the shower, the pain as the hot water scolded the wounds exhilarated her again.

She had tried to resist for days, but a new voice joined the Amish and the Rebecca telling her to do it. They were still present, but in the background and silent. The new voice appeared to be her own, but outside her head, whispering in her ear.

It insisted Marco didn't love her; that he and Ebe would be better off without her, and that cutting herself would show everyone how she felt. Everything would be better if she just let it happen, let herself do what she yearned for, the voice had implored; and it had become so.

The voice disappeared as soon as she obeyed its whims, as did the other two hallucinations. And now, in addition to the immediate reward, she was being taken out with the help of baby sitters. It seemed the voice was right, and even Carys could see this was a dangerous direction for her thoughts.

Fully rested after her break from Ebe by early afternoon, she fed him sitting comfortably on the sofa with a smile on her face. Noticing her fidgeting, Marco suggested they make a move before they missed all the sunshine on this clear spring day.

Ebe was buckled safely into his car seat and they were ready for the short journey to Dan Paulo's large house on the edge of town. Carys was surprised as they pulled up into the driveway that they were not the only ones there. Two other cars not belonging to the Paulo's were already parked in front of the house. "Are you sure your mum and dad are expecting to babysit?"

"Yeah. We're a bit early, I suppose," Marco explained. He unclipped the car seat, which handily turned into a rocker, and took Ebe and his bag of everything to the front door. Carys rang the doorbell as Marco no longer had any digits free.

"Hello," Marco's mum, Natalia, greeted as she answered the door. You can tell she had been a statuesque Italian lady in her youth, now, as seemed so often the case with older woman from Italy, she was becoming much stouter, and beginning to grow hair in places which had previously been smooth. Carys found the bushy eyebrows and beginnings of a moustache hard to look away from.

Ebe was removed to the lounge and plonked with one of the people whose cars were present in the driveway who Carys recognised from church. Carys looked around for Dan to thank him and Natalia for their help babysitting for them this evening.

"Where's your dad? We should thank him."

"Er, just in his study, I think. Hold on and I'll come with you," Marco answered strangely. Something was going on, Carys suspected. But then she shrugged. She was a paranoid schizophrenic, after all. But then the voice in her ear grew louder "Don't go in there. You won't like it!" it hissed in her own, disparate voice. As she tried to halt, she felt Marco's hand push her gently in her back.

"G… go on in," he stuttered.

What was going on? Carys wondered as she tried to turn and leave, but Marco was flanked by his mother. Another couple from church brought up the rear, and more people were coming from other rooms to join them.

She'd been ambushed. Her heart rocketed from 60 to 230 in a second and she tried to wriggle away. "What are you doing?" Carys demanded. "What is going on? What are you doing to me?"

She was bustled and cajoled into the study where a chair, absconded from the dining room, stood central to the darkened room. It took Carys's eyes a little time to adjust to the curtained window light, and before she could object, she was sat on the chair facing Dan Paulo in full robe holding a crucifix in her face.

She wanted to protest. The voice hissing in her ear certainly objected to the proceedings.

"In the name of Jesus Christ, Our Lord, I command you to leave Carys's body and leave this house!" He thrust the crucifix further into her face, making her flinch.

Part of her was angry they would simplify her complicated, genetic, mental health condition to a ridiculous demonic possession. But these were people she trusted and loved. It couldn't do any harm, could it?

Still aware of the voice in her ear hissing away indecipherably, from the corner of her eye she was also aware of the other two, the Amish man and the Rebecca doing nothing, standing outside the group who joined in the chanting

"In the name of Jesus, we command you to leave the body of Carys Ellis in peace, now!" over and over again. "May the name of Jesus compel you!"

The well-meaning chanting was having an effect. Gradually, she relaxed, and soon felt comfortable enough to let out the rage that dwelled within her. It amused her that they would see her purging primal screams as the demon fighting back.

As she screeched, "AAaaarrrgghh!!" for as long as her lungs could sustain before gulping more breath to maintain the yell, the chanting continued. The crucifix thrust purposefully and constantly towards her whilst splashes of holy water rained on her head and body.

From nowhere, Amish man made a grab for the crucifix whilst Rebecca lunged his hands to Dan Paulo's neck. They made no effect, and as they failed in their attempt to sabotage the exorcism, they disappeared.

Overcome with relief, she let out uncontrollable laughter and couldn't stop. She laughed until her sides ached and she was gasping for breath. As she laughed, the exorcists relaxed. The chanting continued for a short while before Dan changed it to a blessing that would protect her from the demons returning.

They all hugged her, and her manic laughter turned to racking sobs

"We'll have to get you baptised, and soon. This wouldn't have happened if you'd been baptised," her father-in-law admonished. "We'll get little Ebe dedicated as well." Carys nodded.

"Thank you, thank you," she spluttered through the sobs. She turned to Marco to thank him personally. "Thank you for what you organised here. I wouldn't have come if I'd had any inkling of what was to come, but I feel so much better." And she did.

But deep, deep inside a resentment of the dishonesty and trickery used to get her here was being logged. Unexpressed it could grow and fester for months, or even years, before surfacing, all the uglier for its repression.

For now, although a tiny awareness of the demon of festering bitterness manifested in the bowels of Carys's mind, she continued with the plan to walk on the beach, a little later, but a lot happier than she had anticipated.

"Maybe we could eat out properly, if your mum and dad wouldn't mind, and you think I look okay?"

Marco was thrilled. Of course, she looked okay. She was the most beautiful girl in the world.

CHAPTER
TWENTY-NINE

Babysitting

Eleri, the CPN, still called round regularly, several times a week. The emergency appointment from the consultant psychiatrist had been and gone and medication adjusted because she'd resolved, reluctantly, to stop breast feeding Ebe.

The midwife assured that because she had done for more than a month, she'd passed on plenty of precious antibodies to her son, and that stopping wasn't as drastic as she feared.

She had even wondered if upping her medication wasn't necessary after her exorcism. Apparitions and voices hadn't troubled her since, but upon consideration, or because she recognised a growing jitteriness, her worries dwelled now not on herself, but Ebe. He really did have a worryingly large head. The midwife had mentioned Hunters Syndrome, but it was too early to tell. A condition typically diagnosed as facial features changed between two and four years old, whilst a large head was part of the visible signs, it didn't fit perfectly with Ebe's condition, and his head was even larger than expected for that ailment anyway.

Appointments were made with paediatric specialists who arranged tests. The health visitor, a very nice lady who wore nothing but purple whenever Carys had seen her (even her car was purple), now called round in place of the midwife. She wasn't so concerned about Ebe. As he seemed perfectly healthy in all other respects, she thought a large head might just be a hereditary condition.

'You don't know how bloody right you are!' Carys thought.

The health checks had baby Ebe well above the upper percentile for weight in his red hospital records book. This was, of course, attributed to his head. All other tests revealed a healthy baby.

The usual assessments continued at three and six-month intervals and concern emerged that Ebe's facial expressions didn't seem to change. He never smiled or gurgled as other babies. He seemed to recognise familiar people, but didn't look at them with pleasure. Family members of a certain age joked about him being 'The Mekon' (a comic book villain from the 1950's, nemesis of hero, Dan Dare) were all too accurate.

The large head and disparaging appearance were almost identical. Sitting in his rocker or baby walker he looked like every picture of the creature from Venus in his flying chair. The family joked that all he needed was green skin to be a double.

Carys wondered if his appearance would lead him to be super intelligent. She hoped the expression he perpetually wore didn't demonstrate the contempt it appeared to.

His hand-eye coordination at his six-month visit had impressed the health visitor. He demonstrated knowledge and ability expected from a one-year-old. He had grown into his head somewhat. That, and the growth of some hair, made him far more appealing. If he were to smile, perhaps he'd look less like an evil villain, and more like the cute baby he actually was.

He delighted in technology, and despite never smiling, his eyes would burn with a passion if ever he was looking at anything mechanical. He loved wires, and would follow their course along the skirting board, or from pylon to pylon when travelling in the car.

The health visitor arrived for his one year check. Unpacking scales and books from her bag, Ebe watched intently, eyes flashing as the electronic scales beeped as he was laid on them.

Included in her bag were some wooden blocks. As he grabbed for them she laughed. "What are you going to do with those, Ebe?" she chuckled. But when instead of thrusting them to sore gums for a chew, he stacked them one on top of another, her knees buckled and she fell back on her cushion. "My goodness! I didn't expect that. I wouldn't worry too much about his head. I think he needs it for an oversized brain. He's going to be a genius!"

Knocking them down, he stacked them again, this time with decreasing numbers as the tower grew for stability.

"He's built a pyramid! I can't believe this," she scribbled in her book. "I've been doing this for twenty years. Babies twice his age can't do this. They'll stack three or four bricks, but nothing like this. He's going to be an architect, I think."

And because of this near genius ability, she wasn't overly concerned that Ebe was yet to utter a single sound. "Einstein didn't speak until he was four years old," she imparted. "They thought he was a dunce at school."

And whilst concern had grown to apprehension by the eighteen-month check, excuses were still made. "Brains develop differently in different children, I suppose," the health visitor advised. "His brain is definitely developing other areas of skill first. Get him to toddler groups. Book him a place at nursery. Seeing other children talk will soon get him going," she reassured. "I've seen plenty of children develop speech late and go on to speak perfectly normally, if not better than those who started earlier."

"Mix with other people. See how Ebe compares to other little ones. You'll soon see that there are all different times of development and be re-assured. Chat with the other mums and make friends with similar interests."

It all sounded like good advice, but the thought of meeting new people had become a big stumbling block.

Marco offered to take the morning off work and take him to the first one, which became the last one, for a while at least.

"It's no longer running," he'd reported after a quick return. "Some problem with the room being too cold and not having found alternatives yet. I bet you're right though. I bet they would have been cliquey as anything anyway."

"Bunch of bitches, is what I said."

"Yes, that. You're probably right. And I'm sure you do talk to Ebe enough. I'll make sure I do my bit too and before you know it," he was about to say, 'He'll be off to play school,' when alarm bells rang and he was reminded of being told how tough his mum had found it when she had let him go to nursery having had him with her twenty-four hours a day until then. "Before you know it, he'll be talking so much we'll wish he'd shut up!"

Carys grinned. You're right.

When, sometime later, Carys and Ebe attended a different nursery used by a mum from church, the main thing she gained were nudges and scathing stares from the clique of other, apparently childhood-friend, mums. It reminded her of the horrible outsider feeling she had always endured living in the fens of Cambridgeshire.

Determined to carry on going; determined to do the best for Ebe, the other children ignoring him saddened her. On reflection, she thought, the only thing she enjoyed about toddler group was sticking it to the other mums with Ebe's superior intellect.

Whilst the other children argued over driving the tractor and trailer, wearing the police helmet, or having their turn in the Ty Bach Twt (Wendy House), Ebe would fix the broken toys or construct things. He was becoming popular in a strange way as they all enjoyed the fruits of his labour.

It wasn't long before he progressed to nursery school, run by the same lady and held in the same building. Although mums weren't encouraged to stay with their child, for Ebe they made an exception. He seemed so different and needy. Attempts at tried-and-tested measures for weaning children away from their parents had failed. But as long as he could see his mum, he was content.

Whilst the other mums enjoyed the break from the care of their little ones, Carys was secretly gratified at how Ebe needed her. It made her feel loved and useful.

One day, after he had been going for about a year, and was more than three years old, he did something astonishing. Selecting some empty toilet rolls and kitchen rolls that were being saved for recycling, he constructed a chair.

It was held together simply with sticky tape, but it could hold the weight of a grown adult! The other mums (some of whom after a year occasionally spoke to Carys) were stunned. The playgroup leaders were so impressed they called the Western Telegraph who sent their photographer to do a piece on Ebe and the nursery.

Ebe was pictured in front of his construction with the nursery leader perched comfortably on top, beaming down the lens, happily promoting the academic benefits of her nursery group. But what pleased Carys and Marco, and Ebe's family, was that for the first time they had ever witnessed, Ebe was smiling!

He had found his niche. The other children loved sitting on his self-crafted chair, and they'd all fetch broken toys for him to mend. But he still hadn't spoken, not even a syllable, and remained very attached to his mother. And he was still rather odd looking, attracting jibes of 'Gollum' rather than the long forgotten 'Mekon.' Carys tried to see it as a step up.

Even three years on, the health visitor and CPN were still frequent callers. Carys's mental health continued to be a concern, but she hadn't suffered any major blips. The medication was doing its job (although, she could tend towards what Marco and her parents described as 'touchy.')

None of her hallucinations: of The Amish man, or The Rebecca, or any aliens, had reared their ugly heads. Her psychiatrist suggested she might (as he was sure her mother did) suffer also with 'borderline personality disorder': a condition whereby the sufferer reaches a certain level of stress at which point they begin to experience audio and visual hallucinations. Carys's borderline of stress seemed to be a little higher than her mum's, so the condition was proving easier to control.

Carys wondered if everybody suffered from this condition, but people's borderlines differed. Everyone could be pushed to breaking point with enough stressors. It made her feel normal.

The purple health visitor, since her advice had been taken and not worked, was more concerned than ever with Ebe's lack of speech development, particularly as school age was rapidly approaching. But there was another more crucial problem causing stress in the marital home: Ebe just would not sleep in his cot.

It began early on. Dan and Natalia scolded them for 'making a rod for their own back,' by letting him settle snuggled up to Carys. She agreed, but continued the bad habit out of desperation.

"He just needs a little cwtch before settling," Carys defended to her mother-in-law one night when Marco had invited her and Dan for dinner.

"And he settles in his cot okay then, does he?" Natalia probed, already knowing the answer. Marco had been bemoaning the poor sleep routine over the dinner.

"Er… no. We try, but he gets distressed… and I tend to pick him up again," Carys admitted.

"And then I'm pushed to the side of the bed and don't sleep," Marco moaned, trying to pass it off as a joke.

"It's dangerous. You shouldn't do it," Natalia admonished in archetypal mother-in-law style. "Babies are killed all the time by parents inadvertently rolling on them! And what are you going to do when you have more children? They can't all sleep in bed with you!"

Marco snorted in disgust "More children! That's a laugh. We'd need to have sex occasionally, or at least once, for that to happen!" he roared a little too readily. Carys wanted the ground to swallow her and glowered at her husband.

"I'm sure he'll settle soon," she mumbled.

"Not unless you do something about it," came the stern rebuke. And then, without consulting Carys, she ordered Marco and Dan upstairs to move Ebe's cot out of the marital bedroom and into the nursery. It had always been the intention for Ebe to sleep in there, of course, and it was decorated beautifully for that purpose, but Carys seethed with resentment.

It was worse because part of her wondered if her mother-in-law wasn't absolutely right. She hoped she was, but begrudged it already. Once the cot had been moved, Natalia got herself involved in Ebe's routine for bed.

"Give him a lovely warm bath. Drop some lavender in, and then, one last feed. Pop him in his cot. If he cries, go back to him but don't make a fuss. If he gets up, lay him down without being friendly or cross, no emotion. That's important. You don't want him attention seeking."

He's not attention seeking! She felt like screaming, but had nothing to fight back with. Ebe was nearly four and would only sleep on her chest. It didn't make for a happy marriage. She decided just to give in. There might be something in it.

"He's nearly four," Natalia echoed Carys's thoughts annoyingly. "He won't fit in a cot for much longer. If he can't settle on his own, how is he going to settle in his own bed?" she said, shrugging her shoulders in violent jerks.

After his bath, Ebe was presented to kiss Marco, Nana and Grandpa goodnight. Carys carried him up, and took him to his nursery.

"This is your new room," she encouraged. "How grown up are you?" Ebe didn't respond in any way and Carys had to assume he didn't understand. He did look as worried as his non expressive little face could demonstrate. Carys almost laughed to herself as she imagined him looking to her and Marco's room and saying "Precious..."

"Bad mother," she admonished, using humour to cover her anxiety. "Come on, little man," she said, hoisting him over the bars of his cot. She bent over and lay him down. He stared up at her with his big, dark eyes.

"Now, you be a good boy. Maybe one day Mummy and Marco will make you a brother or sister to play with." He looked blankly back at her with all the understanding of a new born child. Carys winced at the oddity of his three years. She wasn't shocked when he was crying by the time she reached the door.

"Leave him," Natalia commanded. Carys jumped as she hadn't been aware of being followed upstairs.

"I can't just leave him," she insisted. "It hurts my heart to hear him cry. He doesn't understand the world like other children."

"I can't say I'm surprised with the way you've molly-coddled him," she said harshly, before correcting to a less offensive tone. "Don't blame yourself. You're a new mum. But you must leave him to it now. Trust me. He won't cry forever."

Carys sat in the lounge with her husband and his parents, becoming unbearably tense. All she could hear was Ebe crying. The cries turned to screams, and she was on the edge of not coping. Marco leaned across to his mother and whispered something in her ear. She responded by nodding agreement.

"Carys, dear. He's sensing your tension. You're making him cry."

Carys didn't get up and punch the woman who

all of a sudden was the world's foremost expert on bringing up children. Nor did she question where that interest had been for the previous three years.

Both sets of grandparents had been a disappointment during Ebe's short life. To be fair, they had been more enthusiastic at first, but Ebe never rewarded their eagerness with any affection. He cried constantly when Carys wasn't in sight, so she had learned to be grateful for the occasions when they did baby sit. She knew Ebe was difficult. That's why she needed more help.

Dan and Natalia, or Natalia at least, had clearly decided that Ebe's problems were due to Carys's poor parenting skills. As insulted, unsupported, and misjudged as she felt, she couldn't help wondering if it was true and felt grateful for the attempts at help offered tonight.

"You go off out with Marco somewhere. Have a drink, I bet you could do with one. Go for a walk. Go far enough where you can't hear Ebe crying. I'll stay here with Dan so you won't have to worry, and when you get back, he'll be zonco. Guaranteed!"

Carys accepted reluctantly, with constant backward glances until they were out of sight. She and Marco headed off down The Drang towards town. The elevation as they walked out of the covered ally gave inspirational views across the valley of farmland with an occasional tree. The obligatory smattering of sheep dotted about made them smile. Away from the close, there was no sound of Ebe at all.

"Thank you. I needed this. It'll be so nice if it works, and we get back to a silent house, won't it?"

"If it works?! Of course it'll work! We can enjoy a snuggle tonight."

Carys wasn't sure if snuggling was what she fancied, more than a bloody good sleep, but she didn't say. She knew how frustrated her husband had been. They walked arm in arm down the hill to the little town centre, past the cross of the war memorial and towards the town hall above Rebecca's cell where Carys had suffered her breakdown nearly four years ago.

Feelings of wellbeing since, she put down to her love for Ebe, but more importantly, his love for her. She felt needed; loved. For now, that was enough to keep her stable.

A better bedtime routine, and the possibility of more children would be a benefit that fitted nicely into her life now. With Ebe starting school soon she was expecting to feel the loss badly. Maybe Natalia's help could be just in time.

They walked through the town and decided on one of the numerous public houses to venture into. Carys chose the sturdy stone façade of The Dragon Inn. She'd have a pint of best Brains bitter and feel good, relaxed, and Welsh.

Surprise that just a couple of pints intoxicated her, as she walked back, arm in arm, with her handsome husband, she thought he might get his wish tonight. She was feeling a little frisky.

As they walked up the steep hill back up to the Drang, and back to their town house, Marco had to steady a tipsy Carys, who giggled at her unsteadiness.

The carefree inebriation was rapidly replaced with taut sobriety less than halfway along the alleyway, as the unmistakable screaming of her son filled her ears and head. She broke free from Marco's arm and dashed for home.

The screaming became louder and more distressing with her proximity. She was certain he was noisier than when they left.

As she reached the house, Marco arrived half a second later as the door flew open to a flustered looking Natalia. "He hasn't stopped!" she accused, before altering her tone to portray a pseudo-calm. "I'm sure he'll exhaust himself before long."

Carys continued rushed past her mother-in-law, and up the stairs to her son's bedroom. As she summited the stairs, Ebe's screaming deafened her. Even Carys flinging open the door failed to silence him.

What she saw shocked her: Ebe standing up in his cot, covered in blood, and dripping with sweat. The foul smell of urine and faeces almost knocked her out as she rushed over to see where the blood was coming from.

As she reached the bed, she clearly heard it.

CHAPTER THIRTY

Wool

The dreadful humming noise, that only ever meant imminent disaster to Carys, filled the air comprehensively with no clear source, as it always did. She didn't know if it had been there all along, and she'd somehow managed to ignore it.

With hairs on end, she scooped smelly little Ebe from his cot, and had the presence of mind to notice he wasn't little any more as she struggled to carry him to the bathroom for a clean. He was still screaming as she ran the bath. She held him close and squeezed him tight.

"It's okay," she soothed. "It's okay, my Ebe." She kissed his head over and over. Slowly his sobbing abated as he calmed to his mother's presence. As he sat in the bath, she could see no sign of where the blood on his bed had come from, until she spotted it coming from his mouth. He must have hit his teeth on the side of the cot, or bitten his tongue. She tried to open his mouth to check how bad it was, but it was clamped firmly shut now that he wasn't crying.

A sudden increase in the volume of the humming noise caused Ebe to scream out again. He looked to his mother for reassurance but found none in her anxious expression. His large open mouth provided the opportunity for examination.

She was trembling with fear, but knew she had to see if Ebe needed a doctor. Blood was visible in his mouth, so he must have bitten his tongue. He may have a couple of loose teeth as well, she thought, but it looked okay. Recognising the negative effect she was having, she made concerted attempts to quell her fear, but another sudden increase in volume made them both cry out.

Marco rushed into the doorway. "Is everything okay?" The lack of a reply didn't surprise him. "I've put Ebe's bedding in the wash," he announced helpfully, taking the blame for his mother's interference. "Mum meant well. I don't think she understands Ebe's..." he struggled to find words to sensitively describe what he meant. "...difficulties," he settled on.

"That isn't fucking obvious much, is it!"

"I'll go and put the kettle on."

The humming noise drilled into Carys, loosening her grip on her sanity. It always had, but with her son to protect, it distressed her worse than ever. Placing a fluffy towel around him, she waddled him along to her bedroom and her bed. Lifting him up on top of the covers, she finished drying him, dressed him in clean pyjamas, still conveniently located in her bedroom wardrobe, and decided what to do.

After his reaction to being put in his own cot, and now with the awful humming, the decision was obvious. She wouldn't let him out of her sight, and that was that.

Ebe was tired after his second bath, and from being up much later than his regular bed time. Carys thought that if she left him in her bed he might settle to sleep just fine, but she wouldn't leave him.

She lay on the bed too, arm loosely around him, and he cuddled into her, falling sound asleep with his face touching hers. She smiled to herself as much as she dared, knowing that one false move could wake him.

Keeping his sleep routine was important. If he didn't sleep well tonight, he'd catch up during the day tomorrow after nursery, and then he'd struggle more tomorrow night; but that wasn't why she stayed with him. She knew, as her mum had always known, that she was right to be scared. Lying awhile, listening to Ebe's gentle snoring, she was relieved. But that left only one thing to hear: the incessant, excruciating hum.

Waking at dawn, she scrutinised the silence. It

was definitely quiet. Breathing out slowly, she was satisfied the humming had gone. With a frown she saw the empty space beyond her son. She didn't remember if Marco ever came to bed. Was it before or after he would've looked in on the two of them asleep that she'd stretched out and taken up the whole mattress, blocking his entry? Whatever the reason, he wasn't here.

A glance at the glaring red numbers of the alarm clock declared 6.00am. More time in bed. Without the hum, she might relax, she thought, her heavy lids closing.

She awoke to a moody Marco tapping her arm. "Do you want a cuppa before I go to work?" he asked sulkily.

"Yes... please," she remembered to add. "You okay?"

"Yeah," Marco answered before correcting himself "Actually, no. My back aches from sleeping on the couch, and I'm bloody knackered. I could see you'd managed to settle him. I couldn't get in, so I thought it best to just leave you both in peace."

It was obvious he wasn't happy. Carys paused a moment. "Sorry if I blocked you from getting in. Once Ebe was asleep, I just completely flaked out." Marco's expression softened. "It took me a while to settle him. It was that bloody humming noise," she excused, but really she was probing Marco for a response. "Did it disturb you?"

Irritation returned to Marco's face, knowing

exactly what the humming noise meant to Carys. Filled with worry for her mental health, he felt an irate disappointment that her born-again-Christian life wasn't protecting her from these demons. "No, I didn't hear any humming," he said with ill-contained exasperation. He disappeared, and returned with tea, which he placed noisily onto the bedside table, spilling a little as it splashed over the rim. They air-kissed unaffectionate goodbyes.

Carys lay seething for another fifteen minutes before Ebe's nursery.

She must have pressed the wrong button on the alarm clock, she would later suppose. Easy enough. It was a ridiculous design where the snooze button sat next to the off button. They were labelled of course, and after nearly four years of ownership she might have expected to be pretty sure whether it was the right or the left button, but she never was.

The shrill noise of the telephone ringing from its base next to the icy cold tea Marco had left for her, is what startled her awake. She struggled to comprehend who could be ringing. Her blurry eyes unable to read the caller ID on the handset. Without knowing who to expect, she anxiously answered.

"Hello?" she said, realising too late that she sounded like she'd just woken.

"Er, Mrs Ellis?" (She had kept her maiden name

despite desperate persuasion from Marco to become Carys Paulo) "Er... is Ebe coming into nursery today? Is everything alright?"

Carys panicked "Yes, what's the time then?" she looked across at the alarm clock. After ten! Where was Ebe?!

"I have to go. Sorry." Carys put the phone down without saying whether they should expect her and Ebe or not.

"Ebe!" she called. Hearing no reply, she called again, rushing out of the bedroom.

It didn't take long to see that since waking before his mum, Ebe had been busy. The first thing she noticed was how she could barely make her way from the stairs because the way was blocked. Tied to the bannister was wool. Lots and lots of wool.

Threaded through every bannister rail, up to the ceiling light and down again before looping through every conceivable hole. Around and into light fittings, through door handles, around pictures, round and round the bookshelf and through the doorways to the kitchen and the lounge and the toilet. She didn't know she owned so much of it. The balls went further than she ever would have believed.

Carys expected more of the same as she tentatively made her way through the woolly web to the kitchen. "Ebe? Where are you, cariad?" she gently called as she moved. When she adjusted her eyes past the obstruction in the doorway, she couldn't believe what greeted her.

Stacked high on the kitchen table was a pyramid, constructed from the chairs that usually resided firmly on the kitchen floor. Heavy, solid wooden carver chairs with bulky arms were stacked one on top of another until they touched the ceiling.

The wool around the ceiling light and back to the low protuberances of the room she had seen in the hallway was repeated here, wrapping round and round the stack of chairs making them immovable.

"How on earth have you done this?" she asked out loud. He couldn't reach, could he? He couldn't possibly lift one of those chairs onto the table, and then another one even higher, with skill and core strength to balance them?

She glanced at the centre ceiling light. How could he reach? Could he have used a broom handle or something? She couldn't imagine what level of dexterity would be needed to tie or loop the wool to the broomstick, and then release it keeping it secured to the light.

Relieved that nothing was damaged, it seemed, as the height Ebe had tied wool, and the risk from the huge weight of the heavy chairs slipping, or even from manoeuvring them in the first place, he probably hadn't come to any harm.

Carys walked, pushing aside carefully Ebe's astonishing work as she went. Fighting her way from the kitchen, back through the hallway and past the toilet, she arrived at the lounge. No furniture sculptures bedecked the family room. Everything was in its place but similarly festooned with a web of wool.

With a gasp of joy, she saw her son, at last, sitting happily on the rug in the middle of the floor; and in the middle of the wool web, looking thoroughly pleased with himself. A thrilled, electric look burned in his brown eyes, turning them a vibrant hazel.

"What have you done, Ebe?" He made no sound in response, but smiled immensely at her. She had never seen him happier. Despite the inconvenience of the woollen mesh, and the anxiety she had momentarily felt, seeing Ebe's delight was infectious and she began to laugh. At this Ebe delighted even more and chuckled, too.

It was a deep chortle that didn't fit his slight frame. The incongruence amused Carys, and she laughed harder. Before long the pair of them were hysterical with mirth. Carys's sides ached with the exertion and she gasped for breath with Ebe grinning up at her from the centre of the room.

He launched himself from his sitting position and hugged Carys hard. Taken aback after the distress of last night's bedtime, she squeezed him back. She loved this funny little man with his big head and dark eyes (not so dark today though!)

They enjoyed little rapport: Carys understanding only his basic needs for food and drink preferences, and not his innermost thoughts and dreams.

Today's construction was a revelation. She couldn't begin to imagine how, or why he had done this strange thing.

"Let's tidy this away, shall we?" she asked, whilst moving to what appeared to be the beginning of the web tied round the lounge door handle. As she touched it, intending to untie it, Ebe rushed to her and stopped her, placing his hands on hers. He didn't say "No," or make any sound to indicate his distress, but Carys got the message and moved away.

All the furniture was covered by wool. The doors were blocked too. She had little option but to join Ebe on the floor. "What's this all about, cariad?"

He wouldn't answer, of course. His communication problems had become more troublesome the more information he tried to give, and he was distraught with his failure to convey his feelings.

He had received a diagnosis of a 'speech and language disorder,' by the paediatric specialist. You don't say! Carys scoffed when they told her. It meant that once a week, she was able to take him to a class at the hospital for some lessons.

There had so far been nothing to report regarding any sort of progress. They were beginning to give up on Ebe ever talking and started declaring him mute. There was no obvious physical reason for his disability, but eventually they had been forced to concede, he probably wasn't ever going to speak.

As she daydreamed about Ebe's lack of progress, she was unaware of him getting up. He fiddled with some of the wool in the hallway. Carys's maternal instinct to panic roused her to jump up and stumble towards her son. Before she reached him the front door, apparently in response to whatever Ebe was doing, burst open, flooding the room with bright sunlight.

Somehow, the direct light from the kitchen window combined with sunlight from a different angle flooding through the front door, had a most curios effect on the shadows cast by the wool upon the walls; and in particular, the centre of the floor where Ebe was again sitting, grinning.

The pattern, indiscernible looking at the wool, but in looking at the walls and floor of the lounge appeared very mathematical. The perfect circle in the middle was clearly planned. Surely not, Carys quickly rationalised. The light would have cast the shadows before and Ebe must have noticed.

Scouring the room to see what could be causing the gap in the shade, it was a mystery. So perfectly round, so something already round like one of the light fittings made sense. Carys waved her arms in front of different lights to try to impinge on the area of light, but couldn't find the source. It was baffling.

The sun had already begun its move in the sky. The shadow would be very different before long, and Carys desperately wanted to understand what it was. As the shape moved slowly across the carpet, Carys spotted the silhouette of something else, she recognised as the kitchen door. She now knew the direction she had to look.

Waving her arms confirmed it. The circle pattern: the perfect circle of light in the centre of the lounge was being cast by the sculpture creation of chairs on the kitchen table. Carys swooned with the incredulity of it all.

Had Ebe really planned this? To use wool to make an incredible pattern whilst creating a small circle with heavy chairs across the hall? And why? It seemed outlandish.

Putting her in mind of an ancient stone construction, she shook her head. How did they do it? Impossibly heavy boulders, weighing several tonnes, balanced on one another, even heavier upright rocks by supposedly primitive people who didn't possess the technology to possibly achieve what they did.

She remembered briefly, and pondered the significance, that the bluestones forming the inner circle of the world famous Stone Henge, originated from the Preseli hills here in Pembrokeshire! They were clearly visible from her parent's house, and from the nursery window upstairs. The kitchen chairs were not ancient megaliths, but to a three year old, a skinny one at that, they might as well be.

After a while, the sun moved further round the house, as it tended to do, and the shadow picture was lost. Ebe got up from the floor and came over to Carys. "Are you hungry, bach?" Neither of them had eaten breakfast, and it was well after lunch time now.

Carys looked around the wool filled kitchen. Buying lunch out would be easier. "Do you want to walk, or go in your push chair?" she asked. "Please don't walk there, then insist on being carried back, because Mummy's tired." She had to decide without any input from Ebe, so she took the push chair and let him walk beside. If he didn't need it, she could use it as a little shopping trolley.

Walking down through The Drang she felt a horrible self-consciousness at the memories of her mental breakdown. It was years ago now, but she always worried who had witnessed her fall from sanity. And who had she assaulted? She was hopeless with faces. It could be anyone: someone serving her in Spar, or in Liz's bakery, or in the post office?

Not knowing made her uneasy. And whilst she'd be the first to admit to being paranoid, at least some of the whispering she heard whenever she came across the good people of Narberth was likely about her.

Marco made things better. He seemed well liked

in the community. But today, walking with Ebe, the two of them were ripe for gossip. The 'Nutter,' and her alien looking, mute son. Why did she even care what these strangers thought of her? She wouldn't recognise them again. Such superficial judgements meant nothing.

As they made it past the war memorial with its views of the castle, and then past the town hall with Rebecca's cell underneath, she shuddered, struggling to swallow. "What food do you want, my love?" she hiccupped, pointing at pies in the butcher's window. The scent of olives and Mediterranean food drew her into the deli, whose toilet had been where she'd first glimpsed the proof that Ebe was growing inside her. Opting for a takeaway selection, she didn't fancy mingling with the crowd.

Food in hand, she walked with Ebe to the town moor. Deciding against the dilapidated playground, with its crowds of rowdy children and accompanying mums, she wanted as little social interaction as possible.

Instead, she followed the path into the small wood at the edge of the moor, dark and unknown. It'll be peaceful inside, and there are wonderful views of the valley on the other side.

Ebe, perhaps detecting her trepidation, clambered into his push chair. Strapped in, he regarded the world with dark saucer eyes. A field of cows jostled for their attention just before the path veered into the woods. Carys paused a moment for Ebe to look at them, but he showed no interest.

Sighing, she pushed his chair over the ruts in the muddy path, threatening to dislodge her carefully selected Mediterranean lunch. Tutting, she screwed the bags tighter in her grip.

The sound of cows mooing gave way to birdsong, and Carys stopped to listen. No traffic, no boisterous children, just nature at its most splendid. She recoiled at the hammering of a woodpecker above her head. Realising at once what it was, she smiled.

"Mummy's really on edge today, Ebe!" Skurfing hair from her face, she leaned into her son. "Do you hear that, Ebe?" His mouth had moved into a micro-smile, but his expression didn't change in response to his mother's voice. "We'll be through the woods in a moment, bach," she persisted. "We can have our lunch then."

After a pleasant meander through mixed deciduous and coniferous woodland, the path yielded to the open hilltop. The valley in bright sunlight took Carys's breath away. A farm house, a mile away, cast stark shadows on the green pasture, accented by fluffy clouds of sheep, and sparking white-blue of the stream, snaking its way along the valley floor.

Basking in the quintessential Welshness of her surroundings, her thoughts caught her as she realised today's date: the twenty first of June - Summer Solstice! Had Ebe built his woollen construction because of that?

Confusion at her failing comprehension turned abruptly to terror as the humming, from no-where, filled the valley. Isolated and vulnerable, she had to protect Ebe.

CHAPTER
THIRTY-ONE

Night Terrors

It was loud. Whatever was making the noise was close. Carys imagined the quintessential UFO from films: an enormous saucer, bright lights glowing from every surface.

Thrusting the unopened sandwich bags into the basket underneath Ebe's stroller, she pushed for the safety of the woods as the best place to hide from a flying object.

Civilisation was but a brisk few minutes away. The chatter of rowdy children, and even condescension from the mums held an unprecedented appeal to Carys, recoiling from the vibration filling her head.

The hum grew suddenly louder. Carys's racing mind prayed it was what it often appeared to be to those not giving it their full attention: just a diesel engine, or a helicopter. But she knew the noise well enough not to risk stopping to listen for its unfindable source.

'Keep going. Not much further.' Rushing past the cow field, the hum was deafening to her ears now. Nothing else could penetrate her senses. Tears streaming down her face, she squealed as the wheels on Ebe's pushchair seized up in the dusty path. Dragging the immobilised frame up the hill, she was desperate for the safety she hoped a crowd could offer.

Reaching the clubhouse for the Royal Antediluvian Order of Buffaloes, (known locally as the RAOB, and more affectionately as 'The Buff Club') a group of female patrons sat outside partaking in their nicotine addiction. "You all right, bach?" a large, shorn headed woman asked.

Grateful for the safety even speaking to the small group potentially offered, Carys hesitated. "It's this bloody noise. Doesn't it bother you?"

The women looked thoughtful for a moment. "It's just a helicopter," one suggested.

"Or a tractor," said another.

"No." said Carys. "If you listen…" They listened. "It has no source. It's not coming from anywhere."

One of the ladies shuddered. "That's well creepy, that is!"

'Thank you!' Carys thought. But didn't say out loud. Instead, she smiled her appreciation of their ratification.

The group began discussing among themselves some possible causes of the noise, the orange glow of cigarette tips adding to their gesticulations.

People around was better than alone on a hill, but a pang for home surged her forward. The hum followed her all the way, the rise in volume had settled to a consistent droning.

Throwing open the front door, she struggled to manoeuvre Ebe's push chair though the gap. "Shit! What are you doing?" she berated. Unstrapping Ebe outside and folding the frame made a lot more sense. Rushing through had cost her a valuable minute; one that seemed vital.

Forcing the buggy through, scraping against the wall and catching her blouse on the front door handle, she slammed it shut with a sigh of premature relief. Sanctuary wasn't achieved as she had foolishly expected. Why would it have been? As a child, she'd been removed effortlessly with no chance of deliverance, while her protective parents slept only feet away and she screamed her broken heart out.

Far from being refuge in fact, the house may well be the last place she should be. But she had no choice. There was nowhere to hide; nothing to do to keep herself or her son safe.

If she ran, they would find her. How could Ebe cope then? The distress of her panicking would be as hard to endure as whatever was to come. She had to provide a convincing façade of normality.

She decided to clear the wool. Marco would be

home soon, and she couldn't cook dinner with it as it was. The moment she touched a strand, Ebe screamed at her. His vocal expression was so unusual, she conceded to his desire.

Might the woollen web offer protection from their would-be abductors? Maybe the very particular design interfered with the frequency they operated, and they'd be forced to retreat.

She almost laughed at the absurdity of an alien invasion thwarted by wool, but left it in place, for Ebe. That way, any silly thoughts of a woolly force-field could exist unjustified by her struggling mind.

Now without the distraction of cooking dinner, Carys had little option but to venture back upstairs. She ran her and Ebe a bath for something to do. She expected it might relax her, but it wasn't enough. They lay together wrapped in towels when Marco arrived home after a long day at work.

"What on earth…!" he exclaimed in reaction to walking into unanticipated wool. "Carys?! Where are you?" he called.

"Upstairs." She answered. "We've just had a bath."

Sounds followed of Marco fighting his way through the woollen impediment and walking up the stairs.

"What happened here?!" he yelled. Guilt Carys may have felt for her husband coming home to the mess and no dinner dissolved by his irksome tone. He didn't know what she'd been through today. And he didn't seem to appreciate how amazing Ebe was.

"Perhaps you shouldn't speak to me in that tone of voice before you've heard the explanation." Marco looked as if no explanation would suffice, and when she had elucidated his face was even more scathing.

"Ebe did not do that. It isn't possible!" Marco fumed.

"I know. That's what I thought when I came downstairs."

"You're not listening. It's not possible. You must've done it. Maybe you did it in your sleep." He ignored Carys gesticulating her dissention.

"Whoever did it, why the f..." he controlled his language by biting his lip, "is it still there?!"

"Ebe built it. I don't know how. When I started to tidy it he was so upset. After the turmoil your mother caused..."

"My mother was just trying to help! She was trying to save our marriage!" he said, and regretted it instantly.

"Me caring for my baby is jeopardising our marriage, is it? Well, I suggest you just fuck off then," she answered calmly and coldly. "Because there is no way I'm distressing Ebe for your comfort." Marco winced.

Heartened by the effect, Carys continued. "When I tried to tidy it, Ebe screamed out. I thought it *must* be important. We went out for some lunch and the humming noise… do you hear it?" Marco shook his head. Carys tutted and carried on. "That awful noise started when we were in the woods. And other people noticed it too because they were sitting outside the Buff club. They agreed it was really strange."

Marco was losing patience, but forced himself to listen.

"It was driving me crazy, and I had to get home. I wanted to clear the wool and cook, but that's when Ebe screamed. I half wondered if the web of wool was offering protection…"

Marco snorted, "Protection from what…? Oh, let me guess, UFOs by any chance?" Carys sat stony faced, incensed by the mockery. "You're mad! You are actually insane," Marco fumed. "Do you need to go to the nut-house? Should I call the doctor? Or the police?"

"No!" Carys squealed.

"I won't bother asking what's for dinner! I can smell, or rather I can't smell. It's nothing isn't it?" With that, he grabbed a holdall from under the bed and proceeded to chuck clothes into it.

"I'm going to my 'terrible' mother's for some food. Don't expect me back." He paused, noticing tears trickling down his wife's face, but it was too late. He'd had enough.

A glance towards Ebe showed him oblivious as always, and he left. Stomping down the stairs, yanking viciously at the wool on his way past, he slammed the front door hard behind him.

Carys was left, unsupported and alone to care for Ebe, and endure the unceasing humming.

Aware suddenly that she was rocking back and forth, she tried to quell her fear for the sake of a pretence at reality she must perform for Ebe.

Ordering a pizza from the local 'pizza, burger, kebab, chicken' shop, she rushed downstairs, clutching her bathrobe around her when it duly arrived. She paid and brought it back upstairs, and she and Ebe ate whilst watching a film.

The sky box announcement it would switch off unless someone pressed 'back-up' went unnoticed by the sleeping pair. Now the room was dark, which meant today, the longest of the year, it was late: after eleven.

Carys stirred, alerted to a sound somewhere. A neighbour coming back from the pub? Or someone slamming a car door? She snuggled back down with Ebe, pulling the covers over them more.

Searing light broke through the curtains and Carys sat bolt upright. Glancing down at her son sleeping peacefully, she frowned at what the noise could be. A distant siren concluded her consternation. That idiot Marco must have called the police! 'My wife's gone crazy, you have to help her,' she could imagine him exaggerating.

If they took her away; if they sectioned her, what would happen to Ebe? Would Marco take him, or would he go into care? What had led him to betray her like this? His bloody mother no doubt. Well, she wouldn't let them take her. She'd leave now.

Jumping up from the bed, she hunted on the floor for wearable clothes. She wouldn't need much on this warm night. Getting Ebe ready quickly would be virtually impossible though. The lights brightened. The police car must be just outside the house. She had to go now!

A clattering made her jump. Was it coming from downstairs? Were they in already? What had Marco told them to make them force entry without knocking? She had to get away, but how? There wasn't time! To give herself a fighting chance she heaved the wardrobe in front of the door. She didn't know why.

Perhaps she could assure them of her well state of mind with enough time to do it. The woollen blockade might give her that. She'd explain how she thought it might be burglars, and she didn't realise it was the police breaching her home.

But then it occurred to her, she knew who it was. And why they hadn't knocked or rung the doorbell.

She scooped up Ebe, surprised how heavy he weighed in her arms, her shoulders straining. Head jerking one way then another, she didn't know what she was doing but she felt stricken. She gasped at a sound.

Footsteps on the stairs!

Counting every one, hairs stood so far on end they pulled at the follicles, her whole body prickling in an unearthly shudder. Struggling to hear over the pounding in her chest and her ears, she knew when they'd reached the landing. The distinctive creak of the floorboards which usually meant Ebe was sleep-walking or Marco was on his way to the toilet was unexplainable.

Unless.

Someone was there.

Someone was on the landing.

The footsteps advanced towards the bedroom door.

Boom-boom, boom-boom, so loud whoever was there could surely hear her chest thudding. With a futile scuttle to the corner of the room as the furthest point from the door, Carys huddled and tried to slow her breathing in an instinctive attempt to hide and to hear vital sounds. Breaths came in jagged sniffles as a panicked cry rattled behind her lips. Acutely aware of the smell of leftover pizza broke her fixation with the door broke just for a second and seemed to be the catalyst for them to find her.

The door handle rattled.

The hinges creaked at pressure on the door, but the bulk of the wardrobe kept it from opening.

There came no calls for her to, "Open up, Police." No banging on the door.

The cry that had filled her mouth now screeched into the room as Carys's disbelief at seeing the wardrobe slide back towards the corner transported her to a world where nothing made sense. Petrified to the spot. She had to become un-petrified quickly, or risk being crushed by the kinetic weight of her wardrobe as it pitched towards her.

Leaping to one side as it rammed the wall, a silence cleaved only by the echo from the spent force was filled with dread.

An involuntary yelp might have given her location away, but she was sure they had always known. Recalling her fear at the police, she felt a fool, wishing it was them in her house, full of concern for her.

Instead, held back by a meagre two inches of wood, was Carys's worst nightmare; here again to torture her and have everyone question her sanity.

She stood, placing Ebe behind her, and braced herself as the door handle began its descent to the position that in a micro-moment, without the barrier of the wardrobe to protect them, would provide access to her and Ebe by whomever or whatever was waiting on the other side.

With a burst of brightness, the room filled with the all too familiar, searing white light and the door creaked open as if the hand pushing it was doing so especially slowly for dramatic effect.

It continued its arc, and for a moment Carys forgot how the wardrobe had moved by itself, and almost managed to convince herself it was falling open naturally, like it had been blown from its catch by the wind and was now simply continuing that motion.

The doorway appeared empty for a second. Carys stood blinking in the light, steadfast before the inescapable entry of the figures that had plagued her life entered the room and did whatever they wanted. She wouldn't go down without a fight.

And then they were there. The grotesque, bald, pale-skinned, huge-eyed creatures; just as she remembered them. And just as others had described them on The Discovery Channel.

"Go away!" she screeched. "Leave us Alone!"

The creatures, she wasn't counting how many, moved towards her undeterred. Peering down on them, they were considerably shorter than her. She was surprised as she remembered them taller, but of course, she'd been a child then.

Looking at her son in the same room with *them*, she shuddered at the intimacy she must have shared to create him.

Where were these meandering thoughts coming from? Was it her life flashing before her? Was it about to end; here; now; with them?

She knew she had to fight. And she had to win.

Checking Ebe behind her, she was shocked and relieved that he was still sleeping and she was the barrier, the only obstacle, between the creatures and her son.

Lunging forward, she struck at one in its huge eyes sending it reeling. Others rushed towards her.

She lunged again, but found she couldn't move. Her arm remained stuck at her side, and her legs wouldn't do what her mind wished them to.

The small creatures parted, allowing a similar looking figure, but far taller, taller even than her, to bisect the group and stand before her. "You must do as I say," a thin line of a mouth warbled. "You will remain unharmed if you do as I say." The creature's animalistic voice, like a wounded animal, could be heard distantly; as though she were in a box and the creature was outside. Inside the box she heard the words in perfect English.

"You must do as I say," the creature reiterated needlessly. "We want the boy. You must give us the child."

Every muscle in her body strained against her paralysis to lash out at this beast who wanted to take away from her the only thing that made her life worthwhile. Her limbs cramped, but she achieved no perceptible movement. From her, the creature was perfectly safe.

"You must give the boy to us. He will not be harmed." The assurance unexpected and welcome. She didn't trust them, but given she had no choice, the idea Ebe would be okay was a straw upon which to clutch. Tears streamed down her face, their saltiness giving a tangible taste to her terror. Screams of 'Get away from my son' remained in her head as her voice was as immobile and useless as her arms and legs.

There nothing she could do against her viola-tors.

A jolt in her head gave sudden hope. She had her thoughts. They weren't controlling those. And she was the wife of a minister's son, for god's sake. That must count for something in the realms of the Divine? She prayed.

Nothing happened.

But then, from the corner of her eye there was movement!

She allowed faith to flood her mind and im-agined an angel with the Will of The Almighty on its side, smiting these demons back to where they came from and freeing her and her son.

Hope was short lived as she comprehended the movement she'd peripherally witnessed. It was Ebe. He hadn't woken. He wasn't moving of his own volition. More, he was floating, still unconscious, from the falsely perceived safety provided by him having been behind her legs. He floated in mid-air and over her shoulder to within easy reach of them.

"Nooo!" she yelled, but still no sound came out, not even into the space she imagined as a box. The scream lingered firmly within her head. It didn't matter. She had long since understood she was on her own. Her parents remained sleeping feet away when she'd screamed out as a child. No-one would help her now.

They didn't touch Ebe. There was no need. They simply allowed him to float through the door and away from her, so paralysed she could not even cry.

Then they all left.

The door closed, and the light dimmed, leaving her welded to the spot in the corner of the room, and all she could do was stare at the space she'd last seen her son.

Expecting at some point the paralysis would wear off, she didn't know what she'd do when it happened. An overwhelming apathy washed over her. Nothing mattered but Ebe. A hollow emptiness in the pit of her stomach would never be filled by mere tears. But none came anyway. Just an ache like she'd never known.

When at last, the paralysis did lift, she crumpled to the floor, barely able to breath, the depth of her grief a chasm with no floor.

Where had they taken him? What would they do to him? Would she ever see her funny little boy again?

She lay on the floor after an eternity of silent grief, clutching at the promise they wouldn't harm him. But they'd taken him and that was enough.

Empty of sobs, empty of hope. Now she could physically move, emotionally, she was spent, and she didn't know if she would ever move again.

There was one change she noticed through her numbness that would usually bring relief, but now its absence made her even more desolate:

the humming noise had stopped.

CHAPTER THIRTY-TWO

*The Feather
in the river*

Carys was unaware, but it returned in the night. She had fallen into a deep sleep that, she would believe upon waking, had been forced upon her. Whether the noise had anything to do with her experiences, and if it ever had, could be argued and probably would be over the coming weeks and months. Especially in relation to Carys's sanity; or lack of it.

When she awoke, she couldn't believe her eyes. She was in bed, but had no recollection of moving from the floor.

And then she saw him, and wept.

Breathing peacefully, Ebe lay beside her. Her sobbing woke him and he shuffled across the bed to cuddle her.

How?

Had it all been a terrible nightmare? No, it

wasn't possible. She may as well believe her entire life had been a nightmare as to imagine last night hadn't happened. Wasn't that always the way? They plonked her in bed and put things back to normal. She trembled at the thought.

Why didn't they erase her memory? Perhaps they tried, but she wasn't susceptible. Or maybe they didn't bother, and just didn't fear her telling. Her credibility had never been high.

She considered possibilities. Either it was real, or she was completely insane. Both options entirely plausible, and both horrifically objectionable. She noticed from the corner of her eye a mark on the wall. It must have been caused by the wardrobe hitting it! Looking to the floor, she saw definite scuff marks on the carpet.

A tear of relief cleansed her eyes and purged her doubts. She wasn't insane. It was all true. The horror she'd endured her entire life was real, and she was glad. She hadn't realised, but facing adversity with full use of her faculties was preferable to her lack of faculties *being* the cause of her adversity.

Well, it was over for now, and Ebe was lying unperturbed in her bosom. As with her other experiences with her unknown adversaries, she just had to carry on. There was nothing she could do, no-one she could tell.

She woke Ebe and got him ready for nursery. They walked down the stairs through the wool, partly destroyed by Marco's flouncing off last night. Carys wondered if the damage to Ebe's web is what allowed the creatures into their home, and if the parts left undamaged were the reason Ebe was safe and sound, then shook her head. Maybe the strange patterns were magical; like crop circles. She'd seen discovery channel's explanations. A mix of utter scepticism with testimony from hoaxers, while other testimony from equally credible sources declared them to be everything from extra-terrestrial portals, to time machines, to force-magnifiers. It was entirely possible that Ebe's amazing web of shadow casting wool could be just about anything.

Leaving it in place, she declared they'd have breakfast on the way to nursery. Carys erected the pushchair and Ebe walked beside it. They ambled down the hill, the streets empty and cool in the early morning sunshine.

Pleased not to be rushing she decided upon an alternative scenic route past the church to breathe much needed calmness into her shattered nerves. Skirting steep fields to a small rapidly flowing river at the bottom of the valley, she expected Ebe to tire quickly, but he impressed her with his stamina. In one field they passed a horse who plodded over to them for a fuss.

"Hello, bach," Carys clucked to the lovely old bay Cob. She took a sharp intake of breath that was almost painful in the cold morning air as Ebe put his hand out to the gentle horse and fed it grass plucked from the ground on his side of the fence. After the complete disinterest throughout his childhood, it was quite the revelation.

"You like the horse then, Ebe?" she asked enthusiastically. He smiled up at her and actually made a sound. Nothing discernible, but a noise in response to her question. Chest tightening, she struggled to speak. "That's lovely, cariad," she said, finally, and a large droplet of salty tears ran down her cheek, dripping off her chin. She wiped it away with a laugh.

"Bye, bye, Mr Horse," she said as they left towards the stream at a stride down the hill into a copse of trees after which the path led along the river.

They hadn't gone far before Ebe became agitated.

"Do you need your pushchair, sweetheart?" Carys asked, but he wasn't placated. Whatever is the matter, Ebe?" she asked, becoming concerned now. She was busy examining his legs and arms for signs of nettle stings or something similar when disbelief collided with her expectations once more.

"Oh!" shouted Ebe. His first almost-word before his utterances became too much for Carys to bear, and she broke down into joyous sobs.

"There's a wuffer in the wooper!" Ebe exclaimed. Carys could barely regain her composure to answer before he spoke again.

"There's a wuffer in the woooper!!" he said more

agitatedly.

Carys calmed herself enough to realise that Ebe was pointing. She followed his finger to a point in the river. Water rushed, white, over a pile of rocks in the centre, and something else. Something white, of no significance to Carys, but she strained to see what it was.

A feather, large and white, trapped between the rocks, being battered by the rushing water.

"Oh No!" Ebe yelled now. "There's a wuffer in the wooper!!" And it clicked.

"There's a feather in the river!" Carys cried. Ebe nodded in agreement.

"There's a wuffer in the wooper" he said again, but calmer now.

"It's okay Ebe," his mum reassured. "The feather can't feel any pain. Maybe a bird will fly down and use it for its nest or something. Don't worry though. It's just nature. We should leave it as it is."

Ebe, reassured by his mother's quickly cobbled explanation, smiled and nodded.

And they were Ebe's very first words.

By the time he'd reached nursery he'd said all sorts. "Is there nonan in my gink?" he had asked with his drinks bottle in his mouth. After many repetitions, Carys deciphered that to mean 'is there orange in my drink?'

And then she cried again, when for the first time in his three years on the planet he uttered the word she had been yearning to hear every day: "Mummy."

When Ebe said it, he elongated the sound to 'mumaaay,' and repeated himself over and over to the point where Carys suspected that very soon she would be harking back to the good old days of silence.

When they arrived at nursery, the nursery staff were soon in tears as well when they heard Ebe talk for the first time. "What's happened to him?"

Carys didn't know, and what she suspected, she was keeping to herself.

Later, when she returned with Ebe, she began the laborious task of removing the wool. Untying it proved more difficult than she'd imagined. Once she'd given full appreciation for Ebe's incredible dexterity and knot knowledge to be able to tie them in the first place, she began cutting each one with a small paring knife.

Ebe gave no objection to the removal of his whatever-it-was, and happily sat watching the television news. As Carys snipped and cut away, she appreciated afresh just how much time and effort it must have taken him to construct it.

A new wave of wonder immersed her as she looked across at her remarkable son, watching television unremarkably; apart from the choice of programme: he'd never shown much interest in children's programmes.

A flush of excitement reddened her cheeks at the thought of showing Marco Ebe's incredible development. As if reading her thoughts, Ebe jumped up.

"Mummaaay? Mummaaay?" he repeated a few times to make absolutely sure he had her full attention before asking, "Where Marco?" It was perhaps the clearest thing he had said. Carys supposed he'd heard her calling Marco more than Marco had referred to her as mummy.

"I suppose he must be at work, cariad," she suggested, realising her assumption everything was still okay between them might be optimistic.

"Marco angwee," Ebe attempted. "Him not like Ebe's wool formation," he said matter-of-factly.

Carys literally took a step back in astonishment. "Wool for… *mation?*" she broke the word into two parts, so unfathomable was its emergence from Ebe's lips. He was an enigma, that was undoubtable.

She thought she better phone Marco, just to let him know the wool would be gone by the time he came home, and dialled his direct number. Carys detected reluctance, but he agreed to come home for dinner.

"You won't believe what Ebe can do now!" she gushed, excitedly telling him about his speech: his clear 'Marco,' and 'wool formation.'

"Wool formation? He's never uttered even a grunt, and now you expect me to believe he said that? You're reading too much into it, I bet. It's good he's making sounds though. Nursery is paying off."

Carys couldn't help but be insulted, but didn't bite. Get him home then he'll see for himself.

She was in the middle of organising the ingredients for her speciality, 'Moules Mariniere,' when the front door flew open to a cheerful sounding Marco. "Something smells fantastic!" he proclaimed as he bounded into the kitchen flourishing fresh flowers from behind his back. "I'm sorry I left you to cope on your own last night,"

She bristled with anger now. Trying to control it, not wanting to discourage the magnanimous gesture of his apology and flowers, she found she couldn't stop herself from saying, "Why didn't you believe me?" Her stare would pierce lead. "Why would I make up stories about Ebe? To impress you? Or do you think I'm just sooo screwed up...?"

Marco struggled to answer. Mouth opening and closing in an attempt to speak before his brain had constructed anything, he was forced to listen to more from his furious wife.

"And, if you did think I was cracking up, why would you leave me on my own? You know how I can get! You know what can happen!"

Things were not going how he'd planned. Perhaps he shouldn't have left last night, but he'd needed some breathing space. It had been selfish but necessary.

Carys could see her insistence Ebe constructed what he had was laughable. More than that, it was a physical impossibility. He wasn't tall enough to reach, and as for balancing the chairs on top of one other? Well, he had enough trouble sitting on a chair without falling off. How was Marco expected to believe that suddenly he'd developed super-human strength and dexterity?

He couldn't put his own clothes on, and was not even vaguely capable of tying his shoelaces. Now she was expecting him to believe he'd constructed something with intricate knots she herself would find impossible?

She knew she was being unreasonable, but it was the truth. And she desperately wanted him to believe her. She'd trust him whatever he said. Maybe.

Her doing it in a bi-polar frenzy, and forgetting she'd done it seemed more plausible. It wasn't just that it made more sense. It was the only explanation that made any sense at all.

But she knew the truth. She couldn't stop herself from knowing just to make it convenient for Marco to believe. And so she continued letting him know just how he had wronged her.

"Because you disrupted the formation..." Carys persisted, "They made it into the house. They almost took Ebe!" she finished tersely.

"Wa... Wait...What? Who?" he must have been sure it would be something nonsensical from his crazy wife. Carys knew that it sounded insane. Marco had called her that only last night. But if he was going to be a crutch in her times of need, then he needed to accept her, and she needed to be honest.

She took a deep breath. "The woollen structure Ebe made, it was special." Marco raised his eyes. Regretting it at once, he tried to recover by coughing and covering his mouth. Carys glared at him and continued.

"You can scoff, but you only saw it later. You didn't see the patterns, like corn circles. When the midday sun struck the kitchen window, Ebe seemed to know it was time for... I don't even know, but he opened the front door and all these shapes appeared.

"Ebe sat in the middle of the lounge in a circle he'd created by moving the chairs on top of the table," she babbled on. "It was the only spot downstairs that didn't have any of the patterns on. He sat there until the sun moved, and then we went out for lunch. That's when I realised it was summer solstice! He'd done all of it to take advantage of the sun in a very particular way. It really is incredible, Marco."

Marco listened patiently in silence. It was preferable to becoming involved in a crazy conversation. When would she stop this outlandishness?

"Then, the humming noise came. I know what you think about that, but I've heard it a lot in my life, and it always means the same thing." Marco stifled a sigh. "When I was a child, not much older than Ebe is now, they came for me. The humming noise had been around for days. Everybody heard it, not just me. They came for me and did awful things to me."

"Did what things?"

"Oh, I don't know. It's only snippets of memory, now. Them standing over me; futuristic looking machinery."

"And by 'them' you mean…"

"Yes, I can't think of anything else they could've been. They were aliens, yes." It felt good to be honest.

"The humming noise came again when I was with that arsehole, Stephen Holmes. He can't remember what happened but we both saw indiscernible figures. I remember waking up in my bed, not a clue how I got there, and then," she paused for breath. "I moved here, and discovered I was pregnant! Stephen isn't Ebe's father. One of *them* is. You must believe me now."

Expectation for Marco's response grew unbearable. He was clearly delaying. Was that a squint or a frown? What was he thinking?

"They came again last night and tried to take Ebe," she said when her pause was left silent for too long. "I think his wool thing was designed to stop them somehow, but you damaged it! I thought I'd lost him forever… that they'd taken him away from me and I'd never see him again. But this morning, he was back in bed with me!" Marco snorted, but nothing could suppress her wide grin at the next revelation. "And now he can speak. He never spoke before, and now he can, he really can!"

Was she having some sort of bipolar episode? Marco wondered. That was one of her symptoms, wasn't it? Fast talking and strange conspiracy theories? He decided to try to help by giving an alternative, more plausible explanation. There was no benefit in pretending she had a point. It was important to confront her and make her see sense. Only then would she be willing to get the psychiatric help she so clearly needed. "Listen," he began, ominously. "I'm not sure I believe in all this alien stuff. Hear me out though."

Carys sat, prepared to listen. "Go on."

"We may as well start at the beginning," he said calmly, trying not to sound patronising. "You've told me about your experience when you were Ebe's age. You said how everyone had told you it was just a dream. A waking nightmare. Well if we assume there's no such thing as aliens, just for a minute, then 'waking nightmare' doesn't sound too bad an explanation, does it?" He raised his eyebrows. He didn't wait for Carys's agreement before ploughing on. "Your mum's reaction made it seem real to you, because you were so young."

"When you were raped by that - and I won't believe you weren't," he said in reply to Carys's widening eyes, "he took advantage of your beliefs to get himself off the hook. It's so obvious, I didn't think you actually believed what you were saying. I thought you just didn't want that boy involved with Ebe. Especially as you'd just met me. You can't really believe Ebe has an E.T. for a dad?! Come on! I know he's a little bit strange and his development has been, shall we say 'challenging'; but you were raped by that boy and that's all there is to it."

Carys nodded slowly.

"With all those thoughts in your young head, it's no wonder you've seen things the way you have. As for Ebe's web. I think you must have made it yourself," he asserted. "You must not remember doing it, that's all."

"Why would I do that?" Carys asked indignantly.

"Why would Ebe? How could he possibly understand things you don't?" he stressed. "You must have subconsciously known it was summer solstice, and made your wool creation, and then, I don't know. You must not be well."

"What about the carpet scuffs? And the marks on the wall?"

"I'm not saying things didn't happen," he soothed. "I'm not saying the wardrobe wasn't moved. I'm saying that I think you did it. You did all of it, and you just don't remember."

"But Marco. I saw them! Very clearly, I saw them. Creatures with big eyes, and grey, hairless skin. There were even taller ones who seemed to be in charge. I saw them, Marco. I didn't imagine it!"

Marco didn't want to upset her too much, but had to sustain his explanation in order for it to be of any use. "It isn't the first time you've 'seen' things, or, people, though is it? It probably won't be the last. You know with your borderline disorder that when you get too stressed you have hallucinations, don't you? That humming noise, whatever it is, must be an instant trigger because of your past. It doesn't make it real though." He smiled reassuringly.

Carys began to object. She knew what had happened, even if Marco didn't. Just because it sounded like nonsense didn't mean it was. Expecting her rejection of his theory, Marco gave her an ultimatum.

"I know it all seems real to you. I know," he said with false authority. "I just can't accept that aliens are what all this is about. No-one will," he stated assuredly.

He was right about that, conceded Carys.

"If you can see... If you can see I'm right, well," said Marco. "I can get you help. Everything can be alright."

Carys thought for a moment. There was nobody to tell and nobody she wanted to tell. No-one could do anything. She didn't want to lose Marco for no reason. Her own beliefs were of little consequence, weren't they? "Yes. Of course, you're right."

Beaming at her, weight lifting from his shoulders, he distinctly relaxed. Reaching out, he put his hand on hers. "Thank you," he said, recognising how hard it was for her to go along with him.

At just the perfect moment to break the tension, Ebe came rushing in.

"Mummaay! Mumaay? Wot iss dinner?"

"Moules mariniere," she answered, and not waiting to see if he understood she simplified it, "Mussels, a type of seafood, in a creamy source. Yum Yum!" she declared, and he grinned at her.

"Yum yum," he repeated. He turned to Marco. He appeared not to have noticed him come home. Turning back to Carys he said. "Marco no angwee anymore?" he turned away from Carys again but not quite back to Marco.

"Sorry, Marco. I know you not like Ebe's woollen formation," he said, addressing Marco but not making eye contact.

Marco looked at Ebe in stunned silence. Where he should have reassured him, or at least accepted his apology, he said nothing. He teetered on his chair. "Bloody Hell!" he roared, inappropriately for the son of a minister. The tension broken, Carys began to laugh. Ebe joined her, and poor Marco had no choice but to join in too. Ebe's laugh was very infectious.

CHAPTER THIRTY-THREE

July, 2019

Marco's Surprise

It had been a difficult year. They thought it was just another symptom of her ongoing mental illness. Why it would suddenly rage again, when it had been so well controlled for such a long time, was a subject Geraint and Carys were considering taking legal action about.

It was too painful to drag it all up and go through all the details, but there was still time. But if they could prove it was the fault of the medical profession, it wouldn't offer much comfort now. Diane's enormous raging tumour took hold of her brain, and ultimately killed her within months of being diagnosed.

If things could have been different. If when her speech started to slur, someone had suspected the truth instead of blaming side effects of her medication as the culprit. A *C.T.* scan was booked a couple of times, but then been cancelled due to unforeseen circumstances. There was a letter asking if she still required an appointment, but Diane had ignored it.

She suspected all was not right, and quite frankly did not want to know. But if she had known, could they have removed more of the tumour? It was all conjecture, and unbearably painful at that. Today, Carys was determined to be cheerful.

She had surprised herself, and Marco with her coping skills. She'd stayed out of hospital, and not resorted to harming herself, remaining on a surprisingly even keel.

The Amish man and the Rebecca still showed themselves, but hadn't much to say. She could see them from the corner of her eye drifting to sleep, but they weren't real, and she was determined to take no notice of them should they spout forth their usual venomous counsel.

Perhaps that was why they'd remained silent. More likely, it was the tweaking of her medication after telling her psychiatrist her concerns. He'd said grief was natural and would take its time. It was unavoidable, but to make some adjustments to see her through was probably a good idea.

She had packed everything with her because they were staying the night at a quite magnificent country hotel on the outskirts of the university city of Cambridge, according to its description online. It seemed most appropriate, given the nature of their visit.

She was so proud of her son. Now it was his graduation, from Cambridge no less, she couldn't help but think back to when he couldn't even speak at all...

Having spoken his first words, he carried on learning more and more, but still pronounced words oddly. He had joined school at the same time as the other children. A recommended delay for him to catch up with his speech after all the problems hadn't proved necessary. Whilst he was behind the other children, the education authority had noticed he was a clever boy and would be able to attend mainstream school, with help. He was awarded twenty hours a week Learning Support Assistant help, plus additional lessons specifically targeting his needs.

He made it most of his way through his first few years with a continued diagnosis of a speech and language disorder. The school staff talked, and Carys and Marco talked, and at the parents evening at the end of one of the spring terms, they talked to each other. There was, they all agreed, something more going on.

"He's a genius," his teacher announced. She was new to Ebe and still getting used to his funny ways, Carys remembered. "Don't get me wrong," she had said. "He has his difficulties. There was a time when I thought he might be..." she struggled for a polite way to express her initial impression. "Lacking in intelligence. He wouldn't tackle the maths problems set, and we assumed they were a little advanced for him. Not a bit of it! They must have bored him to tears." She paused for breath and actively calmed herself before continuing

"We were using the computers, if you remember signing a form allowing Ebe to have lessons browsing the internet and such like?" Carys and Marco nodded their recollection, and Miss Simpson continued her narrative.

"Well," she said, "Ebe absolutely loved it. He doesn't much enjoy playing outside with the other children. He prefers to stay near his LSA, so it wasn't a great surprise when he seemed to want to stay and use the computer over his lunch break. Sarah, the LSA agreed to stay with him. It was just so nice to see him so animated."

Carys and Marco carried on nodding.

"He managed to negotiate the web effortlessly, and it started to become a bit of a regular thing. As his competence became more established, Sarah took more of a back seat. To be honest she said he was better at it than her."

Marco and Carys had grinned, expecting this was the reason for her having declared him a genius. They were wrong.

"He started to do a bit more with it, exploring the other functions of the computer. Within a week or so he seemed to know what every button on the windows platform did and started looking at the code behind it. That's what he told Sarah, anyway." She could barely contain her excitement as she told further of Ebe's success.

"We do little talks in front of the class once a week. Children might bring something in from home, or just chat about something they like to do. It's kind of 'show and tell' but they don't have to bring anything." She looked intently at Ebe's parents.

"Ebe has, understandably, been reluctant to become involved. We try to encourage him because it is a good way for the children to get to know one another," she said.

"With his speech difficulties we didn't push him too far, but one day he announced he had something to show us. We were all intrigued as he guided us to join him at the computer where he showed us..." she was overcome with pride and excitement.

"Showed you what?" asked Carys. Miss Simpson led the pair of them over to the computer in the corner of the room.

"I hope I can demonstrate," she said. "Ah yes. Here it is." And she clicked on something with the mouse cursor. "It isn't that clear," she said. "The graphics need some imagination to interpret."

Carys and Marco looked at the monitor. Miss Simpson was right. It wasn't clear what they were looking at.

"Ebe explained what was going on, surprisingly eloquently. No, actually, incredibly advanced for anyone," she amended, "Not just someone with his difficulties. He used words I just did not expect from him."

She pointed at part of the screen. "It's a simulator. A kind of game. The aim, I think is to guide yourself, that is, the point of view of the camera, into a portal, or black hole or something. Once the portal is discovered the graphics disappeared. Ebe explained that he didn't know what was through the doorway so he hadn't made it. He said we could use our imaginations!"

The three of them looked in stunned silence.

"Ebe made this?" Marco asked in disbelief. "But he's only nine! He can't even tie his shoelaces! I can see why you say he's a genius!" Marco shook his head slowly in delighted disbelief.

"That's not even it!" Miss Simpson announced. What more could there possibly be, wondered Carys.

"We were stunned, obviously," his teacher said. "When we asked him to explain how he had done it, I really thought he must have stumbled upon some sort of 'make your own game' website or something. I couldn't believe it. He showed how he'd had problems. The software code required in-depth mathematical knowledge: advanced trigonometry and algebraic equations."

She gave an ironic look to her audience of two open mouthed parents and continued. "It won't surprise either of you to learn, I'm sure, that we don't teach trigonometry or algebra, let alone the type of advanced equations Ebe demonstrated knowledge of. When we asked him where he'd learned it, he replied he'd *worked it out!*"

The incredulity turned to hysterical elation as other teachers passing the class heard them talking and offered their own opinions, all citing Ebe as a prodigy, the like of which they'd never seen.

Carys smiled to herself at the memory. She kept it to herself as Marco drove through the evening traffic. Rush hour wasn't a reality in the same way she'd known it in Cambridge, but the little traffic there was, particularly at this time of year with the tourists flocking to the county, was a little busier at this time. It had been unavoidable. Marco had been unable to leave work earlier, and it really wasn't worth planning to avoid.

Going back to Cambridge was strange for Carys. Less so today than the first time a few years ago when they'd travelled to inspect halls of residence for Ebe.

A proud Diane and Geraint came along then, and thought it might be nice to show Ebe where his mum had grown up. They'd parked in the driveway of Nutters, and were appalled unanimously at its new pink colour. The house in Royston had not provided similar distaste, but to Carys, the memories were unpleasant to say the least.

No detours through her home town were planned on this trip, but she anticipated the same odd feeling when they drove past it on the motorway.

The traffic crawled round the one-way system of Narberth and the couple remained silent. She was sure Marco must be pleased with how she'd coped with the loss of her mother. He hadn't demonstrated pride, but perhaps that was because he'd not wanted to pre-empt things: to put ideas in her head.

Communication had been lacking for some time, truth be told, Carys mused. They went for romantic meals together; they demonstrated unity at church and work functions, but in reality, they'd grown apart.

Ebe hadn't been the most loving child. He'd insisted throughout his childhood upon calling Marco by name, despite plenty of encouragement from them both to call him Daddy.

They tried for children of their own, but there seemed to be a problem with Marco's reproductive capabilities. Help with IVF and even adoption hadn't got very far because of Carys's sectioning and ongoing mental health problems.

It must have left Marco feeling unfulfilled and resentful, Carys supposed. Carys in return felt guilty, and had reacted badly to Marco making her feel that way. It was a chasm that had become difficult to bridge.

It was too late now to expect Ebe would ever

call Marco Daddy, but he had long since become resigned to the fact. Carys hoped he was immensely proud of his stepson, and he certainly couldn't have treated him any better if he had been his own.

It would be good if they could talk. As the journey progressed it might become easier, but for now, Carys resolved to reside within her own thoughts. She thought back to Ebe...

After everyone agreed there was more to his developmental needs than a simple speech and language disorder, further appointments with specialists were made. It took an unfortunate while; eighteen months before they sat in front of a multi-disciplinary team, comprising a Consultant Paediatric Psychiatrist, Psychologist and Child Psychologist.

After an hour or so of asking questions (which they must have seen the answers to in the various forms they'd completed over the years already), a preliminary diagnosis of Autistic spectrum disorder, possibly vying towards Asperger's syndrome, was offered.

Whilst they were curious about Ebe's unusual appearance, they seem to have ruled out any condition that fit that and his developmental issues together, because they simply knew of none.

Nothing happened as a result of the diagnosis, apart from a small amount of financial assistance, and the occasional holiday camp break being taken at the tax-payer's expense. Ebe's education remained much the same.

As he began GCSE studies, he was provided with a lap-top computer as his hand-writing became less and less legible and caused him more and more distress. The Asperger's label at least gained him help, where without it he would have been admonished for his messiness.

They became excited at the idea of him doing his exams early. He certainly had the skills. But he wasn't able, or willing, to apply those skills to questions asked of him in exams, or even in the classroom. He seemed capable of almost any sort of mathematical conundrum if it related to something he wanted to know, yet unable of anything that didn't directly concern his immediate requirements.

It was all part of the Asperger's condition, apparently. Instead of taking exams early, he ended up struggling to gain much in the way of qualifications, and had even been allotted extra time to complete what he did achieve.

Whilst his speech was remained poor, it seemed related mainly to a lack of desire to communicate rather than a reduced vocabulary. He could read a very thick book in one five hour sitting, and was a zealous stickler for grammar. As such he passed English with ease. Along with passes in the sciences, he gained a fantastic grade in Maths, so much so that the prestigious Cambridge University had offered him his place.

There had been tears when Ebe moved to Cambridge. His Asperger's diagnosis granted him a direct payment scheme where carers based in the city came and cooked for him, and, it amused Carys to think, help him tie his shoelaces. A feat he was destined never to master.

Leaving his mum behind was another matter however, and Carys had made the long journey to Cambridge on the train lots of times, just so Ebe could have a cuddle.

She had liked being needed. But over time, as Ebe became busier with his studies, he fell more and more in love with maths and seemed not to need Carys at all anymore. She choked back her sadness at how distant he'd become. Holidays from term time, which Ebe had always yearned for, to be home in the loving bosom of his family, had been missed more and more.

He'd stayed at university one Easter because of the work load, and then the summer holidays too. It had been a struggle to persuade him home even for Christmas. It was what every parent wanted, and also dreaded, for their children. Her little boy had definitely grown up.

Incredibly, he had obtained a Ph.D. in pure mathematics, and later, a masters in applied mathematics, for which the graduation ceremony was tomorrow, and for which they were travelling this evening. Carys felt pride and excitement for the coming events, but it covered an underlying anxiety about Ebe's future plans.

Her fear was not that he wouldn't find work, but more that he'd find it all too easily, and it might be very far afield. He'd already received offers from scientific institutions in the United States, Russia, Germany, and even India and South Korea. Carys fought back tears as she thought of how little she might see her son. She spoke in a controlled monotone. "Where do you think he'll go after tomorrow?" she managed to utter.

As Marco edged towards the roundabout on the by-pass for Carmarthen, he considered his answer. "You can't molly-coddle him, babe," he said affectionately. But really, he wanted to side-step the topic threatening to breach the surface of calm that existed tenuously in the Paulo-Ellis household. "He'll do whatever he wants. We need to make sure we put his needs first, and offer him advice that reflects that. Whatever's going to make him happy? Yes?"

Carys could only nod, too choked to verbalise her agreement. Of course, Marco was right. They had no choice but to support Ebe. She could hope that what he wanted to do was to work very close to his mother though, couldn't she?

They drove on in silence for a while, past Carmarthen and Cross Hands and on to the M4 motorway. Carys stared out of the window at the changing scenery. The foothills of Black Mountain and the mountains around Swansea and Port Talbot stood in defiance against the heavy industrial scape of the steel works with their metal pipes and chimneys scratching the sky, spitting flames like shiny cylindrical dragons.

Still silent, Carys was grateful for the, "Look at that," direction from Marco as they sped past Kenfig sand dunes that had buried a village a long time ago. The spire of the village church could still be seen poking through the sand like the mast of a tall ship sailing through the dessert.

Having gained the most animated response of the journey, Marco decided enough time had passed to broach a touchy subject. "Once Ebe has decided where he wants to go, we can decide on our plans, can't we?"

"I won't want to leave Wales, Marco. I've just lost my mum. My dad needs me, and Ebe will need a base, wherever he ends up working." Carys fidgeted in her seat. "You don't know how he'll cope being away from home. University halls is still institutional. It's not the same as proper grown up living on his own. You can be so insensitive sometimes!"

"He seemed to settle perfectly well in Cambridge. And institutional as it may be, he's done better than you said he would. You just can't stand that he doesn't need you anymore." He was tired of putting first the wishes of his wife whose son had never called him Daddy, and who herself had never ordained to even share his name.

The pride he'd felt when she'd first agreed to

going for a coffee with him, and then when she agreed to marry him had kept him going. Still incredibly beautiful, he'd often receive envious looks from other male diners whenever they went out to restaurants and other social gatherings, and he'd give a knowing smile. But it was bravado. In truth their intimacy had never felt that. Her first experience being involuntary seemed to have affected her forever; understandably, but it still left Marco feeling distant.

And now he had been offered an opportunity for a different life in Alaska. Away from any other distractions they might build on a new closeness. Wilderness and self-sufficiency was the dream he tried to sell his wife, but she made excuse after excuse why she couldn't.

There had been a time when she'd had tentatively gone along with the idea, but recent events had made her more homely. Silence prevailed on the journey as neither wanted to rattle the other's cage. They passed the capital and then Newport. They were rapidly approaching the first major milestone of the mammoth drive to Cambridge.

The impressive Second Severn Crossing loomed into view. It was Carys's cue to exercise her vocal cords. She was determined to sing, as she always did when she crossed into England. She always would have with her mum and dad, and now it was a point of principal. She didn't expect Marco to join her after his going on about leaving

Wales, and she was correct.

He allowed her to finish singing of her Hiriaeth - home sickness, and how a welcome would be kept in the valleys before snorting his retort.

"I always sing that song as I leave Wales, and so does my Dad," Carys cried.

"You say we can't move to Alaska because your dad might need you?"

"That was one of the reasons. Ebe might need to touch base occasionally."

"He might, but he hasn't really needed to while he's been in Cambridge, has he? As for your dad. He's planning a trip back-packing around South East Asia! He's been bending my dad's ear about it for weeks. He doesn't want to be in the house without your mum; says he finds it impossible. So, there's no actual good reason we can't go." He drummed the steering wheel anticipating an objection.

He looked away from the road to glance at his wife. Her eyes were moist and glassy. The tears she held back, painfully apparent. Marco softened his tone.

"Sorry if I spoke out of turn. I just thought you should know. When you've been saying how you wanted to be here for your dad and Ebe, and I knew that neither of them wanted or needed you to, it annoyed me. That was unfair, though. I know you mean well."

A tear found its way from Carys's eye and trickled down her nose dripping noisily onto her handbag in her lap. Marco reached out and squeezed her leg. She grasped his hand for comfort and they were good. For a while.

Dusk fell as they drove further into England. It coincided with the scenery become blander. Carys pressed the buttons on the car stereo until she found music she liked. A few songs into her listening, as though a higher power wished to pique her distress, ABBA played. Memories of her mum flooded intolerably into her mind and she crumpled.

Marco did his best to comfort her, and debated stopping the car. Being on the motorway made that impossible and he opted for further squeezing of her leg.

Unresponsive, she appeared to have moved into one of her catatonic states. Marco had to remain calm and concentrate on the road ahead. He was becoming tired and couldn't allow any distraction or the stress of worrying about his wife's mental state.

After a while driving without looking at her, he risked a quick glance. Her eyes were closed, and she appeared to be sleeping. He relaxed into the drive more as he made the turn for the M25 London Orbital motorway. The music carried on blaring distractingly through the speakers, but Marco left it playing. He thought Carys might value the rest. Grief was something no-one really knows how to deal with, but he'd seen plenty of sufferers seek the church over the years, and expected the distraction might help.

His own thoughts turned practical and he was pleased that, as planned, he had timed the journey just right to miss the motorway rush hour, and before long he was turning off again onto the M11 motorway that would take them to Cambridge and their hotel for the night. Darkness was falling fast and Marco was feeling all the more fatigued for it.

On and on they travelled, north from London towards Cambridge. The M11 had still not benefited from street lamps along most of its length. Marco, took the turn towards the city which were the directions indicated by the hotel's website. They wouldn't reach the city centre and its charming aged architecture until the next day, but the hotel looked lovely in the photos. He hoped Carys would still be in a mood to enjoy it after their spats along the way.

"Are we nearly there?" she asked with her eyes still closed.

"Nearly!" Marco declared enthusiastically.

Carys, noting Marco's placatory tone, allowed herself to open her eyes, ready to enjoy the night and coming day, proud in her boy's success. "What's the name of the hotel again?"

"The Felix, or something. It's an attractive country house just outside the city." The roads twisted a little more as they drove out of suburbia. "It's not long now."

Carys nodded. Fully open eyes appeared to be

playing tricks on her. She had become accustomed to a lack of light pollution, she knew.
South West Wales population was tiny compared
to here, but surely that couldn't account for the
light sky she was seeing now.

Peering hard through the window, perhaps expecting some vast industrial estate or retail park
to have been built since her last visit, all she
could see were country houses and a few street
lamps. The city wasn't like Swansea or Cardiff or
many other of the British cities with bright lights
and tall constructions. The countless listed
buildings ensured that.

And then she heard the unmistakable sound of
the hum. Panic flooded her body with a fight or
flight injection of adrenaline. Her mouth filled
with saliva that warded off the bitter bile that
squeezed into her, a manifestation of the dread
she had never learned to control. The door handle escaped her fevered tapping as the car felt
like a trap she must escape before her hands responded to the screaming logic that it was probably a lot safer whizzing along in a metal box
than outside. With a gulp, she breathed deeply
and shuddered against sudden cold. "Do you hear
that?" Marco may have responded, her thoughts
were racing too fast to comprehend, but she
felt unanswered. It had to be a helicopter flying
an emergency into Addenbrookes Accident and
Emergency Department, she forced herself to believe. But not for long.

Through the windscreen it was clearly visible; the size of a football pitch and oval in shape. Lines of red lights glowed, not a regular pattern, more randomly functional, like a flying city. As it moved closer, she was certain she was staring at the underside of a huge spaceship.

Did the shape change? Or was it just so large, and so close to them now that the form had become indiscernible. Glancing at Marco, his calm countenance made her flinch almost as much as seeing the craft.

"You can see that, right?" she asked, seriously concerned for her sanity if he couldn't. If she'd been calmer, she'd have seen his expression betray his dilemma of whether to toy with her or not. He decided not to.

"Yes. Of course, I can see it. It's bloody massive!" he said, but he didn't seem at all afraid. Mocking laughter filled the cockpit of the car. "It's not real, you silly girl!" she looked at him bewildered. "It'll be one of the student balls. Just a laser show, or a holographic display. You remember? Like they did at Oakwood theme park that time? Over the lake?"

Her failure to answer was not because she couldn't remember, but because she could. The display of laser projected holograms onto dry ice pumping over the water was impressive, spellbinding even, but it lacked realism. Whilst she had been impressed, she had not been fooled.

As if answering her unspoken disbelief Marco

added,

"Of course, this is a little better done. There's a lot of money available to these big universities from businesses courting the best students for job commitments."

Whether that had any basis in truth, Carys didn't know. It seemed unlikely businesses would spend more money than a theme park on a simple student ball. What would be the point? Who was Marco trying to kid? Could he be just so unwilling to believe anything she told him, he'd excuse the very obvious right in front of him? He wouldn't be the first to deny the truth because it didn't suit him, and he wouldn't be the last. What could she do? What if they had come for Ebe again, could she do anything? She knew the answer was no. Nothing. Her face glowed hot, now. If she kept raging from one extreme to the other she feared she would snap as surely as copper fragment in a spent bulb.

"You must let Ebe go," Marco interjected.

What was he bringing that up again for? Carys glared. Did he suppose pressuring her to move to Alaska, while a god-knows-what hovered terrifyingly above their heads, would take her mind from it?

As they continued to the hotel, the enormous craft seemed just as close, reminding Carys of how the moon always appears the same no matter where you travel. How big was this thing?

She allowed herself a tentative glimpse through

trembling fingers to look firmly at it, fear making it as difficult to bear as staring at the sun. It could be man-made, she decided. Not a hologram as Marco suggested, but something. She imagined a bushman seeing a helicopter; he'd be terrified, wouldn't he? Because he wouldn't know what it was? If this behemoth flying craft was some secret new invention, it shouldn't make it something to fear.

She forced her gaze to examine it further. As she peered, she could make out windows where they were close enough; and then figures, moving behind what she still assumed to be glass.

It was too far to be absolutely certain, but to Carys's eyes they were not human figures. They were the same creatures who had visited her all her life; now clearly here for all to see.

The smell of sweat made her wince and she became aware of her blouse clinging to her back and she rolled her shoulders to free it and ease the tension. She felt the juddering before she saw it, and when she looked, her hands were shaking violently. It was too much. She clawed at the handle of the door again. Of course, opening it would be a bad idea at even the reduced speed the car was forced to travel on these windy roads on the rural outskirts of the city, so it may have been good fortune her quivering hands proved too weak and clumsy to be effective.

She slumped heavily back in her seat, pushing back hard into it with her feet planted firmly on the floor of the car's foot-well. Trying to achieve nothing that made any sense, she fought against her own physicality as though she didn't recognise from where a threat could come.

A glance at her husband showed him smiling wryly as he drove, as if everything was totally normal. Was he whistling?

As she thrust back in her seat and peered at Marco, she jolted with alarm. A squeal escaped her lips as she couldn't trust her eyes. She shook her head, desperate to bring reality back. What she witnessed now couldn't be real.

Marco wasn't himself.

His features changed.

For a mere micro-second, he morphed into *something else.*

She couldn't tear her gaze away as his features morphed before her eyes. Aware of her staring, he stole a glance from the road towards her. His features immediately returned to normal, but Carys trembled, snot streaming from her as her unblinking eyes widened, keeping the threat in strict view and alert to peripheral peril as well. Marco saw her terror, and smiled broadly and, still looking directly at her, his features transformed once again.

At the first sign of the change, Carys's heart burst into overdrive, fuelling her desperate escape. As she strove to tear her eyes away from the morphing face of her husband, she clawed at the door handle with a panic that was unlikely to afford her success.

She kept scrabbling, and Marco kept smiling. His face now completely resembling that of a reptile.

Not a lizard, or a snake, more a reptilian human. Why he appeared this way Carys didn't have time to decipher. If she hadn't seen the change, she could almost believe it to be a joke. A mask from a film set, or something that he'd worn in some sick attempt at humour.

Her mind clutched any logical straw it could conceive, as sweating and shaking, Carys's terror consumed her.

As if to quell any doubts, Marco allowed his forked tongue to slither in and out of his scaly mouth.

Unable to run, she lunged at the monster that used to be her husband and punched him firmly in the jugular, the scaly neck absorbed the blow, a cold, smooth, armour. The car swerved, but it failed to have the debilitating effect of her past strikes and now she knew she was powerless.

Prizing her stare from his repugnant features long enough to be sure she had a firm grasp on the door handle, she yanked it hard, but the door failed to open. Marco had deployed the child lock, a feature operated by a switch on the driver's door.

Carys wrenched the door handle a few more times before her cramping brain allowed her the realisation of what must have happened. She lunged at the monster again, this time her furious fists struck at his large, lidless eyes. As her hand grazed the eye's roughness, she thought she must have hit out in vain, but he winced and she was certain she had caused him pain, so she frantically persisted, punch after punch to his vulnerability.

It was time for Marco to flail at buttons. Upon recognising the familiar click of the child-lock deactivating, Carys pushed hard with her feet against the centre console, simultaneously snatching the door open.

She thrust powerfully with her legs and launched herself from the car. Marco grabbed at her with reptilian webbed fingers, but he was too late. She was free of his grasp and free of the car.

With no thought to the speed they were travelling, or whether there was traffic ready to cut her down, she had to get away.

Sharp stones bit into her hands as she thrust them forward to protect her face. Tumbling over and over, thudding onto hard tarmac and softer grass of the verge she came to an agonised halt. Breathing hard, but definitely breathing she let out a cry of laughter. She had escaped, and she was free, but at what cost?

Her arms had broken her fall as she tumbled spectacularly into the ditch. Adrenaline stopped her feeling the worst of the pain, but she knew something wasn't right. Her head. Yes, there was definitely pain in her head, she managed to think before looking at the bright lights of the UFO. Or was it a police car? Or an ambulance?

She couldn't tell.

Her eyes closed, and she didn't care anymore.

CHAPTER THIRTY-FOUR

Carwyn is an Alien

Memories of the night were hazy. The looming face of a policeman peering at her; people asking her name; prodding and poking her as she lay immobilised, strapped to a bed.

She flinched at the memory. Was it them? Had it been *them* that had done things to her again? Suppressing a scream, she was petrified who would come in response to her cries.

The constant beep, beep, beep of a machine nearby and people, yes definitely people; not them, she was sure. Retching, recalling bland, tasteless food, brought her to her senses.

After jolting up to clear the choking, she slumped back down. She remembered where she was, and her thoughts stalled. She couldn't raise enough consciousness to be bothered. Her limbs lay motionless at her side as she muttered obscenities, she fell back asleep.

She stirred at a figure looming over her what could have been minutes, or hours later. "Come on. You're being moved today. Back to Wales. St Cara-dogs, to be precise."

"St Ca-radog's", Carys corrected the poor Welsh pronunciation, emphasising the penultimate syllable. She needn't ask what that meant. It was the secure mental health unit at Haverfordwest, back in Pembrokeshire. The mental health ward had recently been extended. There seemed to be a need for it.

Carys was guided groggily to a waiting ambulance. Someone helped her up the steps and strapped her into a chair where she promptly fell motionless again.

Her consciousness clawed its way back to the surface of her mind's mire just in time to see the tall struts of the big bridge - the bridge, across which, lay her home. But was it still a home anymore? Where was Ebe? Where was Marco?

A sudden recollection of his last appearance to her made her scream out, legs flailing in a futile attempt of escape.

"Pipe down, you. Do you need another shot?" the menacing sneer of her chaperone threatened.

"We'll keep a welcome in the hillside…" Forcing the words through parched lips, she was determined not to be repressed.

"Pipe down, I said!"

She mumbled the rest of the song welcoming her back to Wales under her breath with tears streaming down her face. They crossed the bridge, and the toll was paid to allow them entry to the Principality.

She was in trouble again, wasn't she? Just as she had been more than twenty years ago when she'd traversed the vast Severn estuary to her new home

"Did I miss my son's graduation?" she spluttered.

"I have absolutely no idea. Now hush, will you? I'm trying to do a crossword here," the crewman grumbled. As tears streamed down Carys's face, tissues were fanned in her face along with instructions to blow her nose.

The scenery flashing past now failed to inspire her as it had on the opposite journey yesterday. Was it yesterday even, or some day in the past? She didn't bother asking. The ambulance crew wouldn't know; she wasn't sure she could cope with knowing either.

They arrived, after several hours, at the familiar buildings of Withybush General Hospital, and a new renal unit. Opposite that, bright and new, almost cheery, stood Bro Cerwyn day centre for the mentally ill; its cheer, a vain attempt to inject optimism into the patients. Beyond that, the secure mental health facility didn't bother with such niceties.

Carys peered at the barred windows and wondered which would be her home, and for how long. "Why am I here? How long am I expected to stay?" she asked with a child-like innocence. The prick of tears burned the back of her eyes. Why *was* she here? If she didn't know what had led to her being forced to stay here, how could she know what she had to get better from to be allowed to leave.

"You'll have to ask the doctor when you see him. Now come on. Don't dawdle."

Carys did as she was told. She had no fight left in her. Stood with the driver and the other crewman in the foyer of the ward, they exchanged words with the nurse behind the glass window. A small flap opened like the parcel pass-through of a post office, and some paperwork was passed through.

The same nurse, wearing everyday street clothes of jeans, trainers and a hoody, came out, typed something into the keypad and the door slid open.

"Hello, Carys. We're all ready for you," she declared, before turning to the ambulance crew. "Thank you. We'll take it from here."

They left without word to Carys. No well-wishing, and no good bye. Carys couldn't care less. She preferred the calm woman before her than the morose company she'd been forced to keep for the past seven hours.

"Come on," she smiled. "Let's get you settled in." Carys followed her into the corridor.

Suddenly, a tall man, probably in his late thirties, burst from a door, guitar at his chest, greasy brown locks curling into his eyes as he shook hair from his face. Strumming loudly whilst devoid of talent, the noise he produced was more than unpleasant, but at least it went some way to drown out the shrieking of his vocal proffering. He strutted up and down the corridor as though performing to an adoring crowd.

The nurse with Carys walked on un-phased. When the guitar legend made level with them, he thrust out a friendly hand for Carys to shake. She took it reluctantly.

"Hello, I'm Mike," he declared. "Do you like music?" he asked, as if what he had been playing related to music in some way.

"Er, no. I'm okay thanks," replied Carys, not wanting to encourage another un-musical outburst.

She continued ambling with the nurse, leaving a despondent Mike standing in her wake. She followed the nurse into a small room. When the door was closed, she heard Mike's guitar mutilating cacophony revive.

"Now then, Carys. My name is Andrea. I'm one of the psychiatric nurses here." She glanced down at paper on a clipboard. "You'll continue on the chlorpromazine 1000mg until Doctor Lewis's ward round on Monday. Your room is just being checked, and then I'll take you down there." Carys stared blankly. Andrea continued, undeterred.

"I have a few things for you to sign, and then

I can show you around if you like?" She thrust some papers towards Carys.

"What are these?"

"Just papers agreeing to access your medical notes, that type of thing. We don't want to give you medication that won't agree with you, now do we?"

Carys's hand hovered, holding the pen above the page. "And if I don't sign?"

The nurse shrugged. "It'd be best if you did… Avoid any unpleasantness." She smiled.

Lips pressed together, Carys closed her eyes and squiggled mainly in the box over which her hand had lingered.

"Thank you." Andrea reached to take them and slotted them into a file which she gripped hold of. "I'll show you where you can wait until we finalise your room," she said, leading her to a room near the front door containing a pool table and a television, and in the darkest recess, a shelf with some dog-eared books and tatty board games.

A shudder clutched Carys's heart at a childhood memory of a very similar room from one of her mother's falls from sanity. Now she'd never see her again. The spike of emotion crippled her. Dropping to the floor, she broke into uncontrollable sobs.

"What is it Carys, bach?" Andrea asked, bending over her. Carys sobbed silently. A primal yell emanated piercingly from her lungs as she let out a cry that had been trapped too long.

"I want my mummy!" she screamed, repeating the cry over and over.

Andrea called short the tour, and getting the nod that her room was ready, took her promptly there. "I'll go and get your medication for you. I don't think you'll be up for queuing with the rest of them tonight."

Carys lay on the bed, foetal, waiting for the kind nurse to return with her pills. It wasn't long before she arrived with a cup of water and a smaller cup containing a few tablets. Carys took them greedily, as if they were the answer to all her problems.

Andrea helped her put on some pyjama's that she didn't recognise as being her own, and invited her to settle down. She reassured she'd be around if Carys needed her, and with that, she left Carys to her woes.

She lay on the bed and waited for the medication to take the edge off her pain, and to allow her sanctuary of sleep once more.

Jolting back to full alertness, the door to her room banged against the wall as it flew open, and in walked a rather short gentleman of senior age. In a thick Welsh accent he announced "Carwyn is an alien. Carwyn is an alien!" before dropping his trousers and urinating on the floor.

Carys screamed at him "Get Out!"

"Carwyn is an alien," he insisted, turning from side to side, spreading the foul liquid liberally.

A male CPN and another female nurse rushed in, muttering their apologies and ushering Carwyn from the room.

"Come on now, Carwyn. You mustn't do that."

"Do you want to pop down to the rec room whilst we clean this up?" the female winced at her. Carys had little choice. "I'm so sorry," the female nurse apologised. "It used to be his room, you see."

As an explanation, Carys felt it lacked satisfaction, but nodded and smiled her understanding nevertheless. The new nurse showed her down to the rec room, which was the room she'd seen earlier with the pool table. It was empty, and she had to fumble around for the light switch.

Shuffling over to the squalid sofa, she peered at it before deciding its stained grubby fabric was not something she'd like to touch. She seethed at the sickening filth, not just of the couch, but of the reason she was stood facing it – fresh and pungent urine.

The room was plunged into darkness. And then the lights flickered on again; then off, then on again.

"Leave the bloody light switches alone, Raymond!" it was Mike's voice again, mercifully this time, without his guitar to accompany him. Carys looked up at who had been messing with the light switch to see a slight built man of restricted height. A pointy beard gave him the appearance of a wizard or an elf. Raymond replied in an indiscernible mumble that still managed to convey his displeasure.

"You get out, you!" Mike ordered in what seemed to Carys an unreasonably aggressive tone. He used his arm to guide Raymond from the room. Raymond left under the coercion, and proceeded down the corridor switching on and off and on and off any light switch he passed along the way.

"He's my brother, he is," Mike garbled "I'm sorry about him. I'm Mike," he thrust out his hand again. Carys reluctantly shook it for the second time.

"Yeah. I'm sorry about him," he repeated. Carys reassured it was okay. She didn't care about the lights.

"He doesn't look like your brother," she commented. Mike insisted he was, and seemed hurt at Carys's scepticism.

"Never let 'im get you in a corner!" he blurted from nowhere. "He'll 'av you by the throat!" he hissed, hidden behind his hand. Carys's first thought was, whilst that would be unpleasant, she felt sure she could overpower the weedy little man. "He's stronger than he looks," Mike declared, as though privy to her thoughts.

Slouched over the pool table, he pushed what balls were still present from the majority of absentees, from one end of the table to the other.

"You like to play pool?" he muttered, setting the scant remains into the surprisingly present triangle.

"Okay," she agreed. He looked delighted.

"You'll never beat me," he announced proudly. Carys didn't care. It was still a distraction.

After a few shots, it became clear Mike's prediction of invincibility was wildly exaggerated. He was quite hopeless. Connecting the cue with the white ball was dexterity which escaped Mike. Coaxing it in the right direction to strike another ball of the appropriate colour, and guide that ball into any of the pockets, looked unlikely ever to happen.

Carys, who had until now felt lacking in pool skills, was winning effortlessly. Watching Mike's growing agitation she decided she should probably let him win when he dug his fingernails into his face whilst letting out a tormented squeal of anguish.

As his fingers returned to the cue handle, blood trickled down his face in dirty lines, giving him the appearance of a horror film poster.

Mike perked up quickly as Carys struggled to let him win. She decided it would take forever for Mike to pot all the balls. He kept miscuing and insisting Carys take the extra penalty shots won from his fouls. Eventually, her own skill severely wanting, she managed to pot the black and then the cue ball into the same pocket, immediately forfeiting the game. Mike beamed.

"I told you you wouldn't beat me. I always win." He began chalking his cue again. "Best of three?"

he offered. Carys was horrified.

"No, no. You're too good for me," she blurted. "I hate losing."

"I'll go easy on you, if you like," Mike offered magnanimously. Carys struggled to stifle her own distress when she was rescued, sort of, by another figure entering the rec room.

At first she assumed the nurse had returned, coming to tell her the room was clean—a disadvantage of staff wearing no uniform—it didn't take long to work out who the patients were, though. This particular woman made it clear by loudly proclaiming herself to be God.

She invited Carys to pray to her and was very offended by her reluctance. She was then torn away by another distraction, the entrance of Carwyn announcing himself to be an alien again. Mike and 'God' flew for him, forcing him back into the corridor.

"Don't you piss in here, you stupid fucker!" Mike yelled at him. 'God' was compelling him to leave in the power of her name (which Carys thought she heard was actually Helen) and inviting him to kneel before her for forgiveness.

They forced him into the corridor where he was intercepted by Raymond who grabbed him by the throat and proceeded to try to choke him to death.

It took four nurses, three of them hefty looking men, to prize weedy Raymond's hand from Carwyn's oesophagus. Once they prevailed, one of them helped Carwyn limp, choking the while, to a side room whilst the others tried to subdue Raymond.

He skipped out of their grasp and ran back down the corridor, finding the time, still, to fumble with every light switch as he went.

Carys couldn't stay here. She would speak to the doctor, and find out how she could get back home. And then she remembered home, with no Ebe, no mum, a dad planning to leave the country because he couldn't deal with the memories in his marital home; and a hideous reptilian husband. Where even was home for her now?

CHAPTER THIRTY-FIVE

The Visitor

Carys was called into a small room for Doctor's ward round sometime after breakfast, having stayed in her room after the events of the nights before. "Come in, Carys. Take a seat," the soft spoken doctor invited. "Are you settling in okay?" he asked.

Carys burst into tears. He didn't try to stop her, but passed her a tissue to wipe her eyes and blow her nose.

When sobs subsided, he carried on as though it had never happened. "I'm Doctor Lewis," he introduced. "I want to get a sense of how you're feeling, so we can decide what treatment is going to be most appropriate for your rehabilitation." Carys nodded. "So, how *are* you feeling?"

Carys had no answer. She shrugged.

"You're on quite a high dose of chlorpromazine at the moment. Do you know why?"

Carys shrugged a second time.

"You had a bit of a violent outburst, didn't you? Do you remember?"

Carys remembered the UFO, and Marco's metamorphosis. She didn't know how to put it into words, so she shrugged again.

Undeterred, Doctor Lewis explained for her. "Your husband says you're troubled with visions of extra-terrestrials? That you even believed *he* was an extra-terrestrial. Is that right?" he asked calmly.

Carys was about to answer that it was right, wondering if the most reasonable explanation wasn't that she'd hallucinated everything. But then a thought struck her. "How did Marco know I thought he was an alien? A reptile to be precise?" she demanded. "I never said to him *why* I had to get away from him. How did he know?"

Doctor Lewis looked unperturbed by her outburst, and suggested that perhaps she'd accused him of being an alien, but didn't remember. Carys sighed. There seemed little point arguing it was real. No-one would ever believe her.

"I think I'll try you on Quetiapine. It works as an anti-depressant combined with a mood stabiliser and anti-psychotic in one. I'm not sure if your symptoms present as bipolar, or not, but I can see you are prone to depression. We know you're susceptible to psychotic episodes, and they seem linked to your depression, but perhaps more to your anxiety," he conveyed in a monotone.

"I see from your notes you've had 'borderline personality disorder' mentioned to you before. The hallucinations, and ultimately your psychosis could be connected to that." He closed the file and seemed to be preparing to excuse Carys, so she felt compelled to ask.

"How long will I have to stay here?"

Doctor Lewis remained silent for a while. He leaned back in his chair as steepled fingers prodded his chin, as though the question was a new concept to him. He sighed before speaking. "Well. It will take a while for the medication to take effect. Give it some time and we'll talk again."

"But I don't need to stay here for the medicine to work, do I? I feel okay now, apart from the fact that everybody here is nuts!"

Doctor Lewis reddened, stumbling on his words. "Carys. You are not here *voluntarily*."

A gulp dried her mouth and she sat speechless. Why hadn't that occurred to her? Of course, she wasn't! She wasn't here after a long-drawn-out fall from sanity. Just a rapid disagreement about what sanity is, because she was still absolutely sure she had it right.

There *had* been a spaceship, and Marco *had* shown a side to himself she'd never seen before. But it sounded crazy. Even to Carys, it sounded crazy

Gratitude for a change in medication was the only glimmer of hope. Perhaps that would provide the answer.

"You have been sectioned under the mental health act." Raising her eyes to the ceiling, she had gathered that already. "Until we deem that you are safe to be allowed out, or there is some-one willing to care for you at home… well, like I say; give the medication a chance to work, and we'll see."

Carys got up silently and left the room.

Helen/God stood along the corridor arguing with the coffee machine. Frantically pressing buttons, her hair wafted in the movement of her burgeoning rage. "Bloody thing!" she screamed, grabbing the brightly coloured machine in both hands and shaking it from side to side.

"Leave it alone, Helen," one of the female CPN's ordered. She walked over and pressed buttons, as if Helen might have been doing it wrong. "I'll have to call someone. Shaking it won't do any good," she admonished. "Go and use the kettle for now." As she walked away, Helen stuck her fingers up behind her back and mouthed some obscenities.

She saw Carys approach and indicated for her to follow her. Helen put the kettle on in the small kitchen for patients, and leaned back on the worktop, arms folded.

"What are you in for?" she asked, making it sound like a prison sentence. Carys shook her head and shrugged. Satisfied for now, Helen began to tell her story. "I've been in this shit-hole for... how many years is it? Probably getting on for ten," she answered her own question. Carys swayed in her disbelief.

"What on earth has kept you here for so long?"

"I'm not safe on my own. That's what they say. I get delusions of grandeur, suddenly think I can fly and stuff. I've been pretty messed up."

A huge crashing noise stopped them dead. Peering from the safety of the kitchen, they could see down the corridor through the small wired window in the door.

The coffee machine lay on its side. A large man was being wrestled to the floor by two other men. Carys gawped as an injection was produced and stabbed into the man's leg. His struggling abated, and he groggily accompanied the other men away from the corridor through key coded doors to the secure rooms.

"He always has to break everything!" Helen fumed.

Without further word, she shuffled away to another side room, leaving Carys alone in the kitchen. Helen hadn't offered her a drink. She probably would have declined. No-one here assumed hygiene standards sufficiently to relish them touching anything she was about to put to her mouth. Rinsing an already washed cup under the tap, she re-boiled the kettle, and as she turned to find teabags, she heard someone enter the room.

"Do you want a cuppa?" she asked whoever it was, without looking round.

"Carwyn is an alien," the other occupant announced.

"Do you ever say anything else?" Carys muttered.

"Carwyn is an alien," he repeated, wandering from the kitchen again. The kettle boiled and Carys popped a teabag in her cup, and spooned in a couple of sugars.

She heard Carwyn re-enter the room, but didn't bother speaking. As she turned to fetch the milk from the fridge she was startled not to see Carwyn, but Raymond standing there.

He began fiddling with the light switch. Carys ignored him and opened the fridge. There was a small dribble of semi-skimmed in a four-pint bottle. As she closed the door and turned back towards her cup, Raymond's hand thrust forcefully into her neck. Carys grabbed at his arm with both hands to prize him off, but he was too strong. Eyes bulging, she could see her life slipping away. How was he so strong?

As he choked the life from her, she grabbed around instinctively for something to hit him with. It was her only hope. Her hand grasped something, and she thrust it round to hit him before she'd realised what it was.

As the object arced in the air to make contact with Raymond's head, Carys flinched at a burn from scalding splash. Raymond squealed out in agony as the full kettle of near boiling liquid emptied over him.

Releasing his grip at once, Carys shoved him away, rubbing at her throat, gasping for air. She made it almost to the door when she was blocked.

"Carwyn is an alien. Carwyn is an alien."

"Oh, fuck off, Carwyn," yelled Carys, before suddenly feeling very light-headed and drowsy. She hadn't seen the needle, nor felt it penetrate her leg and relinquish its liquid load. Staggering forward, supported by two indiscriminate figures either side, she recognised the route.

She wasn't going back to her room, which used to be Carwyn's, but the other side of the key coded door. The secure section. Soon she would wonder no more what secrets it held. As the doors opened, her limbs lost all function, and the nurses dragged her through.

She was woken by the aroma of food on a tray. The secure section seemed much the same as her usual room, except there was no storage to keep sharp objects, and no privacy through the glass wall.

While she ate a surprisingly tasty curry and rice, she was watched. It was in the guise of company, but Carys knew the CPN wasn't sitting on the edge of her bed for fun. When she had finished, she made to clear away the plates and cutlery. "I'll come along a bit later and take you outside, if you like."

Carys nodded. "Raymond attacked *me*. I was

just defending myself," she grumbled her indignant explanation.

"We do know. We have cameras everywhere. Having seen the situation unfold, we were on our way to assist, but your way of dealing with it, well, we have our concerns."

Days of the same solitary confinement passed before she returned to her former room. She didn't care. Time away from the other patients, particularly at meal times, was welcome. They hadn't proved to be the most relaxing dinner companions. Thrown food, tossed tables and loud shouting from less than pleasant smelling comrades wasn't something she wanted to get used to.

She was beginning to give up hope of her lot improving when a nurse popped into her room.

"You've got a visitor. Follow me." Carys gladly followed all the way down the corridor, through more key coded doors and to the interview rooms. Anticipation of who it could be turned to distress when she saw the familiar figure of her husband waiting behind the glass.

The nurse unlocked the door, this time with a key and encouraged Carys inside. She went in with her, beamed at Marco, and announced that she'd leave them to it. Before Carys could even think to object, she was alone with Marco in edgy quiet.

"Are you okay?" he asked.

Carys didn't know what to think or what to say. Was he the person who had supported her for twenty plus years, or was he... what she saw that night?

"Are you settling in alright?" he asked. Carys looked sardonically at him before answering.

"No! It's horrible. I don't know what I'm doing here." Marco looked thoughtful. "Do you remember what happened? You attacked me whilst I was driving, and then threw yourself from the car. You narrowly escaped being killed by an on-coming Range Rover!" Carys didn't remember much and raised her eyebrows in mock concern.

"You were pretty hurt. You told the ambulance men I was an alien! That a massive UFO flew overhead, and that I had morphed into a reptile! Insane!" he added gauchely

They sat in uncomfortable silence for a while before Marco revealed his true purpose. "The reason I came to see you today... well... promise you won't flip out?"

Carys promised nothing.

"Well. Enough of this nicey, nicey nonsense," he declared. "Just to let you know, I've filed for divorce. I was reluctant. I didn't know how my father and the church would react, but they are all in agreement that you have made things impossible. We couldn't possibly carry on."

Carys was stunned. She stifled tears and looked away from his gaze.

"Furthermore, I will be moving to Alaska."

Marco smiled. "The opportunity is too compelling and I've decided I have to take it." A cold stare challenged her as he added, "You won't like this, but Ebe is coming with me."

"What?" Carys stood, desperate to run, or to lash out at her cruel tormentor, but with nowhere to go and fear that any threatening behaviour would hurt her more than Marco, she sat slowly down, defeated as blood rushed from her head, robbing her of the impetus. "Why?" she said at last. "Why on earth would he do that?"

Marco bobbed his head from side to side and grinned. "It's not the tranquil, get-away-from-it lifestyle I suggested it was. In fact, I'll be working there on a project. And, Ebe will be a big part of that project. He is a genius you know."

Carys's thoughts raced. Too many questions, so she picked the most urgent, if not the most important. "Where does that leave me?"

Marco's smile turned to a cruel chuckle. "I think you're better off in here, don't you?"

Carys began to shake. It was too much. It couldn't be true, but she'd lost touch with what was real anymore.

Marco spoke over her objections. "You believe in aliens; that your own husband, soon to be ex-husband, of course, is an alien, and you've always said Ebe has a questionable father, haven't you. Oh yes. You're definitely better off staying here, no?" he said in a questioning tone, as if fishing for agreement.

"But, the least I owe you though, as I have condemned you, is the truth."

Carys's shaking stopped abruptly. Hairs on her arms and legs flattened from the erectness and a calmness enveloped her. This she had to hear.

"I know you think I haven't believed you and your alien nonsense all these years, but the truth... the *truth* is that it isn't nonsense. You are right. You were visited by creatures from another planet, another dimension as well, if you want to know. As was your mother. We were genetically acquiring Ebe. I love the name, by the way: Extra Biological Entity! Brilliant."

Faintness threatened to take her away. Gripping the arms of the chair so tight, the ends of her fingers were numb, her head spun but she pushed herself to focus on her husband.

"You weren't the only one. But you were *my* project."

"Project?" she mumbled. "Did you ever love me?!"

"Of course!" Marco sneered. "I still do love you. But it's difficult. Because, although you haven't imagined your alien encounters, you are still... unhinged. I don't like treading on eggshells, or worrying when you might attack me, or worse, attack yourself..." His tone lowered as he took a deep breath.

"You have been a liability over the years, but Ebe needed you." He shrugged and pursed his lips. "He doesn't need you anymore. It's time for him to fulfil his purpose, along with all the other 'Ebes' we've made."

"Other Ebes?" Carys breathed hard.

"Yes! Not as clever as my Ebe, and none of them with such an appropriate name, might I add. We are preparing for the supreme race to come again."

"What do you mean, *supreme race*? If they're so 'supreme' why do they need me?"

"A sensible question," Marco nodded. "They are indeed supreme. They're much closer to God than humans. They *know* God. They *use* God. And they've been here before, and utilised minerals, and left a legacy of structures like the pyramids around the world—all used to create a portal allowing them access."

Carys was unaccustomed to anyone else talking in this way. She struggled to ask the questions she'd had tormenting her brain for more than three decades "The pyramids are still intact. Why do they need Ebe?" she eventually asked.

"Ah! They aren't intact. And the Supreme Arian beings…"

"Arian!? You mean like Hitler, and the Nazi's, and their obsession with the Arian race?"

Marco chuckled. "There are no pure Arians here. Not without a disguise anyway. They're over seven feet tall!" he chuckled and slapped his legs, the crack as his hands hit the smooth fabric jolting Carys from her bilious brooding with a gulp.

He continued his explanation. "They use

maths. Everything of God is mathematical: from the shell of a snail, to the turning of the Earth and its distance from the Sun and the Moon, and it's the same story throughout the Universe. They use maths, but they don't understand it. Can you believe it? To them it's almost artistic. And they can't afford to be subjective. It's a very delicate operation. Terribly perilous for everyone concerned. And, Ebe, well, Ebe understands maths!"

"If Ebe is so good at maths because…" she couldn't bear to say his father, so instead, she settled on, "he is biologically predisposed. Then why can't they do the maths without interfering?"

"Oh, they can do the maths, but they lack a certain…" he frowned, "human understanding. They have no capacity for love. They're quite robotic. You know, like a computer can do maths, but it doesn't understand maths. It doesn't know why it's doing maths." He was in his stride now "Ebe has a passion for it. And passion is a very human trait. Now, fortunately, at least for the greater scheme of things – you probably wouldn't think so – The Arians find humans perfectly easy to manipulate. Wait. Manipulate is perhaps the wrong word… *educate*, to their way of thinking. My species, and the Greys, we get our own rewards that I won't go into now, if you don't mind," he said almost politely.

"Why have you not told me all this before? I've

been plagued for years and you knew all along, I was telling the truth?"

"Sorry my love. I shouldn't even be telling you now..."

"Why not?"

"Well, you see... One of the reasons the pyramids won't suffice anymore is that the Arians have evolved. They vibrate at a whole new rate now and... basically, you wouldn't be able to cope with the change of frequency. No human can. So, you might try to stop us."

It took a while to sink in. "No human?" Marco shrugged his sympathies. "No. I'm afraid not."

"Why don't I stop you now then." she announced. "I could tell someone..."

It sounded ludicrous even to her, and Marco guffawed to show his contempt at the idea. "We choose people with your 'condition' for two reasons, my love. Firstly, no-one will believe you. Example: There's a chap imprisoned here by the name of Carwyn, I don't know if you've met him?"

Carys nodded involuntarily, convinced by his charm.

"Well," Marco laughed, "Carwyn really is an alien! And he's been telling them for twenty years. No-one will trust a thing you say."

She knew he was right. "And the other reason?"

"The other reason," Marco seemed glad to impart, "is your high intelligence. It's like cross breeding any species: you start with traits you wish to enhance, and pick breeding pairs accordingly. Didn't you learn natural selection in your psychology courses?"

"Are you not worried Ebe would have gained my other attributes… my bipolar?" she asked.

"He's not exactly normal, now, is he?" he chuckled again. He put his hands up in placatory fashion. "Don't worry," he assured, "The father is so devoid of emotion, it was never a real concern, and, well, he's turned out just great."

Carys sat in stunned silence. She'd been used by these creatures her whole life. Since before her life had even begun. She felt as though any choice she'd ever made had been manipulated and tinkered with to bring results she didn't even understand.

Every decision she'd ever made had really been made for her. She felt a fool. Terrified beyond endurance to give birth to a son who ultimately would be the demise of the human race? Had she got that right?

"How could you do that?" she demanded indignantly "Why would you want to destroy humanity?"

"Ha!" Carys had barely finished speaking when Marco interjected. "*Destroy* humanity? We *made* humanity." He was shaking his head in rueful disdain. We *made* you from Neanderthals! Careful selective breeding again. I'm surprised you hadn't thought of that with your experiences and your intelligence!" he exclaimed.

Carys was at a loss for words.

"It's not *your* planet," Marco said with a sneer of contempt. "We've been here for thousands and thousands of years. Before you were even dreamed up!"

"What about Dan and Natalia?" Carys asked deliriously.

"Human. I wasn't always Marco. Or rather, Marco wasn't always me. We had to cobble together an alternative plan when Andy Walker let us down. Very unfortunate." It took a while for the name to register.

"Andy… Walker..? The boy who drowned?" Marco was nodding and smiling, like he was imparting celebrity gossip.

"That's right, you remember him, do you? Had quite a thing for you. We'd foreseen you getting together. Ebe growing up near Cambridge, with some of the best schools in the country on his doorstep. That was the plan. But needs must, eh?"

Carys was silent. What on earth did this all mean?

"We discovered he wasn't strong enough in plenty of time to come up with Marco, fortunately." Answering Carys's unasked question, he added. "We didn't kill him. He had an accident because he was weak, that was all. But Marco. He had it all. I've scarcely had to do anything. He came up with the whole, "Carys is possessed" thing. That bought us a few years.

"What do you mean? You aren't Marco?"

"I am now. Completely. But there were aspects of, let's say, the original Marco, that were very useful. It's called a walk-in. It happens all the time; and to far more well-known individuals than me. And you know who I really am, don't you, my love?"

Why was he calling her that? Who was her husband?

She had a dozen questions all pop into her head at once when she was prevented from asking them by Marco laughing hysterically. He was rolling in his chair, tears running down his cheeks.

"What's so fucking funny?" Carys demanded.

"Sorry. I was imagining you telling the staff here about our little chat!" he laughed uncontrollably again. "Sorry…sorry."

"I could find someone to listen. I've got plenty of time to write to anybody I choose," she blustered.

Marco looked taken aback, as though Carys speaking to anyone outside of the facility hadn't occurred to him. He looked sternly at her. "I would just deny everything, of course." He sniggered callously. "Seriously, Carys, you are such a fool. How do you know I haven't just been spouting the same crap I've had to listen to from you watching Discovery Channel for years? Maybe I've just told you all this to mess with your mind." He made a show of crossing his eyes ludicrously and circling his fingers around his temples. "To make the divorce easier. How do you know? Eh?" he prodded.

"Well. Have you?" she demanded. Nothing would surprise her now. "Why would you? You don't need to keep me in here to get a divorce. Why would I want to stay with you if you don't want me? It doesn't make any sense."

"It makes perfect sense," Marco maintained. "I think you'll see the prudence of it." He stood, and in front of Carys's eyes, he morphed instantly and intentionally into a grotesque, inhuman, reptilian creature.

Carys leaped from her chair, shuffling as fast as she could, never taking her eyes from him, she bumped the furthest corner of the room, legs still straggling to get away. Breath coming in rasps, she kicked and squealed, not knowing if she was hitting him, or even if he was near. The taste of iron made her retch as she realised she'd chewed threw her tongue in her panic, blood dripping from her mouth onto her legs.

Pain brought her back to her senses and she saw him, leering from across the room and she clambered up the corner to standing again, clenched her fists ready to fight

Marco rose far taller than his usual frame, his skin was light green and covered in scales. Edging toward her, he let his forked tongue slither in and out of his mouth a couple of times before he reached the edge of her striking zone.

She lashed out, but away from the confines of the cramped car, he was quick and too strong. Her own swiftness was just enough to avoid his scaly grip. She broke free, and hit him in the eyes as she had done in before. Caught off guard, he squealed in pain and she hit out again.

Luck, or super-human strength in the face of adversity, prevailed, and somehow, she knocked the huge creature to the floor just as the door flew open.

Three nurses rushed in and one of them jabbed her with a sharp needled again. As consciousness slipped away, she could hear profuse apologies given to Marco about how she'd been fine for days.

As she was led, supported down the corridor, she looked back at her husband. He was, of course, in human form again and smiling broadly. She knew she had just walked into his trap and he was extremely happy with himself.

CHAPTER
THIRTY-SIX

The truth at last

She was back in the secure unit, and delirious. Hitting her head, she had to remember; were there camera's that would support her wild claims and vindicate her? She asked one of the nurses if they had seen what had happened.

"There are cameras, but by law we have to make it clear to visitors that we're using them. Your visitor was adamant that we were not to watch or film. He cited religious reasons, and we were obliged to respect his wishes.

How convenient, thought Carys as the nurse left her to her disturbing thoughts.

She didn't cope with solitary confinement well this time. Memories of her ordeal with Marco flashed before her eyes whenever she allowed herself to attempt to rest. She was very clear that it had been real in one moment, and totally convinced she was completely deluded the next.

Her fellow patients all seemed utterly convinced by their self-created little worlds too, didn't they. Helen fervently believed she was God most of the time. Carwyn sincerely believed he was an alien (was he though, her mind stalled at trying to comprehend what that would mean?) and Mike believed he was a guitar playing, singing star, pool champion, when he was none of those things.

How can you tell if anything is real, she wondered? What makes it so? If you can see it and touch it but no-one else can, is it unreal? If a crowd, or even the whole world was fooled by the same illusion, did that make the one person seeing it differently wrong?

She wept. Unable to answer her own questions, she felt detached from reality, and didn't know what to do to make it better.

She fretted constantly. Day and night. Haunted by visions of aliens; of herself fighting The Amish man, and the Rebecca; hallucinations she feared weren't real. Sleep evaded her. The only rest she attained was induced by a myriad of medicine, and their effects were fading noticeably.

She cried constantly. Why wouldn't she? Her husband of over twenty years was actually a reptilian extra-terrestrial in disguise and was about to end humanity aided and abetted by her hybrid son. Or, she was as mad as Helen and Carwyn. That was what she'd grown to believe, and when she wasn't crying about it, she rocked in demented despair.

Unaware how long had passed; a week; a day; a month? She was called again to the interview room.

She had another visitor.

The walk along the corridor had her shaking already. She didn't have the strength for more attacks on her sanity.

She winced at smells she'd become acclimatised to; food debris, pungent, stale cigarette breath, bleach from constant cleaning of accident-prone patients, as they struck anew after her isolation. Her mind identified each one with a perverse joy like a child pointing out basic shapes.

It was all a distraction because every cell in her body knew another attack from Marco was the last thing she could cope with. But when she arrived at the door to the room, a sob of tentative delight cracked her chest; it was Ebe.

Rushing over, he stepped to meet her and she threw her arms around him with such vigour, the CPN rocked on her heels, concerned for a second that another incident was imminent. She stepped back as she detected the sobs shaking her patient's body. Ebe hugged her back with his learned response at affection before the two of them sat down.

"Ignore me," the nurse instructed, "But I won't be able to leave you alone this time. I'm sure you understand."

Ebe's eyes widened. He didn't want the woman in with them.

"I'll be fine, I promise," Carys tried her best to smile, but after recent turmoil she wasn't convinced she remembered how.

The nurse shrugged. "No choice, I'm afraid. Sitting in the furthest corner, she picked up a magazine that looked as though it had been left by the very first visitor years ago, and began thumbing through articles and feigning interest so they might feel private. It was far from ideal, but Carys wasn't in apposition to make a fuss.

Taking the furthest table, they huddled together and Carys leaned into her son. "I'm so sorry I missed your graduation, cariad," she said, stroking his hand.

"That's okay. I knew there must have been a really good reason. When Marco told me what happened, I came to see you in hospital and you looked terrible. I visited most days, but by the time I knew you were awake, they'd moved you here."

"Sorry, son. It must have been awful for you. Marco told you? Are you sure? Do you know what happened, Ebe?" she asked.

"Yes. Marco told me."

"Really? He told you the truth? About the huge spacecraft? About me jumping from the car because he'd turned himself into a hideous, reptilian monster?"

Ebe's eyes flashed, "Why did that make you want to get away? Didn't you know about Marco?"

Her face took a while to catch up with her emotions as her forehead creased and her eyes squeezed shut. "You mean you did?" She stared at his dark eyes to decipher the truth. He nodded, and she gasped

"I'm going away with him. To Alaska," he said with the brilliant excitement he always showed when he was really passionate about something, bright eyed, bobbing in his seat.

Carys's heart cramped. It was true. She hadn't dreamt it up. "I can't believe it, Ebe. Why? Marco said we'd all be killed! I've been convincing myself for I don't know how long that I'm just mad, but now you're saying it's true. What exactly are you doing with Marco?"

"They're coming, Mum!" he enthused. "I'm going to build a portal, and then they can come."

"Who are coming, Ebe? Aliens?"

"Not the ones you're used to. Different ones. They've been here before, but their portals aren't strong enough anymore. I'm going to build another one. They'll be here soon, and everything will be different. They know things, you see? They can show us how to do everything better. It's so exciting, Mum," he concluded breathlessly.

Carys was speechless. Was Ebe as crazy as everyone thought *she* was? Everyone agreed he was an undeniable genius. Not crazy. "What will happen to everyone, Ebe? What will happen to you?"

"Oh, Mum, it's state-of-the-art. Technology everywhere! I'll love it."

Carys smiled a brief but genuine smile imagining her son in his element surrounded by flashing lights and wires at every turn. But beneath the table her leg rattled up and down showing her distress.

"We best wrap things up," the nurse looked up from her magazine and said.

Ebe obeyed at once and stood.

"Don't go yet, Ebe. Just a few more minutes. You still haven't answered my questions" Carys gripped her only son's hand. "I'm fine, honestly," Carys implored, eyes bulging with pain.

"The room's booked out, sorry," the nurse interrupted again.

"What, after fie minutes!"

"It's been twenty, and yes. It's not up for discussion. You don't want any trouble, do you, Carys?"

"When they come, which won't be long," Ebe said, squeezing her hand, "I'll come and get you, yeah? And then you can help me. It's going to be the most important and amazing thing ever!" He wrapped his strong arms around her and squeezed her until she pushed him away, gasping for breath.

"You're hurting me, Ebe."

He let go at once. "Sorry."

As they were directed along the corridor, the

nurse a few paces behind, they had almost reached the main exit when Carys gave one last shot at a straight answer from her son. "You can't come and get me. Marco said no-one will be able to cope with the frequency, Ebe. You won't be able to come. I won't be here. No-one will, that's right, isn't it?"

He shifted uncomfortably, as though he hadn't expected her to know so much. "That is a slight risk," he admitted. "I'm quite sure it'll be fine, really. Marco doesn't understand as well as I do."

Carys sighed and shrugged. Stuck here without her family; without her mum, her dad, her husband, or her son, what did it matter? Apart from worrying the two visits might turn out to be some drug-induced dream, she trusted what her son was telling her. "I'll miss you," she mumbled.

Talk of portals made her remember Ebe's woollen structure of two decades ago, so, she had to ask before she lost the chance. "When you were a little boy, you tied wool around everything we own and sat in the middle of it. What was the wool all about, Ebe?"

He frowned, as though struggling to recall. "Oh, that. It was kind of a portal, I suppose. But it wasn't real, Mum!" he explained as if she was being really silly for not understanding. He even tutted good-naturedly. "I was just a kid. I was only playing!"

"But how? How did you do it?"

He beamed at her. "Maths! It's all maths. If you

understand the numbers, you can do anything."

Carys couldn't help but be amused. She had so many questions, but she knew she wouldn't understand the answers even if he'd had time to answer them. She had to be amused. Playing at building interdimensional portals. Ah, bless him, how cute.

Her wry smile never made it beyond a slight turning of her mouth before the crushing reality of her situation hit her hard again.

They hugged more; Carys careful to hold onto her emotions until he had left.

"See you soon, Mum. Real soon, okay?" he promised whilst walking through the door.

Carys nodded with as much enthusiasm as she could marshal.

Escorted back to her solitary room, she at last allowed herself to break down into the emotional wreck she felt. So that's what the future held, was it? Ebe far away, and *them. They* were coming.

Ebe might be excited by the prospect, but she was not. It was her worst nightmare coming true again. Desperate for the truth her entire life. Now she knew it, she wished it could be un-known.

CHAPTER THIRTY-SEVEN

The worst solution

Of course, Ebe was enthusiastic. It was his vocation. He was one of them, half one of them, after all. And she couldn't tell anyone, or they'd just say she was insane

Anti-depressants could do nothing to stem the plunge into desolation that swamped Carys now. Everything was utterly hopeless.

"Are you going to shower today, lady?" a nurse stood at the end of her bed. "We've given you long enough, but everyone's complaining you're rather pongy." The nurse wore a wince of revulsion. When Carys failed to answer again, she kicked the bed. "I'll get help and we'll physically put you in the shower," she sneered. "Is that what you want? Because we've got better things to be doing, believed me." With no response forthcoming, she huffed and stormed from the room, the door closing automatically behind her.

She returned with two male orderlies who stood either side of the bed. "One last chance, Carys Ellis. Are you going to shower, or are we going to move you?"

Carys lay motionless. Slowly, she trained her eyes onto the nurses face. Staring right through her for a moment, she then turned her head away and blocked them by closing her eyes.

"Don't ignore me," the nurse snapped. Grinding her teeth, she pointed at her arms. "Grab her. Let's put her in the shower."

Wary of her putting up a fight, relief when she didn't was short-lived when they saw the mess she'd been lying in.

"Urrgh! You've soiled yourself. What's the matter with you, eh?"

Carys remembered thinking, 'You're the nurse, you tell me,' and then sank deeper inside herself with only vague recollections of being under torrents of water, and now she was back in bed. Clean now, she had lain in her own mess and stared at the ceiling, at the walls and out of the window, without seeing. Just an inky blackness that had swallowed her and was now deciding how to digest her, and which way to spit her out.

More time passed. Medication was tinkered with and therapy offered: CBT, DBT and other initials that meant little to her.

"You have to engage with the treatment for it

to work," she was warned by the nurses and doctors. Why did they bother stating the obvious? She knew that. Who wouldn't know that? She didn't connect with the therapies, because she didn't want to. Everything they said was utterly ridiculous. When she heard the platitudes and pathetic, baby-simple advice 'Is that a way of thinking that is useful for you?', 'What about if you thought this way instead?' she felt like throwing a chair at them.

They accused her. 'You don't want to get better, do you?' which annoyed her further. What was the point of getting better? So, she could engage with the wonderful life of partying with crazy people that Marco had subjected her?

They persisted with stronger and stronger medication, hoping that one day, they'd have made enough difference for Carys to *want* to change, but it just made her numb.

Maybe some of the medication made a difference, and maybe it didn't, but one day Carys decided to take action.

She didn't rush to the nurses' station to sign herself onto one of the therapies. She did something else. She did what she had always done before: found something sharp, and cut herself. It was stupid, she knew, but more than knowing that, she felt pain. And that pushed her head above the fog of her medication enough to feel briefly alive.

But what was the point? Her life was miserable. Yes, she was depressed, but for bloody good reason. Her depression wasn't an illness, it was merely fulfilling its evolutionary purpose: to keep her lying low until things changed.

Things hadn't changed though, had they? Could she make them? That was the crucial question now. There must be something she could do.

Allowing any sort of feeling may well prove regrettable, but something had led her onto the first rung of the very long ladder back to a semblance of normality; of normal feelings. She could take the next step, or she could just as easily slip down again.

Over the coming days she asked to make endeavours to contact Ebe in Alaska. And find her dad, who had seemingly forgotten his daughter on his trip around Asia. That's if he even was in Asia. It was an assumption she'd made when he hadn't shown up to visit her.

Or maybe he didn't know! Maybe Marco had told him a different story. She imagined the torture he could have gone through hearing about her accident, but not that she'd pulled through. Traipsing round the Far East, believing he'd lost his wife *and* his daughter. She had to find him and tell him. There had to be a way.

The staff seemed happy to assist with her enterprise, pleased she'd made plans. It was a good sign, although they had un-voiced concerns she might be a bit manic—a symptom of her bipolar, but they were happy to help for now.

Very quickly nothing happened. Ebe was untraceable, and there was no word from Geraint. And so, Carys's attempts began to receive less and less support. She was sure they were being cagey, holding back; but what could she do?

Weeks turned into months, and still no news.

When would Ebe come for her? Soon, he'd promised. Very soon, she fervently hoped.

She had no other plans. There was nothing to do in St Caradog's. Occupying herself with games of solitaire, walks around the garden, and any other simple pleasure she could rally. She kept out of the way of God/ Helen, Raymond, and Mike with his guitar and screeching songs. And whenever she saw alien Carwyn, her blood ran cold and she walked in the opposite direction.

She waited.

She waited for news.

Of anything that would justify her slow climb from oblivion.

Some validation.

She had done all she could do.

There was no option but to wait.

So, she waited.

She waited for as long as she could possibly wait.

Until it became unfeasible, impractical, and just downright impossible for her to wait any longer.

Inertia being abhorrent in nature, she had to do something; even if it meant falling back down the ladder of her well-being. She'd tried everything in her power to make things better, but it had all been elusively outside her control. So now she had to take control; the only way she knew how.

It began in the queue for medication that she joined whenever she was not locked in solitary confinement. She hadn't had any psychotic outbursts, as the staff called it, or need to defend herself, as Carys herself called it, for a while. Her self-imposed solitude had encouraged that.

She watched as each person in the queue in front of her was given a plastic cup of water, and a smaller cup of medication. They tipped the small one into their mouths, swallowed whatever medication was their individual prescription, and opened their mouths again for inspection, to check they'd actually swallowed the contents. The next person in the queue then took their place at the serving hatch.

Carys had contrived to save her medication. She couldn't be caught with it in her mouth, so she had worked hard on a different plan: concealing the tablets in her gullet without swallowing them completely. She could then retrieve them in her room and save them. Practicing with harder pieces of food and confectionary from the vending machine, she grew steadily proficient.

She still struggled at first. Not swallowing them completely was hard and she couldn't get caught even once, or the game would be up. And her attempts at regurgitation were more like simply vomiting; luckily, something she found easy to explain away. Many of the medications caused nausea as a side effect. But she had to get better, she couldn't arouse suspicion or her plan would never work.

Soggy, but intact, the bounty wasn't as complete as the sweets, due to their propensity to dissolve upon contact with liquid. They tasted foul, but Carys hid it well. Upon regurgitating, they were never perfect, but they were good enough.

To hide them, she hollowed out part of the inside of her shoe, creating a small hole covered by the lining and, her feet, when she wore them. The first reusable harvest was a bit misshapen and mushy but it soon dried.

Day by day she half-swallowed, regurgitated, dried, and stored her medication for use at a future date. It became necessary to hollow the inside of her other shoe too, dispersing the tablets evenly to enable her to walk normally.

She felt absolutely dreadful. Any of the information pamphlets in the medicine boxes would have advised her strictly against stopping taking her medication suddenly. As well as the likely return of symptoms, there was the withdrawal. Quitting an entire cocktail of interacting medication cold turkey would only ever end badly.

Terrible flu aches and excruciating headaches beleaguered her daily. And she couldn't even wallow in her pain; lock herself in her room and pray it would pass soon because she had to keep up the pretence at normalcy.

An ironic smile almost reached her impassive lips when she passed off her headaches as migraine, and received additional pills in her little pot to combat them.

Every day she would queue, and every day she would half-swallow her tablets. Once her mouth was checked, she would take her time, but not too much, and saunter unsuspiciously back to her room.

The sickness, flu aches and thumping headaches symptoms didn't get better for ages. Her self-served sacrifice was almost unbearable, but Carys took pride in it, using it as another form of self-harm as it moved her ever-closer to her purpose.

It began to wear off. The nausea went first, and then the headaches became merely painful rather than excruciating. She left her room, and sought company for the first time in a while. It was, if she'd considered, quite unlike her. If she'd given it any thought, she would have been aware of feeling rather odd.

Compelled, but also reluctant to find any of the patients she knew, she wondered if she should make acquaintance with any new patients she might find. Nerves at her uncharacteristic conviviality made her almost turn round and go straight back to her room.

Her breath was taken away by what she saw down the corridor. Legs buckling, she stumbled on, determined not to let her frailty stop her getting to him. It was over. It was all over, now. Ebe had come for her. She called out to him.

"Ebe, Ebe!" she ran as fast as her aching limbs allowed. He turned and without calling back, ran towards her. Carys couldn't believe it. She had hoped and wished for this day. Things must have gone well in Alaska. He had said, hadn't he, that he was building a portal and when 'they' were here he would be back for her?

She'd always been petrified of what *they* would do. But thinking back over her life, despite the terror, and their disregard for her feelings, had it really been bad? They had planned out her life, but it had been good in places, hadn't it?

And Ebe. He could have been the bastard son of a rapist, which she supposed he still was, but he was special. He was so special.

She'd almost reached him, when he simply was no longer there. Turning her head every which way, she couldn't understand where he'd gone.

"Ebe? Ebe!" she shouted. Wait. She can't have imagined it, because here was Geraint too. "Dad!" she cried. But then, he too melted into the ether right in front of her. She spun round, baffled. Where was Ebe? Where was her dad? Where were they? Where? Where?

"Is everything okay, Carys?" She thought she recognised one of the nurse's voice behind her. Turning to tell her, no, everything was definitely not alright, she broke into a tearful grin. "Mum!" she beamed, as she stood smiling before her. "I thought you had died."

Flinging her arms around her, she hugged her close. Something was horribly wrong. It didn't feel right. It felt uncomfortable.

Pulling away to look at her mum, wondering if she might be hurting her, she was left holding an ashen faced nurse.

"Why did you think I had died?" she asked, more than a little disconcerted by this notably violent patient expressing surprise at her being alive.

"Where's my mum?" Carys said, shoving the nurse away, but by now she was beginning to realise what was happening. She should have expected it.

That was the other downside of stopping her medication. Once the aches got better, the very reason it was being given to her in the first place became all too obvious. The figures she knew were not there, reared their ugly heads persuasively.

She found herself dodging aliens in the corridor. And she spoke to Ebe a few times again before realising he was a hallucination, too. Her dad, and her mum, she also saw, but was by then comprehending the falsity of her experiences.

Treating them as she had always treated the Amish man and the Rebecca: she ignored them.

Despite recognising that they were all hallucinations it always started the same way. Her heart would leap and fill with hope, only to be dashed as Carys's remembered it wasn't real. The crushing sadness which overwhelmed every false hope was becoming unendurable

Apart from hallucinations, she suffered other symptoms. Her general anxiety was high. Someone would recognise why she was so odd soon, wouldn't they? It must occur to one of them before much longer that her medication wasn't doing its job.

She must have enough to implement her plan, but she hadn't quite given up hope. In a desperate, hurried manner, she approached the nurses again and asked for help, but her request to contact Ebe was met with dubious enthusiasm. They said they'd look into any developments and get back to her. She asked daily or more, but was told to be patient. Give it time, they insisted.

Time passed until it felt like an eternity. So much time she could bear it no longer. She couldn't give it forever. It was so awful here. Every day was a struggle not to lash out. She couldn't wait any more. She had to take control.

And so it was, with manic thoughts racing through her troubled mind she took action.

She had help. She wouldn't do it without encouragement. The Amish man, on his own, not with the Rebecca this time, had been around in the corner of her eye for days. He knew when to strike to get the best effect. He was a figment of her own creation after all.

"He ain't never coming back," he drawled "Him or your daddy. They're gonna leave you in here to rot. *They* might come for you though. The funny little ones 'n their bright lights. They might well be coming for you, real soon."

"Shut up!" Carys hissed to the man, and to herself. She shook her head in an attempt to regain her composure. "Just shut up. You're not even real."

"At least I'm here. I'm always here," he said. "I know what'll help too. You just take them pills you been savin,' and it'll *all* go away. It'll be fine, I promise."

She walked down the corridor mumbling for him to go away, but he wouldn't. He told her the nurses were getting suspicious. They knew about her not taking her medicine and they would stop her. Then she'd be at the mercy of *them*. She shuddered.

"Have you heard that humming noise?" he hissed menacingly. "Because I have!"

Carys hadn't, which meant she knew the Amish man couldn't have either. Unless, she'd heard it and blocked it out; and he knew. Of course! That was it.

"They'll stop you, Carees. You godda do it now.

Right now, Carees." She nodded but she was afraid. "Don't you worry none. I'll help you. Come on."

Carys didn't know how far she would go with it, but she'd accommodate him for now to shut him up. Grabbing water from the vending machine, she slinked back to her room and removed her shoes. Placing them carefully on the bed she sat beside them and stared.

Sighing, she picked one up and fiddled with the hole in the lining. The bounty was tricky to release, but once it started coming out, it was a cascade. She was stunned at the quantity of tablets that fell out onto her bed sheets. Emptying the other shoe, she gazed at the mountain of misery, the colours of all the different pills ironically jolly.

She stared at them for a while before reaching out for the bottle on her bedside table and unscrewing the lid.

"That's it. It'll all be all right when you're done. Hell! *I'll* even leave you in peace," he laughed heartily. It all seemed like such a good idea. Tranquillity. Freedom from her heartache. Freedom from… this.

She looked down at the hoard on her bed sheet.

"Go on!" he gestured, smiling at her. She looked one more time. There were so many. So, so many tablets of different shapes and sizes and colours. She must have not been taking her medication for weeks.

And then, she took them all at once.

CHAPTER THIRTY-EIGHT

A New Clarity

As soon as she had swallowed the last one, she regretted it. "What have I done!" she said out loud. She knew of course. She knew with a clarity that was needle sharp. The second she swallowed the last tablet she knew everything. Like coming out of a trance at the click of the hypnotist's fingers.

That number of tablets would kill her, and quick. She wanted to live. Why had she wanted to die? Because she hadn't heard from Ebe? Because her mum had died? Because it was so terrible here?

If it was so awful, why was she not making the most of the treatments on offer so she could leave? She didn't need Marco to sign her out if she was well. If she could prove that she was okay, they would have no option but to release her. It was what they wanted too, wasn't it? She'd been a fool.

Did she want to die to get away from the creatures that had plagued her life? Maybe, but she couldn't. She had to live. For Ebe. How would he feel if he came back for her and she'd done that? And her dad! Returning from his trip to find he'd lost his daughter as well as his wife, he wouldn't cope. It wouldn't be just her she was killing, it would be all of them.

But she had done that hadn't she? She had just swallowed weeks' worth of medicine in one sitting, and was just counting down the minutes until she passed.

No! She wouldn't let it happen. The tablets hadn't been digested yet. She would go and tell the nurses. They'd know what to do. She couldn't be the first patient to take an overdose. It's probably a common occurrence.

As she rushed from her room, her thoughts continued. She was afraid of the alien creatures. A fear that consumed her. The Amish man had known that mention of the hum would push her to the edge. As she had begun to realise when she thought she was seeing her son, nothing bad happened really. Nothing she took from day to day. No injuries or scars. Just the fear of them.

According to Marco they had controlled her entire life. They had done their best to put her back as she was, hadn't they? They tried to wipe her memory and leave her as she had been before. And wasn't everybody's life mapped out by a higher force? Narberth Christian Fellowship certainly believed there was. Or were they all in on it? Were they all there just to acquire Ebe?

Ebes she remembered. She was not alone. Marco had told her, and plenty of testimonies on television concurred, including well-known celebrities. She thought about Marco's metamorphosis, and shuddered. It was real, wasn't it? It was too easy to dismiss it all as her neurosis, but she wasn't alone in that either.

Were she and her mother just crazy people who imagined aliens and saw UFO's and had their husband turn reptilian, or were they sensitive to the frequencies others were not?

How many people were abducted every day, only to have their memory wiped and returned to normal? It could be everyone couldn't it. She neared the nurses' station.

Ebe was going to help them come. He seemed to know it would be good. Maybe he was right. Maybe 2020 would be a new age of Utopia. She needed to be alive for that.

And if he was wrong? If it wasn't a utopia? If it was Armageddon? Well, Ebe and her dad would know and leave her safe.

They might need her. She would get better for them. She would do the CBT therapy and the DBT therapy and the whatever else therapy, and she would get better.

Reaching the nurses, she spoke to one sitting at the desk who had noticed her approach. Reluctant to engage in whatever ridiculous request Carys might be about to make, she kept her eyes down and carried on reading her magazine. Until Carys spoke.

"I've just taken an overdose," she announced calmly. "A big one." The nurse stared up at her. The gravity sinking in. "I don't want to die anymore, so could you help me, please?"

Carys watched as the chain reaction of furious activity began. It appeared that it was happening in slow motion. Sure she would be okay now, she gladly drank the black sooty drink they gave her, and something else, and nodded her compliance that an ambulance should be called.

She'd live, and she would get well again. And if Utopia was reached when *they* came, Ebe and her dad would come and get her. And if it was not as Ebe hoped. If it was as she had always feared? She would leave it up to them to decide.

Maybe, she would be better off staying where she was.

The End

Thank you very much,

Michael

What next?
Well, we all know 2020 was not the utopia Ebe promised.
So, what did happen in Alaska?
Did Ebe build the portal?
And if so, when are the supreme beings due to arrive and what will it mean when they do??
Or, are they here already?

Don't miss the next instalment of **The HUM**,
E.B.E *Extra Biological Entity*.

Available HERE to preorder from Amazon Kindle Store

Note from the publisher. Due to delays experienced since 2019 for obvious reasons, we have elected to set a very long release date as a placeholder to allow for further unforeseen eventualities.
We anticipate the actual release date to be February 2022 with further books in this series due out later in the year. We thank you for your patience.

ABOUT THE AUTHOR

Michael Christopher Carter

The beautiful Pembrokeshire Coast National Park provides the inspiration for Michael's novels, giving a real sense of life in South Wales. A former top performing direct sales consultant from the leafy suburbs of England, Michael was brought up a Catholic with a burgeoning interest in alternative, New Age spirituality, leading him to attain Reiki Master status in 1999.

It's from this unique perspective that he now indulges his one true passion of writing, producing paranormal novels set in his beloved Wales.

Michael lives and works on the fringes of the national park overlooking the Milford Haven Waterway, the Preseli Mountains, and the mighty and historic Pembroke Castle and says anyone would be inspired to write in such an idyll.

When he's not writing you can find him somewhere enjoying the outdoors with his wife, and four children, and little dog, Tedi.

BOOKS IN THIS SERIES

The HUM

A thought provoking horror thriller series of first contact books from Wales's Michael Christopher Carter

The Hum

Just because you're paranoid, doesn't mean they're not coming to get you...

"Wow! This would make a great movie!"

"I've never been disappointed by this author. His books dig deep emotionally, delving into the human psyche..."

Carys is pregnant

But she's never had a boyfriend

Or a one-night-stand

She's never had contact with anyone to explain her condition

Not anyone human anyway

Her wild claims are dismissed as a symptom of her paranoid psychosis, but Carys knows she's not crazy to be afraid whenever the dreadful humming noise fills the air; coming from every-where and nowhere. She knows what it signifies: that her and her baby are in terrible danger...

"Mindblowing. I've never read anything like where the author took this before!"

"This will have you believing in aliens for sure..."

The HUM is the first in a series of thought-provoking first contact books that will have you questioning what is real, both out in the cosmos, and within our own minds...
"Genius"

"A masterpiece!"

E.b.e Extra Biological Entity

On earth, a baby is born every minute.

But not like Ebe.

Not like Ebe at all...

Printed in Great Britain
by Amazon

77154027R00284